Praise

"An introspective, emotional novel that will draw readers in."

— *Kirkus Reviews*

"*Of White Ashes* reminds me a bit of the *tokonoma*, the special place in every Japanese home that displays something beautiful which inspires contemplation. This well-told story of a Japanese-American couple whose love survives a whirlwind of tragic global events leaves the reader with a new awareness of history and a deeper appreciation of the human heart."

— Lois Lowry, author of *Number the Stars, The Giver* and John Newbery Medal winner

"Ruby and Koji's stories are deeply rooted in the trauma of wartime and show the unique forces that affected Americans of Japanese ancestry during World War II. The redemptive power of love allows Ruby to confront her bitter legacy and come through her pain of betrayal and injustice, finding a healing through openness and forgiveness. Lessons for all of us."

— Claudia Katayanagi, director of *A Bitter Legacy: The Untold Stories of American Concentration Camps*

"A stunningly beautiful story. What the Matsumotos give readers is a deep look at an important and troubling period in America's struggle to understand itself. That it springs from their own family history only underscores its importance. From the internment camps to Hiroshima to the Korean War, Ruby and Koji persevered. Their story is the story of all of us."

— Christian Kiefer, author of *Phantoms*

"Sentimental and heartfelt, *Of White Ashes* is a profound exploration of love, loyalty, and duty in the face of unimaginable circumstances. An unfortunately timely debut that forces the reader to question everything they assume about how their one life should be lived."

> — Bradford Pearson, author of *The Eagles of Heart Mountain: A True Story of Football, Incarceration, and Resistance in World War II America*

"*Of White Ashes* illuminates the real lives of those burdened by the weight of war, hate, and one of the darkest days humankind has ever known. Most importantly, it declares that the greatest power of life is to transcend mere survival. A rich and necessary novel."

> — Zach Powers, Artistic Director of the Writer's Center and author of *First Cosmic Velocity*

"The chapters on the Hiroshima bombing and life in the camps raise to best of novel writing. Only a writer with a personal family history could personalize the impact in both despairing episodes. Only the heartless will fail to feel the pain. The useless, unnecessary pain."

> — Mike Malaghan, author of *Picture Bride* and *A Question of Loyalty*

OF WHITE ASHES

OF WHITE ASHES

A Novel

Constance Hays Matsumoto
& Kent Matsumoto

Apprentice
House Press
Layola University Maryland

The chapter titled *White Ashes* was previously published as *Picadon* in the July 2020 Maryland Writers' Association *Pen in Hand Literary Journal.*

First Edition

Library of Congress Control Number: 2022950405

Hardcover ISBN: 978-1-62720-419-4
Paperback ISBN: 978-1-62720-420-0
ISBN: 978-1-62720-421-7

Design by Mary Velazquez
Editorial Development by Mary Velazquez

Published by Apprentice House Press

Apprentice
House Press
Loyola University Maryland

Loyola University Maryland
4501 N. Charles Street, Baltimore, MD 21210
410.617.5265
www.ApprenticeHouse.com
info@ApprenticeHouse.com

For Mat and Reiko

One

1995

TWISTED PEARLS

1995

Airborne. No turning back. The steady hum of the engines permeated the metal cocoon charged with the choreographed energy of flight attendants executing their routine along the aisles. Ruby studied the diverse faces on the plane, knowing that when they landed her physical appearance would blend with the masses. She'd be one of them. At times like this, Ruby wondered why some people found comfort among others who look alike. For her, being surrounded by mostly Japanese faces was a painful reminder.

Flight attendants served drinks. Passengers relaxed into their seats and inhaled deep drags of nicotine. Their journey would be long, and soon the cabin would fill with the fog of cigarette smoke and a cacophony of snores, crying babies, and quiet conversations.

Ruby twisted her pearl necklace, thinking she should have asked for tea to settle her queasiness. *Breathe Ruby. You're not a child anymore and haven't been one for decades. Reach for the joyful chapters of your life. Don't let those other chapters dominate your thoughts and ruin this trip. This is important. It's not about you.* But as her fingers rolled from one pearl to the next, her thoughts drifted to the moments that strung together her young life. So long ago.

Those memories had become a part of her. She placed her hands over her stomach to calm the familiar discomfort spinning within—a torment trapped in her body like a black pearl inside of the grip of an oyster. A piece of her. Enduring. Marking her past.

The string gave way and pearls spilled over her lap.

Two

1939

NAMU AMIDA BUTSU

March 1939 – Waimea, Hawaii

The students in Ruby Ishimaru's fourth-grade class listened to morning announcements and recited the Pledge of Allegiance. Boys threw spitballs and girls passed notes to one another. Ruby sat alone, distracted and indignant at not being allowed to stay home for the birth.

A good student, she was often the first to raise her hand. Not today. She fidgeted all throughout arithmetic and spelling. Instead of following the text during reading, she gazed at the alphabet written in her teacher's flawless cursive on the blackboard and baby names flowed through her imagination. The sharp lines of *K* for Kenzo. The graceful strokes of *M* for Marguerite. The simple curve of *C* for Chiko, her father's given name. Her gaze drifted through the cracked window to endless miles of sugar cane in the distant hills and back to the schoolyard where the crooked trunk of a kiawe tree stood. She daydreamed about teaching her new baby brother or sister not to touch its thorns and hoped the baby wasn't hurting her mother.

"Father, may we stay home from school today?" Mari had asked their father earlier that morning. His forehead furrowed and he didn't respond to her sister, who was fourteen. Ruby knew not to ask again.

After a few minutes, their father spoke, his tone dismissive. "The midwife is on her way. Go to school and pay attention to your studies. In a few hours you'll have a healthy brother to celebrate and love. You will see him the instant you get home." He shooed them out of the house. "Now go," he said, returning to the bedroom from where a soft, steady moan escaped.

• • •

The jarring dismissal bell sounded. Ruby reached under her chair and grabbed the ties of the *furoshiki* wrapped around her now-empty wooden *bentō* box. She and Mama had selected the print fabric from the general store's limited stock—blond girls in smocked dresses petting kittens, fair-skinned boys in knickers and neckties playing ball with a dog, a mother scooping ice cream for her children. No one on the fabric looked like her. Today, she didn't care.

Ruby dashed into the sunlit schoolyard to meet Mari. The girls held hands as they ran downhill past the wood-sided community center, shutters open to the tropical breeze. Breathless, they raced past the Waimea Sugar Mill toward their simple house next to the Buddhist temple. Their father served the temple, ministering to the plantation-family congregation, most of whom were Japanese. Along the path, clumps of ginger flowers grew wild, nourished by abundant sunshine and rain. "They smell yummy," Ruby said. "You pick one bunch for the baby and I'll pick another for Mama." The gifts cost a precious few seconds before they rushed the last distance home.

They found their neighbor, Mrs. Moriwaki, sitting on the front steps and wiping tears from her face. Mari gripped Ruby's arm, as if to stop her from moving forward. The flower bouquets drooped from their hands as the girls stared at the woman, and she at them, her face ashen in the afternoon light. Ruby shook off Mari's grasp and tossed the flowers aside. Her fists clenched.

"Is the baby here?" Ruby asked.

Mrs. Moriwaki removed a crumpled handkerchief from her apron pocket and blew her nose. "I don't want you girls to worry, but the baby's upside-down and isn't coming out."

"Isn't coming out?" Ruby had never heard of such a thing, but she knew little about birthing babies.

"The midwife is here. She'll know what to do," the woman said. She looked away from the girls and stared at the neighboring house. Tears clung to her eyelashes. "My kids will be home from school. I'll be right next door if you need me." She paused. "Stay on the porch. Your father said you should."

Ruby had seen this before. When adults wouldn't look at her, it meant they were lying. She tapped the toes of her dusty shoes together and watched red earthen particles flick away.

The first time Ruby had felt the baby move, "Deck the Halls" was playing on the radio. She had tied her handmade ornament—a chandelier of vibrant *origami* cranes flying from woven string—onto their Christmas tree. On the song's final *fa-la-la*, her eyes had followed the waves of tinsel garland to the gold star that reached for the ceiling.

"Isn't it pretty, Mama?"

"Beautiful, sweetheart," Mama had said, her long eyelashes fluttering as if curtsying after a dance. Her mother's hands rubbed her stomach with a circular motion and her eyes seemed to float from a lacquered tray of ribbon candy on the side table to a starched doily draped over the sagging sofa. Mama had embroidered that doily with poinsettias, and it was Ruby's favorite. Ruby hoped to perfect her own simple cross-stitch to more elaborate split, stem, and satin stitches like her mother's. Mama closed her eyes to the breeze from the open window, and her lashes rested against her cheeks, plump like pink *mochi* balls. A sigh of pleasure escaped from somewhere deep within her swelling belly, and she beckoned Ruby closer with a finger wiggle.

Ruby climbed onto her mother's lap. Nestled together in the cozy chair, slip covered in cotton ticking, she cuddled against Mama's shoulder, twirling the waves of her mother's hair around her fingers. They bathed in the glow of tree lights.

"I like our new reflectors," Ruby said. "They make the lightbulbs look like shiny flowers. Red is the prettiest."

"Red's my favorite too, and that's why you're named Ruby. But you already know that, don't you?" Mama said, with a gentle squeeze. "We never celebrated Christmas in Japan, but Father and I wanted to experience Christmas through your sister's eyes when we moved here. It seemed nearly everyone on the island celebrated the holiday, regardless of their faith. This American tradition has become a magical gift we share with you girls and," she said, shifting her body and placing her hand on her stomach, "this little one."

Ruby snuggled closer.

Mama placed Ruby's small hand on her fertile belly. "There, did you feel that?"

The tiniest of movements fluttered under Ruby's hand. She gasped. "Is that the baby? Is it hurting you?"

"No, sweet girl, he doesn't hurt. He's having fun moving around and growing until he comes out in a few months."

"He's moving around *in there*?"

"All the time. Sometimes it feels like he's doing *taisō*." Ruby tried to imagine the tiny baby somersaulting inside Mama. Feeling the baby move made him more real to her. She kept her hand on Mama's belly, hoping he might move again.

"How do you know it's a boy?"

"We don't. Father hopes so. My hope is for a healthy baby."

• • •

Thunder clapped in the distance, jolting Ruby to the present on the porch steps, now aware she had been rubbing her cheeks a bit too hard.

"If lightning starts, they'll let us in. Won't they?" Ruby asked.

Mari shrugged.

"How long has it been?"

"Too long," Mari whispered.

They waited on the steps, fingers entwined, their young ears absorbing unfamiliar sounds escaping through the open window from the rooms inside—moans, panting, the midwife's demands of "keep going, just a bit more, think of the baby."

And Mama's cries.

The thunder continued its dull and distant rumble as late afternoon changed to early evening. The wilted flowers lay forgotten. Ruby pulled her knees to her chest, wrapped her arms around her shins, and begged the universe to protect her baby brother—or sister.

At last, the screen door creaked open and Father emerged. Ruby shrank at the sight of her father's heavy jawline and appearance—shirt rumpled and half-buttoned, hair uncombed. He crouched in front of them with tears in his raw eyes.

He looked at Mari and his voice cracked. "Girls... *this* is hard."

Never had Ruby seen Father cry. He opened his mouth, but words failed him. Her heart began to beat faster. She hugged her tummy, queasy from the sweaty smell of Father's body odor mixed with something frying in a neighboring kitchen.

Father looked away and seemed to study a streak of dirt on his house slippers. He rubbed his temples with trembling fingers and wandered into the yard as if looking for something. But for her upset father wandering the yard in his slippers, things seemed normal. The chickens were clucking. Some kid yelled "olly olly oxen free" from a Kick the Can game, and she wondered who *it* was. A car drove by and someone waved. She began to raise her hand, an automatic impulse. Mama had taught them to greet everyone with courtesy. But her arm froze.

Mari let go of Ruby's hand. "Father?"

He returned to the steps. The frown around his eyes matched the lone word that slipped through his trembling lips. "Dead."

Ruby's thoughts scurried. "Who?"

Mari blinked hard. "The baby?" Her tears flowed.

Father slumped on the stairs. "Both. They're both gone." His words seemed to come from far away, as though through a tunnel.

Ruby felt detached from her body, as if her mind had come loose. She no longer felt the steps under her. Through her tears, the yard blurred. Father caught her as she crumpled into his big, comforting arms. Tears and perspiration ran down his face and onto her cotton blouse. She tried to swallow, but couldn't.

Father slowly removed his arm from her shoulder and rubbed his tanned hands together. "There's only sorrow now."

Here was a man who had led the temple's worship services, performed rituals and ceremonies, and preserved the Dharma through ministry, week after week, year after year, delivering calm words. "We must seek comfort in our faith and value every day as precious," he told the girls. "Awakening to radiant health in the morning, we accept the possibility of losing life's glow by evening. And so, we entrust ourselves to *Amida* Buddha and the afterlife."

He had entered his internal, sacred space, putting on his mantle as minister. The girls folded within the present, yet distant embrace of his arms.

The midwife stepped out. Her wide frame struggled to stoop to their level. She began wringing her cracked hands. "Girls, I'm sorry about your mother and sister. I tried my best to save them. Truly, I did." A tear trickled down one of the many wrinkles on her weathered face. "I'm nearby if I can do anything for you. Anything at all."

A sister? "What? Not a boy?" Ruby asked.

The woman didn't answer, and it was far too late for her to be helpful. Ruby watched the midwife walk away, her generous hips swaying, her sobs trailing.

The girls tiptoed into the house and found their mother lying on her bed, covered in crisp clean linens with the swaddled baby beside her. A small Buddha statue nestled in the pillow by Mama's head, her hair matted with sweat. They looked peaceful, as though sleeping. But Ruby knew their life essence was gone.

She understood from other deaths in the community that Buddhists believe in giving spirits time to leave. Since Mama's soul would take hours to depart, free from the day's trauma, she and Mari remained at the deathbed as their father chanted sacred and protective verses from Buddhist scripture. Studying the tiny face of her baby sister, Ruby wiped tears that wouldn't stop and imagined having a baby in the house, whether she would have been a good big sister, and what they would have called the baby. The graceful strokes of *M*. Might they have called her Marguerite?

Ruby kept her eyes on Mama and the baby, except for a quick glance out the window as light broke through a passing storm, changing from tangerine to the purple shadows of sunset. Soon, darkness crept in and Mama and the baby's faces seemed to disappear into the sheets. Above their still bodies, the rise and fall of her father's chants resonated—a string of words with meaning beyond her grasp.

A knock at the front door disrupted his ritual. Her father placed his hands on his knees as if to steady himself and strained to stand. "I called the funeral home. That must be them. Mari, look after your sister."

Two somber, stone-faced men entered the room—funeral directors from the mortuary in Old Koloa Town—to take Mama and her baby sister to the mortuary to rest in a refrigerated coffin. They would return to the temple in three days, their bodies prepared for their service.

Ruby had never touched death before.

Through her tears, she squeezed Mama's hand, but it didn't squeeze back. She kissed her rigid cheek, which lacked the plumpness that had always yielded to her cuddles and smooches—no trace of her soft and affectionate mother. Mari took Ruby's hand and led her to the door, where they stood, watching the men carry the stretcher cradling the sheet-covered bodies to the hearse. Ruby wanted to cry out, to run after them, to hold onto her mother, but somehow her bare feet stuck to the floor like a bird ensnared in the sticky fruit of a pisonia tree.

The vehicle groaned away, and their father followed in his faded Chevrolet.

The girls returned inside where anxiety and grief bled into the sanctuary of their bedroom. After ranting about who was to blame—the midwife, the neighbor, Father, even her dead baby sister—Mari faced the wall, hunched in the shadows.

Ruby's questions alternated with bouts of crying. "Who will tell us stories? Who will make our food? Tuck us in?"

"I... don't know," Mari said, her words strangled by tears.

Unfamiliar words overheard that afternoon—*hemorrhage, breech, condolences*—cluttered Ruby's mind. They didn't matter. Dead was dead. Her loving Mama would spend the next few days in a Frigidaire and then vanish from her life, reincarnated into another time and place.

Ruby's ten-year childhood had been all she ever wanted. Sweet. Secure. Until today. The day she learned the world could be hard.

• • •

The night before the funeral service, Ruby had watched her father stare at a blank sheet of paper, his elegant calligraphy brush in hand. He seemed to struggle for words. He said sharing tragic news with family in Japan must come from his heart and be of his hand. The speed of a telegram was too curt and disrespectful.

Ruby's Uncle Ishimaru lived with Father's parents in Hiroshima, where he served as the minister at the Mangyoji Buddhist Temple, like his father had before him. Mama's parents lived in Ehime Prefecture, where her father was the town doctor. Father said the Doctor would blame the island's poor medical care for the deaths. Or worse, blame him for bringing Mama and Mari twelve years ago to what Mama's father considered a primitive island.

Mama and Father often reminisced about being seduced by the opportunity to build something new among Kauai's lush mountains, forests of sandalwood, and dramatic vistas of saturated color. They were proud of Father's stature as leader of the temple and the nearby Japanese school. They also enjoyed exploring Waimea Canyon, swimming in Hanalei Bay, and forming friendships in the plantation community.

Now, a pall rolled over their home. Under the rusted sheet-metal roof, gloom slipped through the shuttered windows and settled into the walls and crevices, its presence blunting the neighbors' attempts to ease the family's pain. Expressions of sympathy and kindness packed the refrigerator— macaroni and potato salad, chicken adobo, *musubi* rice balls with *umeboshi*, and *kimchi*. At any other time, Ruby would have relished these delicacies. She was an avid lunch-trader with her classmates, many the children of immigrant parents from Japan, Portugal, Korea, and the Philippines. But her appetite seemed to have died with Mama.

In the morning, Ruby's puffy eyes squinted at the early light. Within moments, reality washed over her and she sank into the mattress with the heaviness of sorrow. Three monotonous days had passed since the deaths, and today was the funeral service and cremations. Never again would she wake to the aroma of Mama's waffles. Never again would she hear Mama singing to the radio. Never again would Mama greet her in the kitchen with a tickle and a smile. She pulled the bedquilt around her heart and rolled onto her side.

A few minutes later, she dressed in shorts and a top, left the bedroom, and found Mari staring at the contents of the refrigerator. "What is all this stuff? It will spoil."

Knowing Mari wasn't looking for an answer, Ruby stepped outside and slipped onto the swing under the canopy of the monkeypod tree shading the yard. She pushed off, pumped her legs hard, and took flight—back and forth, sailing and falling, higher and higher—until she put as much distance as possible between her and the earth where Mama no longer walked.

She soared with the breeze on her face until the tension in her body lightened and she spotted Mari in the yard. The swing glided and settled.

"Hey. You okay?" Mari asked.

"I guess." Ruby twisted the ropes on the swing until her feet left the ground. Then she let go, spinning around and around.

"I know," Mari said. "And today will be the worst."

The girls had attended funeral services at the temple before, but those people were old, expected to die. No one close to Ruby had ever died before. "Where's Father? In the temple, getting ready?"

"Yeah." Mari offered Ruby her hand. "Let's go. I'll braid your hair."

"I can't say goodbye to Mama. I don't know how."

"Me neither. But come on anyway."

The girls took extra effort dressing in white, the Buddhist color of grief. They wore simple cotton skirts, plain blouses with puffed sleeves, bobby socks, and sandals. Their father came home and tapped on their bedroom door before entering. The white neckline of his suit was a sharp contrast to his ceremonial black robe.

"Girls, are you ready? It's time to go."

How can we ever be ready? They would walk across the yard to the temple, to the finality of death. Ruby's entire body filled with dread.

• • •

Bathed in candlelight, the Higashi Hongwanji temple glowed. The pews were full, and people stood in the side aisles. Ruby and Mari followed their father up the center aisle, passing under the serious gaze of the founding minister's portrait. The coffin rested at the foot of the elaborate altar Father had brought to Hawaii from Japan. Centered on the ornate table was an intricate oversized *butsudan*, shaped like a pagoda with a Buddha statue in the center. Cascading gold filigree ornaments hung from the ceiling, framing the altar. An aroma of white plumeria, ginger, and anemone wafted from the vases lining the altar and the front of the coffin.

A picture of Mama, wearing a serene smile, rested on a small table. A lei of orchids—Mama's favorite—was draped over the edge of the frame. Inside the open coffin, she and the baby were cold and expressionless. Mama wore white, cotton everyday clothes and the baby wore a long white gown, handsewn by a member of the congregation. On Mama's chest lay a paper scroll of calligraphy characters inked by Father: *Namu Amida Butsu*—I take refuge in *Amida* Buddha.

The girls joined their father in the front pew. A deep lingering chime rang from the patina shroud of the brass bell suspended from the temple's porch rafters. The service began.

Father stepped forward and greeted the congregation. He struck an enormous brass bowl, and its deep tone reverberated throughout the room. He chanted the Sanbutsuge, affirming intention and determination to become a Buddha. The melodic calm of his trance-like Japanese chanting continued for fifteen minutes, ending with a phrase the Japanese-speaking congregation understood: "Though I must remain in a state of extreme pain, I will endure all hardship."

How can we continue in this extreme pain? Endure more? Ruby couldn't imagine.

In place of her father's Dharma message, someone from the congregation read the Diamond Sutra. Only certain words registered with Ruby. *"Death. Journey. Star at dawn. A flickering lamp, a phantom, and a dream."*

Was it a dream? Please let it be a dream.

The congregation became a chorus, chanting and taking solace in the Buddha, the Dharma, and the Sangha. The mourners followed Ruby's family to the altar, where one by one they offered incense and bowed to honor the impermanence of life.

Father's voice was steady and his face impassive as he concluded the service with words of appreciation. "My wife, Akemi, was a lovely woman. Her life was full of good deeds, and she was well-loved by our family and you, our friends. She was soft-spoken and patient. She loved and cared. My heart is grateful she came here with me to this land of promise. Now she's gone, and we will miss her. As a Buddhist, she moved with grace toward her death with every breath. She and our baby daughter will be reborn in the pure land."

Outside the temple doors, Ruby stood in a daze next to Mari and their father as he greeted the mourners. Nothing felt real. She heard Father thank each person for attending and for their condolence gifts—fresh fruit, flowers, fancy cards. Nothing red, the Buddhist color of joy. They expressed their sympathies with empty words.

"Please let me know how I can help."

"Words cannot express... I saw her the other day."

"Tragic. She sewed such beautiful clothes for the girls."

Their chatter fell without warmth or meaning on Ruby's ears.

When the time came to follow the hearse to the crematory, Ruby felt the mourners' somber gazes follow her and Mari as they slid onto the backseat of their father's car. Never had so many people surrounded her, yet she felt alone. Grief was her closest companion.

• • •

Inside the crematory, Ruby strained not to vomit as the funeral directors opened the arched door of the cremation chamber. They placed the simple wood coffin inside its soot-stained masonry walls, and the hinges groaned as the door closed. The intense heat would reduce her mother and baby sister to bits of bone and ash.

Father wore a look of stoic nothingness. Mari watched with a blank stare from swollen eyes. They would return tomorrow and use long chopsticks to retrieve the bone fragments from the ashes, pass them to each other, and then transfer them to a porcelain urn. Passing anything chopsticks-to-chopsticks was disrespectful in any other circumstance. Ruby had never done this before, but now she had to. Pass her mother's bones. The very idea of it horrified her.

In the days that followed, Father's face seemed to soften as he found comfort in chanting Buddhist scripture. Lost in his world of meditation, he had unquestioning faith in life's infinite cycle. Spirits carried on in other places and times. But Ruby wasn't so sure. She wondered if Mama had attained enlightenment, if she would return to earth as a leaf. Or if she was in heaven as part of God's plan, like her Christian friends believed.

Maybe dead was just dead, and those beliefs were a bunch of hooey.

Ruby hoped not. A burdening scar began to form inside her heart—not only for the overwhelming loss of Mama and the sister she would never know, but also for losing her father. Father seemed not to hear when she spoke to him. Her questions went unanswered. He was often missing when she looked for him in the temple. Several times she found him sitting on the beach, meditating, or staring into the ocean. Ruby never disrupted his meditation, but she sometimes sat with him and watched the waves pitch and break on the shoreline. In those moments, she wished he would put his arm around her, call her his special little Ruby-*chan*, and take away her sadness. He never did.

Reciting "*Namu Amida Butsu*," she willed herself to take refuge in the Buddha and his teachings that human life is full of suffering.

JIZŌ

1939 – Island of Miyajima, Japan

Ten-year-old Koji Matsuo lay at the bottom of stone steps, breathing in dirt. A disturbing ringing seemed immediate and yet far away. *What's that sound? Is it in my head?* He opened his eyes to a blurred army of stone Buddhas, their chiseled faces intimidating.

Where am I?

He reached for the tiny statue lying in the dirt—a bald monk with childlike features. *My Jizō.* His arm slumped against the ground, sweaty.

Hot. I'm so hot.

A hazy memory emerged. An ancient wood temple... sloping roof, fat rope tassels... hundreds of *Jizō* statues standing side by side on an old stone wall. A monk... he said *Jizō* protects travelers and children. Coins chinking as *Otōsan* deposited a contribution into the collection box.

A warm hand caressed his shoulder. Koji heard *Otōsan's* voice, muffled and distant. "Koji... Koji... you okay?"

He coughed out dirt. There had been a hike. Stairs at the Daisho-in Temple. Metal cylinders inscribed with Buddhist scriptures. *Otōsan* telling him and his seven-year-old brother, Naoki, to spin a wheel. They'd receive a blessing without reciting the inscription.

Koji heard Naoki's sniffling voice. "Is he okay?"

Otōsan's firm voice, "Koji... please! Answer me!"

He shook his head. It hurt.

"Can you sit?"

He pressed his palms into the dirt and tried to raise his upper body. He rolled over and lay his head on the hard ground, opening his eyes to his father's worried face.

"It's okay. Give yourself time," *Otōsan* said.

He drew a deep breath and struggled again, pushing off on his foot and rolling to prop up on an elbow.

"What? What happened?"

Koji heard a labored sigh escape from somewhere deep inside of his father, who tilted his head and rested his eyes before speaking. "You were fooling around on the stairs, spinning prayer wheels, showing off. You lost your balance and fell." He pointed to the tall and weathered stone steps, framed with Buddha statues. "From way up there. Thankfully, you were only out for a few moments."

Koji raised his eyes to where *Otōsan* pointed. The stairs were a blur. The bottom stair came into focus in slow motion. Little by little, the Buddha army looked less hostile and became inanimate. A drop of blood fell onto the ground next to a wilted cherry blossom.

"The cut isn't deep," his father said, dabbing a handkerchief on Koji's forehead, "We'll watch it."

Koji rubbed his hands together to brush off the dirt and poked his fingers in and out of a gash in his pants leg. He worried that he'd lost the small statue *Otōsan* bought for him earlier as a reward for his good grades. The statue had been in his hand before everything went dark. "Where's my *Jizō*?"

"Here," Naoki said. "Lucky yours is metal."

His father's soft stare conveyed love and a thousand admonishments. Koji knew it well. *Otōsan* offered his hand. "Come. Let's try to get you standing."

Fleeting faintness overtook him when he stood, so he lowered his head between his knees until his vision cleared. He took his father's hand.

Koji tried not to limp on the hike back to their picnic spot where his mother was waiting. He continued holding his father's hand, something he hadn't done for years, thinking others would label him a baby. Now, he found comfort in his father's steadiness. Their pace was slow and Koji took hesitant steps, his muscles quivering. He'd never had an accident like that before. The fall could have really hurt and maybe have killed him. "*Otōsan*," he said, his voice wobbly. "I'm sorry."

His father squeezed his hand.

For weeks, Koji had looked forward to his family's annual outing at the start of spring recess, a break from his school's confining walls and the strict discipline of his *sensei*. On Miyajima, away from his studies, he explored and played among the stream's small cascading waterfalls. But then he ruined it with his recklessness. At least he and his *Jizō* were okay. Naoki was right. Cast iron was a good choice. A stone statue might have busted.

Scattered sunlight filtered between the trees as Koji released *Otōsan's* hand and followed him along the shoreline's footpath marked by moss-encrusted lanterns. Open windows of hillside houses invited fresh air indoors. Porch chimes joined with bird songs and stream burbles.

Miyajima is paradise, Koji thought.

Utopia, a word he had recently learned, popped into his head.

Miyajima is utopia.

But that was a made-up place where everything was always perfect.

The cut on his forehead stung. Everything that had always felt safe and fine suddenly wasn't.

They crossed the brilliant red footbridge to the shoreline where, that morning, they had skipped rocks and jumped over fallen trees. Koji dipped his hands in the stream through the reflection of trees and splashed water on his face. He rinsed dirt from his mouth and took a long drink. The calming water extinguished the uneasy embers deep in his gut.

The three approached their blanket under a canopy of cherry trees. Koji's mother—named Sakura, for cherry blossom—was unaware of their exploits, having enjoyed a lazy afternoon chatting with other women. Koji liked that *Okāsan* was prettier than the mothers of his friends. An old barrette held the smallest of blossoms in her black wavy hair, framing her face. She waved and smiled when she saw them, but as they got closer, her eyes widened and her smile faded.

She rushed forward and knelt before Koji. Her soft brown eyes examined his scrapes. Her small hands smoothed his disheveled clothes. And her nurturing arms wrapped around him. In the safety of her embrace, Koji's heartbeat slowed. He wanted the hug to last awhile, to stay near her. Safe. But he wasn't a baby any longer, so he pulled away.

"Why such recklessness, Koji?" she asked, looking directly into his eyes. "You're too impetuous!"

Her face softened and she ruffled his hair. "Thank goodness you're all right. Sit here and rest for a little while."

He sat beside his parents at the base of a five-storied pagoda, its tiered rooflines curving upward to ward off evil spirits. Gazing at the Itsukushima Shrine, built on piers centuries ago, he swallowed the lump in his throat. The tide had washed into the holy place of Shintoism, and the red fifty-foot-high *torii* was illusive, floating in the serene water—so different from that morning when low tide revealed the gate and piers anchored in the sand. He dropped his chin to his chest, realizing how much could change between the tide's ebb and flow.

As *Okāsan* packed the leftover *bentō* of rice, dried fish, and pickled vegetables, he and Naoki sat on the blanket with their father, who cleared his throat to deliver what Koji called the annual cherry blossom oration. Koji admired his father's academic achievements and had learned long ago to pay attention when *Otōsan* spoke in his calm and authoritative voice. He wanted to grow to be like him and achieve an advanced education, but he wasn't sure if he wanted to continue as the next generation of farmer. His father said top grades and a good education led to good jobs in the professions, so Koji worked hard for perfection—in academics, attendance, and citizenship.

Otōsan began. "Boys, these new, unfolded blossoms are ephemeral and are a good reminder to us humans, that life is short... and to embrace life fully." *Otōsan* paused, catching sight of Naoki drawing pictures in the loose soil with a stick. "Naoki, quit messing around and listen when I'm talking to you!"

Naoki dropped the stick. His cheeks flushed.

He continued. "Please remember, in your exuberance, to expect the unexpected and keep vigilance of your surroundings. Life is impermanent. Learn to live with honor like the *samurai*, always prepared for inevitable death. You could have been terribly hurt today, Koji. Let this be a lesson to you."

Why, Koji thought, can't cherry blossoms just be cherry blossoms? Like dried fish is just dried fish.

• • •

Later, their boat crossed the bay toward home. The horizon glowed with the vibrant orange of sunset on the ancient forests, rising and falling with the mountainous landscape on the isle of the gods. Dusk and its violet mist soon enveloped the outer islands.

Naoki leaned against Koji, asleep, as the boat powered along the grime-darkened shoreline at the mouth of the Ōta River, one of seven dividing the graceful city of Hiroshima. Koji's skin prickled with goose-bumps and the hard seat irritated his bruised body. He covered his and Naoki's shoulders with his sweater to insulate them against the evening damp and reached into his pocket, where his sweaty fingers slipped around and clutched his protective *Jizō*.

NATIONAL ESSENCE

1939 – Hiroshima, Japan

No school meant more chores for Koji, but he enjoyed working the land even if he didn't want to do farm work forever. Spring recess passed quickly as his family cultivated the terraced rice paddies and vegetable fields for the growing season. His family ate what they grew and sold what remained within their hillside community of Fuchu, overlooking downtown Hiroshima three kilometers away.

He pumped water from the well and filled the cement holding tank, the handle cool in his grip. A nearby chickadee cried a sharp song, no doubt warning its friends of a predator. A snake, he thought. A warning to be careful as he moved to clean the Zen garden after the long winter's neglect. He removed stray leaves and dead weeds from around the plantings, raked the garden's gravel base, and pruned the evergreens. When finished, he wiped his face with his handkerchief, and gazed at the bamboo groves, mature red pine, and gingko trees growing along the hillsides, admiring the artistic composition of rocks, gravel, and plantings. *Okāsan* seemed to cherish her quiet time overlooking the hills and garden from the wide *engawa* that wrapped around their small *minka* home. Koji knew his hard work pleased her.

As Koji put away the garden tools, he reminded himself to study last trimester's notebook before going to bed. Enthusiastic for school to restart the next day, he intended to earn top grades for promotion to Hiroshima's elite middle school. During the recess, he missed his classmates and the challenge of learning, even if his classes were suffocated by the school's overarching mission—to train loyal subjects for the Japanese Empire.

They learned mathematics to engineer new bridges and industries for the Emperor. They learned science to discover new ways of protecting the land, the food supply, and the health of the populace. They learned geography and social studies to spread Japan's influence around the world. And they bowed their heads when they passed the framed photograph of Emperor Hirohito, who was considered divine and a direct descendant of the sun goddess. But Koji's father didn't respect Hirohito's alliance with the military and viewed him as a mere figurehead. And so, Koji left the Emperor at school and kept *Otōsan's* words at home.

Later, seated at the low table for a meal of pilaf, his family bowed their heads in gratitude. "*Itadakimasu*," they said together.

His father began the dinner conversation. "I talked to Wakamatsu-*san* today. He said the *zaibatsu* are taking over everything now—mining, banking, insurance."

Koji swallowed a mouthful of bamboo shoots. "What's *zaibatsu*?"

"Big enterprises organized around single wealthy families. They crushed Wakamatsu-*san's* insurance business and Hashimoto-*san's* garment factory. Such greed. All to consolidate. All to gain power and wealth."

Koji always listened when *Otōsan* spoke. He was named Akio, meaning "bright man," and he seemed to take care in choosing his words. Most nights, *Otōsan* ranted over the news of Japan conquering Manchuria or warring with China. Japan's military was close to controlling East Asia. He blustered, "Japan's war fever is perilous! I don't respect this path of nationalism... this uncontrolled military." His words mattered.

Naoki gulped his rice as if to escape the table as fast as he could, but Koji pushed food around in his bowl. The National Mobilization Law forced people to make do with less, and less again, directing Japan's resources toward the war effort, all in the Emperor's name. He sometimes had scary daydreams where he envisioned working in a filthy factory, assembling weapons for soldiers to brandish. Other times, he was in a faraway field harvesting crops to feed Japan's soldiers. And other times, he donned a uniform. In his imagination, an officer thrashed him for stepping out of formation or for missing a spot of shine on his boots. Thinking about being mobilized in his teenage years killed his appetite. He pushed his rice, eating a single grain at a time.

•••

The next morning, Koji and Naoki walked to school with their friends. They threw rocks into the Enko River, targeting the distant fishing boats, never believing the rocks would strike. But today, Naoki had a direct hit, and they ran on.

At the school's *genkan,* they removed their caps and leather knapsacks, changed into slippers, and bowed to *Sensei.* All students wore starched uniforms, but the brass buttons on Koji's jacket shined brighter than the others, at least in his eyes. Along with academics, *Sensei* taught them to eat well, exercise for fitness, obey the rules, be orderly and industrious, take responsibility for one's education, and pledge allegiance to Emperor Hirohito, and *yoi nihonjin*—be loyal to and honor Japan. Koji became better and better at acting the part of a good Japanese.

The classroom smelled of *Sensei's* familiar stale tea. Here, Koji felt in flow with the universe and the promise of his potential. He was excited to get started on Earth sciences. The climate, weather, landforms, and water interested him far more than the Emperor. Instead, *Sensei* began the day by introducing a new government-issued textbook, *Fundamentals of Our National Policy.*

The words slipped out of Koji's mouth, "What a title," not realizing he was within *Sensei's* earshot.

The abrupt stinging slap of *Sensei's* hand across his ear arrived from behind.

Koji shielded his watering eyes from his classmates and rubbed his ear. He slid down in his chair to endure *Sensei's* description of the book's doctrine, realized his mistake, and straightened his posture. The book, also known as *Kokutai no Hongi,* espoused a national essence and the qualities that make Japanese uniquely Japanese—collectivism, conformity, patriotism, a spirt of harmony, and absolute loyalty to the Emperor, including the sacrifice of one's life.

That evening, Koji learned his parents were aware of the new text-book. How they stayed attuned to current events while spending most of their days farming baffled him. They either met neighbors for tea and secret conversation or possessed a special sensor, like the newly developed radar. He fiddled with his chopsticks, thankful his parents hadn't learned about *Sensei's* slap. Their shame would hurt far worse than a whack on the side of the head.

After dinner, *Otōsan* asserted his feelings about *Kokutai no Hongi*. "Hirohito promotes an anti-democratic ideology, an unrestrained imperialistic government with military rule." Naoki tapped his chop-sticks as if to say, *oh no, here he goes again.*

Otōsan continued. "Boys, the school requires you to learn and follow the imperialistic doctrine in public, but do not embrace or accept this doctrine as unequivocal truth. Enviable democratic governments exist in our world—where citizens rule, through elected representatives. I hope one day you will enjoy the freedoms of a democratic form of gov-ernment. At school, focus on your studies, exemplify good soldiership, and exercise obedience."

Koji rubbed his tired eyes and forced himself to listen as *Otōsan* continued.

"I know it's late, but stick with me. You're both intelligent, so focus energy on your studies. Consider democracy, imperialism, and other forms of government. Ask yourselves what kind of world *you* want to live in. Above all, value knowledge and the competence it brings you. With it, you have the power to transform our world."

Koji put his hand over his mouth to hide a yawn, but despite his efforts, *Otōsan* must have seen the yawn.

"Okay, that's enough for tonight. Off to bed."

The boys entered their small, shared bedroom and opened their bed rolls on the *tatami* floor. Naoki was soon fast asleep, but restless thoughts kept Koji awake. *Sensei* would find *Otōsan's* ideas disloyal, per-haps even treasonous. Japan was a good and divine country. But *Otōsan* knew what he was talking about. Was *Sensei* wrong?

The compact house offered little privacy between rooms divided by sliding *shōji* doors made from *washi* paper and wood. He usually ignored and wasn't interested in his parents' hushed conversations, but *Otōsan* spoke louder than usual. Koji overheard every word. "I hate the military's grip on Japan's politics. And I never intended to escape one economic depression for another. Sakura, I miss our life in California, the sunshine, our car, and your studies. Most of all, I miss the chance for a better life for our children."

Koji tiptoed to the door. Hardly breathing, he didn't want to miss a word.

Otōsan continued. "May the swells of militarism not become a tsunami that destroys us and our American son."

"*Shikata ga nai*," *Okāsan* said. It can't be helped.

The confusing conversation that Koji could never unhear seemed to have ended.

Moonlight flooded the tiny room. His head and heart scrambled like an out of control motorcycle race on quilt-patterned urban roads with no street signs. *Am I the American son, or Naoki? Or... do we have another brother somewhere?* Koji didn't resemble the Americans they studied in schoolbooks, but neither did Naoki.

Weren't Americans white or brown? He and his brother were neither. They were normal-looking Japanese brothers with heads almost too big for their bodies, wide noses, wavy midnight hair, deep eyelid folds, and ears that stuck out. *Okāsan* said protruding ears were a sign of good fortune. Now he felt duped, and anything but fortunate.

He whirled the tattered globe resting on the simple *tansu* where his folded clothes were neatly stacked in the drawers. Tears of frustration rained on the model Earth. He wondered what kids did in America and if they studied like Japanese kids. And he wondered if America was east or west of Fuchu. He figured it depended on how one looked at and spun the globe, with every point on its sphere an equal distance from the center and its every rotation fueling change.

• • •

The next day after school, Koji was alone in the house. His parents were working in the fields, and Naoki was outside playing with his friends. He eyed the door and approached his parents' ornate *tansu* in the living room—an obvious place to hide something important. He didn't know exactly what he was looking for, but if there was something to be found, this was the place he would find it. A flowered filigree latch camouflaged the keyhole of a locked door. *Okāsan* kept the skeleton key in a small box tucked inside of her cherished *furoshiki*, and she stored the scarf in one of the unlocked upper drawers for safekeeping.

The loud tick of the living room clock was a tyrant, mocking his transgression. He wiped his hands on his pants, and his fingers sifted through treasures that didn't belong to him.

He found and set the *furoshiki* aside, inserted the key into the antique lock, and turned it clockwise. One turn, one gratifying click, and the door swung open, revealing three drawers. Old letters and his grandmother's diary filled the first drawer. Another drawer held his grandfather's calligraphy ink and brushes. Last chance. He opened the bottom drawer and discovered a tattered photograph among a small stack of papers.

Koji's much younger father stared back at him wearing a relaxed grin. He was seated behind the steering wheel of a black automobile with a light-colored roof. His mother leaned on the car, her elbow resting on the frame of the open window. A tiny pocketbook dangled from her delicate wrist, and her scarf lifted in the breeze. They looked out of place, yet strangely in place. Koji had never seen that expression on his parents' faces. Carefree. The headlamps looked like bulging eyeballs he'd seen in comic strips and bookended a rectangular plate with English letters and non-Japanese symbols: WYOMING.

Okāsan had taught him and Naoki how to write and sound out the English alphabet, to recognize their names in English, and to sing the ABC song, but he had never asked how she learned English. Under the photo were loose papers. A slip of paper with perforated edges and *Okāsan's* name: *RECEIPT—Seattle Evening Schools, January 9, 1920.*

He unfolded a stiff, official looking tri-folded paper but didn't understand it. Written in English, the document read *STATE OF CALIFORNIA, Department of Public Health, Vital Statistics, Standard Certificate of Birth*—a bunch of gobbledygook. He recognized his parents' names, but the rest made no sense, except for his name and the date, February 9, 1929—his birthdate.

The dimming daylight alarmed him. He had been looking in the *tansu* too long. He took care returning the papers and photos to the drawers, locked the door, and returned the key to the small box in the *furoshiki*.

A floorboard creaked.

"Koji, what are you doing?" *Okāsan* demanded.

Startled, he choked on the giant lump in his throat. His palms sweated, his chin dipped to his chest, and he stared at the floor. His response was feeble. "I... don't know."

"What do you mean you don't know?"

He couldn't tell her the truth. "Um, I made a gift for you in class, and I was... um... looking for a *furoshiki* to wrap your gift. I'm bringing it home tomorrow."

Okāsan shrieked, "Pack it in your handkerchief if you must, but get out of that *tansu* this moment! You know better than to go in there."

Okāsan was seldom harsh or yelled. He closed the drawer and scurried away, sorry to have upset her and yet relieved she hadn't caught him with the papers. As he left the room, he felt the penetrating energy of *Okāsan's* stare on his back.

• • •

In art class the next day, Koji made a flower bouquet by cutting colored paper scraps into strips to create flower petals, pasting one end to the center and then curling back and securing the other end. Old red buttons created the center of the flowers. Once the paste dried, he'd wrap it in his handkerchief for *Okāsan*.

He remained in the classroom during recess to erase the blackboard, but he was really there to look. With the boards erased clean, he sat at his desk with the Statistical Atlas of the United States, published in 1874, containing maps of populations, forests, climates, metals, and crops. Having studied the United States before, Koji knew it was a country of states, like Japan was a country of prefectures. But the straight-line borders of the large western states surprised him. The smaller eastern states seemed congested and the borders shapeless, more like the prefectures. He ran his chalky fingertip across the page and found CALIFORNIA— pale green and shaped like a bent leg with a long calf. Not too far away, his finger found WYOMING—a light yellow square. His eyes bore into the map, searching for Seattle, and found it on the top left pink corner labeled WASHINGTON. He wondered what the subdued colors meant. The area to the north and south were colorless, as if unimportant.

Koji heard footsteps in the hallway. Recess was over. He put the atlas back on the shelf and returned to his desk. From there, he studied the world map tacked on the wall. He had never realized how small Japan was. If inverted, Japan fit inside of CALIFORNIA.

FIREWORKS

July 4, 1939 – Waimea, Hawaii

Ruby hated Japanese school. Year-round, for half a day on Saturday and two hours each weekday, girls and boys studied Japanese thought and culture and learned to read and write the Japanese syllabary systems, *hiragana, katakana*, and *kanji*. Classes were held in a small nearby building and her father served as headmaster. Only Japanese kids attended. With no desire to visit Japan or practice its customs, Ruby didn't see the point in attending. *She* was an American.

When Ruby returned to school a few days after the deaths, she felt the stares of her classmates. Living in a small community, everyone seemed to know everything about everybody. Most kids didn't know what to say, and when she made eye contact, they looked elsewhere. A girl in her class mocked her. "You don't have a mother! You don't have a mother!"

She sassed back, "You're stupid and your mom is ugly!" That ended that. Except it didn't. It crushed her. And the girl had glared at her with a look that said she would strike back. Harder.

Adhering to Buddhist tradition, Ruby's father held a memorial service for her mother and baby sister every seven days, attended by the family and a few others. The entire congregation and other community friends joined the family to honor and celebrate her mother's and sister's lives on the forty-ninth day after they died. Father had said by then it was time to replace grief with acceptance.

Now, four months after the deaths, wild roosters continued crowing at dawn. Neighbors returned to their routines, and their gestures of kindness slowed to a trickle. Ruby and Mari cared for one another and for their father. They cleaned the house, did the laundry, and prepared simple meals, taking care to soak the rice early in the day.

Most days Ruby's grief faded to a constant dull ache. When the stabbing pain returned, she found sanctuary in the temple storeroom where Mama had kept the dolls she'd made with lifelike heads imported from France. Ruby brought Penny with her, the doll Mama had made for her when she was born. Penny had long, shiny black hair. Her glass eyes were green and her lips a pale shade of rose, her dress sewn of pink and white silk with a delicate black stripe and lace sleeves.

Ruby eyed the dolls and chose Sophia, a fair-skinned, blue-eyed redhead with peachy lips. She closed her eyes, fingered the black satin bows that speckled the doll's garment, and surrendered to the darkness. Black, the absence of light and life.

After a few moments, she opened her eyes to Sophia. "Sophia, meet Penny. Mama made both of you." She smiled. "Father's taking Mari and me swimming at Poipu Beach this afternoon and to the fireworks tonight."

"Two weeks ago," she continued, pretending Sophia and Penny were intent listeners, "Father took us to the Kōkeé mountains and we stayed in a cabin. The Nāpali coast is pretty. We hiked and roasted marshmallows over the campfire. It was such fun. And when we got back, Father gave us each a quarter to go watch the new *Wizard of Oz* movie at the Waimea Theatre. We even had a few coins to spend at the candy counter. The theatre is fancy. I'm not sure, but I think the seats are velvet."

Ruby's eyes welled with tears. "Mama knew all kinds of fabric. She would have known if it was velvet. Mama knew everything." She took a deep breath to stifle the brewing sob storm. "I'll take you sometime. The movie was about a girl named Dorothy whose house blew away in a tornado and she landed in Oz—a strange land of good and bad witches. Dorothy woke up and learned the story had been a dream."

A tear slid down her cheek. "I pretended the good witch was Mama."

Realizing crying was pointless, and with chores to finish before Father came home, Ruby put away Sophia, wiped her eyes, and returned home to sweep the floor.

Their father kept his promise and took the girls to the beach for the afternoon. Under a cloudless sky, sunbathers relaxed beside picnic baskets, lovers walked hand in hand along the edge of the gentle turquoise surf, and children dug moats to protect their sandcastles against the incoming tide. Ruby sat under a coconut tree, reading *Bright Island*, a book set on the other side of the mainland. Laughter erupted from the water where Mari and Father body surfed. Since Mama died, Father's sadness came in waves followed by periods of stillness, like the ocean's current had stopped. But in the past month, the crinkles around his eyes returned and smiles began to ripple through their home again.

Ruby waved to them and they gestured for her to join them in the water, but the sun was scorching. She had read in a magazine that girls should stay as light as possible. She didn't know why, but the magazine said so. She returned to her book.

In the late afternoon, they moved to a bluff offering the best spot for viewing fireworks and enjoying a simple picnic supper. Father complimented her potato salad. "Ruby-*chan*, it tastes like Mama's."

His compliment was the nicest thing anyone had ever said to her. She looked at him with great affection. "*Arigatō*, Father." Her father was quite handsome, with chiseled features, dark brown eyes, long lashes, and a stylish mustache. He enjoyed looking at himself in the mirror and always had his camera with him, inviting others to take *his* picture. A man at the neighboring picnic spot humored Father and photographed the family nestled together in the sand, among the sea grass, with the vast Pacific Ocean as a backdrop. Father looked dapper in his fedora, pressed shirt, and tie. Barefoot and happy, they smiled for the first time in months. She was eager to see the photo, but knew it would take weeks for it to be developed.

As the sun set and the shadows appeared, Father told stories about living and studying in Kyoto, where he had met Mama. He talked about visiting Manchuria and the valet who cared for him. He told them how he wasn't used to doing things for himself. After marriage, Mama had laundered and ironed his clothes, cooked his meals, cleaned the house and the temple, and took care of Ruby and her sister. Ruby believed she and Mari would now take care of the housework, their father, and each other.

His segue was masterful. "I'm going away for a while... to place Mama's ashes in the crypt at my family's temple and to visit my mother. She has screened eligible women identified by a *baishakunin*. I leave tomorrow for Hiroshima to honor Mama and to meet the woman chosen for me. As a forty-one-year-old man with a ministry to manage and daughters to raise, I require a wife. And you girls need a mother. The temple ladies will take turns supervising you while I'm gone."

Their smiles vanished, and they cried their protests. "We don't need a new mother!"

"We can take care of each other!"

Father wouldn't listen to another word. His decision was final.

Around them, families lounged on their blankets. Some played games. Others listened to stories read from well-worn books. Everyone was smiling and enjoying the evening as Ruby and Mari brooded in silence, waiting for the fireworks to begin. Ruby scowled and stuffed her feet in the sand.

People cheered when the colorful fireworks illuminated the sky, but tears and anger obscured her vision. She saw only blurred streaks of color. The explosive sounds made her jump, and the acrid smoke suffocated her ability to cope with her own world blowing up.

That night, Ruby stared at the ceiling. Mari was asleep, so they couldn't talk about their father's plans. She gave up on sleeping, slipped out of bed, and sat on a small toy box under the open window where a lone silverfish sped furtively across the windowsill. The breeze echoed the chirping crickets and all of nature playing in the black shadows of swaying palm trees under the brilliant moon. She longed for Mama to tuck her in and tell her everything would be okay. Maybe tell her a story. Mama told the best stories.

Ruby's favorite was *The Bowl Princess*, a story about a wealthy young princess whose mother died. Before her death, the mother had placed a wooden box on the daughter's head and covered it with a large ugly bowl. The mother said, "Someday when you're older, you will understand why I had to do this." Although the princess could see through the bowl, it hid her face. No matter how hard she tried to remove the bowl, it wouldn't budge. The girl's father remarried, saying his daughter needed a new mother. The princess's new stepmother was a horrid woman—mean and unkind—so the princess ran away. She kept her royalty a secret and worked as a bath girl for a rich and powerful feudal lord. Despite the bowl on her head, she and the *daimyō's* son fell in love. Their love caused the bowl to break apart, uncovering a box of rich treasures and displaying the princess's dazzling outer beauty that matched her beauty inside.

Ruby no longer believed in happy endings anyway. They happened only in fairytales.

MELE KALIKIMAKA

1939 – Waimea, Hawaii

During their father's absence, the temple ladies competed to stay overnight with the sisters. Unlike most of the plantation homes, Ruby's house had modern plumbing. An overnight at the Ishimaru home offered respite for these hard-working women—a flushing toilet, a warm bath, a quiet night's rest away from snoring husbands. The women spoiled the girls with kindness and as with their own children allowed them to run wild.

After play, Ruby often passed a Hawaiian hog farmer known by the locals as Pig Lady. The woman kept her pigs on the beach where the animal waste contributed to the brown discharge from the Waimea sugar plantation. The woman's uncombed hair was stringy, she dressed in tattered housedresses, and she was often overheard hollering, "Get back here, you stupid swine!"

Their friendship began with a wave, and then a smile and a hello, and then Pig Lady called her over. "Hey kid, you're the Ishimaru girl, aren't ya? Want to see my pigs?"

Ruby nodded.

"Sorry to hear about your mom passing and your father going off to Japan. How ya doing?"

Ruby didn't wish to talk about Mama to dirty old Pig Lady. "I'm okay." She turned and walked away.

The woman called after her, "Don't worry, kid. It'll be okay. I heard your father is remarrying. She'll be a good enough woman." Ruby continued walking home.

They began seeing more of each other, and as Ruby warmed to the woman's friendly overtures, she was soon learning how to make tofu. Together, in Pig Lady's garage, they cooked soybeans to slurry and added lemon. Pig Lady passed her a long-handled spoon. "Here, stir this nice and gentle until it curdles."

The science of cooking fascinated Ruby. "How does stirring make it curdle?"

"It's all about the lemon, which is acidic. This curdles the slurry, but you got to stir it so pay attention."

She focused on the task at hand. "But why does it need to curdle?"

"Goodness child, without curds there wouldn't be any tofu."

They placed the strained curds in wooden blocks to cool and cleaned up the pot and utensils. Ruby bent down to sop up a spill she'd made on the concrete floor. "Never mind the spill, that's what floors are for," Pig Lady said. She tucked Ruby's hair behind her ears to get it out of her eyes the same way Mama used to, and gave her a kind smile. "You did a good job today, child. You come be my helper any time you like."

As Ruby was leaving, Pig Lady's son, Kalon, came into the garage and kissed his mother on the cheek.

"Any tofu up for grabs?" he asked, poking around by the wooden blocks.

"Soon," Pig Lady said. "Now get on out of here."

Ruby could feel the blush of her cheeks as she waved goodbye. Kalon was Mari's age and one of the best-looking boys in the school. Ruby knew Mari had a secret crush on him.

For a rough woman, Pig Lady was as gentle as a piglet. Their unlikely friendship and the nurturing warmth of the woman's attention filled an empty spot in Ruby. And she drooled for the creamy tofu, and sometimes for Kalon. Occasionally she accompanied Pig Lady on deliveries to bustling and more remote parts of the island. Her beat-up truck jounced along the narrow and rutted roads, passing pineapple plantations, miles of beaches, and roadside farm stands. After crossing the iron truss bridge leading back to Waimea, Ruby ducked to avoid being seen by anyone who might recognize her, knowing Father would not approve of her being with the woman or acting like a ragamuffin. Whatever a ragamuffin was.

· · ·

The letter from Ruby's father arrived in December.

November 23, 1939

My dearest daughters,

Your new mother and I are scheduled to arrive in Kauai on December 21. Her name is Taeko, and like me, she graduated from Ōtani University. She is a Buddhist priestess and managed a household of girls in her job as a school dormitory housemother. I believe her to be a suitable fit for our family. She looks forward to meeting you and helping me manage the temple and language school.

We will celebrate the Christmas holiday together. Until then, continue to study hard in school, be obedient girls, and enjoy Thanksgiving!

Love,
Father

· · ·

Excited to see their father, the girls swept the house and porch, polished the furniture, and scrubbed the bathroom to a sparkle. They prepared a light meal of miso soup and *tamagoyaki*—Father's favorite—with Mari taking care to roll the sweet omelet without it breaking apart. After setting the table, Ruby walked along their dusty lane and cut as many pink anthurium as she could hold in her hand. Her mother had referred to the heart-shaped flowers as "flamingo flowers" and showed her how to snip the stems at the base of her palm before releasing them to spill from a simple ceramic pitcher. Mama always said not to try too hard, that the prettiest flower arrangements were the ones that fell into place the way nature intended.

She placed the pitcher of flowers in the center of the table and changed into her smocked dress with sleeves trimmed in eyelet. The dress matched the color of her doll Penny's eyes, and it was the last dress Mama had made for her.

Their neighbor pulled up in her father's Chevrolet and honked the horn, and Father jumped out to open the car door for Taeko. Out stepped a homely and stiff-backed woman. Glasses framed her small, close-set eyes. She parted her hair in the middle and wore it in a severe bun. The hairstyle accentuated her wide nose. Deep furrows in her brow made her appear much older than her young age of twenty-six.

Ruby and Mari raced into their father's arms. He tickled Ruby, and her giggles seemed to delight him. Taeko smiled and nodded at the girls. "*Konnichiwa, hajimemashite.*"

"Nice to meet you too." They offered Taeko polite bows and helped carry the luggage inside.

Taeko glanced around the house, nodding and uttering a brief *hmm* of approval here and there. "Thank you for making lunch, girls. The flowers are lovely. Where is the toilet?"

"I'll show you," Ruby said.

They walked into the shiny bathroom. Taeko pointed to the bathtub. "What's that?"

"Um... the bathtub?"

"A Japanese home with no *ofuro*?" Her tone suggested disappointment.

Ruby knew of, but had never seen, the deep wooden Japanese soaking tubs.

"Nope. Just the tub."

"It's so long and not very deep."

In the confined space, Ruby got a whiff of Taeko's body odor—the faint smell of fish rotting on the beach. Squinching her face and turning her nose away to escape the stench, she gave Taeko her privacy and closed the door, wondering if the woman stunk from the lengthy trip or from a rot inside of her.

She stepped into the living room and joined Mari on Father's lap. He gave their shoulders a squeeze to draw them closer. "How I missed my girls. You both did a fine job keeping the house nice and preparing a lovely lunch. You made our homecoming special."

• • •

On Christmas Eve, Ruby crossed the temple's weed-infested lawn to call Father to supper. A neighbor was out for his walk on the quiet dirt road and waved her over.

"Want a candy cane? I have extra." He wore the same flowered shirt as he'd worn last year at the community luau, where he played Santa and distributed candy canes. His fat stomach had jiggled with each "ho-ho-ho."

Ruby accepted one of striped delicacies and began licking the straight end into a sweet point. "Thank you," she said.

"Ho-ho-ho! Mele Kalikimaka, Ruby!" He continued on his way.

The wind rose with the setting sun and whipped her hair around. A storm was coming. Birds flew from higher branches into the shelter of dense flowering shrubs. Ruby kicked the ground. *Figures. Rain on Christmas.* Her family had always hiked the lime and papaya-hued hills of Waimea's forested plateau, where Father claimed their Cook pine with the swift swing of his ax. Later, they had decorated the wide-spaced boughs with *origami* Santas and festive paper balloons filled with air and giggles. But Taeko refused to celebrate a Christian holiday with no meaning to Buddhists. She objected to bringing a dead tree in the house and refused to go to the luau. And Father did not challenge her.

Ruby opened the side door of the temple to the reek of cigarette smoke wafting with the uneasy energy of raised voices from her father's office. Here, he spent long hours thinking big thoughts and meeting other influential men and didn't allow interruptions.

About to return home, she heard her father's distinctive orotund voice. He enunciated each measured word. "What do you suppose might await us back in Japan?"

She couldn't believe her ears—*await us in Japan?* No way would her family would move there! Nor could she comprehend the few words she overheard.

"State Shinto."

"An ideological roof over Japan."

"Decorated and uniformed military officers on majestic white horses."

She backed against the wall and listened as their bluster continued.

"Regime in step with Hitler."

"Dominate Korea."

A sudden pounding punctuated the air. *A fist pounding the table?*

"Invade China."

"People suffering."

The conversation quieted and someone asked for the time. Chairs scraped the floor, drowning out murmurs of *sayonara*.

Acting fast, Ruby pretended she had just arrived. She softly opened the door and slammed it closed with a confident bang, stepping aside so the men could exit the temple. When the last man had left, she removed the candy cane from her mouth, having forgotten it was there, and stepped into her father's office where he was straightening the chairs.

"Father, supper's almost ready."

Her father tousled her wind-whipped hair. "Okay, Peppermint Stick, let's go. It's Christmas." She smiled at his new pet name for her and his playfulness, unsure how he shut off the air of masculine intensity with the closing of his office door.

They dashed across the yard in a torrent of rain.

After supper, Father tried to make up for the lack of Christmas festivity with gifts he had brought from Japan. Taeko sat on the far side of the room, stitching embroidery. Father was in a spirited mood, and only when he involved Taeko in their merriment did the scowl she wore with ease disappear—if only for the moment. Ruby and Mari tore the pleated Japanese paper from their presents—jump ropes, *juzu* prayer beads, and *beigoma* tops. Father showed Ruby how to spin the disk-shaped toys to make a humming sound. From over his shoulder, Taeko's muddy eyes stared at her.

Ruby discovered joy wasn't found wrapped in beautiful paper or disguised by toys that hum. Her eyes made a quick escape to the dark corner of the living room where the tree used to be. Where the tree should be. Where the tree would be if Mama hadn't died. Even in death, Father said no one ever really dies. Was Mama in the spirit realm? Might she be right here? Right now? Ruby closed her eyes and imagined herself snuggled on Mama's lap and surrounded by colorful Christmas lights. She felt Mama's presence and heard her kind voice. *Okāsan doesn't mean to be harsh. Remember making tofu? Even acid has merit.*

• • •

Later, Ruby brushed her teeth and put on her pajamas. She discovered Mari sleeping, despite the raging storm and its orchestration of spooky sounds. Twigs banged into the house, wood siding rattled, and air hissed through exposed openings. As the flexible midribs of palm trees breathed heavily and bent in the violent wind, Ruby wrapped her arms around her tightening stomach. She was more fascinated than fearful of storms, but the men's unnerving conversation swirled in her mind. Why would Father talk about going back to Japan? All of her friends were here. And from what she knew of Japan from Japanese school, she didn't like it. Not one bit.

The loud crash on the tin roof above her head sent her flying out of bed and into the living room where her father and Taeko were reading. Father looked up from his newspaper. "What is it, Ruby?"

"Something crashed on the roof," she said, with a shiver.

"It's probably just a coconut."

Taeko closed her book and set it aside. "The storm is a fright, Chiko. Especially for a little girl. I'll tuck her in. You finish your article."

She took Ruby's hand. "Come with me, little one."

"Thank you, dear," Father said. "Goodnight, Ruby-*chan*. Sleep well."

Taeko's hand was cold. A moment later, Ruby felt the tips of Taeko's fingernails—filed into the shape of pointy almonds—dig into her palm. Ruby wanted to run back to her father, but sensed that would cause more trouble. Instead, she held her breath.

They entered the bedroom to the sound of Mari's restful breathing.

Taeko closed the door, released Ruby's hand, and flung back the covers.

She pointed toward the bed. "Get in."

Ruby got into bed and pulled the covers up to her quivering chin.

Taeko lowered her face to within inches of Ruby's. Her breath reeked of fermented soybeans as she spoke with a whispered hiss. "That will be enough of your whining. Not another sound out of you."

Taeko closed the door as she left the room, leaving Ruby in darkness. Rubbing the dents on her palm, she felt a sudden urge to pee. She didn't dare leave her room again, so she squeezed her legs together and jiggled her buttocks up and down against the mattress, determined to make it through the night without wetting the bed.

Soon, her thoughts drifted to Mama.

Mama would have asked Ruby if she needed to tinkle before going back to bed, tucked her in, and sat with her for a few minutes. She would have stroked her hair and told her a story, maybe the one about the boy who had been inside of a peach. Mama's kindness would have washed over Ruby like the calm of a long bubble bath. When everyone in the story had lived happily ever after, Mama would have kissed her forehead and said, "Sweet dreams, little one."

The storm blew away, and Ruby drifted into sleep to the sound of drizzle pinging on the metal roof. Cocooned in a fuzzy peach, she bounced along ocean swells until carried ashore on the shoulder of a tsunami. She landed in a water-colored orchard and emerged from the peach's flesh surrounded by *oni*—Japanese ogre warriors wielding bayonets and metal-studded clubs—vibrating with saturated color. She darted into the light-filled rows of the orchard, but her legs struggled to move as if racing within a weighted sack of rice. From behind a translucent gnarled tree trunk, the lumbering *oni* kept pace at a menacing distance. The trees trembled, and blushing shades of vibrant coral rained from the branches.

The lead warrior raised his eyes and met hers.

Warm urine streamed down her legs and pooled around her feet. The warrior sneered, raised his club, and advanced toward her.

Three

1940 – 1941

OKĀSAN

1940-1941 – Waimea, Hawaii

Head under her pillow, Ruby cried herself to sleep, comforted by the photograph of her as a baby in her mother's arms, which now hid under her mattress. Earlier that day, she had taken the picture from the drawer where Taeko kept Mama's framed photographs. *How dare she disrespect her mama that way—tossing her pictures upside-down in a drawer among scrap paper, matchsticks, and other meaningless stuff they never used—not even bothering to wrap the delicate frames for protection.*

Father offered a single comment when the girls objected to her tossing their mama's photos aside like used birthday candles. "This is her home now. Give it time."

The tension in their home gave Ruby a stomachache. Taeko refused to learn English and demanded they speak only Japanese. And she had strict rules for everything—even the order of their toothbrushes in the holder. Father allowed Taeko to get away with everything. It seemed to Ruby that he looked the other way, expecting her and Mari to obey.

To Ruby's amusement, Mari mocked Taeko behind her back. "She treats us like we're her dorm girls. I guess *liking* children isn't a requirement for schoolteachers in Japan!"

Taeko insisted on being called *Okāsan*, but Ruby would *never* accept her as her mother.

"Please, may I, *Okāsan?*"

"Yes, *Okāsan.*"

"No, *Okāsan.*"

"Thank you, *Okāsan.*"

"You're welcome, *Okāsan.*"

Taeko didn't play games with them like Mama had. She told them to be quiet when they laughed at something silly. Mama had always wanted to know what was so funny and joined in their laughter. If they sassed Taeko, she slapped them in the face. With Mama, there were few reasons to sass, and she had never hit them. Not once. Mama had wanted to know what they were thinking and feeling, even if they disagreed or were angry.

Ruby sighed. *Through the universe, can she hear our hearts breaking?*

Mama had corresponded often with her parents in Japan. The grandparents used to send Ruby and Mari cute pop-up cards and silk kimonos on their birthdays. Sometimes they sent small trinkets for no special reason. But when their grandparents learned Father had remarried, they sent him a letter saying they would no longer stay in contact with his family. Their granddaughters had a new mother, which left no room for them. Ruby thought it unfair to lose her grandparents too. She told herself she couldn't make them love her if they didn't, and she tried to pretend her grandparents didn't matter. They were old people whom she never saw anyway.

• • •

As Ruby snapped and washed green beans for supper, she thought of how Mama had pulled the string off the beans and snapped the tough end with the ease of water flowing over her graceful fingers during the rinse. Encouraged by Mama's smile and affection, she had learned love was the secret ingredient in cooking. A breeze of spicy sandalwood wafted from the wild naio hedge through the open window above the sink. Mama used to say the aromatic hedge served as protection around their home.

The hedge now served as a barrier between them and the neighboring house, concealing Taeko's hostility toward Ruby and Mari. Mrs. Moriwaki had been close friends with Mama and spent many overnights with them during Father's absence, but they didn't see much of her anymore, their friendship reduced to an occasional wave.

Taeko walked into the kitchen. "Did you soak the rice?"

"Oops, sorry *Okāsan.* I forgot. I'll do it now."

Taeko pounded her fist on the table, shaking the ceramic bowls set for supper. "Stupid girl! Now the rice will be hard."

Ruby looked at her feet. "Sorry, *Okāsan*."

"It's too late for sorry. Get out of here, I'll finish this myself. I expect your father home soon and you'll own up to your stupidity if he complains about the rice!"

On Ruby's way out of the kitchen, she overhead Taeko mutter under her breath, "Never have I experienced such unruly children. He said the girls were well-behaved. No child of mine would behave that way."

Ruby walked into the living room repeating her stepmother's nasty words in her head. She was secretly glad to get out of bean snapping and know her father would join them for supper. He had been spending many more nights out at meetings in the temple or at neighboring temples with other ministers and heads of the Japanese schools on the island. She thought about her stepmother's words. What if Taeko had a baby? Babies are innocent. Would Ruby be able to love Taeko's child as she imagined loving her baby sister who died? What if the baby killed Taeko, like the baby had killed Mama? Dark thoughts like that were too evil—even for Taeko—and Ruby pushed them from her mind.

She found Mari in their bedroom, reading.

"What was all of that about?" Mari asked, never taking her eyes off of her book.

"I forgot to soak the rice again."

"Hm. What a shrew. Looks like one too, with those little bitty eyes of hers."

Ruby laughed. "Yeah, until Father's around, fanning him with her fancy fan on hot days, laughing at his silly jokes."

Mari closed her book and faced Ruby. "Yup, she's a chameleon all right."

"A lizard?"

"No, silly! Someone who changes her behavior to suit a situation... like a chameleon reptilia. She's so phony... mean to us, but a sweet and proper Japanese woman around Father."

Mari returned to her book, but Ruby continued fretting. They had told their father when Taeko hurt them, but he always took Taeko's side.

Two days ago, Taeko hit her with a spatula when she forgot to take out the trash. The wide metal utensil had landed on her arm, leaving a red rectangle and a cut, destroying all fond memories of making *okonomiyaki* with Mama. She howled in pain and ran to her father, disturbing him in his office.

"Father! *Okāsan* hit me and made me bleed. I forgot about the trash. I meant to remember."

Her father had looked up from his papers. His tone was sharp. "Ruby, I'm busy and you know not to disturb me in here. I will not get in the middle of things between you and your mother."

"But she hurt me, Father. And she's not my mother!"

"Nonsense. She *is* your mother now. Accept that and stop provoking her."

"But..."

"Enough. And *Okāsan* hasn't felt well, so be kind to her."

Ruby had noticed the baffling cycles of illness Taeko seemed to experience. She seemed fine for weeks, then she was throwing up. She wept for days, and complained her right side was numb. Each weird cycle resulted in her becoming more intolerable.

"What's wrong with her anyway?" she had asked.

He opened his mouth as if to say something, but stopped.

"Nothing that time won't heal. Now do your chores when you're supposed to and stop bothering me! I must prepare for my trip to Honolulu."

She had sulked away rubbing her arm. The vibrant bruises from Taeko's smacks faded in time, but the bruises inside never faded and her father couldn't see them. Red. Purple. Black. Layers of thickening adhesions.

INTELLIGENCE

1941 – Hawaii

Chiko lowered the brim of his hat against the blinding sun as he disembarked the ship at the Honolulu harbor. Having spent months calming his congregation's worries over Japan's war fever and deteriorating relations between Japan and America, he was eager to visit and talk with his university friend, Reverend Miyamoto.

It seemed the entire Japanese community was worried about their loved ones in Japan, including their *kibei* children sent to Japan for formal education and who lived with relatives there. Families in Japan wrote of people struggling with food shortages and reading news they suspected the government filtered. Increasing numbers of teenagers were being conscripted into service. Those in Japan knew better than to speak against the war.

In Hawaii, many of his congregants devoured multiple newspapers— *The Garden Island, Hawaii Hochi,* and *Nippu Jiji*—and many were in close contact with worried relatives on the American West Coast. People whispered among themselves and to him about yellow peril intensifying in America.

Chiko couldn't understand why their pure race was singled out. The west wasn't that far from the east. *Issei* like him were no different than first-generation Irish, German, and Polish—all doing their best to raise their children in a two-culture system, one foot in their native country's strong culture of pride, honor, and spirit of community, one in the melting pot of America.

Deep in his furrowed brow, he imagined the pot boiling over. *How would he treat the burns?*

···

An hour later, the two friends enjoyed tea on the *engawa* at Miyamoto's temple.

"*Sensei*, I hope the tense situation between our two countries improves, but relations have sickened in the last decade like a fallen ginkgo berry," Chiko said.

Miyamoto took a sip of tea from the cup cradled in his delicate palms and paused, his words interrupted by the train's low whistle from the nearby Oahu Sugar Plantation. "*Hai*," Miyamoto said, tilting his crewcut skull. "*Sōdesune*. That's so true," he said, switching easily between Japanese and English. He took small, quiet sips. "America has been providing her allies arms and supplies, including weapons to China—to use against Japan." His brows knit together. "Roosevelt inflames tensions, freezing Japanese assets and cutting off steel and oil to Japan."

Chiko nodded. "How can Japan hold on?"

"I don't know. We didn't learn war strategy in university, but Japan's obsession with becoming the modern Asian power has become their vulnerability. Who knows when, or if, America will enter the war. And if against Japan, what that means for our families and friends here and there."

Chiko rubbed his forehead and drew in a lengthy breath. "*Sate*," he exhaled. "Well now," he repeated, this time in English, "My brother's temple is in the heart of Hiroshima. He writes to me of troublesome times and is concerned for his congregation. He claims the Empire expects the people to work harder, sacrifice more. People are starving and fleeing to the country where they might grow their own food. But like us, my brother has a responsibility to stay with his temple. He maintains they will make do and get by with the help of the congregation. I worry a war between our countries will divide my family. Only my youngest daughter, Ruby, was born here. She's an American."

"My friend, I'm in the same rotting *wasen*. Regardless of where we're born, we'll all look like the enemy if there's war."

"Indeed. And the boat we're in together will be easy to find."

With their friendship entwined by beliefs, worries, and national identity, they attended a rally sponsored by the Oahu Citizens Committee for Home Defense at McKinley High School as the guests of Dr. Shunzo Sakamaki, the committee's chairman. Standing under a bronze statue of President McKinley, Dr. Sakamaki delivered inspiring words to thousands assembled on the school's manicured lawn.

"We are here to re-pledge, one with another, our unreserved loyalty to the United States of America."

The mostly Japanese assembly thundered its approval, some waved American flags, and small children perched on their father's shoulders clapped their hands in delight.

"There are those who question our sincerity, who doubt our loyalty. But if they would only pause and reflect, they would realize there is no justification for such an attitude. We realize how fortunate we are to be living in this, of all the lands of the earth, and we cherish our heritage as Americans."

Intent listeners, who had previously heard the Army officials declare fair treatment for the Japanese if war started with Japan, nodded their heads.

"If war comes, we will give our lives in defense of the democratic principles for which other Americans have lived, fought, and died."

The crowd exploded. Chiko bowed his head. *"Amida Butsu,* show us the way."

• • •

The next morning, Chiko and Miyamoto sat beside each other in silence before the Oahu Hongwanji altar. Aware his meditation was ending, Chiko savored the quiet within his body before the slow and natural shift from deep relaxation to a gradual re-orientation to the here and now. Thoughts and sensations had come and gone as he wiggled his fingers and opened his eyes. He gazed at the brass candlestick on the altar, a crane standing on a tortoise. Symbols of happiness and longevity.

He closed his eyes, pressed his palms to his heart, and reflected with sadness on the babies Taeko had lost. A month after they returned from Japan, Taeko experienced severe nausea, vomiting, and weight loss. It delighted him to learn she was with child so soon after their marriage, but she miscarried as easily as she'd conceived. Two miscarriages and a procedure followed. His wife was barren. Yet again, Ruby and Mari would be denied a baby brother or sister.

With no babies to care for, Taeko had time to devote to their ministry and the Japanese school. For a year, she had pushed him to allow her to get more involved. Selfishly, he welcomed her help. Once Taeko earned the respect of their congregants and parents of the children she would teach, things would settle down. Until then, he vowed to honor his intention, to ignore the annoying harsh words, protests, and histrionics of Taeko and his daughters. It wasn't his fault Akemi had died and left him to find someone to care for the girls. He was lucky Taeko had agreed to marry him and leave her country and family behind so he could focus on his priority. The temple.

• • •

He soon returned to Waimea, where his wife and daughters lay sleeping, hoping his birth and adopted countries would continue earnest negotiations and find a peaceful compromise. Instead, the bombastic rhetoric worsened, and within days, Chiko began to notice things. A white man he hadn't seen before appeared at the back of the temple during services, then disappeared. He spotted a different stranger standing across the street from the Japanese school. When leaving the bank, he observed a parked car. Someone sitting inside wore sunglasses and seemed to be waiting. Waimea was a small town and people knew each other. Suspicious, he would glance over his shoulder.

As quickly as he had begun noticing the strangers, he stopped noticing them. He concluded his worries were figments of his imagination.

They weren't. The FBI dossier on Chiko Ishimaru was complete.

AMERICAN SON

1941 – Hiroshima, Japan

Koji carried a heavy knapsack and his *hi no maru* lunch—white rice with a red plum in the center resembling the circle of the sun—in his metal *bentō* box. He followed a worn path along the glistening Enko River toward Hiroshima Itchu, the coveted and elite school run by the government where he'd begun the previous year. The fishing fleets had departed for more open waters before dawn, but the river and its industrial shorelines buzzed. Factories spewed a gauntlet of fumes polluting the morning sky, and workers loaded cargo ships with pallets of war machinery. Japan was blowing China to bits. The world was in chaos. And America was the latest enemy of the Japanese Empire.

Otōsan's diatribes had been right—the regime now controlled his school. A shrine was displayed with prominence at the front of the classroom. Koji's *sensei* insisted the students worship the Emperor with their whole hearts, reject any notion of self or independence, and be ready to kill themselves when necessary for Japan. *Sensei* had declared America's democracy a joke and rejected the notion of individual rights and welfare. He believed America's Yankees sat on the sidelines, interfering, weak, and contemptuous.

The school day was much like any other, until late afternoon when Koji returned to his classroom for blackboard duty. After erasing and wiping the boards free of chalk impressions and smudges, he found the next day's class message in the regular place on *Sensei's* organized desk. In his finest calligraphy on the clean slate, and with little verve, he wrote: *I fight with enthusiasm.*

He left the building in the shadows of dusk and began his walk home, thinking about the skeleton key missing from the *tansu*. *Okāsan* must have found a new hiding place for the key, and despite his best efforts he couldn't find it. It had been two years since finding the papers, and he had given up trying to discover more details about what "American son" meant. It seemed the trouble with truth was it somehow made all else feel untrue. Not knowing the full story nagged and frustrated him, and he wondered what else his parents might be keeping from him. But it would be disrespectful to question his parents. Sometimes he wished he'd never heard *Otōsan's* hushed words.

• • •

Weeks later, Koji arrived home to find his flush-faced mother placing a flower in a simple lacquered container, alongside a single curved branch that reminded him of a graceful ballerina's arm. *Okāsan* was skilled in the art of *ikebana,* and he watched her finish the floral arrangement as if she were putting the last touches on a piece of artwork. She placed the flowers along with candles and incense on the family altar.

Otōsan sat at the table reading the newspaper. He had more color in his cheeks than he had that morning when he was up at dawn, retching. Koji had begun noticing *Otōsan's* lack of appetite a few months ago. Usually a voracious eater, *Otōsan* said he was full after eating small amounts of food and complained of indigestion. His body seemed to be working overtime to fight whatever ailed him and his muscular physique had become weak and skinny. The vomiting was something new and worrisome, and Koji felt compelled to tackle more and more chores around the farm.

The newspaper's bold first-page headline faced Koji. The words seemed to fill the page—MILITARY ISSUES NO-SURRENDER POLICY. Koji shook his head. *What's a soldier to do then?* But he knew. *Sensei* often bragged about soldiers who took their own lives. Unthinkable to Koji. He knew the rest of the articles sensationalized Japan's many victories and growing restrictions.

Suddenly, *Otōsan* tossed the newspaper on the table and ranted aloud to whoever was listening. "The government looks to control everything, from labor unions to the allotment of rice people eat. Times are so hard in the city. We farmers and others living in the countryside have enough to eat, but other people rely on paltry rations of rice, barley, and vegetables. These nationalists and militarists are destroying Japan!"

Koji squirmed. He knew to stay quiet and allow *Otōsan* to rant until he was finished.

His father continued. "And over two million teenagers and young adults mobilized to work in factories and bolster the war effort!"

Koji dreaded the call to mandatory service and hoped the war ended before derailing his education. "*Otōsan*, will they mobilize me?"

"I think not. You're far too young." *Otōsan* hesitated and stroked his chin. "It couldn't possibly go on." His voiced drifted away.

Otōsan pointed to an article about government-imposed and voluntary austerity campaigns needed to support Japan's warring. "Ha! Voluntary! What a joke!" He motioned for Koji to join him.

Koji assumed proper *seiza*—knees folded, heels directly underneath his buttocks—at the same table where *Otōsan* had eaten meals since he was a boy. Made of cedar, the sturdy table had developed a patina of scratches, heat stains, and built-up wax. Koji wanted to change the subject. "Where's Naoki?"

His mother slipped to the floor and joined them. "The vines were yellowing. I asked him to start digging up the sweet potatoes."

Otōsan closed the paper and looked at him. "It's good Naoki is out. *Okāsan* and I must speak to you about something important."

For some reason, the taste in Koji's mouth soured at *Otōsan's* serious tone. He felt as though something was wrong, like he was in trouble for something.

Otōsan leaned closer. "Life confronts us with obstacles and tragedies when we least expect them." He rubbed his stomach. "I've had this upset stomach for a while, and the doctor has now diagnosed my stomach pain as a malignancy."

"A what?"

"It's a disease where cells grow out of control."

Koji conjured images in his mind of what multiplying cells looked like. He swept a clammy hand across his forehead to wipe off the sweat. "What causes it?"

"The disease is peculiar and there's no explanation why one person gets sick and another doesn't."

His mother sat motionless, her back straight and head bowed. Silent tears fell and moistened her hands curled together in her lap. She didn't cry often and when she did, Koji felt helpless. He wanted to console her and wished to close the distance between them, but his legs seemed glued to the floor.

"Will we get sick too?"

"No, don't worry. It's not contagious, but it's also not curable. It's treatable, though. Our family must be strong to cope with this illness."

Otōsan reached for and squeezed *Okāsan's* hand.

"You're old enough to hear what you need to hear, not what you want to hear," *Otōsan* said. "The hard truth is I'll have fewer years with you and Naoki than I dreamed of having. But that's life—fleeting—like cherry blossoms. We'll take one day at a time." He cleared his throat. "There's a price to pay for being the eldest son. As *chōnan*, you must assume more responsibility. This will be good for you, Koji. By helping our family through these tough times, you will strengthen your capabilities and build moral fiber."

His father's features were soft and his speech had been unhurried. *Okāsan* wore an empty stare and blinked the wetness from her dull eyes. Helplessness made Koji feel small, yet he had a sense of being taller and stronger at the same time. His words came with difficulty as he looked *Otōsan* in the eyes. "You can count on me."

Otōsan folded the newspaper in thirds. "We have something else to tell you." He paused and stared at the paper.

"Koji, Japan isn't the only country where I've lived. As a young man, I left Japan to work in America and returned in 1920 to find a bride. After marrying *Okāsan*, we left Japan for a city called Seattle, a port city in the United States. Unlike me, *Okāsan* spoke no English, so she attended night school to learn the language. We kept a voucher from her school, stamped *Valuable Receipt—save it!* I'll show it to you sometime. It's funny." *Otōsan* chuckled.

A sudden loss of balance and a whirling sensation stifled Koji's ability to return the chuckle or speak. It felt like he was looking down from a great height and seeing a small detail one shouldn't be able to see from such a distance. His body went limp, realizing his dishonesty had cheated his honest father. Here was *Otōsan* sharing serious, adult things with him while he feigned ignorance.

"Koji, are you listening?"

He kept his flat gaze on the table and nodded. "I'm sorry." He raised his eyes and looked around the room without actually looking at anything and then focused on *Otōsan*.

"After a few years in Seattle, we moved to a place called Superior in the state of Wyoming. There, we opened a laundry and washed the coal miner's clothes. Many were Japanese. We saved enough money to purchase an automobile in 1924—a Ford Touring model. Few people had the money to buy a car, so your mother and I were quite proud. Not long after, we packed our car and drove west to much warmer, southern California to work on a flower farm."

Otōsan was perspiring. His hand no longer comforted *Okāsan*, but clasped with his other on the table. "Koji, you were born in a city called Los Angeles, in a state called California, in the United States." He paused. "You're an American citizen. You have an American birth certificate."

Koji's eyes widened.

His parents had never talked to him as a grown-up or told him secrets. He didn't realize he had been tapping a pair of chopsticks onto the tabletop until *Otōsan* rested a hand over his.

"Sorry," Koji said, trying to force himself to stay calm.

He wanted to know more. "Why did we leave?"

"You were a toddler when we returned to Hiroshima to care for our aging parents. We loved America and wanted to raise you there. But the Great Depression brought hard times, and it became too difficult to make a living. We always intended to move back, but your grandparents begged us to stay in Japan and we were obligated to them."

"As the second son, I wasn't entitled to the family property after our parents died, so I used the money we had saved in America and bought the property from my older brother. We built our life here and your uncle is happier working in Kyoto for a department store and living near his wife's family. He was born too soon. I was born too late."

"What does it mean to be an American citizen?"

"It means you can travel to the U.S., live there if you like, and enjoy the country's freedoms. You're a lucky boy. We never told you because you weren't old enough to know, but you are now. We live in troubled times between Japan and America. You must keep our secret. Don't tell anyone, including Naoki, that you're an American citizen. You may put us all in danger if word got out."

The kitchen faucet dripped. *Okāsan* sniffled. In the distance, he heard the familiar grinding of gears from his neighbor's pickup truck.

Otōsan stood. "We will tell Naoki about my illness when we feel the time is right. For now, let us offer intentions to *Amida Butsu* for our family's well-being."

Koji popped up. He helped *Okāsan* to her feet. She placed a hand on his shoulders and looked up to him. When had he grown taller than her? She moved a hand to his cheek and offered him a weak smile. "You're a good son."

He took her hand and they knelt before the altar with their *juzu* beads. Together they inhaled the aromatic incense and repeated the mantra to Buddha. "*Namu Amida Butsu, Om Amideva Hrīh*"—to overcome all difficulties and give them strength for the days ahead.

PEARL HARBOR

December 7, 1941 – Hawaii

Pearl of beauty, pearl of life
Within your channels deep.
Rest the men and tools of war
For you and God to keep.
—*Cornelius Douglas*

Abundant forests, majestic mountains, and dramatic canyons concealed the scars of violence that had formed the Hawaiian Islands over the course of five million years. Microscopic flecks of energy and explosive volcanic activity had matured into a lush paradise. The islands were tranquil in the early Sunday hours.

Ruby finished her breakfast of fried eggs and Spam marinated in soy sauce. She spent extra time selecting her shorts and top for later, laid the garments on her bed, and pressed the wrinkles with her hands. Invited to lunch and play at the home of her friend, Louise, she wanted to be ready for a quick change of clothes after service. She dressed in a simple cotton frock, slipped on her sandals, and hurried out the door to join Mari, who was already in the temple.

Service was about to begin, yet Ruby's gaze lingered on the glistening dew in the peaceful morning. Flowers had become a jungle of twisted colors with leaves and vines, reposing along the hedge. Beyond the hedge, magenta and flaxen flowers hung like ornaments from a young koa tree, their beauty quietly strangling the tree's tender limbs. The sun peeked through the clouds, and she dashed into the temple.

• • •

On the other side of the Kauai Channel, at Pearl Harbor Naval Base, unsuspecting sailors played craps on the deck of the USS *Arizona*. Others in the ship's belly spruced up for a day of leave in Honolulu. Japanese *sampans* were returning to port from several days of ahi fishing.

A few minutes before eight o'clock, the officer on deck of the hospital ship, the USS *Solace,* focused his binoculars on a swarm of planes with distinctive red dots approaching through the morning mist. He blinked, incredulous. Nurses in starched white uniforms had begun their morning shift. Within moments, the nurses shielded their ears from the deafening noise as they witnessed the USS *Arizona* explode into flames. Powerless to help, they choked on the blinding black smoke, unable to see the dead and dying.

Amid the smoldering wreckage, U.S. soldiers fired anti-aircraft guns. Their desperate and impotent attempts to defend their ships, airplanes, and country resulted in minimal losses for Japan. When the catastrophic attacks ended, 2,400 American civilians and military personnel had died, leaving 1,100 wounded. Hardly a single U.S. vessel escaped destruction.

As the vibration from the temple bell found Ruby and resounded its message of impermanence, Japan's treacherous surprise attack propelled America into war.

JAP!

December 7, 1941 – Hawaii

On her beat-up Dixie Flyer bicycle, Ruby bunny-hopped over the lawn-less plantation grounds and curbs in town and sped toward the taro farm owned by Louise's family. Cruising on the coast road, she passed Fort Elizabeth. The red walls of the star-shaped Russian fortress stood strong after one hundred and twenty years on the shores of Waimea Bay, framed by the Pacific. The sun kissed her round face, and she soaked in the island's perfume, a cocktail of fragrant bougainvillea and salt air. Sea breezes tousled her chin-length black hair.

She glided on her bike with outstretched arms mimicking the wing-span of a mōlī. A well-worn set of jacks and a ball nestled in her pocket. The undefeated champion against her other friends, Ruby hoped to impress Louise with her skills. With any luck, she'd win the flip and go first. She navigated the long driveway framed with banyan trees to Louise's house with its welcoming white porch. Her stomach was grumbling by the time she arrived, and she wondered what Louise might offer for lunch. She rested her bike against a tree and rang the doorbell. Ruby expected Louise to answer the door with her ever-present smile. Instead, her friend was cry-ing. Before she could ask what was wrong, she heard the sharp voice from inside. "Be quick about it, Louise!"

Ruby put her hands in the pockets of her shorts and rubbed the top of her legs through the fabric. The rubbing soothed her.

The door opened. Louise blew her nose and held an embroidered hanky in front of her mouth, mumbling, "I'm sorry... I can't... my mom said I'm not allowed to play with you. She said you have to leave."

"Why? What's wrong?"

"My mom says you're a Jap and I can't be friends with you."

Louise's mother appeared in her housecoat with not a single blond hair out of place. Her steel-blue eyes bore into Ruby. "That's enough. Goodbye, Ruby."

She closed the door in Ruby's face.

Ruby stared at the closed door. She lowered her lashes to her dirty Keds. Never had she suffered such embarrassment. Her cheeks burned. *A Jap.* No one had ever called her a Jap.

She wiped her tears on her sleeve and pedaled furiously home to an empty house. It was just as well no one was home since she didn't know how to explain what had happened. She crumbled onto her bed and grabbed her pillow to hold across her belly. Her trembling body faded into the soft quilting.

The screen door banged sometime after her tears had dried, and Mari entered the room, still wearing her clothes from temple. "Oh good," Mari said, pausing to catch her breath, as if she'd been running. "You're here. The men with Father left. He wants us in his office."

"What for?"

"Jeez... you don't know?"

"Know what?" she asked, hugging her pillow.

"Japan attacked us. Come on, let's go!"

The scent of incense from the morning's service greeted them inside of the temple. Their father was seated in his swivel chair behind the substantial pedestal desk, amid a fog of cigarette smoke that lingered from his meeting. Taeko stood beside him, the veins in her neck pronounced. Her father's eyebrows were lowered, framing his sullen face.

"Sit down, girls."

The girls sat in chairs opposite his desk. Ruby clasped her hands and waited for him to say something.

Father wrinkled his brow. "Japan bombed Pearl Harbor this morning in a surprise attack for reasons impossible to understand. The news is sketchy, but many American soldiers suffered and died. There are rumors the Japanese in Hawaii somehow aided the attack." The chair creaked as he moved closer, and he spoke to them as if they were members of his congregation. "As Buddhists we believe all life is precious, including soldiers. We know suffering is part of life, but we believe in peace. We must hope the will to attack and kill is abandoned."

To Ruby his words sounded hollow.

Taeko held a handkerchief to her mouth and gulped back tears. Ruby had never seen this side of her before and was frightened.

"What's Pearl Harbor?" Ruby asked.

"It's a naval base on Oahu, but don't worry. We are safe here. Run along now, I have calls to attend to."

Ruby wanted to stay with her father, sit on his lap, and be told more about what it meant when countries attacked one another. She wanted to tell him what had happened to her at Louise's house and have him reassure her. That's what Mama would have done. Oahu—right next door, thought Ruby as she walked across the yard. *Was the attack why Louise's mother was so mean?*

That night, bonfires burned throughout the plantation community, fueled by Japanese books, photographs, correspondence, and anything that might give authorities the false impression of one's loyalty to Japan. Father said not to worry. But smoke permeated their walls and Ruby's dreams with fear.

The next morning, Ruby arrived at school to find boys zooming around the yard pretending to be airplanes, blowing raspberries to make the sound of gunfire. Others pretended they were firing machine guns at make-believe enemies. A few played dead. Tension seized her classroom. Teachers seemed distracted and kids eyed each other with caution.

"I pledge allegiance to the flag of the United States of America... "

With her hand on her heart, Ruby recited her loyal conviction to America.

Her seventh-grade homeroom teacher smiled and treated her with kindness, saying Japan's actions weren't Ruby's fault and her feelings toward Ruby hadn't changed. But some of Ruby's white classmates taunted her with chants of "You're the enemy!" and "Go back to where you came from!" Others avoided her altogether. When she felt their stares and looked at them, they looked away.

She bristled. *If they won't see me—see me for who I am, the same girl as yesterday— they should stop staring!*

Mid-morning, her class filed across the schoolyard to the upper school to attend an assembly in the auditorium. The principal approached the lectern and thanked the school secretary for transcribing every word of President's Roosevelt's radio address, delivered hours earlier to the joint session of Congress.

The principal read the President's words:

"Yesterday, December 7, 1941—a date which will live in infamy— the United States of America was suddenly and deliberately attacked by naval and air forces of the Empire of Japan. I ask that Congress declare... "

His words were clear. The United States was at war with Japan, and the Hawaiian Islands were under martial law, with strict travel and curfew restrictions. Teachers passed around blackout schedules, still damp from mimeographing. Windows must be blacked out between 7:15 p.m. and 7:15 a.m. The light inside of Ruby dimmed.

• • •

As dusk settled, Ruby washed the dishes. Mari nailed quilts over the windows—a temporary solution until they made blackout shades. Their father answered a knock at the door. Ruby dried her hands and stepped into the living room to see who was there. Her father greeted the sheriff, who was his friend, and two strangers wearing suits and ties—all three of them white men—and invited them inside.

The sheriff's tone was serious. *"Sensei*, I hate to do this." The sheriff looked at the two strangers. "These men are with the FBI. We have a warrant for your arrest on suspicion that you are an enemy alien of the United States, pending final action by the Commanding General, Hawaiian

Department, United States Army."

Her father's angry voice quivered. "That's absurd! I've done nothing wrong. I'm as outraged by Japan's strike as you are, and I am not an enemy of the U.S."

One of the men pulled handcuffs from his pocket. "Turn around, sir."

"Please," Father said, stepping away from the door as they approached him. "I'm a Buddhist minister. We don't believe in killing."

The sheriff put his hand on her father's arm. "*Sensei*, you must come with us. It's best."

Father's heavy exhale filled the room with resignation, and he turned and put his hands behind him as instructed.

Ruby flinched at the sound of the cuffs locking and felt the living room walls close in around her. Her father's watery eyes looked back at Taeko, but he seemed to avoid making eye contact with Ruby or Mari.

"Don't worry, everything will be okay," he said.

The men escorted her father out.

"Where are you taking him?" Taeko demanded. Mari interpreted her stepmother's irate Japanese to English. The men didn't answer.

Ruby ran to the open door and watched her handcuffed father disappear into the dark night.

SHRILL IN THE AIR

December 8, 1941 – Hiroshima, Japan

Koji woke to a heavy heart in an empty house following a fitful night's sleep. Throughout the night, his thoughts had leapt from his secret American citizenship, to *Otōsan's* illness, to his additional household responsibilities. Like a hamster was caged in his head, his thoughts jumped from one wheel to another.

To escape the quiet house, he stepped into the raw, cold drizzle.

Fuchu seemed on edge that gray morning, a distinct fervor was in the air. Koji crossed the dormant yard and opened the rusty gate to the communal road. He was accustomed to seeing the predictable patterns of people leaving for work and school. Today looked out of kilter. Even the chirping of the birds sounded discordant. Pockets of men congregated up and down the hills of their lane. *Otōsan* huddled with their neighbor, Watanabe-*san*, and some other men. Everyone talked in hushed, serious voices. Animated gestures and furtive glances punctuated their conversations.

Ear-piercing pronouncements yelled by neighborhood men interrupted the gloomy silence and shrilled through the morning air. "We hit the Americans!"

"Japan started war with the United States and Britain!"

"Our bombardiers... are heroes!"

"Japan attacked Hawaii yesterday without warning!"

Koji watched his father and Watanabe-*san* freeze. News of the victory seemed to inflame the passions of many as the quiet street erupted—a volcano belching anxious cheers of *"Forget self. All out for our country!"* People retrieved their Rising Sun flags from porch holders and waved the symbol of the Empire, creating a dizzying and fiery display of red rays. Others wore the strained smiles of dread disguised as joy and hung back.

Koji couldn't believe his ears. *Japan had bombed the United States.* He shrank away from the crowd, retreated through the gate, and ran toward the distant fallow fields behind his home.

• • •

Koji entered his classroom to find the cheer he'd heard earlier—*Forget self. All out for our country!* —written across the blackboard. He settled into his seat with a dull headache, the remnant of a sleepless night. Around him, his classmates exchanged warmongering banter.

"Kaboom!"

"Take this you ugly Yankee!"

"I'm going to cut you in half with my *katana*," a boy said, waving a pretend saber.

A boy playing with a pinecone pretended to blow up an American battleship with his imaginary grenade. *Sensei* stepped through the doorway. He was quick to end the boys' foolishness and high-pitched laughter with a thundering smack of his meterstick on the desk. "Boys, your attention! Our great Empire has shown magnificent power. We have much to be proud of. And much will be expected of you." He pointed at the class. "*You* must willingly do whatever the Empire asks of you. *You* will train as home soldiers."

A knock at the classroom door interrupted *Sensei's* rallying lecture. He opened the door a crack and the teacher from the neighboring classroom passed him a newspaper. His eyes danced across the headlines, and he turned the paper around for the entire class to see—JAPAN DECLARES WAR AGAINST THE UNITED STATES. JAPAN VICTORIOUS! He then read the front-page article out loud.

"The Imperial Navy executed a crippling attack on the Pearl Harbor naval base in Hawaii at 2:48 a.m. Japan Time. Destroying America's Pacific Fleet, a singular threat to Japan, will weaken the resolve of the American people and halt their interference with

Japan's expansion! Japan's key to success lives in our nation's faith in this triumph. "

The classroom responded with roaring applause, but Koji rubbed his thigh to settle his knee caught in an involuntary bounce. For the first time, he dreaded the remainder of the school day.

• • •

That evening, the Matsuo family nestled in the warmth and safety of their home under the darkening sky. *Otōsan* picked up and put down the newspaper every few minutes, as if the headlines might have changed since the last time he looked. Koji sat next to his mother. She must have sensed his anxiety and put her arm around his shoulders. He inched closer to her. The news was a lot to absorb, yet there wasn't enough information for him to understand what the news meant for him.

Intrusive and unwanted thoughts began with *What if? What if I'm found out? What would they do to me? What would happen to my family?* The questions spiraled, and each rotation increased Koji's unease. His mind ran continuously, like a machine. The gears in his head turned over and over. The smaller gears moved and connected with bigger gears, until his entire head was filled with gears connecting to and moving with other gears. The gears of war were in motion. Torque increased.

What if Japan was wrong about the United States? What if America had the strength to strike back... and hard? Then what?

He answered his questions with resolve. Like the teeth on a gear, he must work harder to fit in—he must show patriotism and wave the Japanese flag. Under the Rising Sun, this American son would soldier on.

Four

1941 - 1942

SAUDADE

1941-1942 – Hawaii

Ruby and Mari waited. And waited longer. Weeks passed with no information about their father—what had happened to him, if he would return home, if the men had hurt him. Each morning Ruby set her father's place at the breakfast table, only to put the clean dishes back in the cabinet later. She did the same at supper. When she wasn't at school or doing her chores, she waited for him on the porch—pleading, longing to see him in an approaching car. And the next morning and the morning after that, she had listened for the sound of his voice or his distinctive footfalls on the wood floors. She would jump out from under the covers and look in his bedroom and in the temple to see if he had returned during the night. He never had.

Meanwhile, Taeko's mood worsened. More than once, Ruby heard Taeko complain to her Japanese friends about having come to Kauai, the unfairness of her husband's arrest, and the many obligations imposed on her. And her hatred of America.

While in class, Ruby daydreamed about returning home to find Father in his arm chair, with his stocking feet crossed on the hassock, reading the newspaper. Before drifting off to sleep, she imagined his return the next day. She bargained with herself, promising things she'd give up or do if *only* he would come home—she would strive to be a better Buddhist, give up candy, forgive him for marrying Taeko. His homecoming became a chimeric dream.

New Year's Day—a special holiday for the Japanese—came and went. With no minister, the temple closed and its bell didn't toll at midnight. No one visited. They didn't serve special foods on their best lacquerware. They didn't eat with fancy chopsticks to celebrate a new beginning. There was no *ozōni* soup, no sweet *mochi* cakes, no challenges of who might beat Father by surrounding more territory in a game of *Gō*. There was no joy.

But they honored one tradition—cleaning. Taeko demanded it. The girls beat rugs, washed windows, scrubbed floors, cleaned cabinets, washed and hung their bed linens and curtains on the clothesline, and polished the furniture. Their stepmother insisted they rid the house of old spirits and start the new year clean. Their father would come home soon.

• • •

Ruby pushed the hair off her face and dipped a paintbrush into a pail of white paint. Father would be so mad! She was applying the third coat of paint and still hadn't covered the words NAZI! and JAP! graffitied on the temple's sign overnight by a vandal. It wasn't the Buddhists fault the Germans had hijacked and turned the left-facing *manji* into an emblem of hate. An adult view of complex new realities had unfolded in front of twelve-year-old Ruby. The government ordered Japanese Americans to surrender to the police their short-wave radios, firearms, cameras, and even binoculars. Actions of prejudice and a climate of fear pervaded Waimea and destroyed everything she had learned about democracy. Overnight, law-abiding Japanese had become criminals—guilty by association. To one another, they expressed shame, humiliation, and fear.

She stepped away from the fence to examine her work. The last coat of paint had erased the words. If only a paint brush could erase the attack on Pearl Harbor. The plantation community was outraged Father had been arrested, and they supported their Japanese neighbors, but ignorance bred fear beyond the sugar mill. Ruby's white classmates avoided her as though her disgrace was contagious. At least some had the courage to say it was too dangerous to continue their friendship.

She heard comments at the grocery and on the street. "Japs are dirty, traitorous double-dealers." And "Japs have taken over the islands." The Filipinos who owned the fruit and vegetable stand in town hung a giant sign: WE ARE FILIPINO! A classmate wore an I AM CHINESE button his uncle in California had mailed to him. Ruby wore the face of the enemy.

Longing for Mama and her father, she spent time alone in the storeroom. Here, she promised her attentive audience of dolls that she would not allow herself to love another person again. It hurt too much when they left. Her Portuguese friend's mother told Ruby she experienced *saudade*— the presence of absent loved ones.

Ruby's teacher promoted civility among the students and read a newspaper article to the class about the Japanese American Citizens League's allegiance to the United States. After the bombing, the League sent President Roosevelt a telegram:

In this solemn hour we pledge our fullest cooperation to you, Mr. President, and to our country. There cannot be any question. There must be no doubt. We, in our hearts, are Americans and loyal to America, and will prove that to you.

The words were meaningless to the Japanese-haters and to those Japanese who remained true to the Emperor. Having felt jubilation at the news of the attack, Japanese loyalists began feeling betrayed by Japan for attacking and abandoning them with the Americans. But hatred swirled around divided loyalties, and the article did little to soothe Ruby's fears.

In mid-January, they received a letter from Father with a return address of the Wailua County Jail. He was one of fifty Japanese-language school teachers, clergymen, and other community leaders on the island rounded up, arrested as enemy aliens, and deprived of liberty without due process. In his letter, he complained about being held in a rank, noisy, crowded, and gloomy concrete cell, where he slept on a hard surface covered by a single blanket and shared a metal bucket toilet with the other inmates. Why did they suspect her father, a dedicated and committed teacher of the Buddha, of being a spy or anyone's enemy? No one told him anything. Yet they held him, behind iron bars in despicable conditions.

His next letter arrived weeks later.

January 28, 1942

My dearest family,

Regrettably, I write with disturbing news. Today I appeared, without the benefit of legal counsel, before an all-civilian board comprised of the president, recorder, and two other members. Based on meritless findings, the board determined me a devotee to Japan's Emperor and recommended my continued incarceration. I did my best to convince them I have not and would not engage in any subversive activities against the United States, but my fate seemed pre-determined. I am labeled an enemy alien and will remain imprisoned.

With our bank account frozen and my inability to lead the temple, I trust the good graces of the congregation will come to your aid.

All my love, Father

· · ·

Mr. Masaki, the local grocer, began taking Taeko to visit Ruby's father in jail on his weekly trips to the eastern side of the island. Taeko took her father treats and clean clothes from home, they visited for a few minutes, and she returned with his dirty laundry. Father had asked to see Ruby, and she was thrilled to be singled out to visit her father on a crisp, sunny March morning. Seated in the bed of Mr. Masaki's rattling truck among empty produce crates, Ruby gazed beyond the unspoiled terrain of red-dirt interwoven valleys, up to the forested Mount Kawaikini, soaring over five thousand feet into a shroud of mist.

She wondered what lay beneath the verdant peaks, if it was light and flourishing, dark and scary, or mystical. Did the mythical Menehune live there among the exuberant forested canyons? Father used to tease that if she misbehaved, the mischievous leprechaun-like creatures would dart out of the forest gorges and kidnap her. He said the Menehune were three feet tall, had gigantic eyes, and no hair. Some were small enough to fit in her palm, but they possessed super strength.

The truck sped along the single dusty road that hugged most of Kauai's perimeter. In the front seat, Taeko's small head bobbed along with the truck's movement. Like a mountain peak, her stepmother's stern and despairing persona showed only the tip of her mean-hearted true self. She had become increasingly bad-tempered, and Ruby had overheard her grumbling, "I'm an educated woman. They've stripped me of my dignity. I'll bring shame on my family. I *never* should have left Japan. Never!"

If Ruby didn't finish her chores on time, Taeko smacked her. And sometimes she smacked her or Mari for no reason. She called Mari *baka-yarō*—a stupid fool who would never amount to anything—and ridiculed Mari's slightly buck teeth. But Ruby knew Taeko was the unattractive one, uglied by her disagreeable demeanor. Everyone loved Mari. They didn't care if her teeth weren't perfect. And didn't Mari's friends just celebrate her sixteenth birthday with a homemade cake? Fat chance anyone would do that for Taeko!

While Mari was at the library studying or looking for odd jobs to make extra money, Ruby hid from her stepmother's storms in the temple store-room among her mother's dolls. Like a puppy who finds comfort in a small den, Ruby crouched in a corner, surrounded by empty floral vessels, candle supplies, and the calming scent of incense, and spoke to each of her artfully clothed friends who brightened her darkness.

Now, Mr. Masaki pulled in front of the new two-story jail, and Ruby jumped out of the truck bed onto the dirt parking area. With her shoes and white socks enveloped in dust, she faced the concrete block fortress, where bars covered the windows and an American flag fluttered rhythmically in the steady breeze.

In recent months, people of the town had built the new jail to improve living conditions for the Japanese inmates. Inside were toilets, a bathhouse, bunk beds, a kitchen, and a modest community room where her father honed his *sumi-e* skills. In his letters, he had boasted that his peers envied his brushwork—shades of black brushed over a muted pastel.

They stepped inside of the building, registered with the man in charge, and entered the visiting room. The room reeked of hot sweat and cold metal. Although frightened to be inside of a jail, Ruby was filled with joy to see her father. But she wasn't prepared for his appearance. He was pitifully thin and the color of his skin seemed to match the gloomy shade of the gray block walls. Ruby moved to hug her father, clad in dizzying black-and-white zebra stripes. The guard's voice boomed, "No touching!"

They sat across the metal table from Father. His beard was stubbled and the area under his eyes was dark and puffy.

"Ruby, are you keeping up with your schoolwork?"

"Yes, Father. All A's."

"And are you helping *Okāsan*?"

"Yes, Sir."

Taeko patted Ruby's hand. "She's been a big help."

Ruby hated when her stepmother acted like this in front of her father, since she never showed Ruby an iota of appreciation when they were alone.

"That's my girl," Father said, and presented her with his latest *sumi-e* of a butterfly kissing periwinkle wisteria alongside a poem about spring, inked in perfect calligraphy.

"This is for you," he said, offering her the delicate piece. "When we endure difficulties with grace, we change for the better. Beauty emerges from darkness, Ruby."

She smiled and her heart swelled.

Father turned his attention to Taeko. He looked at and spoke only to her from that moment on. They rattled on in frantic Japanese—something about a lawyer, something about the temple. He never looked at or included Ruby in their conversation. Not once. It was as if Ruby wasn't there. Did he think she was invisible? That she wouldn't understand his words? That she had no feelings? From behind the steel door, she heard the sound of keys jingling, followed by the reverberation of what could only be the slam of a cell door. Father must have seen her flinch. He reached to hold her hand, but he quickly pulled his hand back, as if suddenly remembering the no touching rule.

His words alternated between Japanese and English—much easier for Ruby to follow. Less so for Taeko. "It seems the U.S. is using the war to get rid of the Japanese," he said. "Ah, the sentiments of mistrust from the angry media fuel an angrier public, who fuel an outraged Congress."

Tendons rose to the surface of his neck as he picked up a *San Francisco Examiner* newspaper. He shook the paper. "This newspaper calls for the ouster of every Japanese on the West Coast!" He pointed to an article which reported: *Herd 'em up, pack 'em off and give them the inside room in the badlands. Let 'em be pinched, hurt, hungry and dead up against it.* Ruby didn't understand what the article was saying or where the badlands were, but her vision of badlands and being hurt or killed made her retreat deep into the back of the chair.

Father stared at his small hands, tipped by chewed fingernails. "I have news."

He leaned forward as if signaling his desire for them to listen carefully and then spoke Japanese words that Ruby didn't understand.

Taeko let out a wail, followed by unintelligible Japanese words, sobs, and snivels.

Were they about to be pinched in the darkness of the badlands?

Suddenly, the gray walls lurked with the shadow of something bad. Ruby's voice quivered. "Father, what did you say?"

"They are moving me to a Justice Department detention center somewhere on the mainland. I'm not sure when I leave." He began popping his knuckles one at a time.

Ruby cringed at each crack, a sound as annoying to her as the metal on metal grinding often heard from the sugar mill.

He continued. "I understand President Roosevelt signed an Order allowing the Secretary of War to designate military areas where Japanese people torn from their homes and businesses will be housed. He's given full control to a Commander DeWitt of the Western Defense Command—a hardliner who says, '*A Jap's a Jap*' and all Japanese are alike. We are traitors and must not be trusted."

Ruby shouted over her stepmother's cries. "You've done nothing wrong!

It's not fair! People are supposed to be innocent until proven guilty."

The guard approached the table. "Time's up."

Her innocent eyes met those of the burly uniformed man and pleaded for forgiveness for her outburst.

The guard made his position clear. "Visit's over, folks." Ruby would never know if her shouts ended the visit.

Taeko struggled to stand through her hysteria. Ruby took her by the elbow, and they bowed a respectful goodbye to Father. The guard escorted him through a rear door, returning him to confinement. The door slammed.

Ruby picked up the *sumi-e* and led Taeko through the front door to exit the jail. Mr. Masaki was waiting. Moments later, the truck kicked up dust driving away, and Ruby leaned into the side walls of its bed.

Trying to block out Taeko's howls of anguish, Ruby stared at the *sumi-e* in her hand and worried if, when, and how the authorities might come for her and Mari. *Take them to the badlands.* She rolled up and gripped her father's precious artwork. The breeze had strengthened, and she tucked the gift down the front of her blouse between her budding breasts—the image of Father's art blowing away unimaginable. The white scroll was crisp against her skin. She closed her eyes and reflected on his words. *Endure with grace, change for the better, for beauty emerges from darkness.*

SHIKATA GA NAI

1942 – Hiroshima, Japan

It began as a mutter two nights ago. "*Shikata ga nai,*" *Okāsan* had said, as she gathered the family's metal possessions. An armload at a time, Koji had helped her carry cookware, bells, garden tools—anything and everything metal—from the house and outbuildings to the cart in the front yard. Japan suffered from severe metal shortages, and the government compelled every household to relinquish anything made of metal to make more armaments for Japan.

Even the temples were ordered to donate their precious bells. How Koji would miss the resounding sound of the Take Shrine bell. Every Sunday, they walked under the massive stone *torii* gate, marking the divide between the physical and spiritual worlds, and climbed seventy stairs to the shrine where Emperor Jimmu had visited during the Goto era while settling Japan. At the top, they washed their hands in the stone basin shaped like a curved boat hull before entering the wooden temple for service.

The bell shelter stood apart from the temple, its sides open to the universe, its roof curved skyward in Japanese tradition. *Otōsan* loved that ornate, bronze *bonshō*, having rung it with pride throughout his own childhood. Koji and Naoki, too, grew up ringing the bell. How it thrilled them to strike the instrument with the long wooden log and melt into its deep reverberating sound. Each year, they looked forward to taking turns at the tolling ceremony on New Year's Eve when bells rang one hundred eight times at midnight from temples all over Japan, symbolizing the cleansing of an equivalent number of evil desires for the upcoming year.

Koji had helped his father, weak from cancer by now, and some other men remove the bell. The men lubricated and loosened the ancient bolts with hand tools powered by their physical strength. The stubborn bolt *Otōsan* had attempted to loosen wouldn't budge. "Hard to dislodge something that's found its home here for so long," he said.

"I'll get that last one, Akio," Watanabe-*san* offered.

"Arigatō, my friend."

Otōsan stepped out of the way and wiped beads of sweat from his brow. Watanabe-*san* freed the seized bolt with ease.

Koji joined the men, surrounded the bell, and counted in unison, *"Ichi, ni, san."* They lifted the sacred bell from its frame, and carried it—some walking backward, some sideways, and others forward—toward Watanabe-*san's* truck, where they applied more lubricant and unbolted the bell from the wheel that had enabled its rotation. After removing the cast-iron frame from the bell tower, they wrapped all the pieces in blankets and placed them in the truck bed.

In the eerie quiet of dusk, with their work complete, they bowed to the empty space where the bell used to hang. The enlightened voice would cease to open ceremonies, invite protective forces, or prompt people to contemplate the emptiness of all things.

They muttered a collective *"Shikata ga nai,"* and went their separate ways.

Watanabe-*san* drove away leaving tire tracks in the dirt. He would deliver the bell and its components to the metal collection center in the morning. Koji and his father descended the long stairway for home. *Otōsan* was quiet on their walk. Like many other Japanese farmers, *Otōsan* complied with most government mandates, but resisted others in subtle ways, like selling or giving away vegetables from their farm to neighbors and friends, rather than turning the produce over to the government as required. Since *Otōsan* wasn't conscripted or didn't serve meals, he couldn't shake dandruff into the rice of unsuspecting military officers, as some were known to do. But he often joked how he'd love to show his contempt for the regime by joining with the soldiers in this gross practice. Some men *Otōsan* knew conspired on tactics and strategies to thwart the military's enforcement of laws and regulations—a dangerous business that *Otōsan* shied away from.

They returned home to find *Okāsan* eyeing a handful of hair pins tipped with cranes and filigree fans, some that had belonged to her mother. She released an exasperated sigh. "How dare they take something so small! What can the blasted military make with hair pins, anyway? I'm keeping them!"

Koji chuckled. *Good for her!*

She shoved the hairpins in the pocket of her apron. "Koji, I've been through everything but your room. Please gather your things and add them to the cart."

In his room, Koji dumped his miniature tin trucks onto the floor, adding a small metal box that held his *Gō* stones. He unscrewed the iron hardware from the drawers of his *tansu* and tossed them on the pile, not caring if they damaged his toy trucks. He rifled through the drawers, messing up the neat stacks of clothes, hesitating when he discovered his *Jizō*. Verdigris had formed on the tiny statue since they brought it home from Miyajima three years ago.

He found *Okāsan* outside adding an old teapot to the groaning cart. He placed the *Jizō* in her small hands, weathered by years of hard work.

She looked into his eyes and nodded her head softly. "Hmmm. Yes, you can keep it. But son, please," *Okāsan* said, her hands trembling, "you must keep our secret. Holding onto the *Jizō* is a small offense. I don't know what would happen if the authorities learned of your American citizenship."

"I will. I promise." Koji well understood how the Japanese authorities and the public viewed the thousands of U.S. citizens living in Japan—with rancor and suspicion, thinking them spies of the American government. He'd be careful.

She offered him a weak smile and whispered, "*Shikata ga nai.*" The heavy emphasis on *kata* seemed to release her frustration. "Koji, slip it into one of your old socks and hide it in your room. And remember, nothing goes on forever. We *gaman*. Everything ends and we must endure the hard times with grace and strength."

• • •

The next morning, Koji tethered their donkey to the rundown wagon—bulging with his family's belongings—and headed downtown to the metal collection center. The facility buzzed with organized chaos, processing a daily stream of donations from hundreds of people in a building that housed a tire manufacturer before the British Malay ceased rubber exports to Japan. No rubber, no tires. Cherished belongings arrived by automobile, pickup truck, and carts pulled by tractors and animals, generating clouds of dust that commingled with dour gray fumes spewing into the damp spring air from nearby factories. Small children brought wagons overflowing with toy trucks, figurines, and *beigomas* that would no longer spin. The children left their wagons at the facility to bolster Japan's war effort, but took their disappointment with them, knowing they couldn't do anything about it.

The donkey was panting from the exertion of pulling the cart into the city. After filling a bowl with water from his canteen to satisfy the donkey's thirst, Koji watched the selflessness of the people around him. He stared for an overlong moment at a bronze statue and garden chime that had been in his family for generations. The Japanese people seemed to comply with everything asked of them and possess a bottomless pit of fortitude to accept hardship. Annoyed by the public's inability to stand up to the regime and fight to keep what belonged to them, he wondered whether things were different in America. Feeling like a coward and hypocrite, he waited his turn in the line wrapping around the building and down the street, afraid and helpless to change anything.

Koji glanced around and recognized Emi Watanabe and her older brother, Itsuki, in the neighboring line. Although the Watanabe farm was nearby, he and Emi hadn't seen each other for over a year, and she looked different from the elementary school friend he remembered. Emi's heart-shaped face was unblemished and framed by shiny black hair cascading over her slender shoulders and down the curve of her back. Her lips were full and pouty. He, too, had changed, having grown taller, his scrawniness replaced with muscles, and he sensed a pleasant arousal in his body. He shifted to hide his growing excitement.

"Hurry ahead," the man behind him said, jarring Koji back to reality.

After waiting for hours, he reached the officer in charge. A cigarette dangled from the man's wrinkled lips as he barked brisk orders to subordinates, all scrambling to manage yet another disruption in the lives of Hiroshima's residents. The man's eyes never shifted from his clipboard. "Head of household name?"

"Akio Matsuo."

"Address?"

"Block No. 6, Fuchu."

The official examined the cart's contents and logged items onto an inventory sheet on his clipboard. "Do you affirm this donation represents a complete inventory of metal possessions from your property?"

Donation? Koji tried not to roll his eyes.

He hesitated, knowing his *Jizō* hid under a floorboard. *What was done was done.*

His voice was confident. "Yes, Sir."

The man looked over the eyeglasses sliding down his nose. "Are you sure, boy? There are serious consequences if your family didn't turn in all of their metal."

He looked the man in the eyes. "Yes, Sir. I'm certain."

"Sign here."

He signed the paper and helped to empty his family's possessions into the mountain of cookware, housewares, and tools. As he turned to leave, Emi's brother approached. "Koji-*kun*, how are you, my friend?"

"Good, thanks."

Koji's eyes met Emi's. "Nice to see you, Emi," he said, his heart beating fast.

Emi blushed and offered a brief wave, and her brother interrupted their kittenish exchange. "Koji-*kun*, will you do me a favor? That blasted line. I'm late and don't have time to take Emi shopping for our mother. Will you take her?"

"Sure! And I'll see Emi gets home before dinner."

Itsuki reached in his pocket and retrieved a piece of paper and some money. "Buy only what's on the list and maybe a small snack, okay Emi."

"Okay," she said.

"Thank you, Koji-*kun*. I'll tether your donkey and cart with mine and tell your mother to expect you by dinnertime. *Sayonara!*"

They parted ways. Without the burden of the cart or animal, Koji and Emi strolled along city sidewalks, lanes, and the banks of the Motoyasu River, following its gentle curves under the Heiwao Bridge. Fishermen descended old wooden ladders from the bridge to the dock below, home to fishing boats in various states of disrepair.

Koji and Emi stopped to rest at the Aioi Bridge, where the Hon and Motoyasu rivers combined to create the Ōta River to the north. Upriver, dozens of sailboats were docked along the small wooden houses dotting the bank. Other boats skipped across the water with the wind. Koji closed his eyes and drank in the rich smell of the river flowing through the city from the fertile Chugoku Mountains visible in the distance.

He opened his eyes to Emi's smile. "Hiroshima's river system resembles the shape of your hand," he said, trying to impress her.

She giggled. "How so?"

He held out his hand with his fingers separated and pointed down. "Well, each of my fingers represents a river in this part of Hiroshima's center city. My fingertips flow into Hiroshima Bay." He pointed to the fold of skin between his middle and ring fingers. "We are right here, at the Aioi Bridge."

"Oh Koji, you're so funny!"

They walked east and paused at the Hiroshima Prefectural Industrial Promotion Hall. Koji had always admired the unique European-style building with its curved corners, soaring windows, and spectacular dome. As Emi looked up, taking in the architecture's dome roof, he took in all of Her—her lightweight coat, belted at her tiny waist, and her dusty brown loafers. Her petite body was fit and strong from farm work. She raised her delicate hand to shade her brown eyes, flecked with amber. The brilliant sunshine illuminated his first perfect moment—enjoying the building's architecture, the fragrant breeze, and the charm of this lovely girl.

She broke the spell. "Did you ever go inside the Promotion Hall before the government claimed it?"

"Once, when I was little. I remember the oyster man and wondered who buys oysters in a department store when you can get them fresh off the boats."

"Oh, but vendors also sold beautiful woodworks and unique musical instruments. There was always something new to discover. Even if I never take up an instrument, those visits inspired my love of music."

"Now that our government has commandeered the building along with many others, I guess I missed my chance to see those things." *Shut up,* he told himself. He didn't mean to speak negatively.

Emi nodded. "It's all so very sad."

Having escaped the cluttered clouds, the sun came out to play.

They continued toward Hiroshima's vibrant downtown shopping area. The roads were congested with trucks, trams, and bicycles whizzing by, but the traffic quieted as they approached Hon Dori, the street restricted to pedestrians and bicycles. Ornamental lanterns arched over the entire length of the street. The white globe lanterns resembled clusters of lily of the valley with a mesmerizing, infinite repeat. The Rising Sun hung from storefronts and flapped in the breeze, some tangled around their poles. Parked bicycles with rear cargo baskets and empty wood pallets scattered along the street. Vendors pushed and pulled carts transporting enormous barrels of *sake,* as people bustled about in diverse attire. Men and women alike wore traditional kimonos and more modern suits, hats, overcoats, and dresses. Signs in a riot of color advertised goods for sale in the food, dry goods, and craft shops.

Because of rationing, Emi carried a short list limited to staples, but the smells and tastes of Hon Dori were varied—and tempting. Their first stop was at a tea store where the intense aromas dominated Koji's senses. He held Emi's basket while she selected her father's favorite *sencha.* At the tobacconist, they breathed into their sleeves to filter the pungent odors while she bought her father's cigarette papers.

A block later, Emi rested her forehead on the window of a parasol shop and shaded her eyes with her hand to peek in. "Let's look!" she said, and disappeared inside. Koji wound his way through bouquets of paper and silk parasols. A few were brown and muted, but most were patterned with flowers, bamboo foliage, and long-necked cranes hand painted in vivid coral, mustard, and fuchsia over delicate frames. He found Emi in the back of the store, where she eyed a dainty parasol with blushing cherry blossoms over an opaline background.

He could tell how much Emi liked it and wished he had the money to buy it for her.

Her eyes sparkled, as she spoke to the parasol. "I'll see you next time."

She smiled at Koji. The sparkle in her eyes flowed through her voice. "Let's go!"

At the end of the block, the shopkeeper greeted them with "*Irasshaimase*," and a wave of his heavy chopsticks, as he turned savory *senbei* on the grill. Koji's mouth watered. They eyed jars of crackers lining the shelves, and Emi purchased a small bag of the ones sprinkled with seaweed. The shopkeeper wrapped two crackers hot off the grill and wished them a pleasant day.

With their shopping finished, they strolled to the tram stop, yielded to exiting passengers, and jumped on a crowded tram for the short ride to Hiroshima Station. Seated in the middle of the car, they were surrounded by a sea of women with shopping bags, men clutching newspapers in one hand and smoking cigarettes with the other, and children enjoying spring recess. Outside the windows, cars crisscrossed with other cars, trams, and carts, and people darted across streets beneath a web of wires crackling with energy.

At the next stop, they offered their seats to an elderly couple. Holding the circular straps suspended from the ceiling and pressed against strangers, they shouted with delight each time the tram operator pushed the lever to speed up. Their arrival at Hiroshima Station came too soon.

From the busy station, they walked past rickshaws and automobiles with spare tires on the rear, parked in perfect straight lines. The caramelized aroma of *yaki imo* seduced them, and they followed the scent to where the sweet potatoes nestled to roast on a bed of pebbles over hot coals inside the deep cavity of the vendor's cart. Emi bought one of the delicious treats wrapped in a square of day-old newspaper to share. Koji slipped the basket handles up his forearm as he accepted half of the treat, careful not to drop the basket or the potato. He sank his teeth into and gobbled the potato flesh except for the last bite, which he kept in his mouth and savored a bit longer.

The late afternoon sun kissed their backs. Cars and trams whizzed past the crowded sidewalk where their shadows lengthened as they moved closer to the hills and mountains. The salt air was heavy with exhaust fumes and cooking smells wafting from ramen and *okonomiyaki* shops. Nearing the end of their three-kilometer walk, their conversations of school and family shifted to war, disrupting the bliss of the perfect day that Koji didn't want to end. At the entrance to Emi's farm, he dithered over how to say goodbye, but Emi snatched the basket from his hands and skipped down the driveway.

"No," he whispered, as she skipped farther away. The clench in his stomach released to a quiver at her backhanded wave. Halfway down her drive, she stopped and turned to face him. "I had fun! Thanks for everything!" She took off running down the drive.

He shoved his hands in his pockets and felt the wad of newspaper rolled around the uneaten potato skin. Although food was scarce, Emi disliked the skin too, so he intended to dispose of it later.

The magic of the afternoon faded as worry caught up with him. What if the officer who had questioned him earlier about the completeness of his family's metal donation thought he'd lied and came to search his house? What if the authorities found his *Jizō* and his mother's hairpins? Or his American birth certificate?

A stray dog, probably smelling the potato, darted from a bamboo grove and followed him. He tossed the potato skin to the dog, who devoured it and lost interest in Koji. He shoved the newspaper back into his pocket and murmured the truth. "*Shikata ga nai.*"

Worry followed him home.

SPLENDID LITTLE CHILDREN

1942 – Hiroshima, Japan

In the amber and russet autumn, the boys brandished their homemade spears and practiced skewering straw bale targets screaming, "Savage Americans!"

"All of you boys are home front soldiers now. You defend our homeland!" Koji's school military officer shouted. In the humid days of summer, the boys had stripped bamboo and whittled the ends into pointed spears. "Sharper!" the military officer had ordered. "When our enemies drop in parachutes from airplanes, you will attack them."

The officer had stomped his foot. "You will kill them or die!"

Koji aimed for the circle painted in the center of the bale, threw, and missed.

"Do it again!" the officer said. "Together, we protect our divine country. No sacrifice is too great for our Emperor!"

Koji hated the practice sessions, but enjoyed the invigorating physical activity. Stoked by frustration, he lunged forward and nearly impaled a classmate, knocking him to the ground. The other students cheered, and the ruckus brought him to his senses. He helped his friend to his feet, bowed, and apologized. "*Gomennasai.*" Ashamed, Koji hoped the boy accepted.

After an hour of spear throwing, they moved on to throwing rocks. Once all their rocks had been thrown, they retrieved them from around the bales for round two. By lunch time, Koji's arm was exhausted.

Rudimentary military training and air-raid drills had replaced academics. *Otōsan* had said the schools now shaped young minds like *bonsai* trees, pruning splendid little children for obedience, selflessness, and loyalty.

Students also practiced semaphore, using handheld flags as visual symbols to convey information. They honed basic evacuating and marching skills. His friends thrived on playing war games and many longed to serve their Emperor as soldiers, some seeking revenge for the deaths of their fathers and brothers.

In the afternoon, the class marched through Hiroshima's streets, their feet crunching in unison across dried leaves. As they marched toward the Moto-machi military facility, next to the sixteenth-century Hiroshima Castle, Koji recalled the stories his father had shared with him and Naoki about Japan's storied past. *Otōsan*, a historian by nature, regaled them with lore of the lengthy Edo Period when the Shogun, Japan's top feudal military commanders, controlled the country. *Otōsan's* stories inspired hours of playtime along the outer shore of the castle moat, where Koji and Naoki pretended to be warriors and let their imaginations of the *shogunate* life run wild. At the abolishment of feudal domains in the late nineteenth century, the castle had become the Imperial General Headquarters and now served as the Headquarters of the Second General Army commanding all of southern Japan. Then and now, Hiroshima enjoyed military importance, in sharp contrast to its graceful beauty. A leading military garrison and key port for shipping, Hiroshima swarmed with war activity. Moto-machi was the center of the hive.

They found deafening artillery training underway when they reached the Moto-machi Western Drill Ground. Koji and a dozen other boys climbed high up a tree to gain a better vantage. From tree limbs nearly bare of foliage, they glimpsed into their future. Every day the army conscripted thousands of men and boys. Japan's people revered the magnificent power of its imperial forces. With inspiring public spectacles, they honored military sendoffs with farewell parties and family processions extending from the conscript's home all the way to the train station.

And they celebrated their dead. Most soldiers didn't expect to return home. The war ministry's *Senjinkun* Field Service Code of 1941 No-Surrender Clause ordered Japanese soldiers to show honor and take their lives rather than surrender to the enemy. The flapping of mourning flags was constant throughout the city, along with elaborate ceremonies honoring the deceased. Soon after their chance meeting at the metal collection center, Emi's brother had left Fuchu for the navy with much fanfare. Koji wondered how long it might be before flags fluttered in Itsuki's honor.

From their perch, the students observed a sea of men, clad in khaki uniforms with standing shirt collars and helmets covered with camouflage netting. Hundreds of soldiers carried battle-ready swords with wooden handles and long curved blades. Hundreds more carried rifles. Wearing tall, shiny boots, with leather binocular cases hanging from their necks, the officers ordered the enlisted men to toughen up and destroy Japan's enemies.

A few boys broke off small branches and pretended to shoot rifles. Others mimicked the soldiers on the field by resting pretend rifles on their shoulders. A soldier below spotted them, elbowed the soldier beside him, and pointed toward their tree. Both soldiers laughed at them. Koji knew these soldiers might one day kill Americans or be killed by them. At least for today, they had a good laugh. He wondered if he would become one of them—a killer. Or, if he might survive the war and live in the United States someday. But he couldn't imagine how he would get there. It was so far away. And what would Americans think of him? Could he possibly fit in?

Over the past year, he had spent rainy days studying pictures in a university press series titled *The Chronicles of the United States*. His parents had brought the books from America, kept them hidden in a closet, and now allowed Koji to look through the pages as long as he returned the books to the closet immediately after he finished.

Holding the books in his hands brought a comfortable warmth to his body. He'd run his fingers over the smooth leather covers and drank in the scent of glue and brittle paper. As he turned the pages and skimmed English words he didn't understand, he developed a deep respect for the knowledge contained within a book's spine. Someday he would learn English and know important things. Until then, his parents answered his questions as best as they could. He admired illustrations of the U.S. Capitol and imagined what it was like inside. He marveled at the engineering of the towering obelisk honoring America's first President. His first glance at the Grand

Canyon was one of wonder and disbelief. How could something that huge and breathtaking be a mere dot on a United States map?

Now, the kid on the branch next to him jabbed his elbow into Koji's side, taking him out of his daydream. "Hey, have you been here before or not?" he asked.

"Sorry. Where?"

"Right here on the soldiers' field, dummy... but when they held *Shokonsai* Festivals. We went every year. You?"

Koji nodded.

"I liked the food stalls the best." The boy laughed. "My mother isn't a very good cook."

Koji best remembered the motorcycle races. The same competitors raced every year, and fans shouted and cheered from grandstands constructed of logs encircling the track. But elaborate festivals and competitions ended after Pearl Harbor was bombed. His eyes raked the rows of soldiers standing at attention, and he wondered if any of the celebrated motorcycle racers were there.

On the march back to school, he inhaled the aroma of dead leaves and visualized their dry and curling debris trapped along buildings and fences as the millions of people trapped and dying for Japan's cause. In another year he could be mobilized. Each day drew him closer. Nothing was within his control. He wished the madness would end, but was confident his wishes wouldn't do any good.

STAR CROSSED

1942 – Waimea, Hawaii

Weeks and then months had passed, and Ruby's hope for her father's return faded. Since visiting her father at the jail, she had developed an insatiable appetite for news. She listened to broadcasts on radio station KGXO and stopped by the general store nestled among the plantation houses to glance at newspaper headlines. Vibrant flowers burst from giant pots, welcoming customers to the dandelion-yellow store, its doors open to the sea breeze. Inside, printed labels identified contents concealed within the hefty built-in cabinetry. Behind the glass of an oversized case, Chuckles, Mary Janes, and Bit-O-Honey candies in colorful wrappers tempted children. War was absent in the cheerful store except for the daily newspaper's saber-rattling headlines.

Sometimes Mrs. Sato, the store owner, offered Ruby a leftover newspaper at closing time. She always allowed Ruby to save face. "I have too many newspapers, Ruby. Will you please take one off my hands?" Other days, she would insist, "The newspaper boy delivered more papers than I ordered. Grab one to wash your windows with." She also gave her a free treat to enjoy on her walk home, sometimes a strawberry licorice string or a five-cent Coca-Cola from the bright red cooler.

Ruby had read about a patriotism dividing her world as America kept its promise to achieve victory against Japan, no matter how long or difficult the effort, and no matter how far Japan expanded into the Pacific Islands with victories in Singapore, Java, and Bataan. She read about and saw in her daily life how anger and determination replaced the gripping panic and fear immediately following Pearl Harbor. The Stars and Stripes flew in front of most houses. People purchased war bonds to help pay for the war effort. Families planted victory gardens to supplement rations. On the mainland, women found jobs building military weapons and equipment.

No eye could avoid the headline: OUSTER OF ALL JAPS IN CALIFORNIA NEAR.

"Mrs. Sato, what's ouster?" Ruby asked.

"It means to get rid of. Horrible times we live in. Just horrible."

The article said General DeWitt commanded the strategy to evacuate and detain 120,000 Japanese, two-thirds of whom were U.S.-born citizens. *Herd 'em up and pack 'em off'* in California, Washington, and Oregon had begun, as her father had said it would.

It seemed those at the center of the herd—where there was safety in numbers—believed their obedience and cooperation was necessary to survive. The authorities corralled and jailed the few resisters who left the herd. The plantation community worried when the government would begin herding them from the security of their homes to places unknown. Ruby refused to believe the evacuation had anything to do with national security or keeping people safe.

As the months passed, she devoured articles recapping the Doolittle raids when Army planes bombed Tokyo and inflicted a psychological blow on the Japanese, Japan's defeat in the Battle of the Coral Sea—crippling Japan's Navy despite heavy American losses—and America's decisive victory at Midway. She understood that newspapers fed what was important to Americans. Revenge.

While America's navy was on the offensive attacking in the Pacific, the War Relocation Administration executed the weapon of mass incarceration on American soil. Her anxious mind did its best to digest the news, but her stomach couldn't keep up with her brain.

Her family had always depended on the congregation's offerings. But the temple was closed, and the bank froze their account on the day of her father's arrest. No father, no minister, no money. To support the household, Taeko donned a hairnet that accentuated her ugly features and went to work at the pineapple cannery. Not a day passed without her reminding

Ruby and Mari how she hated the job and was forced into grunt work—to support *them*. Ruby and Mari had also taken part-time jobs after school, apprenticing at a dress shop owned by a woman sympathetic to their circumstances. Together, they spent hours sewing darts and hems and cutting patterns for women who had means.

Now, Ruby rubbed her sore fingertips, inflamed from needle and pin pricks, and gazed at the ocean swells and into the November sky. Spellbound by amber and persimmon rays illuminating the horizon, she rested her head against Mari's shoulder. Mari would graduate high school next spring, but she seemed to have given up on her dream to attend college. Selfishly, Ruby was relieved that her sister wouldn't be an island away at school. She liked her right here. They wriggled their toes in the sand and watched the ocean's undulating surface reflect charcoal clouds dancing on the polished silver sky. The symphony of dusk caressed them. Gentle waves lapped the shoreline, joining the incoming tide. Someone sounded a shell horn as darkness erased the day. The calm of the harmonious day-to-night rhythm did little to soothe Ruby. She snuggled closer to Mari as the evening stars appeared. They took their chances violating curfew to compete for star formation sightings as they searched for the elusive Canoe-Bailer of Makali'i star line, a sign of the season changing to winter.

"I call North Star," Mari said.

"The Southern Cross is mine," she volleyed. "Mari, do you think Father sees the same sky from prison? Is it possible he's seeing the same stars as us at this very minute?"

• • •

Transferred and imprisoned in a Department of Justice detention center, Ruby's father had no rights or privacy. His infrequent letters bore the postmark of Lordsburg, New Mexico. He wrote of his mundane prison routine—sweeping, cooking, and creating art from scrap wood in his scarce available time. Sometimes, simple black and white drawings were tucked inside of the envelope. One was of a *butsudan* he had carved from orange crates. Another portrayed him sitting on the cot where he slept, side by side with other men. In the drawing, which appeared to have been hastily created with single sharp strokes, the cots lined both sides of a barracks, army-style. With his brush in his hand, her father worked on something on his lap. His *sumi-e* supplies were organized on a small table. Even in prison, he wore a shirt and necktie under his pleated black Buddhist robe. A robed man sat on the bunk next to him. The man's back was turned. Ruby wondered who the robed man and the artist were, and if they, too, were fathers.

Her father's latest letter, long overdue, arrived in early December. Someone had stamped the envelope PRISONER OF WAR and U.S. CENSORSHIP—Examined by 439, whoever 439 was. He had been gone for a year. Ruby and Mari had ventured to the sugar cane fields early in the morning to watch the harvest. Days earlier, they had seen the smoke curling skyward as the growers burned the mature cane to remove unwanted spiny-needle leaves. High above the fields, lying on the red-chocolate earth among dozens of other kids, they watched the laborers swing razor-sharp machetes and whack the twelve-foot stalks close to the ground. The workers then bundled and dumped the cane into a truck and transported it to the mill. There, massive iron rollers pulverized the cane and squeezed the succulent juice from the fiber. Soon the aroma of juice boiling to thick syrup would permeate the air.

Cheerful and covered in chocolate dust, the girls had returned home to find Taeko furious, having read the letter from Father. Taeko grabbed a hand-painted lacquered tray that belonged to their mother and threw it against the wall. "I hate this country. Home of the free. Ha! And to think I gave up everything to move here—my family, my job, my self-respect!"

Mari snatched the letter out of Taeko's hands and read it to Ruby. It took her awhile to read, translating from Japanese to English. Taeko stormed out of the room.

October 30, 1942

My dearest family,

Far away from you, in New Mexico, the air becomes colder, and the days grow shorter. Being fenced within ███████ *is chilling, but the warmth in my heart remains. Soon, winter will be upon us. Tucked under a wool blanket at night, I dream of endless summer on Kauai and long to be home with you.*

My faith in Amida Butsu anchors and calms me. I spend my free time creating art and in meditation with the other ministers here. These unexpected circumstances disrupt our lives and our expectations of what America represents. However, we must accept, persevere, and create something positive from our grim circumstances. I transform boredom into harnessing the power of clarity and write sermons to share when these tragic times pass.

I'm sorry so much time has passed since my last letter. The enclosed drawing is of me in the infirmary, where I've spent the past few weeks resting and receiving ultraviolet light treatments for an unknown ailment. I suffer from malaise, anemia, and respiratory issues. The light warms, heals, and soothes, and I'm feeling better now.

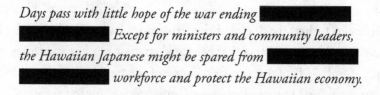

Days pass with little hope of the war ending ████████████ ████████ *Except for ministers and community leaders, the Hawaiian Japanese might be spared from* █████████ █████████ *workforce and protect the Hawaiian economy.*

I worry for your well-being and ability to support yourselves in my absence. Only we can relinquish our power of choice to decisions when subjected to the worst of those who control us. And so, I have decided it is in your best interests to join the Japanese in a camp where you will have dependable food and shelter.

Watch the mail for an envelope from the War Relocation Administration with instructions for your move from Waimea to the mainland. Please write to me of your safe arrival when you settle in.

All my love, Father

Fear and rage burned in Ruby's heart as she picked up her mother's now-fractured tray—split down the middle. Just like her.

ALOHA

December 1942 – Waimea, Hawaii

The rickety Nawiliwili pier was devoid of celebration, of laughter. With her face to the morning sun, Ruby tried to find comfort in fond memories. How often had they greeted guests coming from Honolulu or seen them off from this harbor? Hawaiian ladies had welcomed visitors on the pier with fragrant leis of plumeria or crown flowers of pikake. The laughter of people saying hello, saying goodbye, had filled the air. When a ship was ready to sail, the captain had sounded a deafening blast, sending Ruby and Mari jumping and squealing with delight. That was how it used to be. Before Mama died. Before the war. Before Ruby's world shattered. Before her memory began the harsh trade-off, from the way things used to be to the nip of reality.

Now, Ruby was leaving for an unknown destination on the mainland. She sat on her tattered green footlocker, eating her *bentō*—tofu and cucumber salad—prepared by Pig Lady. Ruby had been surprised to find the woman on her porch when she answered the door that morning. Although their friendship had faded since Taeko arrived, Pig Lady always stopped what she was doing to talk when they saw each other on the beach or when Ruby snuck away to her garage on tofu-making days. Full of grief from the recent loss of her son to the war, Pig Lady's heart still made room for Ruby.

Taeko had been busy and paid no attention to their visitor. Pig Lady asked about her father and how things were at home, encouraged Ruby to think positive, and told her Taeko's mean streak wasn't Ruby's fault. Before saying goodbye, she had given Ruby a bag of firm, pink lychee nuts. "Put these in your basket and don't share them with you-know-who!" she'd said with a wink and a crooked smile. "I know how much you love them."

She'd wrapped Ruby in her fat arms and squeezed her tight. "Now you be careful and do your best while you're gone. And sail back to us someday. The pigs and I will be waiting for you."

Finishing her last bite, Ruby tucked the memory away. She and Mari wore new dresses sewn by neighbors from the same bolt of periwinkle cotton, and despite the warm temperature, they wore hats, white cotton gloves, and lightweight sweaters to conserve precious packing space.

Ruby shuffled her restless feet along the dock, waiting for the boat that would take them to Honolulu. She rubbed her cheekbone to soothe her toothache, which had begun yesterday after cracking open a pistachio with her teeth. Taeko told her she would have to wait until they arrived at camp to see a dentist.

Two weeks before, Taeko received notification from the War Relocation Administration to pack and prepare for their journey to Honolulu and then onto San Francisco. Her stepmother was not told their ultimate destination, only when to report and what the government permitted them to take. They were each allowed forty-eight pounds and what they could carry. The family sold their remaining possessions for pennies or gave them away to neighbors and brazen, uninvited opportunists who peered in their windows and beat on their door to discover bargains. When total strangers admired and inquired about the girls' treasured doll collection, Taeko said, "Take what you want!" And they did. Ruby and Mari saved only the dolls Mama had made for each of them.

As easy as it seemed for Taeko to sell the things that had made their house a home, she refused to leave behind her kimonos, lacquered trays, and the tea set she had brought from Japan, and she divided the heavy items to carry between the girls. Anger and resentment slipped into the space between Ruby's socks and Taeko's teacups as Ruby packed her basket and small footlocker in silence. Scanning her room, she pictured everything in the faraway camp, holding a glimmer of hope she could magically transport everything there. She lifted her mattress and retrieved the cherished photo of her mother. From her nightstand, she grabbed the photo of her, Mari, and their father on the beach. She eyed her books shelved from short to tall and then by color, opened the Japanese children's story collection that Mama had read to her, and placed the photos inside. Worried she might be separated from her footlocker during the journey, she placed the book at the bottom of the basket she would keep with her. With an inch to spare in the footlocker, she chose *The Hobbit*, *Madeline*, and books by Laura Ingalls, and wondered if her camp room would have a bookshelf. She dumped a bowl of sea glass and shells onto her bed and began sifting through chipped bits and pieces, setting aside those treasures that held special memories— the purple sea glass she'd found with Pig Lady, the weathered puka shells she'd traded with her friends hoping to make a necklace someday, and the cone shell Father had found the day he taught her never to touch until she was sure the inside was clear of the poisonous stinging creatures living there.

With her shells wrapped in handkerchiefs, she removed the lone shell displayed on her shelf—a perfect deep-water scallop in the colors of sunrise that she'd discovered with Mama. That one she triple-folded inside of socks and nestled it inside the basket alongside Mama's photograph and her doll, Penny. There was room for little more than her jacks and ball, which she hadn't touched since that horrible day at Louise's house. She thought about leaving them behind, but decided to take them, anyway. In a few months, she would celebrate her thirteenth birthday. Who knew what games teen-agers played at camp, and she was the best player in her neighborhood. She tightened the footlocker's cracked leather straps and felt a sudden naked-ness as she looked around her room one last time. Losing one's home and liberty could do that to a girl.

• • •

Aloha Tower greeted them as they sailed into Honolulu Harbor. Ruby had never seen a building so tall, and thought it grand, even though the city shut off its welcoming beacon and painted it a dreary shade of gray to avoid detection by the enemy—at least that's what she heard from some-one speaking nearby. Taeko led the way as they disembarked, and a military escort showed them to a secure area in the terminal crowded with other

Japanese families. Ruby's family joined the herd, moving from one registration line to the next. The adults muttered an ongoing refrain, "*Shikata ga nai.*"

Why did adults always say that it can't be helped? They should know better.

A frightened boy tugged on his mother's skirt. "Mommy, the soldiers have guns. Are the soldiers going too?"

The boy's crying mother knelt before him and caressed his pudgy cheek. "I don't know."

How could she? They aren't telling anybody anything. Ruby felt queasy from anger's bile.

Heads held high, her family—wearing identical numbers tagged to their clothing—proceeded up the gangway and boarded the *SS Lurline* ocean liner. Ruby Ishimaru was now number H-150—an alphanumeric identifier designating the family. On the ship's deck, she took in a deep breath and whispered, "Aloha, Hawaii. Until we meet again." She closed her eyes to capture mental mini-clips of sledding downhill on palm leaves, exploring jungles of twisted plant life, and swimming alongside rainbows of fish, wanting more than anything to experience the feelings of Aloha again. Love. Compassion. Peace.

She took Mari's hand. "We'll come home soon. Right? Our house will be waiting for us, won't it?"

"I wish I knew, Ruby."

Ruby swallowed her tears.

They lugged their belongings to a tiny cabin in steerage—dark, airless, and cramped quarters with no privacy. They shared a washroom with other passengers, leaving body odors behind long after its users had vacated. Ruby wondered about the passengers and cabins on the upper decks and imagined fancy quarters that matched the finery of their dress and lightness of their skin.

For a week, the ship lumbered through endless waves under the sun's fiery rays. The ship was at the mercy of the ocean, and Ruby at the mercy of the ship. With her tooth aching and feeling as though she didn't fit in with other kids, she spent most of the week alone, transported to the big skies and wilderness of America's interior in Ingalls's adventures on the prairie. When she left the dank cabin—mostly when seasick—a whiff of mildew and fumes and the sting and smell of the salt water seemed to follow her everywhere. The number of murky stews she had lost over the rail measured the days.

In the evenings, Mari returned to the cabin and babbled about how she'd explored the ship with other teenagers as far from their parents' watchful eyes as possible. Surrounded by ocean with no way to escape, the soldiers had lowered their guns and allowed people to move around freely. Mari told Ruby about discovering the dark corners and below-deck nooks overlooked by most passengers where she played card games and talked with other teenagers about the unknown ahead. Taeko spent her days commiserating in whispers with other Japanese ladies.

The groan of the engine room, creak of swaying bunks, and smack of lifeboats against the port and starboard haunted the gray ship. The milky air further weighed down the heavy vessel—a tiny dot of a floating prison on an ocean, where its steerage passengers wore rumpled and stained clothing and shared the same glum and hopeless look in their eyes. Children's cries and an occasional angry outburst punctuated otherwise monotonous voices, but no Japanese spoke out loud about their misfortune. They were a compliant, melancholy herd floating on a monotonous ocean desert.

Alone in a crowd on New Year's Day, Ruby stood on deck to greet the famous Golden Gate Bridge when their ship entered the San Francisco Bay. A light bay breeze flipped her collar up and tickled her cheek. She peeled her last lychee nut, popped the plump translucent treat into her mouth, and spit the pit over the rail.

The fiery color of the bridge stretched farther than she ever imagined a bridge could stretch, disappearing into the fog. Strange, she couldn't see land on the far side, but she trusted it was there. The fog in her head cleared and her heart stirred. Maybe things wouldn't be so bad once land was beneath their feet in the city of cable cars.

Five

1943 – 1945

THE MAINLAND

1943 – San Francisco, CA

S omeone shouted, "Lookie, lookie! Hawaii's Nips are here!"

Ruby, Mari, and their stepmother were at the front of a long line of Japanese passengers, held back from leaving the ship until all other passengers had disembarked. Armed soldiers marshaled them down the gangway to waiting buses. Their process orderly. Their faces unsmiling. Their eyes uncaring.

The faint melody of band music played in the distance. Or maybe Ruby imagined she was hearing *My Country 'Tis of Thee*. The irony of sweet land of liberty registered with her as a mob of white people wearing tight expressions shoved each other to get closer to the Japanese passengers. The horde, teeth bared and nostrils flaring, closed in. They began shaking fists in the air and yelling obscenities.

"This is white man's country!"

"Spies!"

"Lock up the slanty-eyed scum!"

Carrying her basket, Ruby walked as close as possible to Mari. Her eyes wandered to a man's lapel button: JAP HUNTING LICENSE. OPEN SEASON. NO LIMIT. The sneering man glared in return. "Aren't you an adorable little Jap!" He threw a banana peel, hitting her in the temple.

The louse.

And there was that word again. Jap. What was wrong with people?

At the bus, soldiers stowed the larger pieces of luggage in the vehicle's underbelly, and they boarded. After a short and bumpy ride, the bus parked along a dusty railroad siding where the silent passengers stepped off and gathered with their families to claim their luggage.

Ruby released her clenched fists when she took her footlocker from the driver who assisted the soldiers with the luggage. The man smiled. "That's a big locker for a young girl. You must be strong. God bless you, honey." She would always remember the driver's kindness.

They were told to wait in place. Surrounded by canvas laundry sacks, suitcases, duffel bags, and soldiers, she understood they were waiting for a train. But to where? She hoped the train would hurry. Her tongue found the sharp chip in the back of her mouth. The toothache was getting worse. She was reluctant to ask her stepmother for help, but she was becoming desperate. Maybe Taeko had an aspirin.

Taeko was speaking to a woman from Honolulu, so Ruby was polite and waited until Taeko finished her sentence before interrupting. "Excuse me, *Okāsan*. My tooth hurts. Do you have an aspirin?"

Her stepmother released an exasperated sigh. "It's packed at the bottom of my suitcase. Can you wait or must I rifle through my personal things out here in the dirt?"

The other woman flinched. "I expect I have some aspirin right here." She rummaged around in her purse and produced a small Bayer bottle. She opened the bottle into her palm and tapped out two white tablets. "Here you are. I hope they help you."

The stranger's kindness warmed her. "Thank you, ma'am." With no sip of water, she swallowed the medicine and locked eyes with her stepmother's frigid stare. She held the defiant glare until startled by the piercing shrill of a whistle and the rumble of the approaching train. Soldiers ordered everybody to prepare for boarding. The train arrived moments later, screeching and hissing to stop. Mari jumped to her feet. "Look! Look how big it is!"

Ruby didn't share her sister's excitement. She recoiled at the formidable, soot-bearded monster and hid behind her sister.

Mari offered her a hand. "Let's stay together, okay?" They hustled onto the dark train, the window shades drawn. Inside, two soldiers ordered passengers to keep the shades down and prepare for the four-day trip to Arkansas. Ruby was relieved to know where they were going, even if unable to see the journey.

"May I have the window seat?" Ruby asked Mari.

"I don't care. You can't see anything anyway."

From across the aisle, Taeko snapped her fingers. "Girls. Respect the rules. Keep your mouths shut."

The train chugged away.

In the seat by the window, Ruby faced the shade, yellowed with age. She didn't understand why they weren't permitted to look outside the windows. She rubbed her cheekbone and surrendered to the darkness of the space, the rhythm of the movement and the sounds of the engine, the wheels on the tracks, and the unfamiliar whoosh. The aspirin was helping. She nodded off.

Something jostled against her and she awoke, sleep-drunk and disoriented, not knowing where she was. With the shade now raised, the sun shone on her face. On the other side of the window and in the distance, enormous boulders jutted from mountains towering against the sky. The mountains and florae differed from anything in Hawaii. Unlike Kauai's mountains, that kissed the sky with gentle curves of lush vegetation, these snow-tipped mountains pierced right through the clouds. She'd never seen snow before and thought it beautiful.

"Hey, sleepyhead," Mari said. "You've been sleeping for hours. Welcome back. I think those are the Sierra Nevada mountains. Pretty, aren't they?"

Ruby yawned. "I guess. When did they open the shades?"

"A little while ago. It seems we have to close them anytime we go through a town to hide our enemy faces. But as soon as we are in the middle of nowhere again, they let us open them."

Ruby absorbed her sister's words. The shades were ordered to be drawn not to keep her from seeing outside of the train, but to protect those outside of the train from seeing *her*! She slid down in her seat, wanting to disappear.

"Mari, I have to pee. Where are we supposed to go?"

"There's a toilet at the end of the car. Lock the door before pulling down your panties. You don't want some stranger barging in on you."

Ruby walked through the adult chatter. A baby was nursing. Another crying. Men snored, ladies worked intricate needlepoint, teenagers played cards together, and children made friends over a game of I Spy. She stepped around the kids and waited in line for the toilet, pinching her nostrils at the odors leaching from the toilet each time the door opened and closed. By her turn, the acrid smell of urine overwhelmed her. She held her breath and peed as fast as she could.

When she returned, she slouched into her seat. "It's disgusting in there!"

Her sister didn't respond. Ruby stared at the forest in the distance, imagining the kinds of animals and birds that lived there. Her thoughts turned to camp. It was easier to visualize life in the forest.

Hours later, the train slowed and the soldiers ordered the shades drawn. They changed trains in a place called Bakersfield, and without delay were on their way again.

During the night, unbearable pain jolted her awake. She crossed the aisle to where her stepmother lay across the two-seater bench in a deep sleep, her head bobbing against the window. Drool trickled down her chin. Ruby poked her into wakefulness. "*Okāsan*." She paused. "*Okāsan*, please wake up, my tooth is throbbing."

Her stepmother struggled from slumber. "What is it? It's the dead of night."

"My tooth aches terrible. May I please have an aspirin?... Please?"

"Wait a minute. Let me wake up."

Her stepmother sat and rested her head in her hands for what seemed a long time.

"Okay. Show me which tooth."

Ruby opened her mouth and pointed to the injured tooth. "It's the chipped one. Please, it hurts so bad."

In the shadows of moonlight, her stepmother jiggled one of her teeth. "This one?"

She shook her head.

"This one?" When Taeko jiggled the damaged molar, excruciating pain filled Ruby's head with stars. She'd always wondered if that was possible—to see a burst of intensely lit stars that weren't in the sky. It was.

Her stepmother pulled her bag from the overhead compartment and rummaged through her belongings. But rather than offering Ruby aspirin, she revealed a pair of pliers.

Ruby backed away.

"It's obvious the tooth is bad and must come out. We can do that now or you must wait until we can visit a dentist. If we do it now, it will hurt terrible but then it will get better." Moonlight glimmered on the pliers. "Well?"

"I'll wait."

Taeko rummaged in her bag again and handed Ruby two aspirin and a tea bag.

"Take the aspirin and hold this tea bag on the gum above your tooth. These will help with the pain until a dentist pulls it. Now go back to your seat and try to sleep."

Ruby left her stepmother's seat for her own and snuggled up against and sobbed into Mari's small breasts, surrounded by a chorus of snores.

The next day, the Colorado River welcomed them to Arizona, and she wondered how far they were from her father. She would give anything to hike with him through Waimea Canyon, staining their shoes with red dirt. Vivid memories of the canyon overcame her. She and Father would lose their breath overlooking the gorge. Share a *bentō*. Cool off under Waipoo Falls. Laugh at the feral goats. Make a wish on one of the rainbows crowning the falling water on a windy day. She rubbed her cheekbone, feeling relief from the aspirin and tea bags, and the noble truths pushed away her pain. Suffering exists. There is an end to suffering.

Soon after entering New Mexico, the train abruptly halted in the heart of the barren landscape. The toilet was clogged, so the officers ordered everyone outside to do their business. Ruby squatted behind a scrawny desert bush and relieved herself. Startled, she found blood in the crotch of her panties. It was the curse. The period. Mari had told her to expect it some-time—that it would come without warning.

She looked around for Mari but didn't see her. Taeko was beside her.

"*Okāsan*, I think I have my first period. What should I do?"

"Clean yourself up and take care of it."

Ruby inspected the back of her clothing for stains. "How do I take care of it?"

"Ask your sister to help you. Come on, let's go."

Weakened in the knees by the sting of shame, Ruby cursed herself for asking.

But then a solitary white feather floated to rest at her feet. An angel's wing. How did it get there?

Mama?

She looked to the heavens and felt a calming, compassionate presence. A presence that somehow suggested things would be okay. That she would be okay. She placed the feather in her pocket.

Back on the train in the privacy of the stench-filled toilet room, Ruby accepted from Mari a sanitary belt and pad. Mari showed her what to do and hugged her. "You're a woman now. Everything will be okay. I promise."

"How do you know?"

"I just do. I know in my heart this kind of hardship can't last forever. Nothing ever does."

JEROME

1943 – Jerome, AR

The train screeched to a halt, waking the passengers from another restless night. Ruby stirred and snuggled closer to her sister's warm body. A sliver of dawn filtered through the edges of the shades. She willed herself back into the hazy residue of her dream—vague images of tents scattered in a tree-lined camp where she was popular and pretty with straight-cut bangs.

The booming voice of a soldier with an unusual accent snapped Ruby from her dreamy slumber. "Wake up, y'all! Okay, listen up!"

She yawned and stretched the morning fuzz away and assumed they would be told of yet another train change. The soldier continued, "We've done arrived at our destination. Welcome to Jerome, Arkansas—y'all's new home. It may not seem like you're in swampy marshland now, but you can bet your sweet Jap asses that you'll know it when summer comes around. My oh my, the heat and humidity in these here parts will make you beg for Mr. Jack Frost. If you know some geography, you're about twelve miles west of the great Mississippi River, surrounded by Arkansas's finest crooked bayous. We'll be fixing to get off soon. Got to wait for the go-ahead from the boss. Go on and get your stuff together."

Ruby heard someone ask if they might raise the shades.

"Darn tootin'! Go on and open the shades and wait till it's time to get off."

Nothing had prepared her for what she saw when Mari raised the shade. The dark sky gave way to a gray dawn behind a tall chain-link fence topped with rolled barbed wire. An armed sentry stood at the wood railing of a watch tower surveying their train and the bleak sea of tar paper buildings. His watchful eyes bore through her.

She clung to Mari. "The guard up there is looking at us. He's got a gun! Does he keep people in or out?"

"I don't know. Probably both. At least we're together. Hopefully, Father will join us soon. No matter what, obey the rules and do what you're told."

The train doors opened and a blast of frigid air poured into the car. The soldier shouted, "Y'all get in line. Single-file-like. Good luck."

Carrying their belongings, Ruby and Mari followed their stepmother off the train onto frozen mud. The biting wind whipped Ruby's hair around. Her cheeks burned with cold. They trekked behind the others over ruts rigid with ice and past a large sign painted in plain block letters—JEROME RELOCATION CENTER—and through the gate, where soldiers hoisted a U.S. flag and rendered military salutes. Winter gales sent the flag flapping.

Ruby rubbed her arms, jumped around to get warm, and recalled her lessons on what the distinct colors of the flag represented—white for purity and innocence, red for valor, blue for perseverance, vigilance, and justice. She jumped at the startling clang of the gate slamming behind them, and her sudden realization the guards were there to keep them in, locked behind barbed wire fencing under freedom's flag. Standing in a line that stretched beyond her field of vision, she asked for bravery from any higher power who might hear her, and struggled to breathe the air that accentuated the flag's merciless taunts of freedom.

She rubbed her hands to stop their trembling, and the line crept its way into the administration building where the heat did little to warm her chills. Continuing to follow the others, she rested her belongings on the ground for a few moments, only to pick them up—feeling heavier each time—to move from one line to the next, completing forms, answering questions, being categorized, photographed, assigned addresses, jobs, and classrooms.

A man rolled Ruby's fingertips on ink and then on paper, where the unique whorls and ridges of her genetics labeled her a criminal. She wondered if the ink would wash off or if her black fingertips would forever identify her. Another official replaced her temporary tag with a permanent identification badge—W.R.A., JEROME RELOCATION CENTER, RUBY ISHIMARU, and her family number, H-150.

A Red Cross volunteer gave them each a scratchy sweater and cap. Ruby's was the color of hay. She thought it ugly, but wore it anyway, and followed the escort behind warehouses and toward a separate building with a soaring smokestack spewing plumes into the dull light of morning. Inside, they received medical examinations and a series of inoculations.

"Please, no more needles," she begged, rubbing her bottom.

The heavyset nurse had white hair and a kind smile. "Okay, sweetie. Let's try your upper arm."

Soon, her backside *and* her arm ached. And her eyes. *Why did her eyes ache?*

Her stepmother approached the nurse and spoke in rapid Japanese. "The girl chipped her tooth somehow and needs a dentist. She's suffered for days."

"I'm sorry, I don't speak Japanese," the nurse said.

"I chipped my tooth and it *really* hurts," Ruby said. "Is there a dentist here?"

The nurse felt Ruby's cheek the way Mama used to when she was sick. Her hand was soft. "How did you hurt your tooth, sweetie?"

"I tried to crack open a pistachio."

"That'll do it. Let's take your temperature and make sure you don't have a fever."

The nurse took a thermometer from a glass canister, rubbed it with alcohol, shook down its silver mercury, and placed it under Ruby's tongue. Ruby imagined the caring nurse as a grandmother, one who welcomed a crowd of small children onto her lap. The nurse glanced at her watch and removed the thermometer. "One hundred one point five. You may have an infection. I'll check on the dentist. Maybe he can see you now."

They waited a few hours for the dentist, who gave her two aspirin, a shot of penicillin, and numbed her with Novocain. The dentist entered her wide-open mouth with a cold metal instrument he had selected from a nearby tray. She felt force but no pain and thought the dentist might pull her out of the chair by the tooth before it was all over.

With her bottom pricked like a pincushion, cotton packed into the cavity in her cheek, and a supply of aspirin for later, Ruby joined her sister and stepmother as they set out to locate their new home among the grid of crude barracks—Block 38, Building No. 11, Unit F—circled in red ink on a mimeographed map of the prison camp. The map displayed a city bigger than Ruby's eyes could see from one place, organized into blocks, with streets A-I running one direction and First through Seventh Street running the other. A high school, two elementary schools, a store, churches, and open spaces were in the center. Each block contained a mess hall, recreation building, men and women's lavatories, and laundry facilities, and twelve tar paper barracks with six units per building. They found 38-11-F on the corner of First and H Streets.

As Taeko opened the door to their unit, the wind caught the screen door and sent it banging into the front wall, its handle tearing the tar paper. The scarred sheathing suggested this wasn't the first time. A single bare light bulb with a pull-string dangled from the center of the rafters, illuminating their cruel fate. Home was now a twenty-foot-square, one-room unit with unfinished wood floors, exterior walls with no insulation, wood beam ceilings, and only a thin wood partition to separate them from the adjoining unit. The partition fell short of the ceiling. Three unassembled army cots rested against a wall. Blankets were stacked in the corner. A hulking potbelly stove stood against the back wall with a box of matches and a pile of newspaper.

The wind howled, and the freezing air coursed through the gaps in the tar paper and the boards. It was as cold inside as it was outside. Taeko stooped and examined the inside of the stove. "When I lived in Ishikawa, we had a stove like this. The winters were harsh there. Mari, I saw a shovel and a pile of coal on the ground. Get some and put it in the chamber."

But Ruby and Mari stood still. Only their eyes moved, examining the room and looking at each other. To Ruby, the room was a prison cell, but without bars. Without the cozy chair she'd sat in with Mama. Without Mama. Without Father. Without freedom.

At that moment, she hated Japan. She hated the United States. And she hated Taeko.

"Now, Mari!" Taeko ordered.

"Hold the door for me, Ruby," Mari said.

Ruby held the door as Mari stomped in and out.

Taeko ripped a newspaper to shreds. "Girls, watch me so you'll know how to do this yourselves."

Ruby stood over her stepmother's shoulders as she showed them how to open and close the vent and load the coal and shredded paper. She lit a roll of newspaper and inserted the smoking paper into the coal chamber. "Don't touch the stove once it gets going. It'll burn your skin off." The belly of the stove soon hissed and popped, and the winter-long challenge of feeding the stove's insatiable hunger for fuel began.

Mari put her arm around Ruby. "It'll be okay. We'll make it a home and then it will feel that way."

Having missed breakfast, and with empty stomachs, they made their way to the mess hall, where they joined the end of a short line. The lunch service was almost over and few people were around. Cafeteria servers spooned sausages and spinach on their tin plates. Except for Spam marinated in soy sauce and grilled, their family ate fresh fish, vegetables, and fruit. Ruby had never eaten pale and mushy spinach before, and the sausage repulsed her.

"Yuck," she said. "I'm cutting mine up so I won't have to chew it."

An old lady at the next table must have overheard her. "Those are Vienna sausages, child. Eat what you're served, or don't eat at all."

Within hours, they all suffered from diarrhea and raced to the one women's lavatory building in their entire block of over seventy families. They hurried past rows of sinks and open shower facilities to find two rows of five toilets, arranged back-to-back. The toilets sat side-by-side with no partitions and so close Ruby could touch the girl next to her. Ruby hung her head, inches away from her sister, stepmother, and total strangers, as her anus farted and squirted.

Throughout the day, Taeko's skills at overseeing a girls' dormitory surfaced. She told Ruby and Mari everything would get better when Father joined them. That he'd be there soon. They spent the afternoon running to and from the lavatory and purchasing coats, boots, and household supplies from a store, staffed by incarcerees and selling the barest of essentials. Taeko spent every dime of the little money she had received in exchange for their belongings in Hawaii, but said she could earn money working in camp.

Back in the unit, Taeko instructed Ruby to sweep the walls and floors and Mari to take the cot mattresses outside and beat out the dust. Once beaten, they assembled the cots and made their beds with simple linens brought from Waimea. Ruby washed the windows and mopped the floors.

After they settled in, Ruby and Mari took showers next to women and girls of all ages. Only Mari had seen her naked, and she'd been raised to avoid impropriety or indecency. She began to understand how everything had changed and how vulnerable she was in here. She lathered the soap between her hands and turned her eyes and body toward the wall, allowing the tepid water to shower down her bare backside.

That night, searchlights pierced the darkness and crisscrossed the barracks. Stiff with cold, Ruby pulled the blanket up to her chin and explored the new gap in her mouth with her tongue. The aspirin was working, and the pain had subsided. The blustery wind assaulted the building, and the stove groaned and crackled. From the other side of the partition, she heard faint conversations and a baby crying from distant units, and groans of pleasure coming from the banging cot in the neighboring unit. Mari had met the newlywed couple earlier.

Ruby wondered if the couple's lovemaking would become her nightly lullaby and fantasized about what it might feel like to be held and kissed by a boy someday. How long would they be forced to stay in camp? A few weeks, months, or longer? Would she meet a boy and fall in love here? Would she, too, be here long enough to marry inside of the fences and share the private moments of her wedding night with strangers? Raise children here? Grow old here? Impossible. The wedding she had always imagined was in Waimea. She would wear a dress of white eyelet and an orchid lei, her feet bare in the sand. Like her, the neighbors probably never imagined beginning their marriage in a crude barracks surrounded by scary guards.

The pain of hopelessness replaced her toothache, which no aspirin could ever cure. Despair joined her in bed, and she fell asleep.

GIRI

February 1943 – Hiroshima, Japan

To preserve appearances, Koji's family tried to maintain their patriotic public persona by honoring their civic duty and demonstrating the self-sacrificing devotion of *giri*. Within reason, they did whatever the government demanded of them. They were part of the neighborhood self-policing association, supervised by Community Council officials, formed throughout Hiroshima to train citizens as home-front soldiers capable of defending against enemy attacks. They were expected to keep their eyes and ears open for espionage, monitor neighborhood morale, distribute scarce supplies and food rations, and implement Council directives.

Leadership of Fuchu's association rotated among the households each month, and now the burden defaulted to Koji's mother since his father's illness and fatigue prevented him from handling those responsibilities. During February, Koji had always helped *Otōsan* clear debris, prepare the fields for early spring planting, and rebuild fences damaged over the winter. Feeling unwell, *Otōsan* rested for most of the day, and his responsibilities fell to Koji, along with studying and helping his mother.

Anything could happen. The Council could show up for a surprise inspection, so his family always had to be ready. The military might call a boy from Fuchu to military service, requiring they lead the sendoff, recognizing the pain it would cause the boy's parents. *Okāsan* had told him she was grateful their rotation fell during the winter, while there was less work to do around the farm. While Koji spent every available hour helping his mother, Naoki—caught up in the fantasy of war—played soldier and boasted about ways he would defeat Japan's enemies. For months, Naoki

120

had bugged him to build a bomb shelter from within their existing root cellar. A determined and budding engineer, Naoki spent hours drawing various design schemes and figuring out how to stabilize the earth. Despite the increased threat of enemy raids, Koji placed the building of a bomb shelter at the low end of his priority list.

During the month, Koji helped his mother pick up, divide, and distribute rations to neighboring households in Fuchu. On a Sunday night, he had helped her document, in a well-organized ledger, the donations she had received the prior week from each household in their section to buy war-supporting savings bonds. Koji cringed when his mother wrote down the names of families who failed to contribute to the campaign.

"*Okāsan*, do you have to tell on them?" he asked.

His mother had twisted a lone strand of hair that came loose from her bun and her pained gaze met his eyes. "Sadly, yes. Self-policing has intensified and we are expected to do whatever is asked of us." She rested her chin on her hand. "Even if we don't want to."

The next morning, his mother was at the table finishing the tallies of ledger entries as Koji put on his coat and grabbed his knapsack. "Come on, Naoki. We'll be late for school!"

His mother set the ledger aside. She rubbed under her eyes where dark circles had formed.

"Finished?" he asked.

"Almost. I still need to make the deposit at the post office and tidy the house for the neighborhood meeting tonight. And I need to figure out refreshments." She wiped her brow.

"There's a meeting here tonight?"

"Yes. Today is the eighth."

Koji should have remembered the date, since he would turn fourteen tomorrow. Showing reverence to the Emperor, all community meetings were held on the eighth of the month, recognizing the day Japan had declared war on the United States and its allies.

Naoki came running from their bedroom, half awake, his shirt partially tucked.

"We'll help you when we get home," Koji said to his mother, knowing his brother would be off playing war games and the work would fall to him.

• • •

That evening, Koji finished sweeping the *engawa* and checked his watch for the third time in an hour, wondering if Emi would attend the meeting with her parents. If so, he hoped he wouldn't get tongue-tangled and weak in the knees again. He leaned the broom against the wall and went inside to help his mother in the kitchen.

"Smells good," he said.

"Bean-paste soup and pickled cherry blossom tea." She released an exhausted sigh. "How embarrassing."

In better times, his mother would have served their guests plentiful and delicious refreshments on her finest dishes. He put a hand on her shoulder. "Our neighbors will understand, *Okāsan*. They don't have much, either."

She wrung her callused hands.

The neighbors arrived, shared gossip with one another, and divided up yet more tasks within the already overworked community. Emi sat beside her mother as the women agreed to spin silk to fabricate into parachutes. On the opposite side of the room, the men promised more of their labor for the war effort. His mother would later record the work commitment for each neighbor.

With his hands busy clearing and washing dishes, Koji struggled to follow the conversations—some tedious, some hushed, and some passionate. Shocking stories of the Japanese incarceration in America had reached Japan, and outlandish hypotheses circulated their small living room. Many worried about what might become of their families in America. Someone shared a heartbreaking report from Tokyo—zookeepers poisoned the animals for the sake of Japan. With people starving, the luxury of feeding monkeys and zebras was no longer justified.

The Watanabe family was the last to leave the gathering. Koji walked Emi to the gate and his eyes followed her as she continued down the lane. She walked about a dozen steps and turned to wave. Her sweet, dimpled smile brought a silly grin to his face. He thought of the *haiku* he'd written for her, but the wadded paper always ended up in the trash. For that smile, he'd try again.

His mother stood on the *engawa*, rubbing her arms and looking into the yard as if something bad was about to happen. With everyone gone, the quiet seemed to heighten her disquiet. He felt her watching him as he struggled with the fraying rope and lowered their flag. At sunrise, he would wrestle once again with the antiquated pulley to hoist the Rising Sun.

QUESTIONS
OF LOYALTY

1943 – Jerome, AR

Ruby's bare legs were blushed crimson from the hem of her coat to the top of her boots. She'd been incarcerated for over a month and couldn't get used to the stinging cold.

On her walk to school, shadows and the flapping of wings caught her attention as a voracious murder of crows soared overhead and perched together on the power lines laced between coarse utility poles above the barracks. The starkness of the birds' black plumage was so unlike Hawaii's colorful songbirds. Even the crows were cold, facing into the wind and gripping their claws along the line, as they searched for food. Their incessant *caw-caw-caw* mocked the incarcerees confined within steel fences crowned with razor sharp thorns.

A woman hanging dripping wet laundry—scrubbed and wrung out by hand—screeched *"Jōdan deshō?"* And there it was, bird poop right in the middle of one of her freezing dingy sheets flapping in the wind. The woman would have to re-wash the sheet, only for it to freeze again, and later hang inside of her barracks to finish drying amid the soot-filled-air. Coal stoves meant nothing would be white again.

Ruby chuckled. *No, the bird wasn't kidding you. It intended to poop on your sheets! Why haven't you learned English?* Since the government imprisoned them for looking like the enemy, she believed everyone should at least try not to sound like one too. *Oh well, Okāsan hasn't bothered, either.*

She passed the lavatory, having sworn never to go there again without the paper bag she had saved to put over her head for an iota of privacy, entered the school building, and hung her coat on the rack. Like many other kids, she wore the scratchy Red Cross sweater and cap in the classroom. There, the wind whistled through openings in the uninsulated rough timber walls and floors. Someone had pasted learning aids on bright construction paper and hung them around the room. An American flag draped in the corner. A blackboard filled one wall with chalked assignments. She joined other students at one of the long tables arranged in a U. Individual desks always faced the front of Waimea classrooms. It was something else to get used to.

Her eighth-grade teacher, Mrs. Flint, was marking papers at her tattered wood desk. She loved when Mrs. Flint returned papers marked in red pen with cursive comments on the top right corner. Ruby always got A's, check pluses, or stars. Mrs. Flint was a sizeable woman with curly gray hair who wore dresses belted at the waist and clunky shoes. She had left retirement to work for the War Relocation Authority after teaching in Arkansas for thirty years. She often rested her warm, age-spotted hand on a student's shoulder when returning assignments. For Ruby, the touch meant *Good Job!* Mrs. Flint wore a benevolent smile and twice led the civics class in frank debates about the injustice of the camps.

After the Pledge of Allegiance, Ruby twisted in her wood-slat chair to face the front for announcements, including one that might affect families in the camps. "Class," Mrs. Flint announced, "the War Department has reversed its decision to exclude Japanese Americans from serving America's Armed Forces. The Army will soon begin recruiting adult male volunteers from Jerome and other relocation centers to enlist in an all-*Nisei* combat unit."

Anxious, questioning hands flew in the air.

"Does this mean my father will have to fight in the war?"

"They want us to fight for a country that made us leave our homes?"

"Will they fight in Japan? But what if my brother shoots his cousin?"

"Do we have to stay in here if someone in our family is fighting for our country? That's not right."

Mrs. Flint held up her hand. "I understand this is unexpected, and I wish I had answers to all of your questions. All I know is we were told to share this information with junior and high school students because the Administration will begin posting flyers and things will unfold in the coming weeks. Until then you'll hear a bunch of scuttlebutt. Try to avoid forming opinions or getting yourselves upset until things are clear."

"What brought this about?"

"I only have President Roosevelt's statement." She began reading.

"No loyal citizen of the United States should be denied the democratic right to exercise the responsibilities of his citizenship, regardless of ancestry. Every loyal American citizen should be given the opportunity to serve this country wherever his skills will make the greatest contribution, whether it be in the ranks of our armed forces, war production, agriculture, government service, or other work essential to the war effort."

She returned the sheet to her desk. "It seems our President has reconsidered."

More hands were raised.

"Can we leave to work if we want?"

"What kind of work is essential?"

"Can we go home and work on our farm?"

Although some kids seemed optimistic about the news, Ruby wasn't so sure it was positive for her family. Taeko and Mari were not U.S. citizens, and she was just a kid. She glanced around to gauge others' reactions, but it was hard to tell what they were thinking. When all other hands were down, she stopped tapping her pencil and raised her hand. "Mrs. Flint, what... if you're not a citizen?"

"Oh, how I wish I had the answer for you... for all of you."

• • •

Within the week, War Department posters featuring an American Eagle and bold lettering—U.S. ARMY RECRUITERS ARRIVING SOON—were posted around the camp. Now, adults congregated in small huddles and covered their mouths when speaking. Kids talkèd among themselves about their parents' concerns. Ruby overheard whispers from the other side of the partition late into the night. Inadequate information. Fear of dueling loyalties. Violated civil rights. A division between the people for and against the government's decision began to widen.

Taeko seemed to care little about the controversy, dedicating every waking hour to reuniting with Father who remained in Lordsburg. With Mari's help translating Japanese to English, Taeko wrote letters every week to the Director, Enemy Alien Control Unit and the Provost Marshal General pleading for Father's release to join them in a family relocation center. English-speaking neighbors wrote character reference letters attesting to Taeko's *fine* qualities. Once a chameleon, always a chameleon, thought Ruby.

Day after day, they endured roll calls, structured mealtimes, and standing in line—for meals, laundry tubs, toilets. For everything. Ruby found it strange that families seldom ate meals together. Grownups sat with other adults and children of all ages sat with their friends in the mess hall. Since her bout of diarrhea on the first day, she avoided certain foods and enjoyed many of the other meals. Her favorite was Sunday when they served fried chicken, biscuits, and gravy for dinner and Neapolitans for dessert. She loved the pretty ice cream squares—perfect stripes of chocolate, vanilla, and strawberry. Most of the kids that Ruby ate with were from California. Few were from Hawaii. Except for their ethnicity, she had little in common with the California city kids and she felt left out. She missed walking barefoot to school, picking and eating ripe mangoes, and year-round summer—it was so cold in Arkansas. More than anything, she missed her true friends—the ones who didn't turn their backs on her after Pearl Harbor.

Sometimes she would see Taeko or Mari in the mess halls where they worked as waitresses, earning sixteen dollars per month, plus a stipend for clothing. Taeko constantly complained. "I didn't leave my home for this shrunken and imprisoned life. I'm an educated woman! I came for freedom, and now I'm stuck in this prison with you girls *and* have to fill other people's water glasses for money."

Ruby missed Mari, who was always busy—working, studying in her last year of high school, or keeping company with her new beau, a nineteen-year-old Japanese American from Los Angeles named Warren Okada. Warren was the son of traditional Japanese parents who had immigrated to California before his birth, and he had already graduated.

On the night of the school Valentine's Day dance, Mari returned home gushing, "Oh, it was such a fun party and Warren's so handsome... and a marvelous dancer! Look, he made me a Valentine. Isn't it pretty?" She slipped a handmade *origami* card from her small purse. Warren had cut and cleverly folded the red construction paper into a heart secured by a length of old lace tied in a bow. Mari untied the lace and opened the card where he had written *Be Mine*. She leaned toward Ruby and whispered, "He kissed me tonight! I think I'm in love!"

Ruby rolled her eyes. "Oh, come on! You just met him."

"Haven't you ever heard of love at first sight, little sister?"

"In fairy tales, maybe," Ruby said, tossing her pillow gently at Mari.

"You won't think that forever. Well, whatever. Sleep well. I believe I will. Oh, give me my card."

Mari tucked the card under her pillow, undressed, and pulled the string to turn off the light. Taeko snored in her cot with a book flopped open on her chest. Soon, her sister's soft whistling began, and Ruby was alone with her thoughts, illuminated by the dim light creeping in from the neighboring units.

• • •

As the Army's recruitment efforts began, Mrs. Flint did her best to explain to the class why there was such unexpected resistance. Ruby assumed the *Nisei* men would line up to enlist for Uncle Sam. But along with recruiting initiatives, the government required all adult *Nisei* men to register with the Selective Service System by completing a long questionnaire. Mrs. Flint had a copy of the form because school had been closed for a few days while teachers helped administer the process. She passed it around for the students to review while she explained the questions and wrote key issues on the blackboard.

"Class, the survey mostly asks for simple information such as education, past addresses and employment, family names, foreign language ability, religion, other affiliations, and criminal offenses. But it also asks for more sensitive information, such as if people have any money in foreign bank accounts, financial contributions they may have made to societies, and the kinds of magazines and newspapers they subscribed to. What do you think about those questions?"

The kids were slow to raise their hands, but once the ideas began flowing, it seemed there was no stopping their tidal wave of ideas.

"Well, if somebody has money in Japan and not in America, it might mean they think it is safer in Japan and are planning to move back."

"Sure, but I think my parents have a bank account in Tokyo where they keep the money they saved for my grandparents. That doesn't mean they'd want to return! They don't!"

"Why would anybody care if somebody gives money to a *kendō* club? I don't get why they'd ask that question."

"Probably because it means something different than if you give money to the Boy Scouts!"

"I guess if you read only Japanese and not American papers, maybe that means you care more about Japan than the United States."

Ruby wondered about the questions concerning religion. "Mrs. Flint, they arrested my father because he is a Buddhist minister and the authorities charged him as an enemy alien. Are all Buddhists labeled loyal to Japan? Are only Christians loyal to America?"

Her teacher rolled chalk between her hands. "Good question. I don't believe that's the case, but I'm not sure how the government interprets the answers. Some questions are deeply troubling, especially questions 27 and 28." Mrs. Flint glanced down and paraphrased the questions.

"'Are you willing to serve in the armed forces of the United States in combat duty wherever ordered?' and 'Will you swear unqualified allegiance to the United States and faithfully defend the United States against all attack by foreign or domestic forces and forswear any form of allegiance or obedience to

the Japanese Emperor or other foreign governments or powers?'"

She paused. "It appears these questions may determine one's patriotism to either the U.S. or Japan. And *that* will stir controversy."

The *Statement of U.S. Citizen of Japanese Ancestry* form became known as the loyalty questionnaire. It suggested the only path to scaling the barbed wire was to answer the questions the *right* way and volunteer to die for America. But the government was wrong to expect all positive responses from the *Nisei*. Ruby's classmates talked about overheard conversations and meetings where men argued over the government's intentions and their willingness to enlist.

Like many *Nisei* determined to prove fidelity to America, Warren seized on his right to serve the United States and punish Japan for its shameful attack. Others had lost faith in the United States and refused to volunteer for an America that had incarcerated them. They couldn't understand how the United States would dare ask them to show loyalty to America now and forswear allegiance to the Emperor when they had *never* felt devotion to the Emperor in the first place.

• • •

A week later, before bedtime, Ruby visited the lavatory to shower. She preferred to shower in the evening when darkness had claimed the day and fewer old women were around to gawk at her nakedness. With her business finished, she tucked her damp hair into her cap, buttoned her coat, and stepped outside to walk home. Searchlights raked the barracks and caught her. She crossed her arms against the light and ran, knowing there was no route home where the light wouldn't illuminate her vulnerability to the whims of the guards.

She turned the corner of their building and discovered Mari in Warren's arms, her head nestled into his chest. Feeling like an intruder, she slipped into the shadows and peered at them. Warren raised Mari's face with one finger, a tender touch under her chin. When he held her sister's face between his hands and spoke words only Mari could hear, Ruby touched her own face and imagined what it would be like to be touched so tenderly by a boy. When the search light discovered and held its beam on them, it revealed Mari's quivering lips. Her sister was crying. Mari broke away and dashed up the steps into the barracks.

Warren stumbled away on the uneven dirt road and vanished into the darkness. A searchlight threw harsh brightness after him and would likely follow him home. Alone in the dark and in her shame for violating their privacy, Ruby waited before going inside, trying to decide if she should tell Mari what she saw or act ignorant. She imagined Warren was breaking up with her or leaving. Or both. Their stepmother was hemming an apron and ignoring Mari's tears.

Ruby curled up beside her sister in bed. Choked sobs drowned out Mari's words. "He's been... accepted... medical exam... leaves in a few days... basic training."

Sadness welled in Ruby's heart as she enveloped Mari in her arms, but tears wouldn't come. She hadn't wept since saying goodbye to Hawaii. Crying never changed things and it made her feel worse. Ruby caught Taeko's sideways glance, a look more curious than sympathetic. Taeko had given up enforcing her *speak Japanese only* rule since entering camp, so the girls chatted freely without Taeko understanding.

"I'm sorry, Mari." Not knowing what else to say, she held her sister until they both surrendered to sleep.

After Warren left for basic training in Mississippi, people became more embroiled in heated controversy. The WRA had adopted the Selective Service questionnaire, without adequate revision, to survey adult *Issei* and female *Nisei* for leave clearances and releases. The controversial armed forces Question 27 changed to: *If the opportunity presents itself and you are found qualified, would you be willing to volunteer for the Army Nurse Corps or the Women's Army Auxiliary Corps?* Question 28 remained the same, but for deleting *and faithfully defend the United States from any or all attack by foreign or domestic forces.*

The government identified those who answered no to both questions as disloyal—the *No-No's.* Those who answered yes to both were considered loyal. People resented the questionnaire and mistrusted its intent, especially Question 28, which they considered a trick question. Answering yes and agreeing to forswear any form of allegiance or obedience to the Japanese Emperor implied the person had held a faithfulness to Japan's Emperor, even when the person held no such loyalty. Answering yes also left *Issei* without a country since U.S. law barred them from citizenship. Answering no might also cause deportation in a prisoner exchange. Those who stood on principle and withheld answers were labeled as disloyal saboteurs. It seemed to Ruby there were no correct responses.

In response to the incarcerees' continuing protests against the fairness of the questionnaire, the WRA once again revised Question 28 to: *Will you swear to abide by the laws of the United States and take no action which would in any way interfere with the war effort of the United States?*

Ruby had one loyalty—to the country that had betrayed her—but she was too young for her opinion to matter. Her fourteenth birthday on March 25 went uncelebrated but for a single candle in her rice pudding and a warm wish for a happy birthday from her sister who would turn eighteen two days later. Mari completed her questionnaire, answering yes to 27, even though she didn't qualify because she wasn't a U.S. citizen, and yes to 28, out of devotion to Warren and the future she wanted with him in America. Taeko withheld an answer to 27 and answered no to 28.

• • •

At her stepmother's insistence, Ruby missed school to meet with an official in the Administration building. Taeko would not tell her the purpose of the meeting, so Ruby assumed it had something to do with school. Perhaps she was being promoted to the next grade level early since her test scores were so high. Ruby hadn't been in the Administration building since the day they arrived, but she discovered it warm and cozy against the chilly rain. They waited in the receiving area on an uncomfortable wood bench for hours before being called to the desk of an army administrator who was not much older than Mari. He wore a starched uniform and a stern look. Buzzed short on the sides and back, his red hair stood straight up about an inch atop his square-shaped head—flat, like a manicured lawn. Like a blockhead. A stapler, a box of paper clips, and a stack of papers next to a telephone were the only things on his tidy metal desk. He waited for the interpreter to begin, his crossed hands resting on the desk blotter. Ruby assumed Blockhead didn't trust her to correctly interpret Taeko's words.

The interpreter was a middle-aged man with wire-framed glasses, a furrowed brow, and an uncaring demeanor. He translated Taeko's insistent Japanese to English. "We wish to return to Japan. Where do I sign?"

We? What on earth was she saying?

Even though Taeko had often grumbled that her ultimate goal was to return to Japan, Ruby was shocked to learn of her intention to move there. Ruby felt as if someone had punched her in the stomach. She wanted to run. She was desperate to run, but she was surrounded by the interpreter, Blockhead, and Taeko. Powerless.

The men busied themselves with paperwork. Blockhead pulled two forms from his drawer. The other asked and interpreted basic questions— name, age, place of birth, family members, education—while Blockhead typed the responses. Unable to move, Ruby stared at her crossed arms. When Blockhead finished typing, he placed two completed applications in front of them. The form in front of Taeko was titled INDIVIDUAL REQUEST FOR REPATRIATION. The form in front of Ruby was identical, except the man had crossed out REPATRIATION with a series of Xs and typed EXPATRIATION beside it. The interpreter showed them where to sign.

Ruby's eyes bulged, her muscles stiffened, her voice cracked. "I'm not going to... Japan!"

"*Shizukani!*"

She would not shut up. "No! You can't force me!"

Taeko's backhanded slap across Ruby's face silenced her protests.

The men showed no interest in the mother-daughter squabble.

Blistering heat pulsed through Ruby's body. The impulse to bolt was irresistible, and she pushed her chair backward and ran out of the building into the pounding March rain. She ran as fast as she could, slipping and sliding through the mud—past the open area, the schools, and the barracks—all the way to the fence line at East Patrol Road on the far side of camp.

She threw herself onto the chain-link fence. "I won't go! I won't!" She clutched the fence with both hands and shook it, but the fence was unbending. Her screams continued. "I hate you! You can't make me go! Let me OUT!"

Lost in her meltdown, she ignored the guard's megaphoned demand to get away from the fence.

The voice boomed. "MOVE AWAY FROM THE FENCE!"

She released the fence, turned away from the desolate windswept fields rolling into the horizon, and raised her vacant eyes to the guard shouting at *her* from the tower.

"BACK UP AND AWAY, KID! GO HOME!"

Emboldened by fury, she screamed, "I CAN'T! I'M A PRISONER IN HERE, STUPID!"

Suddenly realizing the danger of her circumstances, she walked backward, never taking her eyes off of the guard, and created distance between them. She stumbled on legs that felt too heavy to carry her through the mud and forced herself to keep moving through a grid of barracks away from her own and toward the high school, where school was still in session. She entered a nearby lavatory, where she stood under the shower, fully clothed, and washed the mud from her body and shoes, watching her life spill across the filthy tile floor and down the drain.

Soaking wet, Ruby walked to the high school and entered through a side door. She sneaked down the hallway and hid in a supply closet near her sister's classroom.

The dismissal bell rang about a half hour later. She stepped out of the closet and found Mari smiling and chatting with her friends. Mari's smile faded at her appearance. She grasped Ruby's hand and guided her to an empty bench at the end of the corridor. "Ruby, what on earth? You're drenched!"

Ruby rehashed the events of the morning as water dripped from her clothing, puddled on the wood floor, and seeped between the cracks.

"The nerve of her!" Mari said. "I can't imagine she can make you go to Japan."

Mari took her hand. "Come on, let's figure this out."

• • •

When they opened the door to their unit, Taeko was sitting at the table. Her jaw was tight, and she glared over the rims of her glasses with a flat stare.

"Stupid girl. How dare you defy me and make such a scene. I'd be ashamed if I were you!"

Mari approached Taeko. Her voice stern, yet calm. "*Okāsan*, it's not right for you to make Ruby abandon her birth country."

Taeko smirked triumphantly and handed Mari a letter from their father. Neither sister had seen the letter before. "Here, read this."

Mari snatched the letter from Taeko's hands. The letter was written nearly a month ago in their father's perfect calligraphy.

March 1, 1943

My dearest Taeko,

It causes me great despair to hear of your unhappiness in Jerome. I believed a secure home within a larger Japanese population might raise your spirits. My requests to join you fall on deaf ears and we can't know when they will reunite us. Until we are together again, please resist giving in to bitterness.

None of this is of our doing. The fault falls on two polarized governments, enemies of each other. We couldn't have known any of these adversities would befall us. Thank you for your selflessness. You left everything familiar to you and the life you had built to marry me, raise my daughters, and help lead the temple. I trust you to make reasoned decisions for yourself and Ruby while we are apart, including your heartfelt wish to return to Japan and take her with you. Mari will be of age to decide for herself on her birthday later this month, but I imagine she, too, will accompany you.

*My grateful heart is yours and, until we meet again, we will close
our eyes at day's end knowing we were strong and the powers failed
to break us.*

Please wish Ruby and Mari happy birthday for me.

With devotion,
Chiko

Ruby gripped the table edge. Beads of sweat dribbled over her lips. *No.
Father wouldn't agree to this. He wouldn't!*

Mari set the letter on the table. "*Okāsan*, this situation is temporary.
Things are already changing. People eligible for leave clearance are finding
sponsors and are leaving for jobs in factories and on farms. The war will
end soon, and we will all return to Hawaii with Father and live the life you
imagined when you came here. Please don't be hasty. Japan is unsafe. Don't
do this to yourself and to my sister."

"Ruby's a disrespectful child. She will do what I say. And it's plenty safe
in Ishikawa. At least there, she will learn the manners of a proper Japanese
girl and to respect her elders."

Taeko's five-foot, three-inch frame seemed to tower. She grabbed Ruby
out of the chair by her ear. "Change into clean clothes. We're going back to
finish the paperwork."

Mari turned to Ruby's pleading eyes. "I'm sorry, Ruby. You must not
disobey Father. Go with her and sign the form. As Father would say, we
can't return spilled water to the glass. We must trust the universe will provide a path."

An hour later, Ruby stood before Blockhead. With throbbing heat
behind her eyeballs and a painful lump in her throat, she read the statement above the signature line. *"I have read the above statements... request
is filed voluntarily... does not bind the United States to... my expatriation."*
She signed her name to the form threatening deportation from the only

country she'd ever known. Blockhead affixed his signature as her witness.

With a wheezing breath, she murmured, "It's *not* voluntary. I didn't volunteer. I don't want to leave." But Blockhead had already walked away.

SHELTER

March 1943 – Hiroshima, Japan

Koji welcomed the cooler-than-normal spring temperatures and returned with an empty pail to the hand-dug shelter deep in the hillside. He and Naoki had been working nonstop to expand the family's root cellar deeper into the hill, and they were close to finishing construction of a crude bomb shelter.

Built many years ago by Koji's grandfather behind their home, the root cellar was accessed via a well-worn path through a narrow bamboo grove. *Otōsan* said he and his father had stacked the moss-covered stones shoring up the entrance when he was young. The rotting wood door opened to the cellar's dank-smelling interior, its walls lined with splintering crates connected by an intricate network of sticky webs and filled with dwindling quantities of scarce vegetables—*daikon*, turnips, potatoes, and cabbage.

Bombing raids on other major Japanese cities were common, and the entire country practiced routine air raid drills. Though he was grateful the Allies had spared Hiroshima so far, Koji knew it was only a matter of time before they attacked his city. His family needed a safe place, and so he had capitulated to Naoki's pleas to build the shelter and threw himself into the work. They had begun constructing Naoki's design by digging past the cellar's rear wall and expanding farther into the slope. When complete, the shelter would be about three meters long, two meters wide, and high enough for them to sit. The arduous process required them to penetrate a small section at a time, reinforce the sides and ceiling with tree wood and cured bamboo, and lace the structure together before moving deeper into the earth. One boy dug and filled a bucket with dirt and rocks for removal, while the other removed the full buckets and came back with the empties. Day after day, they made slow progress.

Koji went back inside the dark burrow, and his brain adjusted to the silence of their subterranean world. He no longer heard cars on their road or the hum of tractors from the surrounding farms. The deeper he dug and the quieter it became, the more his mind escaped from everything wrong with the world above the surface.

Everything except for Emi. He'd only seen her a few times, for a quick wave or hello, since last month's community meeting. Now, he imagined them swirling in a galaxy of darkness. Beckoned by a distant kaleidoscope of vivid colors, they held hands, kissed, and floated to a time and place free from war, where kids could just be kids. A place where he might learn English and maybe study another language. A place where he became a diplomat who traveled the world and experienced unique cultures, while negotiating trade deals, treaties, and strategic agreements to benefit humanity. A place where he would bring Japan and its enemies together in peace.

He shifted his body to a more comfortable position and returned to digging. Their progress satisfied him, and he enjoyed the physical exertion of the mindless work in the tunnel. His muscles were sore and his hands blistered from the prior day's work, but the effort was easier this morning—the coarse-grained earth was looser—perhaps because of all the worms crawling around. The tempo of his shoveling increased from slow and intermittent to fast and steady. Until he hit something hard. His spade came to a jarring halt.

He scraped the area and uncovered a sizeable rock. Crouched in the confining space, he used his full upper-body strength to strike the earth surrounding the rock with his handheld pickaxe. Feeling the need to shift positions yet again, he lay on his stomach with his rib cage grinding into the ground and thrashed at the dirt in front of him. He kept hitting until the rock surrendered. The earth above drizzled loose soil on his head. Not wanting to break pace, he had neglected to shore up the excavated earthen walls and ceiling. But the warning was clear. He would reinforce the area as soon as he made more room for himself and Naoki returned with the empty buckets.

As he shoveled dirt into a bucket, his flashlight jostled and illuminated something other than rock and dirt, something incongruous. He set the shovel aside, dug around the artifact with his hands, and discovered a small clay jar. He brushed the loose earth from the jar, revealing ancient markings, removed the lid, and shined his flashlight on a few blackened coins. How had the jar come to be buried here? Had it been part of an ancient ritual to ward off evil spirits, or coins hidden by a medieval *samurai*?

With the jar nestled in the curve of his arm, he crawled backward toward the entrance, emerged from the root cellar, and discovered Emi sitting on a crate with *bentō* boxes on her lap.

"Hi, dirt ball." She giggled. "Wow, the whites of your eyes are really white today!"

Embarrassed for Emi to see him so filthy, he raked his free hand through his hair to shake off the loose dirt, but dirt and grit were embedded in his skin and clothing.

"Hi yourself. What's on your lap?"

"I brought you lunch. But what's that?" she asked, pointing to the jar.

"I dug it up and found old coins inside."

"Wow! How old?"

"Old, I think. Maybe Edo."

"*Samurai* gold?"

"No. I think silver, but they're pretty tarnished. I'll polish them later."

"Thanks for bringing us lunch," he said, resting the jar on the ground. "That was nice of you. Sorry I'm such a mess."

"You're fine. Getting dirty is a testament to hard work."

"I'll admit, it's pretty tiring work, but it will be worth it if they bomb us. I'll wash up and then we can eat."

"Sorry, I can't stay. My mother said to come right back. The *bentō* boxes are for you and Naoki. But show me your discovery before I leave."

Realizing he wouldn't be sharing lunch with Emi, his smile faded.

She reached for the jar. "May I?"

"Sure. Dump the coins out."

But Emi wasn't a dumper. She carefully removed the jar's lid and emptied the coins into her lap. While she held each coin to the sunlight and ran her fingers over the surface, Koji's thoughts returned to what had been front of mind inside of the tunnel, but in the context of found money. He believed finding the coins was a sign. Money was valuable. Maybe the found coins foretold big things in life were destined for him.

"They're old, all right," she said.

"I think finding money is a way for spirits to say something good is going to happen."

The coins sifted through her delicate fingers and returned to the jar. She closed the lid. "I hope you're right, Koji. But my grandmother is superstitious about these things. She says inanimate objects have spirits, and hidden treasure brings the discoverer the luck of the past. Good and bad."

ONE THOUSAND STITCHES

June 1943 – Jerome, AR

They stood outside of a building that was distinguished from the other tar paper barracks by a tattered sign stapled above the door: BUDDHIST CHURCH. Flowering perennials conveyed welcome and softened the building's rough-hewn crudeness. Ruby supposed someone had mail-ordered the plants or seeds and planted them long before her winter arrival at camp.

The warmer weather brought dramatic changes as spring sailed into summer. Bugs crawled through cracks in the barracks walls that had expanded over the cold winter. Sticky, suffocating heat replaced frigid, dry air. Mosquito bites tormented her freckled legs, no longer chafed red. Barren land beyond the fence came to life with vegetable fields and snakes thriving in the swampy lowlands and traveling through the fence with ease.

Ruby faced the sky and gave thanks for blessing her sister with a glorious sunny day, and then placed the bridal lei of fresh wildflowers over Mari's head. Ruby had discovered the playful flowers growing near the southern fence and finished stringing the blossoms together that morning. She kissed Mari on the cheek, and sighed, "Be happy," and beamed, knowing Mari would enjoy the Hawaiian tradition of wearing a bridal lei on her special day.

When Mari hugged her with warmth and affection, Ruby wanted to stay cocooned in their private sister space forever, but it was time to go inside where Warren was waiting. Mari cupped her hands onto Ruby's shoulders and looked deep into her eyes. "I love you, little sister. Everything will be okay. For all of us. I know it."

Ruby extended her hand to Mari—a gesture of joy and trust—and escorted her sister up the steps and into the temple.

A few months before, Mari had received Warren's postcard: GREETINGS FROM CAMP SHELBY, MISSISSIPPI. Colorful vignettes featuring the U.S. flag, army barracks, and marching troops filled each of the fat CAMP SHELBY letters. Warren's message had evoked squeals of delight from her.

My love,

I'm being dispatched to the Rohwer Relocation Center, 30 miles from Jerome, on special assignment in two weeks. I will visit you during my quick trip from Hattiesburg, but we won't have much time together. I yearn to look into your beautiful brown eyes and hold you in my arms.

Love always, Warren

According to Warren, many of the enlisted men at basic training were Japanese Americans from Hawaii—called Pineapple Soldiers—who had avoided incarceration and never visited the mainland before. The happy-go-lucky sort, they had not assimilated well with the soldiers who enlisted from the relocation centers. It seemed they did not appreciate what life was like in the camps or the internal struggle of men like Warren—those who served their country while their loved ones remained imprisoned. And so, Warren's commander ordered several busloads of Pineapple Soldiers to Rohwer, accompanied by soldiers previously incarcerated in the Jerome and Rohwer camps. The commander wanted the Pineapple Soldiers to see for themselves the primitive housing, armed guards, and barbed-wire fences they had avoided. Their empathy and newfound respect for the mainland recruits would make for a successful mission.

But Warren had been more focused on his personal mission, getting down on one knee and proposing to Mari.

Ruby's heart ached at the thought her sister might move away, but she smiled at Mari's joy when Warren slipped the tiny diamond ring on her sister's finger. The mere chip of a gem had taken every cent of Warren's basic training pay.

After Warren returned to Mississippi, Mari had danced through camp on a pillowy cloud of bliss, committed to waiting out the war until they married, until a letter from Warren changed things. He was being deployed to Europe and wished to marry before shipping out. Mari had raced to borrow and alter a suitable wedding dress and to sew Warren a *senninbari*, a scarf she'd embellished with one thousand stiches. In Japan, this traditional gift for departing warriors would have been stitched by one thousand different women.

The scarf draped from Mari's left forearm as she stepped through the door of the make-shift temple. Warren waited at the front alongside a bald elderly minister, who was long retired from the Buddhist ministry, but now served Jerome's Buddhist community. The minister had a tremor and held onto a wooden cane with a quivering hand. He appeared on the verge of falling over at any moment. As if struggling to see, the minister squinted at the sisters as they made their way toward the altar, past Taeko and the few friends attending the wedding. Everyone was smiling, except for Taeko, who was horrified Mari was marrying a U.S. soldier—a soldier who would kill Japanese if ordered to do so. Mari didn't seem to notice, and Ruby tried to ignore Taeko's scowl. In dress uniform, the groom greeted his bride with the widest smile of all.

Ruby wondered if a boy would ever smile at her that way, if she would ever feel love like her sister. Would she ever light a candle or incense at her own wedding as Mari and Warren? Would she someday declare, as her sister would today, a sincere commitment to grow a loving and harmonious relationship with someone for better, for worse, and through life's cycles of continuous change until death parted one from the other?

At the close of the ceremony, Mari presented the *senninbari* to Warren as an amulet to protect him from danger. Ruby embraced her sister and new brother-in-law and wished them well before they waved their good-byes, leaving to enjoy their afternoon and wedding night in the privacy of a unit arranged by Warren's friends. Would Mari make sounds tonight with

Warren like the sounds made on the other side of their partition? Would Ruby make sounds like that someday too?

• • •

After Warren returned to Mississippi, Ruby spent as much time as possible with Mari, trying to raise her sister's spirits. She and Mari started flower and vegetable gardens, sewed window curtains, and leafed through the Montgomery Ward catalog, searching for inexpensive essentials to make their home feel cozier. Dipping into the money she made waitressing, Mari purchased a small electric burner for their room. On rainy days they used it to cook taffy with the sugar and peanut butter they saved from the mess hall, while monitoring the metal buckets that collected rain dripping from the holes in the roof.

Their stepmother expanded her letter-writing campaign to the Director of the Prisoner of War Division, appealing for reunion with Father, hoping they could all be relocated to the Crystal City family camp. The girls appreciated their stepmother's efforts, but wondered if the government ignored her letters because of her formal request to repatriate. Later, when Father's requests for parole-to-family camp were all denied, they transferred him from Lordsburg to another Department of Justice facility in Santa Fe, New Mexico, where he remained.

Ruby's heart shriveled as she listened to Mari read the news of his transfer. In a fit of rage, Taeko tore the new curtains from the windows and threw everything within her reach—a chair, a book, a jar of buttons. Ruby cowered in a corner and waited for the storm to pass. When it did and Taeko stormed out of the unit, Ruby understood the destruction was hers to clean up.

• • •

At Taeko's insistence, Ruby now attended Japanese school in the afternoon after year-round regular school. She despised the Japanese school in Jerome even more than the one in Waimea. In Hawaii she didn't get the point of going. Now, she understood and resented the point—they were indoctrinating her for the eventuality of being deported to Japan as part of a prisoner exchange.

But on her first day of Japanese school, a bubbly girl plopped down next to her and life became far more interesting. The girl wore a snug fitting lightweight cardigan buttoned in the back, a pleated plaid skirt, white bobby socks, and a pair of stylish saddle shoes. At her neck was a gold heart-shaped locket. Her long hair was secured to the side by a tortoiseshell barrette showing off her unblemished skin and regal nose. And her eyes—Ruby had never seen a Japanese with such round, almond-shaped eyes before.

"Hi. I'm Velvet. Velvet Katayama."

"I'm Ruby Ishimaru." Ruby giggled. "Why's your sweater on backwards?"

"The style's all the rage... don't you know?"

Before she could answer, their *sensei* stepped before the class. He wasted no time jumping into the schedule and referring to the blackboard where he chalked months of the year and days of the week in elegant calligraphy between narrow vertical lines. They would learn to write and speak Japanese and to respect Japanese values—reverence for family and authority, modesty, moderation, etiquette.

Freed hours later, in time for supper, the girls walked together to the mess hall. Velvet looked stylish and experienced, and she looked different too, with those exotic eyes.

"Velvet... interesting name."

"Yeah, my Mom named me Velvet because my hair reminded her of a fancy black velvet dress she once wore. We're from Sacramento. You?"

"Waimea. It's on the island of Kauai."

"I've never met a kid from Hawaii before. I bet the weather and beaches are paradise."

"It was," Ruby sighed with a stab of homesickness. "And yeah, it seems the majority of the people here are Californians."

The girls chatted throughout supper, ignoring the other kids around them. When she had cleaned her plate, Velvet returned to the line for seconds. Ruby wondered how the girl ate so much and yet maintained her tiny waist. But instead of eating, Velvet folded the food into a napkin, and slipped the napkin into her pocket. Ruby hoped Velvet didn't notice her grimace.

"Come on, Ruby. Let's go. I want you to meet somebody."

As they headed toward the north side of the fence line, Ruby's curiosity got the best of her. "Where are we going?"

"You'll see," Velvet said, stepping her right foot far across Ruby's legs.

Ruby stumbled over Velvet's foot and nearly fell on the ground. "What are you doing?"

"Walk the wide step with me. It's fun! When I step far left, you step far left too. And then to the right. Get it?" Velvet put her arm around the lower part of Ruby's waist, and Ruby did the same. Together they strutted, legs in unison, across the dusty ground as if they were parade clowns.

Velvet broke away. "Oh look... she's over there. Come with me, or stay behind. I don't care which, but if you come along, you must run like hell from the fence if a guard sees us."

Out of the corner of her eye, Ruby glimpsed a scrawny white girl approaching the fence from the other side. She was about their age and wore pants with holes, a top that seemed too small, her blond hair in pig-tails. Velvet took off running toward the girl, and Ruby ran as fast as she could to keep up with her. When they reached the fence, Velvet pushed the napkin of food through the wire and into the girl's dirty hands.

"Sara-Beth, meet Ruby. Ruby, meet Sara-Beth."

A guard from a nearby tower bellowed, "Hey! What are you kids doing over there?"

As quick as the words, "Let's go!" were out of her mouth, Velvet had turned and was running toward the maze of barracks with Ruby hot on her heels.

Breathless, they sat on a bench in front of the Elementary School. As Ruby caught her breath, she wondered about Sara-Beth. Although she had only seen her for a quick moment, the girl's appearance struck her—a skinny face with sharp cheekbones, hungry eyes, and a grateful smile.

"Who *was* that girl?"

"Sara-Beth? She's a sharecropper kid, says she lives next to a hog farm. I met her by the fence a few months ago. We both kept our distance from the fence but shouted back and forth to each other. First day I saw her, she called me a lucky bitch enemy! She said the fence wasn't fair, that it kept her out while we're in here with food. She said they didn't have enough to eat, and she was always hungry. She questioned why the government would treat us better than her family. So, I told her I'm not the enemy, and I'd bring her food as often as I could. Now we're friends... well, sort of. It's hard to be real friends sprinting to and away from each other. She loves those disgusting Vienna sausages. Do you believe it?"

Ruby cringed at the memory. "Oh, those are nasty. Almost made me poop my pants!"

They fell into a giggle party, and so their friendship began.

MOBILIZED

1943 – Hiroshima, Japan

Koji rubbed his palm across the soft moss covering a rock along the shallow stream, its banks bulging with vegetation thriving in the moist heat of August. Dragonflies buzzed and ruffled the clear water, hunting swarming insects. His forehead and hands perspired, and he was unsure if he was hot and bothered by the day's blistering heat and mosquitoes, or by anticipating his private meeting with Emi.

It was her idea to meet in this secluded spot. He fantasized about kissing Emi and touching her girl parts, but he'd never kissed a girl before. *I'm clueless. What if my breath smells bad?* He huffed into his palm. *It's okay, I think. What should I do with my hands? Tongue? Should I turn my head? What if I bonk her head!* He craved to look into her eyes, lean in to her, and taste her mouth, stroke her hair, breathe her scent. And he wanted her to like it when he did. For certain, the moment would be magical or embarrassing.

He heard the rustle of bushes and stood to greet Emi, wiping his sweaty palms on his pants. She looked fresh, wearing a simple summer dress and sandals, her shiny hair pulled into a ponytail.

"Hi. You look pretty."

Her cheeks flushed. "Hi. Thanks for meeting me here."

"Sure! What a beautiful spot." *More like, tucked away.*

"I'm glad you like it too—it's my favorite. My grandmother used to bring me here to catch dragonflies. Look at all of them dancing today."

He offered Emi his hand and led her to an enormous boulder. They took off their shoes and dangled their toes in the cool stream. As he interlocked his fingers with hers, he sensed her excitement. Her eyes sparkled, and she wore a wide smile.

"I have exciting news," she said, extending her legs and tapping her heels on the water, creating ripples. "I applied to the Hiroshima Electric Company as a tram girl and they accepted me! Tomorrow is my first day of conductor training at the downtown School of Domestic Science for Girls."

Not knowing how her news would change things, his smile was tentative. "I thought only men were conductors?"

She dipped a curled big toe into the water. "I know. It's so exciting! With our boys going off to war, there are more opportunities for girls. I imagined I'd get stuck in some factory job."

"How are you going to get there every day? On your bike?"

"No, silly," she said, wetting her fingertips and flinging water on him. "I'll live in the dormitory. Isn't it great! Now we can both continue our education."

He had imagined today all wrong. She hadn't invited him here to kiss. She'd wanted to share her news in private. But he had to admit, this opportunity would create brighter prospects for her and he'd be a crummy friend if he let her see his disappointment. Not many girls got to pursue their education after sixth grade. Offering the most genuine smile he could muster, he stepped into the stream beside her. "Congratulations, Emi. I'm happy for you."

As if delivered by destiny, a dragonfly landed and hovered on her shoulder. The buzzing insect reminded him to accept the situation and be happy for her. "My father says dragonflies are messengers of illusion," he said. "They teach us about change and transformation. I believe the guy on your shoulder is a sign of good luck. You'll be a great conductor... and," he said, wetting his fingertips and returning the playful fling of water, "we'll see each other."

Her eyes met his. "Thanks. You know, you're so smart... and very cute." She lowered her head and crossed one foot over the other, as if to disrupt their connection. But without lifting her chin, she quickly peeked at him from under the flutter of her lashes.

In awkward silence, they looked at and away from each other and then pressed their foreheads together. Their noses met. He absorbed her jasmine fragrance. Her warmth. Her breath. All inviting a tingling warmth between his legs, thrilling his entire body. His heart beat faster. Surrounded by dragonflies moving like ballet dancers on gauzy wings, he kissed her, ever so gently.

• • •

The next day began a new trimester at Koji's school. First thing that morning, *Sensei* barked at the class, "Boys, all eyes up here."

Koji sat a little straighter.

"I have orders. The government has conscripted the entire class for duty under the Student Mobilization Program."

Koji swallowed the spuming stomach upset that roiled to his throat.

"Tomorrow," *Sensei* continued, "you will report to a factory at this address." He turned to the blackboard and wrote the address of a building in a commercial area along the Enko River. "You will make rifles for the Empire."

A sudden quiet descended over the classroom. Koji looked around at his classmates. Mouths had fallen open. One boy's face was in his hands, another wiped his watery eyes, and others hunched over. He slumped into his chair. The war had upended people's lives all across Japan, some for the better—like Emi—but most for the worse. He had become a magnet to his greatest fear. He would sacrifice his education for Japan. The loud voice in his head uttered his hatred for an Empire that would cheat him and forever alter his future.

• • •

The next morning, Koji arrived for work—three kilometers south of his house—a few minutes early, having heeded *Sensei*'s warning. "Do. Not. Be. Late!" *Sensei* would also work at the factory, but he would be the boss to some of his students. Heavy pants and a white undershirt replaced

Koji's smart-looking uniform and leather knapsack. He already longed for school, and his enthusiasm for the start of another day had morphed into resentment.

Dilapidated buildings edged the banks of the river and housed the rifle arsenal. A crude sheet-metal roof rested on the building's six-meter-high wooden walls. Grimy windows concealed the sweaty work of gun-making inside. A parade of trucks arrived at the loading dock. Disturbed by the frenzy of activity, resident rats dashed around and under stacked, rotting pallets. Lucky vermin. They, unlike the factory workers inside, possessed the raw, unencumbered capability to scurry where they pleased.

He dragged his feet to join his class and *Sensei*, and they entered the factory. The smell of cut wood melding with the tang of burnt metal and gunpowder permeated the air. War smelled foul. Within moments, his shirt stuck to his skin from the oppressive heat and humidity. Koji and his classmates received their employee numbers and work caps, then toured the plant to observe the complicated process of manufacturing bolt-action rifles. Fascinated, he paid close attention. These were extraordinary weapons, complete with flip-up sights and fifty-centimeter bayonets that locked into place at the tip of the rifle, extending the weapon's length to one and one-half meters. He supposed dying by a bullet was the preferred alternative to being impaled or sliced to death by the razor point of a bayonet.

He tried to imagine himself in one of many specialized jobs—machine operators, barrel makers, woodworkers, finishers, and inspectors. Assemblers kept feverish pace with parts whizzing by on a conveyor belt. One job was reserved for highly skilled and senior workers who would imprint, with flawless precision, the royal chrysanthemum on the rifle's receiver. Although Koji would be paid a living wage, with regular raises based on seniority, he didn't want to be there. He understood there would be no rewards without putting in a few years of drudgery, and so he would *gaman* and tough it out, as long as he got away from the factory long before he was eligible to stamp the seal.

He spent the early afternoon hours sweeping. The air was so thick with humidity, the damp dirt refused to lift and streaked the floor. Later, while disposing of trash and debris, he listened to conversation fragments. A woodworker told another about his nephew, shot down somewhere in the Pacific. Someone commented about how busy the farmers had been during August in the wheat fields and rice paddies. He stopped sweeping to pay attention to a conversation between two machine operators.

"I heard they manufactured cork stoppers for beer and *sake* bottles here before the war."

"*Hai*. But we can't get beer and *sake* anymore. Not since they took over with distributive control."

"*Sōdeska*," the man said, shaking his head. "*Sayonara, sake*. Make way for rifles!"

The other man snickered. "To kill Americans."

Koji emptied the bins and walked away.

At the end of the workday, with his mind full of rifle-making images and factory chatter, an irony gelled. He would be making rifles for Japanese soldiers to shoot the enemy. And *he* was the enemy.

TADAIMA

March 1944 – Jerome, AR

The steady drip of rain that had fallen throughout the day now poured in torrents. Finding the damp air much cooler than the 60-degree Fahrenheit reading on the school's thermometer, Ruby tightened the scarf at the neck of her raincoat and trudged home through the mud.

When she arrived in front of their barracks, she shook and closed her umbrella and removed her muddy shoes, giving them a quick bath in a puddle at the bottom of the steps before struggling against the damp to open the swollen door and place her shoes on the mat inside.

The potbelly stove offered warmth, and the smell of cinnamon wafted from a potpourri on the ledge of the stove. Her stepmother was at the table, surrounded by colored threads, working an embroidery project of botanicals and complaining about the miserable weather.

Ruby shut her ears to Taeko's complaints and wiped up the puddle she'd created when she removed her coat. As she was draping the rag over the stove, she heard a thin voice outside.

"*Tadaima!*" Her mind played tricks on her, and the rain distorted the male voice.

Who is home? It must have been the neighbor. But the measured cadence was all too familiar.

Could it be? She glanced at Taeko, who looked equally puzzled.

As if prompted by a conductor, they rushed to the door.

Like moments earlier, the door refused to open. Ruby pulled with all of her strength. Finally, the door surrendered and her eyes locked on the source of the unusual lightness in her body.

Father.

Drops of rain dribbled down his face, now lined and weary. He gripped boxes covered in soggy brown paper and strung with cord, splitting open at the corners.

"Ruby-*chan*."

Was he real? Where had he come from?

"May I come in, please?"

"Father!" she screamed, regaining her senses. "You... you're home!"

She moved out of her father's way so he could enter.

Taeko sagged against the wall and released an enormous sigh, like someone had squeezed her too tightly.

Ruby dove into her father's sopping wet coat and hugged his bony body with all she had to give, and held her breath against his travel-weary body odor.

She clung to him, not wanting to let go for fear he might disappear; that she might wake up from this dream. Having wished for this day for so long, she couldn't believe he had shown up with no notice.

"I can't believe it's you. Oh, Father!"

"Yes, it's me, Ruby-*chan*. I'm here."

She followed his gaze to Taeko, slumped to the floor with her head in her hands. Why did she have to be so melodramatic? Even Taeko wouldn't ruin this moment. Ruby released her father and offered her hand to Taeko, who accepted the gesture, wobbled to Father, and grabbed his hands. "*Okaerinasai*," she said, welcoming him home.

"Tea, I must make tea!" Taeko said, scurrying to the burner.

"*Arigatō gozaimasu*," Father said, as if thanking a stranger.

While Taeko set the teapot to boil, Ruby helped her father remove his soaked and rumpled coat, and she hung it by the stove to dry. He handed her his battered fedora. His hair had thinned and his ears somehow looked bigger, maybe because he had lost weight. He had shaved his once-stylish mustache straight at the vertical in the style of Adolf Hitler's. *Why would he do that? Weren't the Japanese hated enough?*

She removed his wet shoes and gathered his belongings left outside in the pelting rain. After cleaning the floor, she joined him and Taeko at the table.

"Father, how come you didn't send us a letter you were coming home? I would have met you and carried your things."

"There was no chance to write. I boarded a train with ten other prisoners the same day they paroled me from the Department of Justice prison, with little time to pack my few possessions."

"Was the trip okay?"

"Ah, long and uncomfortable, but I paid no attention to the discomforts. It thrilled me to leave Santa Fe and glide across the rails to you."

"What was it like there? You were sick. Are you feeling okay? Your letters were so short and blacked out in big chunks."

He looked down at his teacup. "All in good time, child. My detainment wasn't so bad and I feel better now. I enjoyed the company of about a thousand other Buddhist ministers and Japanese language teachers. From the fences, the beautiful Sangre de Cristo Mountains soared in the distance. The border patrols and their dogs kindled much bitterness within the fences, but seeing the mountains beyond the barbed wire calmed me and took my breath away."

As he spoke, Taeko's eyes softened.

Ruby poured him another cup of tea, hoping he would quickly regain his physical strength and trusting he would undo everything Taeko had done. He was here. He would allow them to stay in America. He would improve Taeko's mood. As her burdens melted away, she floated inside.

But then his tone changed.

"They stripped us of our freedom, money, and future. Within my forty square feet of barracks space, I lost all respect for the United States."

Ruby's ribs grew tight. She held her breath and closed her ears to what she dreaded was coming next.

"Looking at those mountains gave me peace to ruminate. My loyalties forged closer to Mount Fuji."

Her stomach churned. She thought she might get sick.

Father put his hand over Taeko's. "I know in my heart a more promising future awaits us in Japan. There, I will shed this shame of having been labeled a dangerous enemy alien. I'll regain my dignity. We will be happy there."

Taeko's triumphant smile spread across her face. Ruby felt herself go pale.

Father chattered with Taeko as they unpacked his boxes, containing his *butsudan*, *sumi-e* supplies, and his threadbare minister's robe. He said something about having been assigned a job as a hospital orderly. Something about starting tomorrow. Cleaning patient rooms, something about sheets and patient meals. Something about making sixteen dollars per month... shameful... a man with his education and stature.

She wanted to escape and find Mari, but Father was hungry and insisted they eat supper together. They put on their coats and walked to the mess hall in the driving rain.

She had no appetite and was pushing her mushy brussels sprouts around on her plate when Mari came through the kitchen door with a tray of Jell-O squares. Delighted to see Mari was working, Ruby waved her over and watched her sister do a double take, drop the tray on the nearest table, and run to where they were sitting.

"Father!" she said, standing before him with an ear-to-ear smile. She lowered herself to hug him, but his body was stone.

He remained seated at a cold distance and faced her. "Hello, daughter," he said, his manner accentuating a sense of formality bordering on aloof, like a cat expecting fish and turning its whiskers from unpleasant orange peels.

The color drained from Mari's face and the sisters met each other's pained and knowing eyes. Father was silently chastising Mari for having married an American soldier. He had told Mari in one of his letters that he disapproved of her marriage to Warren, but she hoped he would come around in time. As if knowing this day was too soon, Mari dropped her head, stumbled backward, and returned to the abandoned tray of Jell-O.

TULE LAKE

May 1944 – Jerome, AR

Ruby might have felt the tremor from the approaching train had she not closed herself off from its foreshock like a turtle retreating into the hardness and safety of its shell. Although Jerome was closing for reasons unknown to its inhabitants, what she and about one-fourth of the camp's population understood was they would soon be on their way to the maximum-security Tule Lake Segregation Center in Northern California. The remaining Jerome prisoners would move to the nearby Rohwer camp or resettle in states far away from their West Coast homes and communities.

Once onboard and seated, Ruby's feet absorbed the vibration of the cars hooking to the locomotive. The sensation quivered up her calves and froze at her knees, as her body rejected this next leg of her family's journey. With a sudden jolt, the train began its slow roll west toward the second incarceration detour of her early teenage years, with fewer miles between her and Japan.

A trace of body odor invaded her space, but she didn't bother to look at who sat stinking beside her. Looking out the window, her burning eyes scanned the fence line until she found Mari on the other side, waving goodbye. She strained her neck, watching until her sister's faint image appeared to move backward, until she had become a mere speck disappearing in the humid haze.

Far from the swampy landscape, bitter fighting raged in Europe, and Warren's unit had left in April bound for Italy to join the Allied forces. Ruby neither understood Italy's capricious change in allegiance nor bothered using her energy to comprehend the treachery, Fascism, and number of the dead in Europe. Because of Mari's answers to the loyalty questionnaire, she had avoided the forced move to Tule Lake with the *disloyals*, choosing to join Warren's family in Rohwer. Ruby caught sight of her reflection in the window, but missed Mari's warmth and reflection beside her, like when they had traveled to Jerome.

Ruby had no way of knowing when she might see Mari again, and she struggled to imagine life without her and who would take her side. Sensing the familiar quiver of grief, she picked at her fingers and denied her tears.

Seated behind her parents, she eyed Taeko's high bun, twisted and held in place by a rosewood hair stick, echoing the shape of a wishbone with a sharp pointy end capable of poking out someone's eye. The tight bun accentuated her bony profile and compulsive nodding. Ruby had little doubt that Taeko breathed sighs of relief through her pursed lips, having left one of her stepdaughters behind. Beside Taeko, Father's slouched shoulders supported his balding head. He, too, had faced the window so he must have seen Mari's frantic waves of goodbye, yet he seemed to ignore her. Her marriage to an American soldier without his permission and decision to remain behind angered and disappointed him.

In the two months they had together in Jerome, Father did little to compensate for their time apart or to make life easier for Ruby. She dreaded the idea of looking at the back of her father's head for however many days they'd travel. *You don't care about me. It's all your wife's fault we're going to the lake and now it's YOURS too!*

Beyond the boundaries of camp, they whizzed past farms and lonesome scrub flatlands. No fences. No guards. She relaxed into her seat and savored every changing frame. A lovely package wrapped in traditional kimono style rested on her lap, but she would wait until they lowered the shades to open it.

Careful not to tear the paper and savoring the undoing of its perfect folds, she opened Velvet's gift an hour later.

Inside was a letter and a diary, its covers constructed of black walnut.

May 8, 1944

Dear Ruby,

This dump is about to close, and I imagine tomorrow we'll have sundered apart, east and west. I hope you enjoy this diary. I made it for you with my Dad's help. He sawed scrap lumber and drilled the holes in the wood shop, and I bound it together with his old rawhide shoelaces. Ruby, I'll say this—it's strange to me you never shed tears, since I'm such a crybaby. But you are hurting, and I hope releasing your private thoughts on these pages softens some of your pain. Remember, the past is about things we can't change, so once you write it down, try to leave it behind.

Gosh, there's nothing much a gal might say to a close pal because all she feels never quite comes out, but I'll try. Think back to the best friend who used to share her fun with you. Don't forget jitterbugging in the laundry room and squeezing your feet into my too-small loafers, determined to stretch the leather, only to get blisters. I loved our times arm in arm, singing and laughing about who knows what. Something always tickled us despite being locked up, like the screwball comedy movie we saw together, His Girl Friday. Maybe we'll have Rosalind Russell's sophisticated clothes and job someday. How about when we painted the corners of your eyeglasses with red nail polish? A girl named Ruby should always wear some red!

I guess Sara-Beth is on her own now and will need to get along without us pushing sausages through the fence. But she's not really alone, seeing how she's getting fat with a baby in her tummy. Do you believe that? Jeez, fifteen and pregnant. That will never happen to you and me. We won't let it, right? Instead, we'll honor the code and save ourselves for marriage to a dreamboat like Cary Grant. Well, maybe you will.

We talked about many things that scare me, but are you afraid of anything? If you are, I don't see it. I think you're brave, and I'm grateful they didn't exchange you on that last ship to Japan. My mom says your stepmother is damaged goods to behave as she does. In a few short years, you'll get away from her. Until then, I hope your life improves with your father around. Anyway, you're big enough to fight back, and no matter what, look for the humor. I'll always remember the night I stayed over with you and her shock at seeing me wear my Dad's old PJs and the way I tied curling rags in my hair. She looked at me like I was from outer space. I nearly peed in my PJs saying out loud what an ugly cow she is, knowing she chose not to understand a lick of English.

The future seems dark and in such a muddle and we are clueless what to do or think. Let's do our best as we split across the country, perhaps never to see each other again. I will forever envy your boundless energy and ready wit, backed by real brains. Those brains will take you somewhere one day. When you reflect on our Jerome days, remember the pleasant ones with your Pepsodent smile and try to forget the others and keep the faith. You get what I mean, huh?

Here's wishing you the best of everything. My Dad is relieved to be released and eager to work at Seabrook Farms in New Jersey. Once we settle-in I'll write to you c/o Tule Lake and trust the letter reaches you. Please write back to me and let's grow our friendship even stronger in the years to come.

So long until we meet again, dear friend. Someday. Somewhere in a land of sunshine. Like the line in For Whom the Bell Tolls, there's no goodbye, Ruby, because we're never really apart.

With love to a swell girl and always your friend, Velvet

•••

Sunlight streamed into the car, crystalizing an Iwikuamo'o streak of dust particles mingled with cigarette smoke floating in the air. Ruby's hand found her chest. The warmth of her hand softened the pang of nostalgia thinking about the North-South star line resembling a bone back-lizard, as Iwikuamo'o was known to the Hawaiians. As the early navigators who searched for the promise of direction in rising stars, she hoped the train's northwest journey would end in something—anything—good.

Beyond the window, the rugged flat and treeless terrain bored Ruby. Sparse blooms of grasses and sagebrush appeared beaten in the aftermath of a windstorm that had gusted in rage, with nothing to blow but dust. Drowsiness trumped her boredom, and she fell asleep against the dirty window, wondering why sitting was so exhausting. She concluded that thinking sapped her energy.

The Central Pacific Railroad cars traversed Oklahoma's vast wheat fields, Texas's cattle ranges, New Mexico and Arizona's rose-colored deserts, and California's fertile valleys and mountain ranges. Days later, the train slowed and ground to a stop at Tule Lake, built on barren lava fields thirty-five miles southeast of Klamath Falls, Oregon. Ruby shifted in her seat, eager to leave the train and its smells behind—the constant whiff of grease, the distinct odor of the elderly, the stink of feet, halitosis, and the reek of cigarette smoke permeating everything.

The tang of shame—of being labeled *disloyal*—this she still carried.

Outside, soldiers shouted directions and herded them into empty Army trucks parked in rows at the end of the railroad spur. Her family and the other passengers boarded the trucks and were driven to the Administration building, where they waited in line—as before at Jerome—but this time her father completed the forms.

Ruby stuck out and retracted her tongue just before they photographed her, disheveled and unclean from the journey. As she stood in front of a screen with measurement graduations marking her four-foot-eleven-inch height, she cursed the American government in her head. A man with bulging eyes and yellow teeth tucked her mugshot within a badge labeled TULE

Lake Center Identification that included her name and H-150 family number. They were assigned to Ward 6, Block 54 in the maze of barracks at the far northeast side of the camp.

5402-A was now home.

Earthen particles from the windstorm accompanied them to a one-room unit where footprints marked the dirt that would be a chronic and unwelcome roommate. The barracks were constructed in the same tar paper, privacy-lacking configuration as Jerome, with open spaces above thin unit partitions. Except for a hulking four-legged potbelly stove, three cots, and a thick layer of dust, the room was empty. In the neighboring lavatory, Ruby was relieved to find partitions dividing the toilets. At long last, she would throw away her paper bag of shame.

Tule Lake had held the Japanese for over two years, and the incarcerees had done their best to beautify the camp. It was at least twice the size of Jerome and had co-op stores, barber shops, beauty salons, shoe repair and other convenience stores, warehouses, bakeries, a tofu factory, churches, temples, and funeral parlors scattered throughout—all staffed by the incarcerees. Shallow irrigation trenches wove through the camp like veins from a central spigot to the barracks, providing nourishment for flower and vegetable gardens. The Ishimarus settled in to live under indefinite guard and began creating a home.

The next day, while her stepmother sewed curtains at the communal center, Ruby and her father headed out to buy paint and scavenge for scrap wood to build furniture.

Father stopped to greet the neighbor who had loaned him a wagon. The neighbor was hoeing a small garden in front of his unit. "*Ohayō goziamasu,*" Father said, tipping his hat with a pleasant good morning.

"Good morning, *Sensei!*"

"What are you planting?"

"Tomatoes, lettuce, and beans," the man said, wiping sweat from his brow. "Maybe some marigolds and petunias too."

A smile crossed Ruby's face having learned playful flowers would soon adorn their barracks. They passed others preparing their gardens for the growing season, sweeping their steps, and making an already tidy area tidier—everyone doing his or her part to persevere in the slight space over which they had some control in the universe.

Having purchased the paint at the co-op, they continued to a new fire station where construction workers had thrown scrap lumber into a pile. Living in a wood-frame tinder box heated by fire-burning stoves, Ruby took comfort in knowing the fire station was nearby.

She walked to the fence next to the pile and pointed to a huge pock-marked and crumbing rock monopolizing the horizon among enormous white stratus clouds. A massive cross stood at its peak.

"Look!" she said to her father.

His gaze followed where her finger pointed about a mile into the distance.

"They call it Castle Rock," he said. "It's a peninsula that once rose from Tule Lake, when there was a lake. Seems the government drained the lake in a reclamation project, leaving behind this dry lake bed."

She had wondered where the lake was. Darn—no swimming.

He continued. "They say the cross is made from railroad ties. It inspires and gives hope to the Christians in camp."

Ruby didn't believe Jesus Christ was God's son, but what did she know? She turned her back to the cross and they filled the wagon with the best pieces of wood. Ruby pulled the wagon back home, while her father carried an armload of longer boards.

Even in their meager surroundings, artistic details mattered to Father. He allowed her to roll the white paint—the one color available at the co-op—over the blank surfaces while he brushed the paint with razor precision along the edges of the windows and floors. After the paint dried, Father drew and painted the family *kamon* in the center of the largest wall with white paint tinted to a rainbow of colors using pigments he'd brought from Santa Fe. The crest depicted a caterpillar's metamorphosis. The caterpillar kept its legs while delicate purple wings emerged, dancing and smiling.

When finished, he used his smallest paintbrush and replicated the design on the top of Ruby's left hand. He touched the tip of her nose with a tiny dot of paint and lovingly pinched her cheek. His gesture was a smidgen of times past. Her heart fluttered.

There's the old Father. I hope his butterfly never washes off.

He joined her on the floor and met her eyes with a softness she thought she might never see again. "Ruby, our *kamon* symbolizes hope within the borders of our new home." She listened with earnest attention. "The caterpillar's transformation to butterfly teaches us much about change. Losing the protective casings of the life we once knew gives us the opportunity to experience change and strengthen our resilience. I don't know what the future holds, but I believe we must *gaman* and endure these troublesome times with patience and dignity."

She sighed. "But what will become of us?"

"I wish I knew, Ruby-*chan*. They will probably deport us on a prisoner exchange or when the war ends. For now, we live in uncertainty. And dust!" He chuckled. "All we can do is focus on what's within our control. For you, that's your education. I met the *sensei* of the Japanese school yesterday. You will attend his classes in the early mornings before school to prepare for when we move to Japan. I insist you not be an outcast, so you must learn to respect the culture and norms and to be a dutiful granddaughter to your *sofubo* in Hiroshima. As a girl you already have a strike against you. Now, you have two schools to attend and double the work, so you must work very hard to keep up with the students in your regular school. But I have confidence in you and believe you will excel in your high school academics and Japanese school studies. *Shikata ga nai*, Ruby-*chan*."

She wanted more than anything to argue against going to Japan, but knew her father would admonish her for being disrespectful. Instead, she argued with him in her head for the rest of the afternoon. In the argument raging in her mind, she told him to go to Japan if he wanted. Take Taeko with him. Just leave her here.

Later, in the quiet and eerie dark of night, Ruby convinced herself that her father, deep down, wanted to stay in America, despite saying he would return to Japan. He wanted her prepared for success no matter where they lived.

•••

The next morning, while Taeko was laundering, Ruby helped her father make bunk bed frames with the longer scavenged boards and tools he had borrowed from the wood-working shop. She marveled at his meticulous craftsmanship—his careful measurements, confident and straight saw cuts, and expertise with a hammer. She would sleep in the smaller bunk above her parents where the light, odors, and noise crept in from the neighboring units.

Satisfied with their work, her father sat on the bottom bunk. "Ruby-*chan*, come sit next to me." She sat beside him, and he placed a small padlock in her hands. "This is for your footlocker. I understand *Okāsan* can be difficult and it hasn't been easy for you. Girls your age should have some privacy and a place to safeguard their personal possessions." He smiled with gentleness and affection. "Here," he said, while fastening a delicate chain around her neck, "Wear the key. Now let's build a small shelf on the wall at the foot of your bunk to hold your footlocker before *Okāsan* returns and starts asking a bunch of questions I don't want to answer."

She lifted her chin to meet his eyes. "Thank you, Father."

Alone that afternoon, Ruby repacked the contents of her footlocker, taking a long moment to look at the photograph of her as a baby with her mother. She tucked Father's butterfly *sumi-e* and cherished photographs inside of the footlocker lining and organized her seashells from Waimea. In the privacy of her new upper bunk, she felt like a Hawaiian honeycreeper perched in the forest.

She hugged Penny, laid her head on the pillow, and drifted into sleep. Her dream took her back to the swing under the monkeypod tree. "Higher, Mama, higher!"

But the swing slowed to a stop. She turned around and Mama wasn't there. No one was there. A brilliant butterfly landed on the knuckle of her index finger. Its coral wings fluttered. It spoke in Mama's voice. *Put your feet on the ground, Ruby-chan. Mother nature will protect you.*

Her eyes opened to Penny's green eyes. Ruby recalled a fuzzy dream. Something about flying... and a pretty butterfly.

She balled her hands and rubbed sleep from her eyes.

"Now that I have a place to keep my diary private, I can write in it," she whispered into her doll's ear. She smiled, opened the cover, and penned her personal information in perfect cursive on the first page.

Diary of Ruby Ishimaru
Tule Lake Segregation Center
California–1944

PRIVATE!

• • •

May 9, 1944

Dear Diary,

I will try to do what Velvet suggested and write every day. Castle Rock inspired me to write this haiku.

Castle Rock's bleakness,
Diamond Head's lush silhouette,
So close, yet so far.

• • •

May 10, 1944

Dear Diary,

We've been here a week now and I tell you Tule is more of a prison than Jerome. The military flaunts its might from sixteen towers surrounding the perimeter guarding TWO fences. Each fence circles the entire camp completely, as if one isn't enough. Fence One warns you're too close to Fence Two. And Fence Two is higher and about two hundred feet beyond Fence One. But get this—tanks line up between them. Real honest to goodness tanks with machine guns! Father told me not to get too close to the fence because the soldiers wouldn't give much thought before gunning us down. He's probably exaggerating, but I'll take his word for it. For sure, I won't push food through the fence around here. Not for anyone! Oh, and he also said there are over 18,000 people in here, about half the population of Kauai! I live in a big city now, but with no tall buildings, or fancy restaurants, or ladies and gentlemen dressed in finery doing interesting work.

Tule is a lot like Jerome in other ways. Our barracks have zero insulation and zero privacy. The hospital has the same towering smokestack releasing sooty coal exhaust into the sky. Mess halls are the same, just bigger, with polished linoleum floors instead of crude wood planks. The climate is different too. Jerome was either damp-bitter cold or sultry. Here, it's dry and neither hot nor cold, and I heard it's that way all summer, but to look out for biting cold in the winter. Where Jerome's nature was low and swampy, Tule is lifeless and sandy.

Beautiful mountains frame the sky in the distance. Mount Shasta is an active volcano, about 50 miles away, and it soars over 14,000 feet! Lifting my eyes to the top of its silvery snow-covered peak at sunset strengthens my determination to stand my ground. I'm preparing for deportation, but I WON'T go. I haven't figured out how I'll pull that off, but I will. I know it.

There's another mountain looming to the east, beyond the wind-swept, patchy fields. They call it Abalone Mountain for its giant abalone shape, but the treeless mountain's actual name is Horse Mountain. I wonder who the horse is. R.I.

• • •

May 14, 1944

Dear Diary,

Today is Mother's Day so most kids ate lunch with their mothers in the mess hall, which people decorated with flowers and pink crepe paper streamers. Father asked me to make a card for Okāsan. I did, but it's not my best effort. It's impossible to believe five years have passed since Mama died. I miss her so much my stomach hurts, like she died yesterday. Sometimes, I swear I hear her talking to me. Maybe it's not really her, just my imagination conjuring up words she might say. Oh, I don't know. It feels real when it happens.

I start Japanese school tomorrow with calisthenics and worship to the rising sun at dawn, so I have to go to bed early tonight. If they sort out my schedule, I'll start high school on Tuesday! R.I.

• • •

May 15, 1944

Dear Diary,

On my way to morning calisthenics today, I passed hundreds of scary-looking men who wore headbands with the Rising Sun emblem, face the sun, and pledge their devotion to Japan. These hachimaki-wearing fanatics made me shudder. I shook it off and warmed up fast because Sensei made us run around the camp shouting wasshoi-wasshoi to keep our attention and rhythm. He said the exercise builds our stamina and supports good health. It was pure torture! I huffed and puffed behind the others and ended up with my head between my knees with a stitch in my side. I then had to race back to shower, change clothes, and eat breakfast—all before Japanese school started at 8:00!

My first classes at Tri-State High are tomorrow! The building is brand-new and not like the rickety school barracks in Jerome. But the dumb Japanese school is in a tar papered barracks with scrap wood tables and hard, uncomfortable benches. We began the morning by reciting the Kyōiku ni Kansuru Chokugo—Japan's rigid principles of education and the virtues of loyalty to Japan, the Emperor, and our elders and ancestors.

Sensei is mean! The boy next to me slouched during math and Sensei thwacked the table with a meter stick. He scared me so badly I jumped. And he teaches in Japanese! I hope I keep up and earn decent grades. It will be hard, but I'll try if only to make Father proud. History commemorates the gods and goddesses who created Japan. WASTE. OF. TIME! R.I.

• • •

May 27, 1944

Dear Diary,

Sorry I missed so many days. It's hard keeping up. Japanese school is mighty dull, but high school's swell. I don't stick out as the new kid because too many disloyals to count moved here too.

Boy, is this place cliquey! The majorettes are the prettiest and most popular girls. I already hate a few of them in their red and white uniforms, shaking their breasts and pompoms at a school spirt rally I passed by this afternoon. After cheering, "Aquila pride! Aquila pride! Our school's the best, let's shout our pride," a girl turned to me. "Don't just stand there, shout your pride!"

Honestly! Doesn't she know some kids are too busy for silly things like pep rallies?

Father keeps asking if I've made any friends yet, but I have no friends here. What's the point in friendship when I can't tend it? And why does he care since he's planning to drag me to Japan? Plus, how would I ever find another friend as unique and fun as Velvet? Missing her festers like a mean sore before the skin grows back. So, I'll be friendly with everyone and friends with no one. Some girls think I'm quiet. Shy. The reality is I don't care about them or their tittle-tattle.

School is hard and they teach math differently from Jerome. But I'll catch up and do okay. I need to get straight A's to get to college. Father says a solid education is important. I'm glad they have year-round school here too. I like most of my teachers. Some say our incarceration never should have happened and tell us to always stand against injustice. But my PE teacher is this short-haired attack dog who makes me feel less than human. PE is bad enough without being called a filthy stinking Jap! I hate her. R.I.

• • •

May 30, 1944

Dear Diary,

They closed school this afternoon to remember and honor the service personnel who died while serving in the armed forces. Beyond the gates, I imagine families are enjoying fried chicken and potato salad picnics, attending parades, and visiting gravesites of loved ones. But in here, we are one day closer to resuming the lives we took for granted. Hopefully, anyway. We're totally out of touch with the outside world. How do people adapt to the daily routines of being stuck inside these fences? It's weird, but some do. I won't. NOT. EVER. Time and space have changed and yet many of the kids in my high school act as though everything's okay. I guess they've accepted being locked up, and it doesn't bother them. NINCOMPOOPS!

But frustration grows outside of school. They assigned additional troops here, and soldiers are everywhere—inside and outside of the fences. The real thugs with loyalty to Japan have become violent and beat up and harass those loyal to America. I see bloodied men lying in the dirt or making their way home beaten and battered after being terrorized. I hope Father stays out of it all. I think he will. He's busy with his art and poetry and sermon writing. I don't get why he's writing sermons he might never deliver again.

One thing I know for sure, I won't get used to being stuck in this dark chapter. I AM AN AMERICAN, and THEY stole my freedom from me. We're not in here for our own protection! We're in here because our leaders got entangled in hysteria and trampled on our civil liberties! To hell with complacency! I want OUT! R.I.

GO FOR BROKE

September 1944 – Tule Lake, CA

The petite elderly woman in front of Ruby in the post office line mocked her friend at the counter. "Lucky, lucky... a fat package from Sears. You must be rich!" Ogling the package, she persisted. "What's inside?"

The friend, also an old lady, shuffled to the exit and snickered, "Wouldn't you like to know, Mrs. Busybody! *Sayonara!*"

Ruby giggled to herself. *The woman is an old busybody!* The line slowed to an irksome crawl. She had waited in the queue several times a week, crammed between strangers, hoping for a post from her sister or Velvet. She played games in her head to speed the wait by guessing how many men and women customers stood behind her in line and then testing her answer counting in sing-song Japanese—*ichi, ni, san, shi, go.* Then she hypothesized what someone's mail might say or the contents of packages.

"Next!" the clerk said.

She approached the counter. "Hi. Any mail for Ishimaru, 5402-A?"

The clerk, a man with slicked-back hair and slumped shoulders, offered a weak smile and disappeared behind the partition. Strange. Tule Lake's post station was Newell, CA and not Tule Lake. But why and why not? There was no lake at Tule Lake either. The man returned and handed her a single envelope postmarked from Rohwer and addressed to Father in Mari's handwriting.

She ran all the way home. Her father was sitting on the steps of their barracks reading the latest edition of the *Tulean Dispatch,* the camp newspaper covering routine news and feature stories. She smirked at the irony of an independent paper being published within a prison camp.

"Father! Mari wrote!"

Her father glanced up from the headlines—PARIS LIBERATED. NAZIS FLEEING FOR RHINELAND. As the war ravaged, his face was often behind the folds of the newspaper. Some things never changed. It had been three months since the Allies smashed the Nazi wall on the shores of Normandy and stormed into France. In the Pacific, they completed their capture of the Mariana Islands. The victories suggested the U.S. Navy was closing in on Japan.

Bouncing on her tiptoes, her impatience got the best of her. "Open it!"

"Okay, Ruby-*chan*. Sit down and we'll see why your sister is writing to me."

She joined him on the step.

He rolled up his sleeves and opened the envelope.

To Ruby, Mari's address was pure gold, and she was grateful Father was careful not to rip the return address.

He unfolded the letter and began to read silently. It seemed his lips hadn't caught up with his eyes as he lowered his forehead into the palm of his hand.

"What is it? Is she okay?"

"Mari's fine," he said, in a controlled voice. "Here, you can read it."

He handed her the letter.

1 September 1944

Dear Father,

As the days become shorter, your daughter's heart is breaking. On 22 July I received a telegram from the office of The Secretary of War expressing deep regret. Warren died in Italy.

Ruby gasped.

A letter followed from Warren's commanding officer in August. He wrote:

Dear Mrs. Okada:

By this date I am confident you have been officially notified by the War Department that your husband, Private First-Class Warren Okada, was killed in action while serving with the 2nd Battalion of the 442nd Regimental Combat Team, U.S. Army, in Italy on 10 July.

It distresses me to write to his widow, still held in a relocation center, while Warren fought, bled, and died for his country. The 442nd's motto is Go for Broke! Indeed, Warren gave his all and served with great distinction. He was given a full military funeral and was laid to rest by his comrades in the Sicily-Rome American Cemetery.

Please accept my sincerest condolences. You should be proud to be the wife of a fine soldier who gave his life to a grateful nation.

Sincerely yours,
Colonel Daniel F. Anderson
Commander

Father, Warren's parents are crushed. His mother hasn't stopped crying. How does one recover from the loss of a child? How were you able to move on when Mama and our baby sister died?

Warren volunteered and spilled his blood to prove his loyalty to the country that continues to incarcerate his family. The courier delivered the telegram and commander's letter to our barracks where an American service flag fluttered proudly outside the door. Inside of this fog, I feel profound sorrow and loneliness knowing my marriage is over before it really got started. I understand you didn't approve of our marrying, but please respect how much I loved Warren and, to the extent you are able, show empathy for your oldest daughter.

Please tell Ruby I'm sorry for not writing sooner and her sister loves her.

Love, Mari

Ruby leaned into her father, and he put his protective arm around her shoulders for the first time since Mama died.

Determined not to cry, she swallowed the familiar surge of sorrow in her throat.

DIVINE WIND

November 1944 – Hiroshima, Japan

To Koji, survival was the fulcrum underpinning the seesaw between those for and against the war. He watched patriotism gain momentum, as people united behind the country's militaristic goals and their Emperor—the heart of Japan. They pressured thousands of young men to volunteer as *kamikaze* pilots in a desperate tactic to break American morale. The pilots trained as suicide bombers in special attack units deployed to plummet into and destroy American warships. As human bombs with purity of commitment, they resolved to make the ultimate sacrifice for their country, their lives in the Emperor's name. Like shattering the most glorious of jewels, *gyokusai* was the most honorable and gallant of deaths. But Koji couldn't imagine staring into the deck of an aircraft carrier as the weapon he flew exploded into flames. The idea of it haunted him.

Despite widespread loyalty to the Emperor, Koji could feel the brew of feverish dissent sparked by extraordinary sacrifice, food shortages, and poor working conditions. He heard rumors about extremists who plotted to assassinate government and military leaders, risking arrest and death. He watched the calculated resistance of the average Japanese, intent on breaking the rules. Some of his mother's friends defied the government and shopped the black markets for scarce tea and *shōyu*. In the privacy of his neighboring backyards, boys continued using American baseball terminology—strike, hit, ball, run—expunged by the government. Their parents listened to jazz music with the volume turned low, to avoid being caught by local officials snooping around on periodic inspections—or worse, by neighbors who snitched to Community Council officials. The intense self-policing structure seemed to work too well, as no one wanted to bring shame on their family.

Frequent sabotage occurred at the factory. Observant, Koji possessed a keen awareness of intentional go-slow ploys, when workers slowed their line to reduce production. Absence disrupted operations and, some days, workers failed to complete a single rifle. If caught, the accused suffered severe consequences. Bosses thrashed and demoted men for laziness or insolence. They scolded, smacked, and beat student workers. A boy, exhausted from long hours of work, had fallen asleep behind some boxes last week. *Sensei* discovered the boy and kicked him awake with the toe of his heavy boot. He scolded the student and told him to go home and fetch his mother to apologize. Koji's careful behavior helped him maintain his family's strong reputation and avoid the whack of the wood stick, bamboo cane, or the dreaded *shinai*.

Japan had believed a victorious knockout punch would be delivered to the Americans at Pearl Harbor. Instead, the Americans had proven a formidable force. Koji learned early to keep his opinions to himself. Authorities had arrested the father of his co-worker and questioned the man for twelve hours, after learning the man had repeated a rumor that Guam had fallen to U.S. forces. The smallest defeatist talk against the Emperor or Japan's magnificent imperial forces risked punishment and imprisonment.

At fifteen, Koji had become clearheaded and shrewd. He thought before speaking and inspired trust and confidence among the other employees by his words and actions. Constructive manipulation became his unique, teenage version of psychological warfare—choosing his battles with care and focusing on acts within his control and of greatest importance to him. He made friends with ease and worked, often behind the scenes, to garner support and help others look good. Since food was scarce and people were starving, he brought vegetables from the farm to his friends in need when there was extra. One earned loyalty with a potato now and then.

Fairness. Justice. They mattered to Koji. For over a year, he kept his head down and his mouth shut. He worked hard to exceed expectations at the most difficult and mundane factory tasks. When assigned to the assembly line, he competed against his own output from the prior day. In the wood-working shop, he put his full strength into sanding and prided himself on having the smoothest finishes. Days went faster when he engaged his mind and body. His bosses rewarded his conscientiousness and perfect atten-dance with skimpy pay raises and promotions. Now, as courier and direct report to the factory manager, he delivered and retrieved packages and doc-uments around the city. When there was no courier duty, he substituted on the shop floor for absent employees who despised mandatory labor and often faked illness.

At the sound of the factory's midday whistle, they stopped work to eat with dirty hands. Taking time to wash wasted a third of their meager fif-teen-minute break, which workers received three times a day during long work days that stretched into darkness. Most boys ate together, if only to compare and trade *bentō* boxes. Lunches of red plum and hefty servings of white rice were a distant, mouth-watering memory because of the worsen-ing food shortage. Each adult was expected to survive on bean curd, limp vegetables, and a dwindling allotment of hulled rice. The government had replaced fresh fish rations with dried anchovies and fish preserves. But some people continued to fish the Hiroshima rivers, where the fish swam among industrial waste.

It was a warm late fall day, so most everyone was enjoying lunch outside. Sprawled along the riverbank with other students, Koji traded his pumpkin for some of his co-worker's rice. Toma always had more rice than the other boys. The kid's family was *Yakuza*—Japanese mafia—and controlled the black market. Although having more than others was like being a nail that stuck out, Toma never got hammered down. People left him alone. No one wanted trouble with Toma or his family.

A fist fight flared up between two older boys—Hinata and someone Koji didn't recognize. Hinata held a reputation for outspokenness and intimidation. Often absent, he worked on the line installing rifle safety knobs. Another student on the line said something under his breath, and Hinata flew into a rage and slammed the student to the ground, pinning him down by digging his knees into the boy's biceps. He threw punches to the boy's head as the fellow tried in desperation to get away, thrashing his feet and legs.

Hinata screamed, "We hear about victory after victory, but the radio lies. We aren't punishing our enemies. They aren't afraid of us!" He paused his punches long enough to glare at his adversary. "The Americans whipped us in Midway and Saipan. With Guam fallen, nothing stands between them and us!"

The boy spat in Hinata's face. "So that makes it all right for you to install inferior safety knobs in our rifles? You maim and kill our soldiers... you traitor! You have no honor!"

Hinata's fury of punches continued. "Shut up! I'll kill you!"

Sensei rushed to break up the fight, delivering a crushing blow to Hinata's left temple from the center of his four-foot *shinai*. The bamboo sword struck with such force, blood gushed from Hinata's eye socket, his piercing cry of pain echoing across the river. His victim wriggled from under his grasp and escaped. Another supervisor arrived and helped *Sensei* pull Hinata to his feet.

Feelings of admiration for Hinata's passion bubbled up in Koji. Even the crippling blow of the *shinai* hadn't conquered the bully. Hinata may have lost sight in that eye, but Koji recognized something as they dragged him away—Hinata's crazed look of invincibility and determination.

Koji's heartbeat raced. His last swallow of rice stuck in his throat, obstructed by shame, regret, and fear. He agreed with Hinata. The U.S. would win this war, but he didn't dare voice that belief. Rumors circulated that the Americans liberated major Italian cities and Paris and were pummeling the Germans. No one believed The Land of the Rising Sun could be destroyed from the air, and the country would never surrender imperial rule. Japan was a stubborn and dangerous spirit. Surrender was not in its vocabulary. Would the United States invade Japan and engage in savage hand-to-hand combat with tens of millions of patriots willing to die in defense of their homeland? Unthinkable. Trapped in limbo, Koji's future faded.

Work resumed and returned to normal after the fight, but an eerie tension followed the fast-spreading news of Hinata's beating. Koji was glad when his manager dispatched him to the Office of Army Logistics at Hiroshima Castle to deliver an envelope of requisitions for additional materials. He didn't notice the envelope flap was unsealed.

Off on his five-kilometer walk to the castle, he was preoccupied by the possibility of seeing Emi along the way. He had only seen her a few times since her training began, and he craved the tiniest glimpse of her beautiful face. When he last saw Emi, she had looked adorable in her new uniform—a crisp, white blouse under a jacket with an oval name badge on the breast pocket, matching skirt, white headband embroidered with the Hiroshima Electric Railway Company's logo, and proud arm band, inscribed with STUDENTS SERVING THE NATION. Still training as a Hiroden Girl, she worked the port route, transporting soldiers to and from Hiroden and Ujina. Taught to despise the enemy, she and the other girls began the morning singing "Toward Victory." Driving the tram had terrified her at first and she had blushed, telling him how she needed one hand free to steady her shaking thighs. Now, she loved her job.

Along the way, Koji passed several work gangs—kids his age and younger—conscripted by the military to tear down wooden houses. The long and straight firebreaks would protect the city from burning during the much-expected air strikes. After partial dismantling of a house, they attached heavy ropes to the tops of the walls. Teams of five or six kids per rope played tug of war with the facade, pulling in unison, until the wall lost and collapsed. Other kids broke down the wreckage into smaller pieces and threw the wood into piles for burning.

Koji searched the cabs of trams for one Emi might be driving. Over a dozen had passed with no sign of her. With each step toward the castle, among the wreckage and fires, he thought of Hinata and gained confidence to step up and do something, anything to make a difference in this blasted war. If America invaded, he—like everyone around him—would meet with certain death. What would he do? Wave his U.S. birth certificate and pronounce, *I'm one of you?* Ha! American soldiers would laugh in his Japanese face and shoot him between the eyes. Japan had provoked and suffered war for as long as he could remember. Enough was enough. He wanted Japan to surrender, no matter the consequences. And he hungered to experience America.

Turning a corner, he glanced at sparking electric wires dancing above a tram. Once again, the driver wasn't Emi. He picked up his pace. Resolve had come to him in a blinding flash. He saw his internal battle clearly, much like the blue water at Miyajima where he had seen all the way to the bottom. His mind drifted to those delightful and carefree days, wading into the calm, glassy water with Naoki, searching for shells and other treasures washed in with the tide on the sandy floor. Together, they had splashed and played, swimming to where the bottom gave way to the deeper and more mysterious dark water. By the time he crossed the street and stepped onto the next block, Koji knew he would do his part and plunge into the depths of his sphere of influence and take a stand. He needed to figure out how.

Ahead, a gang of kids were halfway through tearing down an entire block of houses. How did people abandon the safety of home, and where did they go? Perhaps they fled to the country? The light winds from the morning gained strength and carried smoke in his direction. Suddenly, his eyes burned and it was hard for him to see as he dodged debris strewn everywhere.

Another tram screeched on the rails. He raced in the tram's direction, stumbled on a wood beam jutting from the ground, and fell. Hard. His palms flew out in front, and only luck saved him from the rusty nail sticking out of the board beneath him. Another centimeter and the nail would have punctured his eye. Feeling weak, he rested and tried to shake off the shock of his fall, only to realize he had dropped the envelope. Pages had spilled and tumbled in the wind.

Frantic, he collected the scattered papers. Some had blown against a wall, but he stared in horror as other pages blew into the fire. He rushed around and gathered as many requisitions as he could find and tried to put them in some semblance of order.

He pulled himself together, brushed grit from his palms, and started walking. Should he return to the shop and tell his boss what happened?

Surely, the man would understand it was an accident. He hadn't destroyed the requisitions intentionally. Perhaps his manager would reward him for telling the truth so they might account for and replace the missing forms.

More likely, his boss would berate him for his clumsiness and demote him to grunt work. He had worked too hard and spent too much time cozying up to the factory manager to be humiliated and lose the benefits of his position.

Down the block, the workers pulled down another wall, all the while screaming, "*kamikaze*." He didn't understand the reference. Stupid kids, they must have meant *banzai*. The term *kamikaze* came from the name "Divine Wind," in honor of an ancient story. Two typhoons, separated by seven years, destroyed Mongol fleets destined to invade Japan. Perhaps today's wind was divine intervention, and a universal energy carried the sheets into the fire and consumed them. By telling no one about the lost requisitions, he would spare himself from discipline. And in some small way within his control, he would make it a bit harder for Japan to continue the insanity of war. If every Japanese took some small action, maybe there was the possibility of a huge outcome. Since keeping secrets had become a strength, he vowed to have the backbone to do what he felt was right, even if it was wrong.

An hour later, Koji locked eyes with the Army Logistics receiving clerk and handed over the thin envelope. Clueless to Koji's transgression, the busy clerk took it, stamped it, and waved Koji away.

Six

1945

FAITH

1945 – Tule Lake, CA

Alone in her unit, Ruby removed the tattered 1944 calendar from the nail on the wall. They had been incarcerated two full years. The *hachimaki*-wearing Japanese fanatics no longer gathered en mass at sunrise to pledge devotion to Japan. She hadn't noticed when they stopped. Her father had not mentioned repatriation for months. As much as she hated and resented her incarceration, in her mind, every month spent at Tule Lake was a month saved from sailing to Japan.

Now a high school junior, Ruby found comfort in the classroom's familiarity and its distinctive Pine-Sol odor. But unlike pine, the disinfectant smelled like an artificial Christmas tree that had lingered too long. Classmates had become friends, yet she still didn't quite fit in. An outsider inside barbed wire, she had forced herself to attend extracurricular activities, including band and orchestra concerts and rallies where yell leaders boosted spirits. She even snuck off to play Spin the Bottle. The promiscuous gals always joined, but Ruby had never kissed a boy, not until Tosh spun the bottle and it stopped, pointing at her. She knew Tosh had a puny brain and she was too good for him, but rules were rules, and her lips met his when his acne-scarred face leaned in. The other kids in the circle had hooted, hollered, and called them "eight eyes" when the embrace resulted in crooked eyeglasses on both their faces. She wiped away the taste of his stale cigarette smoke, watched the bottle spin again, and relaxed when it landed on someone else. But that was all play. Ruby's priority was school. She had thrown herself into academics, earning straight A's every semester, and would graduate in November.

To everyone's delight, an unexpected early Christmas gift arrived—the Army had declared the end of Japanese incarceration in the camps. Two days later, the U.S. Supreme Court issued a decision requiring the release of all Japanese Americans, but a separate Court decision dashed any hope of vindication, ruling their incarceration *was* constitutional.

Ruby's class had been following the case of Mr. Korematsu, who had been arrested and jailed for violating the relocation order. Determined to avoid the camps, his eyes had been surgically altered to change his appearance and he had changed his name to Clyde Sarah. The Court's decision upholding the government's discrimination was a crushing loss for Korematsu and the tens of thousands of incarcerated Japanese Americans hoping for a different outcome—for him and for them. Her mind whirled. How unfair. How unjust.

She hung a glossy new 1945 calendar on the nail and circled January second with red ink—the date the Army would begin releasing them, or so she thought. She assumed they would be free to walk out the gates that day. But would they have transportation home? And where would home be? Japan? Hawaii? The calendar, published by the Travelers Insurance Company and given to her father by a friend for Christmas, featured a quintessential American farm scene. Smoke from the chimney of a farmhouse nestled in pristine snow billowed the warmth of fresh-baked apple pie. In the foreground, the driver of a horse-drawn sleigh loaded with milk cans snuggled under a wool blanket. He waved to a half-dozen children skating on a crystal pond under the freedom of the winter sky.

Ruby salivated at the memory of sprinkling sugar on the cream skimmed off the top of a fresh milk bottle—one of her last memories of freedom in Waimea. She peeked outside to the cheerless filth of reality. Ankle-deep in mud, people navigated ridges of slush that would refreeze overnight and form a new rut of uncertainty.

Ruby turned her attention to her Aquila yearbook, featuring an eagle on the cover.

Latin for eagle, Aquila inspired the students to soar high and achieve their loftiest ideals. She dreamed of leaving camp, finishing high school, attending college, and teaching elementary school—all far from Tule Lake. The students had passed around their yearbooks for autographs, and now she read their words. Most of their messages were cursory.

Best wishes to a swell gal!

Here's wishing you a load of happiness!

Luck and happiness to a real brain.

She leafed through the pages of Student Council and the many clubs she had avoided joining. Maybe it was wrong not to experience the social side of school. Her eyes landed on the Home Makerettes page, featuring the most popular girls, and she read through the short quips to a longer, unsigned note.

Dear Ruby,

It has NOT been great knowing you and being your punching bag. You wait till I fatten-up. Then I'll use you as my punching bag, and you'll know how it feels to be one. To my best enemy pal, have a happy life.

Ruby glared at the page. Concealed in anonymity and in her perfectly inked cursive, Norma Hamasaki had ruined Ruby's yearbook. Ruby had picked a fight with Norma after a row with her stepmother, provoked by Norma's frilly polka-dotted perfection and incessant bragging about boys. *"Oh boy, my love affair with Hiroshi was such a thrill. I told the entire world he was my guy... at least until I broke up with him."* And then there was Norma's relationship with her mother. *"Mommy and me, we're like that,"* she had said with crossed fingers. *"How about you, Ruby? Are you and your mom close too?"*

Perhaps Norma knew her mother was dead, perhaps not. Either way, Ruby punched her as hard as she could, right into her puffed sleeve. Ruby tore the page from the yearbook, crumbled it into a ball, and threw it in the bin. What did she care about Norma? She would leave this place and never see her again.

But she did care. And she felt bad about punching the girl.

∙ ∙ ∙

Months passed with no news of release. People worried Tule Lake would be the last to close because the segregation center imprisoned the most rotten of the bad apples. On Ruby's sixteenth birthday, her father had tried to make the day special despite the dreary rain and clouds of disquiet. After temple and lunch, they spent hours playing *Gō* with bottle tops on a makeshift cardboard grid. Father always surrounded more territory than Ruby captured, but she beat him after hours of play. Likely he let her win.

Later, he surprised her with a cupcake topped with a lit candle and sang happy birthday. Ruby wished Mari was there to celebrate their birthdays together, and hoped she was getting along okay at Rohwer.

Taeko gave her a brooch she had made from bleached seashells long buried in the camp's seabed grounds.

"Here, let me pin it on you," Taeko said.

Ruby was surprised by her rare act of kindness. But then, Taeko stabbed the pin into Ruby's collarbone and glowered at her, defying Ruby to flinch. To say ouch. To draw any attention to the purposeful injury. And then she secured the clasp.

"Isn't that pretty," Father said. "Ruby, what do you say to *Okāsan*?"

Taeko smiled the sweetest of smiles.

"It's lovely, *Okāsan*. Thank you."

Ruby wanted to clobber her.

While they waited for news, her father encouraged her to make the best of things. He believed life existed only in the present. Nothing was permanent. Change was always possible. And nothing was within their control, except their minds and their attitudes. He told her to get more involved, maybe join a club at school, adding that she was living in a community of people like her and she should try harder to make friends.

As the days continued to blend into one, she learned the Home Makerettes were planning a Hawaiian-theme banquet for June's graduating seniors. Having lived in Hawaii, she thought she'd enjoy contributing to the club. At her first meeting, Ruby glanced around the classroom for an effective escape plan when Norma—who didn't seem to notice her—entered.

But Mildred Otogawa, president of the Home Makerettes, quickly called for the attention of all forty-three girls in attendance and announced that Ruby was joining. She then drew labeled columns on the blackboard: REFRESHMENTS. DECORATIONS. SERVERS. PROGRAM.

Mildred rested the chalk on the ledge. Her posture was perfect and she held her head so high she couldn't help but look down her nose as she spoke to the room. "Okay girls, everyone find your way to a corner of the room. If there's a crowd, pick a different corner and work it out until we have equal numbers in each corner. Refreshments front left, Decorations front right, Servers back left, and Program back right. Then write your names on the board. We're not leaving here until we have at least ten names in each column."

The girls scattered throughout the room like Hawaiian cockroaches disturbed from under one of Pig Lady's buckets. Ruby reached the already crowded Refreshments corner at the same time as Norma, who threw a challenging sideways glance without turning her head. "I was here first, Ruby. Best you try another group."

Ruby carried the sting of rejection with her to the opposite corner where she found a friendly face in a girl named Seiko and joined the Decorations team. Mildred joined them, and said, "I've already thought a lot about this and have some ideas. Let's have palm tree cut-outs and paper flowers, and our waitresses should wear flower leis and grass skirts. Agreed?"

Ideas began tumbling over one another.

"I think we should decorate the food tables like tiki huts. That would be cute."

"My father might agree to build the palm trees out of scrap wood in the wood shop."

"Let's make the hula skirts with crepe paper."

Amid the chatter, Ruby warmed at the memory of making leis with Mama and the lei she had made for Mari's wedding, and spoke up. "If someone wants to help me, we can string leis together with whatever wildflowers are blooming."

Mildred strutted to the blackboard and recorded the decorating suggestions. Next to the word *lay*, she wrote Ruby's name. Ruby couldn't help herself. "*Lei* is spelled l-e-i, not l-a-y."

Mildred returned a glassy stare. "What difference does it make?"

"Well... " Ruby crossed her arms. "It's spelled wrong! Haven't you ever heard of a homophone?"

Through her clenched jaw, Mildred said, "Of course I have. But do *you* want to know something?"

"What?"

"I don't think *you* belong here. You're not a good fit for *our* club."

The other girls bit their lips, smoothed their skirts, and exchanged uncomfortable glances.

Ruby squinted. She planted her hands on her hips. "Fine. I'll click better with smarter students than in a clique led by a cluck like you." She shoved her notebook and pencil into her bag to leave. "And, by the way, I suspect that homophone reference also totally escaped you."

Proud of her quick alliterative retort, and with a pounding heartbeat and in a hurried gait, she left the school building.

• • •

Ruby entered their unit and found her father resting on his cot and Taeko sitting at the table sorting seashells for her latest project. A cunning look washed over Taeko's face and she tried to hide an official-looking document lying on the table among the scattered seashells.

But the capitalized words had already screamed at Ruby— INDIVIDUAL REQUEST FOR REPATRIATION. Her brain scrambled. Why would her parents pursue going to Japan now when they were awaiting release? The documents must be old. They had to be. But the feeling of dread in her body said otherwise.

Ruby's body was taut with fear, and she didn't know what to say. Father walked over to the table. She looked at him with imploring eyes. "Those papers. They aren't new requests... are they?"

"Ruby-*chan*, I doubt there's anything for us in Hawaii. I don't know if I even have a congregation left, or if they'd let me lead... " He looked down, as though unable to meet her eyes before continuing. "If they'd let me lead the temple with this humiliating stain. On my character. On my reputation."

His eyes moistened. "Only a locked temple and an empty house remain there. My brother, his wife, his children, and *your* grandmother will surround us Japan. It's where we belong."

A sinking sensation filled her stomach. Her father's once strong shoulders, now hunched and rounded, supported the face of a sad, defeated man. She was truly sorry for him and for all he had lost—his temple, his reputation, his money, his freedom. Yet she could not leave one prison for another, nor could she imagine escaping a massive island prison like Japan.

As much as she wanted to respond to her father's despair with kindness, self-interest and impulsivity took over. "But I'm an American citizen! I'm about to graduate from high school. I hate speaking Japanese. Don't you see that? If we go to Japan, I'll be the enemy! I don't even know *your* family!"

His calm voice unnerved her. "I will not fight with you. You are my responsibility. You are my daughter. You may not understand today, but you will when you're older."

She didn't know what outraged her more—her father's words or his mastery of calm. Anger leaked out of her pores. Her eyeballs. Her nostrils. She couldn't look at his vacant face anymore. She couldn't hear his calm words anymore. She couldn't stand his patronizing anymore.

And she wouldn't. She ran from their barracks to the far side of camp, where a few kids played kickball. Even they angered her. There was not a single place inside of the fences to find solitude. Nor was there a single place to escape the incessant wind assaulting her cheeks and eyes with black tule grit. She faced the rocky shoulders of Abalone Mountain, her throat choked with emotion as thick as peanut butter. She swallowed the painful obstruction for supper. Why couldn't Father see her side? Just because he'd been thrown from his mighty altar didn't give him the right to punish her. She hated him.

The warmth of the sun on her back disappeared with the sudden chill of shadows as nightfall made its silent entrance. Her burning hunger to stay in the United States escaped as a painful howl from her roiling belly. Far beyond the looming and twisted wire, and obscured by the barren loam and rock formations, a coyote echoed her despair.

• • •

Uncertainty over when Tule Lake would close cast a shadow over the camp as time passed. News of President Roosevelt's sudden death compounded her worries. Ruby didn't know any president but FDR. He had been the president her entire life. Truman had been vice president for only a few months, and now he commanded the nation that had done the Japanese Americans wrong. Who knew what would happen with a new leader in the White House.

Nearly everyone in camp distrusted the government, including Ruby. Yet her small inner voice had faith in America. Convinced her family's release would result in them being deported to Japan, she knew she was better off in camp. And so, she began believing in her dreams and Mari's words. Things change and hardships come and go. She would make the best of her situation, finish high school at Tule Lake, and attend an American college. As much as Father valued higher education, she believed he wouldn't make her go to Japan if she was accepted to a university.

Bright and early the next morning, Ruby took her new attitude to school. Light filtered from open door classrooms and her footsteps echoed on the linoleum floors. Ruby had successfully avoided Mildred in the weeks since the Home Makerettes meeting, but now, Mildred walked toward her from the opposite end of the hallway. Pins and needles pricked Ruby's spine.

Not in the mood for dealing with Mildred, she turned her back to the hall, and her eyes landed on a bulletin board poster: THE DEBATE TEAM NEEDS YOU NOW. Behind her, she heard Mildred greet another student, and they walked past Ruby. But turning into the shadows to avoid Mildred haunted her throughout the day. If she was going to make the best of things, she needed to take the first step. Even big changes required tiny beginnings.

After her last class, Ruby visited her social studies teacher, Mr. Wilson, who served as the debate team's faculty advisor. She learned the team was down one person for a debate scheduled in two weeks about Racism in Camps, and she filled the vacancy. Yoshi and Albert would be her teammates, and Henry, Ted, and Martin were on the opposing team. Yoshi and Henry would argue whether the Japanese in America were better off inside of the camps or better off if they had been allowed to stay in their communities. Albert and Ted would argue whether America would continue to discriminate based on race after the war. She would debate Martin, who would argue that the extermination of Jews in Europe could happen here. She would argue that it couldn't—the least defensible position given their imprisonment.

Mr. Wilson described the format. She would either accept and concede to Martin's argument, point out flaws, or ask for clarification before giving her counter-argument. The team winning the two of three arguments, as judged by Mr. Wilson, won overall.

Last November, newspapers had begun reporting atrocities from concentration camp escapees and survivors. Ruby spent the next two weeks finding old newspapers and reading about the brutality of Hitler and his Gestapo and their massacre of Jews. Her father also helped. Through his network of Buddhist and Christian ministers, he obtained a copy of the Auschwitz Report that had found its way into camp from Protestant clergy in Switzerland.

Night after night, she studied the Nazis' acts of barbarity, her face wrinkling in revulsion. Thoughts of concentration camps and murder stayed with her while sleeping. The more she strengthened her debate argument, the more unsettling her dreams of being starved, beaten, and herded into furnaces. The nightmares haunted her well into the wee hours and undermined her confidence.

On debate day, she entered Mr. Wilson's classroom early. She had done her best to prepare for what Martin might say, but she didn't know him well, and the uncertainty of what he might argue had her biting and picking her cuticles for days.

Her mouth was dry and she wished she had stopped for a drink of water. About thirty Honor Society students filed in. With her chin held high and shoulders back, Ruby approached her teammates and offered handshakes. They had met the past few afternoons to quiz each other, and the boys treated her like one of them, except for Albert. A real gentleman, he held doors and chairs for her, and she liked the attention. Ruby hadn't seen Mildred enter the classroom, at least not until she poked her fingers into Ruby's shoulder. She turned to meet Mildred's haughty look, scrunched lips, and whining voice. "Good luck, smarty-pants!"

Ruby returned a suffocated smile.

Mildred took a seat.

Mr. Wilson called for attention, closed the door, and the debates began. During the first two arguments, she silently rehearsed her argument. Mere snippets of what the boys argued registered in her brain. Her team had won the first round, and the opposing team, the second. She and Martin would determine the overall winner. She had to win. She had something to prove to herself *and* to Mildred.

Her eyes followed the steady gait of Martin's long legs to the lectern. He towered over her, and began with a commanding declamation. "They say history has a way of repeating. I agree. History will prove the comparability between the German concentration camps and the American camps imprisoning us. Given the striking similarities we've already experienced, and acknowledging that past behavior is an excellent predictor of future behavior, I believe the U.S. could exterminate the remaining of the 120,000 Japanese prisoners, two-thirds of us American citizens, in these camps, just as Hitler exterminated the Jews in Europe."

His eyes brimmed with confidence as he grabbed a piece of chalk and drew a large triangle, and then another, inverted and overlaid on the first. "They marked every Jew with a garish yellow six-point star, making them targets." He pointed at the audience. "Just as *your* yellow faces identify *you* as the enemy." The students murmured with approval. "The Nazis loaded Jewish prisoners into railroad cars at assembly centers. We, too, were held in crude assembly centers and loaded into rail cars, headed to uncertain destinations and futures. We, too, arrived at prison camps under watchtowers equipped with guns and searchlights."

Ruby wiped her sweaty palms on her skirt. She remembered the fear of uncertainty on those train rides and the fear of certain imprisonment arriving at Jerome and then Tule Lake. Martin was right.

He turned to the next page of his notes with calm. "Jewish prisoners were greeted at the camp entrances with misleading signage, just like we were greeted. The entrance sign at Auschwitz said WORK BRINGS FREEDOM. Ha! The Jews were worked or gassed to death. The sign here says, TULE LAKE SEGREGATION CENTER. Ha! This isn't a segregation center. This... is a concentration camp."

He continued. "The prisoners in the German camps were each assigned a number, just as they assigned us numbers. *Schutzstaffel* officers, better known as SS, closely guarded the prisoners, just as the Army watches us. The SS shot without warning and assigned laborers small squares to stay within while performing their work. Their guards ordered men to fetch things outside of their squares, only to shoot them for stepping out. Our square just happens to be bigger and fenced in by barbed wire."

Distracted by the trickle of perspiration under her arms, Ruby glanced at Henry giving Martin a thumb-up. She forced herself to breathe and not allow Martin's confidence and command of the subject to unnerve her. Listening to each of his words, she jotted down major themes and drew lines from those themes to her counter-points.

Martin continued. "Jewish prisoners were forced to live in degrading conditions just like us. On winter nights, we return to our uninsulated barracks with inadequate heat and huddle with our families around inefficient potbelly stoves to stay warm."

He rested his notes on the table and continued, speaking with ease from memory. "These atrocities occurred within Germany's democratic government. Hitler was elected. So was Roosevelt. And Roosevelt signed Executive Order 9066, violating our civil liberties. Why would Truman be any different? And what do you suppose is delaying our release? The government said they'd begin releasing us in January. It's April thirteenth, people. We're still here! Maybe they've decided to exterminate those of us in here, having arbitrarily determined all of us disloyal. Few Caucasians care about us Japs, and people listen to Caucasian voices. It seems their privilege gives them the power."

Ruby thought Martin had finished, but he continued. "And let's not forget. Who could have imagined rounding up well-respected Buddhist ministers?" He paused and locked on Ruby's eyes. "That happened. In fact, that happened to *her* father." He pointed at her.

The students applauded—some with enthusiasm and others with perfunctory politeness. Ruby's teammates furrowed their brows with concern. Mr. Wilson commended Martin on a job well done and looked at her. "Ruby, time for you to concede, refute, or ask Martin for clarification, after which you may offer your argument."

The stab of Martin's finger-pointing hurt as he intended. She told herself to get it together, breathe, and focus. She would acknowledge the points that didn't harm her position, and then gut his argument. He may have tried to knock her off-balance, but she would defeat his intentions.

Martin may enjoy poking in the sticker bushes, but her focus was on the bigger picture. Despite the looming threat of going to Japan, deep down Ruby always had faith she would avoid deportation and leave Tule Lake. That faith had strengthened since realizing the importance of a positive outlook. She didn't understand what the delays were, but she still had faith and she had convinced herself the delays were in her favor. Faith was the answer.

She looked at the notes of her well-crafted argument, but set them and her fears aside, raising her lashes to meet Martin's eyes.

"Martin, you're right. The yellow stars marked the Jews as open targets, as our faces identify us. But consider perspective." She took a deep breath before continuing.

"I concede we were loaded into rail cars from assembly centers. However, the Jews weren't allowed to take any possessions, as we were. Jews were shoved to stand shoulder to shoulder in cattle cars. The doors slammed behind them, plunging them in total darkness. We sat together with our families and we had windows. We had the freedom to breathe."

"I concede we live surrounded by barbed wire and armed guards in watchtowers with spotlights that sweep and harass all night." Her heart thumped as she recalled her experience being ordered away from the fence in Jerome. Doubt crept in and undermined her concentration, but she couldn't let it get the best of her. Her argument was sound and she must keep going. She paused and made a wide, calming circle on the dusty floor with the toe of her shoe. She was determined to leave her fears outside the circle and have faith in the strength of her argument.

"I concede the wording of the German sign, WORK BRINGS FREEDOM, is ironic. I also agree our Tule Lake sign should be clear—the American camps are incarceration centers, not internment, segregation, or relocation camps." She paused.

"Words matter."

With her heart pounding, she continued. "I concede every family here has a registration number, but those numbers help us receive mail. The Jews didn't receive mail—they didn't know where they were. And their numbers were branded on them. How cruel! We weren't forced to endure that kind of barbarism."

Nerves had raised her voice to a higher pitch. She remembered something Father had suggested and visualized all the boys stripped down to skid-marked tighty-whities. It helped. And then, for a moment, she focused on the inside of her circle—her circle of influence—before returning her attention to Martin.

The pitch of her voice softened. "You're right. If we do anything stupid, like try to escape, we might be shot and killed. If we get too close to the fence, we're ordered away. We listen and do what we're told. You mentioned the work camps, yet failed to acknowledge the difference in working conditions. The brutality under which Jews labored, weakened by starvation, is inconceivable. At least in here, the working conditions are fair and workers are paid—even if the pay is only sixteen dollars per month. And we get to go to school. The Jews didn't." She released her stare at Martin and met all the eyes now riveted on her—including Mildred's.

"I agree our living accommodations lack warmth, privacy, and basic running water. However, we have shelter and a cot to sleep on at night.

Some Jews lived three men to a space that was so small, they couldn't lie down or sit up. When we turn on the showers in the lavatory, water flows, not poison gas. And you're right about Hitler and Roosevelt." She sneered. "Sometimes voters elect the wrong person, even when the person wins by heavy margins in a country fighting a war against fascism. After all," she paused, "democracies aren't perfect."

She stepped from behind the lectern, signaling the importance of her words to come, faced Martin, and hoped his ego would blind him to her trap. "I'll conclude my rebuttal with a question. Martin, do you test the food they serve you at the mess hall for poison before eating it?"

Martin opened his mouth as if to argue and stopped himself. He then gave her a dismissive shrug. "No."

It was time for her conclusion. "Martin made some outstanding points, but he excluded critical facts and his conclusion is wrong. The Jews endured horrific cruelties in the German concentration camps. They lived among the stench of pestilence, were starved, neglected, and brutalized, and lived in unspeakable destitution. We haven't suffered in our camps the way the Jews suffered in theirs. Martin is right. Past behavior can be an excellent predictor of future behavior. The behavior we've experienced from the U.S. government continues to be unjust, but it will not lead to our mass murder."

She launched her final blow. "Despite our incarceration, mass extermination can't happen here, because we have *faith* in our government's *faithfulness* to us as Americans. *Faith* requires trust in our democracy, even if imperfect."

She straightened her posture and made intense eye contact with her opponent. "Martin, when I asked if you test your food, you said no, which requires your having *faith* that our government would not kill you. Thus, you concede in having *faith* in our government. Americans have not and would not commit the same horrific atrocities that the Germans inflicted on the Jews."

Martin's smug cheeks now burned red. He broke eye contact with her and stared at his feet.

Again, the students applauded, but with more enthusiasm than their applause for Martin. Cheers and whistles came from the back of the class-room. Ruby smiled. Martin's teammates frowned. Mr. Wilson compli-mented her on a job well done, and he turned to Martin. "Time for you to concede, refute, or ask Ruby for clarification."

Martin's bewildered teammates exchanged resigned and defeated expressions with each other and with him. Martin's lips were moving, and he stammered a rebuttal, but she picked up only vague words here and there. His weak and brief counter-argument didn't matter. She had crushed him. Adrenaline coursed throughout her tiny frame, and her eyes danced when Mr. Wilson judged her the winner of the round and her team the winner of the debate.

Ruby basked in victory. She believed in her argument. Mostly. The government would never exterminate them. They would be released.

Days later, doubt would creep back into her psyche.

DON'T FENCE ME IN

1945 – Tule Lake, CA

Ruby stepped out of the school and into the warm May afternoon. Motes from yesterday's dust storm caught the sun and shimmered like tiny crystals.

She breathed in the earthy fragrance of tilled dirt and spring plantings, set down a pail of soapy water, and got busy cleaning the railings. Yesterday's powerful gusts had scudded a ravaging wall of dust and debris across the camp for an hour. Last night, she had retreated to her bunk and watched the dust blow through the cracks in the walls and floors. The howling wind and pelting dirt on the window had heightened her chronic sense of isolation, prompting her to curl up against the storm, lost in a desert with no mirage in sight.

The railing was thick with grime. She wrung out a tattered terry-cloth rag and scrubbed, wondering what it would take to remove the years of filth from camp. Her eyes lifted to Albert, who was picking up debris in the schoolyard. In the weeks since the debate, he seemed to be around her more often—in the mess hall at lunch, in the hallway during class changes, and now cleaning up from the same storm. He was tall with a stocky build, straight hair mowed with the buzz of a razor, and wire-frame eyeglasses. When he smiled, his cheeks fattened, and his face looked goofy. He approached Ruby and rested his chin on the railing.

"What are you doing?" Ruby asked.

"Just watching."

"Watching what?"

His face got a bit fatter, a bit goofier.

"Not what. Who. I'm watching you."

Ruby suddenly felt tongue-tied.

"Want some help?" asked Albert.

Ruby tossed him a rag.

They finished in less than an hour, and he offered to walk her home.

Walking across the firebreak, Albert took Ruby's elbow and steered her away from debris littering the open area.

"We haven't received our release papers. You?" he asked.

"No," she said, with a heavy sigh, liking the warmth of his hand on her sleeveless elbow.

She looked toward the fences. "I wonder what it's like out there now."

"I hope we find out soon. Many people are afraid to leave here with the war still raging. My family doesn't have a home to return to. At least in here we have food and shelter."

A piece of newspaper was lifted by the breeze and landed by her feet. "My father insists on returning to Japan to live with his family, but... "

All of a sudden, the jubilant sound of cheering escaped from the military area on the other side of the fence. Ruby's eyes followed the cheers and watched the soldiers wave outstretched arms, hug one another, and hoist other soldiers onto their shoulders. They raised triumphant arms and fisted hands. In a nearby guard tower, two sentries embraced, separated only by their machine guns.

Ruby scanned the concerned and confused faces in the crowd gathering around them. Despite the cheerful sounds from the soldiers, she had a sinking feeling something bad had happened, and she stayed close to Albert.

A man shouted to the guards and asked what was going on. A megaphone amplified the guard's response. *"Germany surrendered! Europe is free!"*

From around the side of a nearby building, a popular boy named Lyle appeared, holding Mildred's hand. The boys greeted one another and then Lyle released Mildred and hustled Albert into the crowd, leaving Ruby and Mildred behind.

"Hey Ruby, we got our release papers. You?" Mildred asked, with a baiting tone.

Ruby shook her head. She didn't want to talk to Mildred, especially about being released. Europe may be free, but they were still stuck behind barbed wire. Wanting to distance herself from her adversary and curl up into a soft place with her thoughts, she continued walking.

But Mildred followed in step. "I wonder why," she said. "Lots of us have them now. Maybe *your* family did something wrong."

Trying to watch her step, Ruby could feel Mildred's eyes drilling into the soft spot of her vulnerability.

Suddenly, Mildred's feet got tangled in a piece of rope on the ground and she fell. Flat. Ruby looked around as if waiting for someone to help Mildred, but not a person was watching. Mildred raised her head and Ruby met the heated glare of her eyes. "You pushed me!"

Though Ruby had done nothing to cause the fall, she suffered a flutter of concern. It would take only a moment to extend her hand to the pitiful girl, lying in the dirt examining her bleeding palm. She could also ignore her and walk away. That's what Miss Snarky, Sanctimonious, Sneaky deserved. It might have been the optimism in the air or Ruby wanting to feel good about something, but she didn't walk away.

"You *know* I didn't trip you," Ruby said, extending her hand. "Here... take it."

A flush swept over Mildred's face, and rather than accept Ruby's hand, she slapped it away. More than anything, Ruby wanted to grind Mildred's face into the ground. Instead, she pushed her way into the crowd and found Albert.

"I've got to get home," she said to Albert.

"There's nothing more to learn here, anyway. Let's go," he said. "See you around, Lyle."

"Not for much longer, I hope." The dimples in Lyle's face framed his huge grin.

They walked to Ruby's barracks in silence, observing more crowds of spontaneous joy. She enjoyed the quiet between them amid the unfolding chaos. When they arrived at her unit, Ruby thanked Albert for walking her and started up the steps.

"Wait a second," he said, taking her hand. His palm was sweating when he invited her to be his date at the junior-senior prom.

• • •

Three weeks later and alone in the barracks, Ruby sat at their crude table and primped at a small mirror. She imagined herself getting ready for prom in a beautiful bedroom with a canopy bed and seated at a kidney-shaped vanity, skirted in pleated organza, like the ones featured in magazines the girls passed around at school. In her imagination, crystal perfume bottles, photographs in fancy frames, and an ivory comb surrounded her. And Mama was brushing her hair. Before she knew it, she had over-teased her hair and had to comb it out and start over.

Having re-teased her hair, she swept the front and sides into pompadour rolls, twisting and securing one curl at a time. The back of her hair fell in soft waves to the shoulders of her blue satin dress, a hand-me-down from Seiko's older sister, which Ruby had altered in the sewing room. Her friendship with Seiko was the only good thing that ever came from attending that Home Makerettes meeting. Ruby powdered her nose and filled in her lips with Victory Red lipstick, finishing with a tissue blot. After rubbing a touch of red onto her cheeks, she gave the mirror a satisfied pucker, happy for splurging on the fancy tube at the co-op with her babysitting money.

Now, for the love bite. Head tilted, she dabbed powder over the faint bruise, using her best artistry to camouflage the proof of heavy necking with Albert last night. He had walked her home most days since she had accepted his invitation to the prom, and they had eaten supper together at the same table a few times. But last night, under the stars, he had caressed her face in a way that felt exquisite. She wasn't used to being touched. It began with him looking at her with his smiling eyes. He had stroked her hair, and then her brows, cheeks, and chin, with his eyes moving little by little to each part of her face as if she was the most beautiful girl he had ever seen.

Then the kissing began. Her body had tingled all over when he began the gentle sucking on her neck. She thought about asking him to stop, but they weren't doing anything wrong, and he felt *so* good.

Her eyes nearly popped out of her head when she saw the result. With the bruise peeking through the powder, she moved a lock of hair to cover it. She tidied the table, and then smoothed her dress, running her hands over the voluptuous fabric, the sensation luxurious on her skin.

The door opened and Father and Taeko stepped in.

"Ruby-*chan*, you look so pretty and so grown up," Father said.

Taeko eyed Ruby up and down. "Yes, but she's missing something."

Ruby's stomach clenched with dread, wondering what her stepmother was about to criticize.

Taeko handed Ruby a small gift wrapped in a remnant of fabric.

"What's this?"

"Something I made for you to wear tonight."

Ruby untied the cloth. Inside was a lovely brooch made of tiny shells into the shape of a butterfly with delicate details painted in sapphire blue, amber, and white. Some shells were as tiny as a pinhead.

Taeko came toward her. "Here, I'll help you."

But Ruby had learned her lesson the last time, and she questioned Taeko's motivations. Taeko never gave freely. She either wanted something yet unstated from Ruby, or the gesture was another show for Father, or she intended to stab Ruby with the pin again. Ruby wouldn't give her the chance or the satisfaction.

They were interrupted by a knock at the door.

"It's lovely, *Okāsan*. Thank you. Albert's here... I'll pin it on later."

Albert said hello to her parents, and after a short walk, they entered the gymnasium decorated with balloon bouquets and swaths of twisted crepe paper. In the air, flavors of dime-store perfumes wafted from girl to girl.

Albert escorted her to the dance floor and the record player blared Frank Sinatra's number-one hit, "Don't Fence Me In."

"I'm not a very good dancer," Albert said.

"Me neither, but let's give it a go."

Albert held her close, and the song's disturbing irony sunk in.

"I want to ride to the ridge where the West commences
And gaze at the moon till I lose my senses
And I can't look at hobbles and I can't stand fences
Don't fence me in."

Ruby glanced around. Everyone was dancing, laughing, and enjoying the occasion. Everyone, it seemed, but her. *Why didn't the lyrics bother them too?*

She pulled away from Albert. "I have to run. It's eight o'clock and my turn to serve punch." Albert looked puzzled. She turned and walked away.

Seiko was standing at the punch table. "Ruby, I heard a rumor your family was denied release. I'm sorry."

"Where did you hear that?"

"Mildred. She's telling everyone."

"That's a lie. We haven't even heard yet! What else is she saying?"

Seiko's eyes widened. Her lips pursed.

"Answer me, Seiko!"

"She said you're going back to Japan, where *you* belong."

To Ruby, a snake bite wouldn't have hurt as bad.

"Where is she?"

"Who cares?"

Ruby cared.

While Ruby was filling a cup with punch, Lyle approached the table. She pretended not to notice him and said to Seiko in a voice loud enough for Lyle and others nearby to hear, "Poor Lyle. Mildred's miss-goodie-two-shoes act is a joke. If he thinks she's marrying material, he'll learn the hard way, maybe even catch a disease from the tramp. That shookie opens her legs for all the boys with no regard to the girl code, ruining things for us nice girls. What do they say? Why buy the cow when the cow gives away the milk for free!"

Seiko giggled. "Oh, Ruby."

Lyle's sudden about-face made it clear he had heard her. As he walked away, two girls waiting for punch whispered behind their hands.

Later that evening when the master of ceremonies announced the crowning of Mildred as prom queen and Lyle as king, the rumor of

Mildred's promiscuity had circulated the room in hushed whispers. As Mildred walked past her adoring court, only Ruby and the boys smiled at her. Ruby's smile was most satisfying. The other girls had stopped talking the moment Mildred walked by, turning their scornful gazes to decorations, other students, anything and anyone but Mildred. Lyle was nowhere in sight.

• • •

Two days later, a letter arrived from Mari. Ruby didn't wait for her parents to open it.

June 3, 1945

Dear Father, Okāsan, and Ruby,

I trust this letter finds you well and experiencing pleasant weather. The Immigration Service has approved my release, along with Warren's parents' release. We are preparing to leave for their home in Los Angeles and will probably be on the train by the date you receive this letter. I plan to find work there as a dressmaker.

Sadly, I've received many distressing letters from friends who returned to California, Washington, and Oregon. They write about a frightening and pervasive anti-Japanese sentiment, people returning to find unwelcome communities and their properties vandalized. They've been spat on by landlords who say they would never rent to a Jap again. Others who had sold their homes, farms, and businesses for pennies, found all of their belongings disposed of or destroyed. Isn't that horrible? They entrusted everything they owned to neighbors and friends. Where has common decency gone? I hope it's not like this in Waimea.

The government gave me $25 and a train ticket to LA. When I *walk out of here, I won't look back. I will step off that train in LA with my head held high as a free woman who will make the most of each day. My heart yearns for Warren's death to have been a big mistake and that he will find his way home to me. My mouth waters for a Japanese breakfast—grilled fish, miso soup, fluffy white rice— but with side orders of waffles and eggs. And hash browns!*

To Ruby: Remember, the future is about hope. The present is about the moment you're in, alive and breathing. Make every day count, my sweet baby sister. And remember, you always have a home with me. I'll write once settled at my address.

Love, Mari

Ruby had folded and returned the letter to the envelope as her father and Taeko returned from running whatever errands they ran, or meeting with whomever they met. His face was taut, brows furrowed, and lips pressed tight together. He clasped an envelope in his hand. His tone was serious when he asked her to sit down.

Taeko wore the insidious expression of a predator, like a hungry jaguar ready to ambush its prey.

Ruby's chest was heavy as she sank into the chair.

He handed Ruby an official-looking document folded in thirds. "There's one for you and one for *Okāsan*."

Her fingers fumbled to open the document and her eyes couldn't read fast enough.

Immigration and Naturalization Service, U.S. Department of Justice.

So far as this Service is concerned, the above-named person, Ruby Ishimaru, may be released.

Signed Z.B. Jackson, U.S. Immigration Officer

Her chest began to lighten.

"What does *Okāsan's* say?"

"Same as yours."

"But what about you?"

The air grew heavy. He opened the envelope and removed another document. Ruby unfolded the paper.

So far as this Service is concerned, the above-named parolee, Chiko Ishimaru, may not be released.

She thought the ache in her throat might suffocate her.

"I'm sorry, Ruby. I know you hoped for a different outcome. You must accept we are stuck here until we go to Japan."

She waited until her father's eyes met hers. "Please, Father. What about Mari? We received a letter from her today. She said I can live with her."

"No. You stay with us."

Taeko smirked. "Of course, you'll stay with us. Japan will be good for you."

Later that night, Taeko would find the brooch she'd made for Ruby smashed and discarded in the trash can.

FALSE ALARM?

August 1945 – Hiroshima, Japan

Koji woke before dawn from a jittery and sleepless night to the intensity of another hot, sticky day. Soon, he would wake Naoki for work. The Imperial Army could have mobilized his brother to anywhere in Hiroshima, including the firebreak gangs, so Koji was relieved they worked in the same factory. Plus, they enjoyed each other's company on their way to and from work. Naoki's rhythmic snoring sent comforting vibrations through their silent, cozy home. Grateful for the early quiet, Koji cherished his time to meditate, cooling his mind and spirit from the rising heat of war.

His parents were in Fukuoka, where *Otōsan* had been receiving cancer treatments at Kyushu University Hospital for the past few weeks. Today was his last treatment, and Koji hoped the University doctors had cured him. His mother's *kampō* treatments had helped his father for a while, but his health continued to decline. Like weeds that destroyed their crops, the invasive and multiplying cancer cells competed for nutrients—one cell divided by two, then four, then eight and so on. Tiny, vigorous enemies inside *Otōsan's* body, sucking the light and life out of him. Koji recalled his first memories of being hoisted into the air by his young, virile father, and he was excited for his parents' return the next week.

Soon, his positive thoughts gave way to anxiety. Even with its strong military presence and war supporting industries, Hiroshima hadn't been a target of the many devastating raids on the Japanese Islands. Since February, the raids had been relentless. He thought Hiroshima's luck avoiding attack was peculiar, since American squadrons flew overhead most days, intimidating everyone below. Yet the B-29 bomber planes continued to spare

211

Hiroshima and Kyoto—Japan's ancient center of art and culture. Koji didn't believe their luck would hold much longer. His family considered each air raid to be *the one* and wasted no time scurrying into the depths of their now completed bomb shelter. Sometimes they surfaced from the shelter to find that the planes had rained U.S. leaflets emblazoned with messages designed to crush the will of the Japanese. The government required citizens to turn over any leaflets to the police, but he hid them alongside his *Jizō*, now under a floorboard in his room. Saving the forbidden mementos gave him hope that one day his experiences might lead to a better life. He imagined showing the leaflets to his American children and grandchildren.

In the evenings before his parents left for Fukuoka, his family had huddled around their radio listening to stories of significant devastation in cities throughout Japan. In the Tokyo raid alone, America's massive firebombing destroyed a fifth of the city and killed 100,000 people—many burned to death in the resulting fires. They had listened to broadcasted stories of people running through the streets and jumping into rivers to extinguish themselves or defend against the flames. His harried father, who had become thinner by the day, would drum his fingers on the table and mumble, "Such horrific ways to die. And the poor survivors live among ashes, starving."

Naoki's eyes would bulge, and *Okāsan* squeezed hers shut as if closing her eyelids would block the painful images, while shaking her head in denial.

During those broadcasts, Koji's heartbeat thundered in his ears, as the news boasted of victory and of the Empire attacking on all fronts. They heard about the magnificent *kamikaze* attacks and their toll on the United States Navy, without knowing what was true or false, or at what cost. Over four thousand *kamikaze* pilots had joined the sea of ghosts in the South Pacific, and despite government censorship, nearly everyone suspected Japan was losing to a powerful enemy. In the spirit of duty, honor, and sacrifice, millions of people prepared for an Allied invasion and a decisive battle on Japanese soil. Even women and young children practiced drills and learned hand-to-hand combat, how to fight and impale with homemade bamboo spears, and how to stab the enemy with a kitchen knife. Without question, the honorable Japanese would give their lives for their homeland.

With rising tension, fear intruded into Koji's life. A week earlier, Allied leaders had met in Potsdam, Germany and issued an ultimatum for Japan's surrender. They gave Japan the choice to preserve or abandon its reign of imperialism, to surrender without condition or face prompt and utter destruction. Prime Minister Suzuki rejected the ultimatum and Japan held firm with no weakening in its determination to continue fighting. Koji believed Japan's leadership had unhinged into complete and total lunacy.

• • •

Three days later, at 6:30 a.m., the air-raid siren blasted, startling Koji as he and Naoki were leaving for work. The deafening noise swelled, contracted, and transmitted the sharp and frightening threat on their fragility. The boys covered their ears against the siren's piercing scream and ran to the root cellar. They threw open the cellar door, latched it behind them, and bolted to the rear wall where they crawled into the reinforced area.

"Aren't *Okāsan* and *Otōsan* on the train now? I hope the planes aren't above them." Naoki said.

Koji worried about that, too, but he didn't want to heighten Naoki's fear. "They'll be okay. Don't worry."

"But how do you know that?"

"I just do."

And deep down, he believed it.

The cleared area was large enough for their family and the supplies stored there. In total darkness, Koji moved farther back and crawled into a spider web. The sticky sensation of the web and of spiders crawling on his face and neck gave him goosebumps. He whacked his face and neck with his hands and shook his head.

Naoki followed behind hm. "What's going on?"

"Spider web! I hate those things!"

He continued crawling forward until his hand found the flashlight. It was where they always kept it, on top of a crate. Once the flashlight illuminated the dank shelter, Naoki lit the candles stuck in old *sake* bottles. They found seats on wooden platforms built a few inches off of the ground and cushioned with old *tatami* and blankets. They had never stayed long enough to use any of the supplies stored there—jugs of water, a small kit of bandages, hydrogen peroxide, Mercurochrome, and dried fish in tin canisters, home-preserved pickled vegetables, tinned *miso* powder, and dried seaweed. Koji rested his elbow on the crate beside him where they stored extra flashlights, batteries, a whistle, and a metal box holding his parents' important papers—including his birth certificate. The box was secured by a keyless lock, and only Koji and his parents knew the correct combination of five numbers. Naoki still didn't know the secret of Koji's American citizenship, and Koji was determined to keep it that way.

"I don't understand," Naoki said, his hands jammed into his armpits as if to protect himself. "Why don't our planes go after them? How else are we to defend ourselves?" He stretched his arms open, but the dirt walls blocked his movement. "*Kuso*! Their planes are this big!"

Ignoring his brother's profanity, Koji said, "Japanese planes can't fly that high, and our anti-aircraft guns can't reach them either. We are powerless targets to their raids. Doomed. Japan will lose this war soon, so keep yourself together and be strong."

"But what if something happens before *Okāsan* and *Otōsan* return? We might never see them again?" Tears streamed down Naoki's face, sweet and innocent, yet adolescent-like with stray facial hairs, acne, and a mouth that spewed obscenities.

"That won't happen. We'll hear the all-clear soon and everything will return to normal, at least until the next warning. Their train arrives in Hiroshima in about an hour and Watanabe-*san* promised to pick them up. You'll see, they'll be home waiting for us tonight, along with a delicious dinner of fresh-picked vegetables and *miso* soup." But doubt hid behind Koji's comforting words. Germany's unconditional surrender in May seemed to destroy any remaining hope for Japan. Yet those in charge refused to surrender, and the country crumbled, city after bombed city, into near defeat.

Koji listened to the silence and to the sounds of his and Naoki's

214

breathing. His eyes followed the single strand of a spider's silk, anchored to a bucket in the corner for latrine emergencies, to bamboo lacings in the opposite corner of the ceiling. The spider was hard at work using its spinnerets to weave its orb-shaped web. He thought about the web he had crawled into and destroyed, knowing the spider had labored for days to spin it. The spider would spin again. Spiders were like that. Resilient.

The all-clear sounded about a half hour later, and they crawled from the tunnel's darkness to sunshine, a clear and cloudless sky, and the tymbal serenade of cicadas flourishing in the sultry weather. They grabbed their heavy civil-defense helmets from the handlebars of their bikes and pedaled toward another day of rifle-making. Along the flowing river, they passed trucks, cars, other bicycles, and people pulling wooden carts of supplies. An old man carrying fishing gear and a little girl swinging a basket walked down the embankment to the shoreline.

Across the river, thousands of soldiers wearing backpacks engaged in early-morning military exercises—saluting, marching, and hurdling over rough timber obstacles. The squadron's war games unfolded against a backdrop of the city's streetcar and traffic sounds and the high and fertile hills of Hiji Park, an oasis amid Hiroshima's military activity and factories. Once again, everyone was back to their busy, normal routines.

LITTLE BOY

August 6, 1945 – Hiroshima, Japan

"When people see things as beautiful, ugliness is created.
When people see things as good, evil is created."
—*Lao Tzu*

American weather planes, responsible for the air-raid alert, departed Hiroshima's airspace and transmitted the excellent news. The sky above the pre-determined city-center target was clear. It was a magnificent day to destroy Japan's unrelenting national pride and bring the country to its knees.

Soaring toward Hiroshima from the island of Tinian, the supercharged engines and spinning blades of three American Superfortress bombers propelled the top-secret squadron forward high above the swells of the azure Pacific Ocean. The sparkling surface and dancing white caps of the ocean— named Peaceful Sea by the Portuguese—hid the remains of savage conflicts sunken deep in the salty graveyard.

Enola Gay, named after her commander's mother, received and acknowledged orders to complete her mission: unleash Little Boy's boundless power of enriched uranium, engineered to annihilate the unsuspecting city without distinguishing between military leaders barking orders, conscripted soldiers following orders, grandparents rubbing their arthritic bones, housewives hanging sheets in the warm sunshine, bank tellers arriving for work, gardeners pruning branches, tram drivers transporting passengers, doctors and nurses tending to the ill, school children learning to read and write, toddlers kicking balls, or newborn babies taking their first breaths.

Among them, a mere speck below the Enola Gay, Koji stood at a table facing one of the few windows in the dark and demoralizing factory. No air-raid siren warned him or hundreds of thousands of other people of the impending doom.

Accompanied by scientific and photography planes, Enola Gay carried the fate of the world in her belly. Enola Gay's anxious crew readied Little Boy's three-meter armored steel cylinder, loaded gunpowder between his tail and projectile, and replaced dud plugs with those that ignite. She reached her destination—ten thousand meters above Hiroshima—aimed her crosshairs at the Aioi Bridge, and dropped her four-and-one-half-ton payload of mass destruction.

Little Boy plummeted through the sky.

SOUNDLESS FLASH OF DEATH

August 6, 1945 – Hiroshima, Japan

Koji stood at a filthy window, sorting metal components for the rifle assembly mechanism. Outside, gangs of student workers pushed rail carts laden with stacked wood crates filled with rifles. His eyes followed an old man in a tattered hat, limping along the shoreline. Koji paused to gaze at the wide, slow-moving river below, where a crew paddled a small *wasen* beside a lone fisherman leaning over his boat to retrieve his straw hat. From a distance, an empty barge approached. Toma sauntered by, swinging his *bentō* box. Koji glanced at the clock's arrowed hands—8:15. Toma wasn't too late. His mouth watered at the possibility of trading his *kabocha* squash for Toma's rice at lunch.

A blinding explosion of light seared across the sky from east to west. Koji's world went dark.

• • •

Four kilometers to the northwest, Sakura wiped perspiration from Akio's forehead as he sucked in labored breaths, frail and nauseated from the lengthy train ride back to Hiroshima. At the end of the dreary underground corridor connecting the north and south stations, they stopped to rest near the stairs leading outside to where Watanabe-*san* agreed to meet them. The hospital's treatments had drained the remnant of her husband's energy, and she looked forward to returning home, where she hoped he would regain his strength. He sat on their small suitcase, removed his hat, and squeezed her hand when she rested it on his shoulder to comfort him. Her eyes wandered to the bottom of the long staircase, the upper stairs concealed behind a water stained concrete wall.

A sinister bluish-white light flashed and sizzled down the stairs.

• • •

West of the train station and northwest of the factory, Watanabe-*san* returned to his reliable pickup truck parked a few blocks from Hon Dori, after completing a purchase at the hardware store. He checked his wristwatch to make sure he wouldn't be late meeting Akio and Sakura's train. He had missed conversing with his old friend about politics and the war during Akio's hospitalization and hoped the treatments might cure Akio's cancer. The hands on his watch read almost a quarter past eight. He must hurry.

Watanabe-*san's* step was brisk and easy. He whistled a favorite tune, delighted at his good fortune because he had waved to Emi that morning as she drove the tram northwest toward Yokogawa Station. She had changed from her usual route between Hiroden and Ujina, and he marveled at the notion of girls working as tram conductors and wondered what might be next.

Along with the entire city, he felt relief. The planes that flew over earlier hadn't unleashed any bombs. They had spared Hiroshima once more. He passed a noodle shop where the owner carried early morning deliveries to the inside, a bank where a stream of employees arrived for work, and a stationery store where a young woman was displaying exquisite fountain pens and paper as smooth as silk in its window.

A garish and soundless flash radiated high above him. The air flickered with the electricity of a light bulb about to explode.

WHITE ASHES

August 6, 1945 – Hiroshima, Japan

"For every action there is a reaction."
—*Sir Isaac Newton*

Curls of gentle sea breezes lifted a ginkgo leaf from its nourishing umbilical cord. The fragile leaf spiraled through the radiant sky, tumbled about, and rested far from its roots and siblings in a dazzling sunflower patch. All of nature and the denizens of Hiroshima were oblivious to the danger above and the reversal of fate that would unfold.

At exactly forty-three seconds, deep inside Little Boy, an ignition launched a chain reaction that released the powerful energy of immeasurable small spinning atoms. The world's first atomic bomb announced its birth one block east of its target, six hundred meters above the elegant copper dome of Hiroshima's bustling Prefectural Industrial Promotion Hall, with a sky-piercing, blinding flash of light, streaking above Hiroshima's exquisite sea, rippling rivers, mountains, and neighborhoods teeming with humanity.

Little Boy exploded. His superheated center—a bubble of extreme air pressure—freed a supercritical mass outward at over 1,400 kilometers per hour. Lethal invisible radiation released in the form of gamma and neutron rays. Shock waves of energy roared at twice the force of gravity, collapsing buildings and reducing steel to shrapnel.

Little Boy's transcendent fireball consumed the sky, and searing heat—hot as the sun's surface—built under the blast. A massive chimney of smoke and gases stalked upward, forming a spectacular cloud eleven kilometers high against the cloudless sky.

Within two kilometers of the blast's radius, Hiroshima was demolished. Seventy thousand people died instantly or were charred to death beyond recognition from severe thermal burns. Those closest to the blast carbonized and vanished, leaving behind atomic human shadows, imprinted on concrete rubble in perpetuity. Survivors within a four-kilometer radius of the blast suffered horrendous injuries. Naked, scalded, blinded, and delirious, they staggered to rivers clogged with corpses. The waters beckoned—a tantalizing escape from the fires igniting and surrounding them in every direction.

A blazing inferno sucked in ground air, generating intense vortexes of wind and fire. Tiny carbon particles, born by the gutting fires, swirled aloft where they reached cooler air and morphed into a violent dance of thunderous inky clouds. Sticky black raindrops fell in torrents over the land. People suffering from desperate thirst opened their mouths to the heavens and drank the deadly droplets—gifts of radioactive poison.

Death rained on the once-graceful city of Hiroshima—its train station where Sakura and Akio had arrived, its shopping district where Watanabe-san whistled, and its rifle factories where Koji and Naoki labored. The ginkgo leaf perished alongside the scorched and blackened sunflowers. Tens of thousands of innocent souls enjoying radiant health in the sunlit warmth of the early morning, departed life on earth. Only their white ashes remained.

ONE WITH THE LIGHT

August 6, 1945 – Hiroshima, Japan

Within seconds of witnessing the flash, Watanabe-*san's* boiling internal organs evaporated. Incinerated and vaporized, he became one with the brilliant light and one with the universe. His body, clothing, bag of screws to fix his tractor, and work boots vanished.

BILLOWING SAVAGERY

August 6, 1945 – Hiroshima, Japan

Amid the rubble and in total darkness, Koji lay unconscious. His head throbbed as he came to, blinking his eyes to force the blur of his surroundings into focus. Jagged and precarious trusses hung above him.

The gaping roof was like a camera's viewfinder, framing a massive cloud engulfing the sky. He must be dreaming. The cloud was a soaring column of vapor, widening as it rose, as though belched by a violent volcano and congealing to form an unusual top-heavy shape.

He faded in and out of consciousness.

How did it get cloudy so fast? The sky had been clear earlier—ideal for kite flying. When did he last hold a kite string on a breezy day and release it to soar into the heights of Hiroshima's picturesque mountains? Kite flying on Boy's Day seemed long ago.

A memory came. He was at a harvest festival and his father was attaching a stalk of rice to a kite, offering thanks for a strong crop. *Otōsan* had painted a bright carp on the *washi* paper skin. Carp swam upstream, against the current, to lay eggs, symbolizing bravery and strength. It seemed all species struggle in their own way. In the high-spirited gales of his imagination, the kite sailed across the sky, twirled over the wind, and carried him to adventures in foreign lands.

The unmistakable metallic taste of blood married with his saliva and slid down his throat. He struggled against the weight of fallen timbers, metal roof fragments, and collapsed shelving. Buried, his left arm ached, and he couldn't feel his fingers. He panicked at the thought they had been severed. Blood oozed from embedded shards of glass and splinters in his right hand. His eyes darted around the workshop. A bucket turned upside-down. A door hung askew by one hinge. Piles of papers and files scattered in the dirt, no longer important. The window where he had been standing was blown out. The table where he had been sorting metal components lay propped on its side. Rifle components were scattered everywhere.

Koji found his voice. "Is anybody there?"

Hammering inside of his head replied.

A feeble voice. "My leg." More frantic. "My leg!"

A booming voice. "FIRE!"

A cry. "I can't move!"

An authoritative voice. "He's over here!"

A lone groan of despair.

Screams of pain.

Smoke burned his eyes and throat. The room spun, revealing a smoky coruscating kaleidoscope of spots of all sizes. He closed his eyes. The spinning worsened.

Single voices expanded to the chaotic sounds of many.

Koji wrestled to break free of the debris trapping his upper body. Pushing beyond the pain, he shoved aside a fallen timber with his free arm, now a pincushion of sharp fragments. He kicked away a chair, a ladder, and building fragments. His torso was still pinned. Across the room, someone knocked the door off its hinge and onto the floor. Toma. Blood trickled down Toma's panic-stricken face. Otherwise, he appeared unharmed. He rushed to Koji's side.

Koji's voice quivered. "What happened?"

"Mega-bomb. And there's this crazy cloud. It's a disaster. Nothing but destroyed or damaged buildings for as far as I can see. Let's get out of here."

Toma ripped off his shirt sleeve and wrapped it around Koji's bleeding forehead. When Koji raised his uninjured hand to hold the bandage in place, he felt a massive bump.

Toma's eyes moved down Koji's legs where a glass shard and an enormous wooden splinter protruded from his pants leg. He didn't ask permission before yanking them out, and he seemed to take no notice of Koji's cries of pain.

Desperate to find his brother, who he had last seen unloading a new shipment of gunstock blanks in the woodworking shop, Koji brushed away Toma's attempts to tend his wounds. "I have to find Naoki. Do you know what happened to the woodworking shop?"

Toma shook his head, helped Koji to his feet, and then left to find his own family.

Koji stumbled amid the debris to the woodworking shop, passing other men—dazed, injured, or deceased. He found the shop demolished with no sign of activity. Entire sections of wall had collapsed into a tenuous maze of angles, supported by boards zigging and zagging.

"Naoki! Naoki! Where are you?... Naoki!"

He moved to the machine shop where heavy machinery and parts had fallen on top of the workers who lay contorted, bleeding, and unmoving. Dregs from chemical barrels puddled and seeped into the dust and debris. The man whose job it was to imprint the royal chrysanthemum lay in a pool of blood with a finished rifle beside him.

Koji stared where an exterior wall once stood at the neighboring building engulfed in fire. The smoke and flames blew toward him. Other nearby buildings were flattened or destroyed. Survivors limped through openings in the rubble and dug through the shambles, no doubt looking for workmates buried in the remains of the once-vibrant industrial center.

He crawled outside through the opening. Across the river, the soldiers who had saluted and marched earlier that morning, weaved in and out of the smoke-filled air, carrying the injured on stretchers made by crisscrossing their arms together. Others ran aimlessly, like the rats living under the factory's rotting pallets. The scene was a life-sized diorama. A frenzied, terrorized squadron in the foreground. The backdrop, a city in flames where terror was left to the wildest of imaginations.

From what he could see, the entire city was ablaze under the darkening shadow of the towering cloud, swirling mysteriously kilometers above. He couldn't believe his eyes—it seemed all of Hiroshima was obliterated. He squeezed his eyes shut and repeated to himself this couldn't be happening, couldn't be real. When he opened his eyes, hot tears raced down his cheeks. When had he started crying?

Feeling faint, he hobbled back inside the factory to search for Naoki. With the aid of other survivors, he freed several boys with minor injuries, who then freed others. Most workers were beyond help. A boy lay lifeless, his head severed by corrugated metal that had transformed into a guillotine. Heavy machinery pinned a *sensei* against a wall. The conveyor system crushed assemblers to their death where they had stood working. An older man lay in a puddle of his blood, still spurting. None were Naoki.

A *sensei* ordered everyone to seek shelter out of the city. Koji ignored the order and continued searching for his brother. He stumbled into his manager's office. File cabinets, crates, and beams buried the man's desk, and maybe the man himself. When he came face to face with the *sensei* who had ordered him to leave, the *sensei* grabbed and pulled him to an exterior opening and screamed, "Go home, or away from the city! Now!"

END OF THE LINE

August 6, 1945 – Hiroshima, Japan

Within the bowels of Hiroshima Station, Sakura's voice trembled, "Akio, that flash. What... was that?"

"I don't know." He took her hand, clutched their suitcase, and rushed her away from the stairwell. The earth shook, and they heard a loud explosion, followed by a shocking roar. The ground heaved, jolting them off their feet and onto the filthy floor where thousands of dirty shoes had walked. Screams echoed down the stairway toward where they cowered with several dozen others. Noxious hot fumes followed. Paralyzed with fear, everyone in the tunnel was still. There had been no sirens, no airplanes roaring, and no unmistakable bombs dropping. No one spoke.

After many long minutes, people started up the stairs to the outside.

Akio patted her hand. "It's okay. We'll wait here for another minute and see if they come back."

The people did not return.

Sakura swallowed a deep breath, mustering her courage and strength. "Wait here. I'll go see what's happening. Things must be okay because those people haven't come back down."

She covered her nose and mouth. Sweat poured down her face as she ascended the concrete steps. Her urge to turn back strengthened its grip on her as the heat of the air intensified with every step. Dizzy, she stopped halfway for a brief moment. Her entire body was trembling when she reached the top and faced west. Their bustling city had transformed into a vast wasteland of rubble and fire. People were sprawled everywhere—wailing, injured, dying. Dead. A weak and polite voice called, "Help me. Please help me." A toddler cried over her mother, lying on the ground, puddled in blood. Sakura looked skyward to a tsunami of enormous clouds, stormy and dark in the center, whitening toward the edges.

She looked at the station's damaged facade. Its wide filigree awning had collapsed. Bloody human extremities protruded from under the awning's edges—a young child's arm, a woman's delicate palm, a man's trousered leg, his shoe missing.

Silent tears, long stifled during years of hardship, spilled down her cheeks. She bent over at the intense urge to vomit. Droplets of grief pooled in dark circles from her wet lashes.

Fumes burned her throat and lungs and irritated her eyes. Now, flames raged from within the gaping holes of the station's upper windows.

Fire! The station is on fire! I must get Akio!

INFERNO

August 6, 1945 – Hiroshima, Japan

Koji staggered to the riverbank and lifted his gaze to the horizon. How could he leave without Naoki? Across the river, flames rose and stretched in every direction, devouring the city and fueling a vicious northward blowing firestorm. The hills of Hiji Park and the Enko River buffered him from being swallowed into the urban furnace. Below, a child stood alone, surrounded by others drinking from the river, lifeless, or jumping into the river to extinguish flames burning the life out of them. He stared at the river where dozens of naked adults and children lay lifeless, drifting on wood fragments. Koji recognized the tattered hat of the old man who had limped along the shoreline earlier. The man lay under a shattered crate of rifles, his crooked fingers in the dirt. Blood trickled from his mouth. The *wasen* Koji had seen earlier was now drifting wreckage. A lone fisherman's boat was upside down, its captain missing. The distant barge was closer, a bed for the injured and dying. People floated on debris. The carcass of a dog floated by.

Unable to imagine their pain, he wobbled away from the factory and joined other survivors headed north along the riverbank. Had Watanabe-san picked up his parents before the explosion? Were they safe or lying in Hiroshima Station—injured, bleeding, dying? He needed to find them. In the destruction, he passed stunned and defeated people, many slumped and standing around glassy-eyed, detached from reality, and others struck down unconscious or dead. He passed a woman—her face singed red and swollen—looking straight ahead as she carried her infant, its tiny head marbled purple and slumped over the crook of her arm. The nightmare worsened the farther north he traveled. He tripped over dead bodies and cringed at the bloody and burned who shuffled in mindless disarray.

At the bridge where the Enko River divided, he faced Hiroshima Station. Below, the river was choked with floating corpses. Coughing, he crossed the span toward the station and blazing city, and plowed forward against masses of scorched and maimed people stumbling away from the fires. Somehow, the painful images blocked the pain of his own injuries.

Sounds of misery—terror-stricken screams, pitiful moans, and pleas for help—assaulted him. Now and then he thought he heard his name being called. He told himself it was his imagination. The shouts built to a crescendo. "Koji. Koji! KOJI!"

In the distance, an apparition of his brother appeared through the dense smoke.

At first, the blurry body looked like it was covered in wooly tufts. The body faded. A ghost, he feared. But then the body reappeared. Naoki. Covered in ash, his clothing ripped, his shattered eyeglasses clung to his nose.

"Naoki!" Koji raced to his brother, clutching and squeezing his bony shoulders and then rubbing his arms to make sure he was real. Amid the chaos, Naoki's head cradled against the quiet strength of Koji's chest, yielding to its safety. Tears of relief welled under Koji's eyelids.

Naoki's breath came and went in gasps. His sobs quieted. "Koji... your head. Are you okay?"

"I think so. You?"

Naoki nodded. He pointed to the sky. "What is that... thing?"

Koji stared at the sky, now congested with smoke, for a prolonged moment. "I don't know," he said, making no effort to wipe the tears streaming on this face. "Where were you? I looked everywhere!"

"*Sensei* sent me to Minami Ward to pick up a part. I was inside a building there when we heard a terrifying roar. The concrete building didn't collapse like all the others." Naoki seemed to struggle for breath, as if he lacked the strength to talk. "Koji, people screamed for help from within collapsed buildings, but there were too many people and too many buildings for me to help. I'm so ashamed. Their screams followed me all the way to the station. I had go there and look for *Okāsan* and *Otōsan*. I never found them. Parts of the station and all of its windows blew out. What's left is on fire."

"That's where I'm headed."

Naoki's breathing was labored. "People are running... escaping the flames... begging for water. Burns are bad... skin hanging from their bones... falling dead in layers on the streets and sidewalks... I had to step over them!"

Now, sobbing muffled his voice. "It's too late. The train station is an inferno."

Koji swallowed the parched air, unable to speak. Unable to fathom.

He looked toward their home, hoping Watanabe-*san* had taken his parents there. He grabbed Naoki's arm. "Let's go. It's not safe here."

They turned east and began the two-kilometer walk, through the gruesome landscape that could never be unseen, toward what they hoped was still home.

SHAMBLES

August 6, 1945 – Hiroshima, Japan

Sakura ran down the station stairs to her husband. Speechless, she held Akio's arm and guided him up the staircase as he peppered her with questions. "Sakura, what's wrong? What's happened?" She couldn't find the words to answer.

At the landing, Akio clamped a hand over his mouth as his unsettled gaze wandered over the devastation. Everything, absolutely everything, was gone. For as far as they could see, all of Hiroshima—leveled, ablaze, and in chaos. Directionless and struggling people moved with the crowds. She followed his upward gaze to the turbulent sky where undulating clouds and soot had formed a colossal cloud in the shape of a mushroom.

Incapable of imagining what force had caused such horror, Sakura squeezed her eyes. "This isn't real. This can't be real." But when her eyes opened, the fire escaping the station's windows must have caught the wind, creating an inferno.

A commanding voice within told her to take her sick husband home. She grasped Akio's hand. "We must go."

They began the three-kilometer journey home to Fuchu, passing building after building demolished beyond any point of recognition. Those remaining stood with an odd tilt, akin to a man in disbelief and utter confusion cocking his head. In the hallowed grounds of a temple cemetery, tombstones lay scattered every which way, among the newly dead and dying. A man entered the graveyard, felt the pulse of a small boy, and crumpled on top of him.

Beyond the cemetery, Sakura and Akio stopped to rest, turned to face the obliterated city, and witnessed the terrifying fires merge into a massive firestorm. The air had become a sooty smoldering mass of swirling ashes. Sakura removed her scarf and tied it around Akio's nose and mouth to protect his vulnerable airways. She closed her eyes. *Namu Amida Butsu, help me undo the act of seeing what I've seen. May my eyes reopen to beauty and light.*

Akio took her elbow, and they joined the masses wearing vacant expressions and wended their way past once-lush trees, now jagged branches akimbo, stripped of foliage. They stepped around people bleeding through rags that wrapped their injuries, people crawling, people dying.

Smoke pouring into Fuchu's lush hills followed them, obscuring and graying the area's former greenness. They passed crumbled buildings beside those still standing. Almost home, they passed the Watanabe barn and farmhouse, both in shambles. They stopped for a brief rest to catch their breath and tried to make sense of a changed world where nothing was as it should be. Bone weary, they trudged up the last hill to their property. The gate hung crooked before the intact house. The shed leaned lopsided. They stumbled across the yard and up the stairs and opened the door to the precious gift of voices.

Koji and Naoki were home.

Inside their sanctuary, the Matsuo family collapsed in a huddle, much like a tulip folding its petals after the sun sets to conserve energy for the next day.

HAVEN

August 6, 1945 – Hiroshima, Japan

Koji stood on a hillside overlooking the firestorms consuming his city, fewer than three kilometers away, his throat and eyes burning from the intense smoke.

Across the street at his house, relatives, neighbors, and helpless strangers trickled in. By mid-afternoon, a dozen people lay on the *engawa* or in their living room injured and burned, some taking their last breaths. All were homeless and thirsty. Koji's mother frantically offered water and cleaned and dressed wounds. She instructed him and Naoki to fetch blankets and countless jugs of water from the well, as the kitchen faucet couldn't keep up with the demand. Koji also kept an eye on the stove, where bandages made from torn sheets boiled on every burner.

Despite his mother's limited first-aid experience and supplies, her effort was tireless, and Koji did his best to help her. His debilitated father rested in the privacy of his bedroom, somehow enduring the anguished sounds of suffering and the reek of burnt human flesh permeating their home.

A soot-encrusted toddler, his face wrapped in cloth torn from his mother's dress, was the first to die. Blistered and struggling to breathe, the child's mother wept over the tiny body. His mother called for him. "Carry the child to the Take Shrine. If no minister is present, leave him. Someone will know what to do."

Koji cradled the lifeless boy in his arms and carried him beyond the stone *torii* and up the seventy steps to the temple. The grounds and building stood unharmed and empty. Quiet but for the gentle tinkling of chimes. With tenderness, he laid the boy's small body at the base of a bronze statue of a stallion, regal and majestic. He believed the statue would protect the boy from harm until cremation. On his knees, he pressed together the palms of his hands over the nameless child. "*Namu Amida Butsu, Om Amideva Hrih.*" He stood and walked away, leaving the child in Buddha's grace.

Koji approached the temple's outdoor basin, dipped a wooden ladle into the remaining few centimeters of water, and rinsed his hands, wanting to erase the stench of death. But it would be impossible to erase from his mind the horrendous things he had witnessed. Fire, raging in the distance, beckoned him to the top of the steps. Vicious, undulating flames rolled, roared, and reached into the sky in vibrant colors of autumn. Gray plumes of smoke billowed into and darkened the sky. The invincible conflagration had swallowed the city below.

He heard a high-pitched scream escape from deep within someone's belly. When Koji realized the scream was his, he was seated on the top step of the long stairway with his head in his hands. He didn't remember sitting. Nor did he understand why his family was spared when so many had perished.

By the time he returned home, the boy's mother was dead, lying with one hand over the other on her chest, as if to protect her heart. Her slender fingers formed a delicate fan under her chin. With Naoki's help, he repeated his climb up the stairs, reuniting mother and son.

Refugees continued arriving at their home. They shared stories of the nightmarish morning—the brilliant flash and ferocious boom, unquenchable fires, raindrops like black gasoline, fierce winds. They told of survivors—many naked or clothed in shreds—who had swarmed to the rivers, leaned over, and fallen off the warped bridges into the water below where the living clung to life among the dead floating out with the tide. They spoke of trams hurled from their tracks and roads blocked by collapsed buildings. Of a man, walking like a ghost, his melted skin hanging. Of people crushed, buried alive. Of wristwatches no longer ticking.

Someone reported they'd seen a naval ship. A crew member had shouted help was coming. But when? And how? The men who were able scavenged for information and supplies and devised plans for identifying and gathering the dead, dragging timber from collapsed houses to fuel cremation fires. With no medicine, organized aid, or basic community structure, the ill-equipped and devastated fought to survive. Without electricity, open news channels, or reliable access to information, rumor and imagination fueled theories. Many concluded the United States had dropped hundreds of incendiary bomb clusters. What else could it have been? But no one had heard enemy planes *or* bombs.

Neighborhood women who had somehow escaped harm helped his mother nurse the growing number of critically injured, transforming their home into a makeshift hospital. Nearby houses, of simple wood construction, had fallen to pieces. Some burst into flames when active cooktops or live wires sparked dry timber. Other houses remained, leaning at precarious angles. Most whose houses were still standing tried to help others, but some closed their shades and locked their doors to keep outsiders *out*.

Koji listened to women gossip over such selfishness.

"What person shuts out the needy?"

"Shameful."

"Karma will inflict revenge."

Hearing their comments, he felt immense pride for his compassionate mother who treated each uninvited houseguest with much deserved care, dignity, and respect.

• • •

At sunset, an unrecognizable girl with hideous burns arrived in a wheelbarrow. Melted skin slipped from her fingers as they lowered her to the *tatami* floor. Sakura tended to the girl at once and applied cooking-oil-soaked rags to the girl's injuries. A tortured voice—faint and familiar—whispered, "Thank y... Matsuo-*san*... Koji?"

Sakura's heart broke as she recognized Emi's soft lilt that had once filled her house with light and laughter.

• • •

Koji didn't hear his mother slide the *shōji* open. He was tending to his father who had spent hours vomiting into a tin bucket beside his bedroll.

"Koji," she whispered.

He looked at *Okāsan*, her eyes wet with tears and her shoulders bowed from exhaustion. Without the door jamb supporting her fragile body, she would have collapsed.

"Emi is here." Her body shivered slightly as if it were winter and not a hot August day. "Son, her injuries are serious."

A wisp of hair hung in front of her eyes. She tucked it behind an ear. "I'm so sorry."

He jumped to his feet.

"Koji, she won't make it. Sit with her, talk to her, soothe your friend's fears. *You* are her family today."

His mother took his hand and guided him to Emi who lay silently suffering in the corner. He lowered himself to the floor next to his dear *kenzoku*, the family he had chosen for himself. Hot tears spilled down his cheeks and over his quivering lips.

"Emi, I'm here. I won't leave you, I promise."

Every inch of her body was burned. He didn't know where to touch without causing her more pain. "Remember shopping on Hon Dori, eating *yaki imo,* and watching dragonflies dance? This war—this thief—steals us from each other."

Her eyes opened to him, ever so slowly, like the lifting of a heavy theatre curtain before the final act. "Don't fuss. Hold me, Ko.."

He slid an arm under her neck, cradled her head in his arms, and gently rocked her. "I love you, Emi. You're so beautiful. I'll always love you."

He strained to hear the tiny hush of her labored cry, "I lo... It's okay... Ko... "

Her light extinguished.

An hour passed. He didn't move. He could no more distance himself from her than from the impossible grief imprisoning his body. When a helpful stranger attempted to remove her, Koji pushed him and screamed, "Get off! She's my friend! I'll take care of her!"

Okāsan shooed the man and embraced Koji, "I'm sorry, Koji. You're much too young for death to scar you this way."

He remained in his mother's embrace until his knees no longer buckled under him. Then he picked up his dear friend, carried her limp body out the door, and up the seventy steps where an open-air cremation fire was now burning. *Okāsan* was right. Someone knew what to do. A stranger helped him place Emi into the blazing funeral pyre.

Koji offered a deep bow, and the flames engulfed his sweet friend.

The coppery effluvia of Emi's burning flesh melded with the smoky air from untold fires lighting the darkness, as people mourned and cremated strangers and loved ones together into a bed of ash.

FISSION

August 1945 – Tule Lake, CA

Ruby experienced everything in slow motion during the summer months, finding it difficult to understand how the world kept spinning when it felt to her as if it had stopped. She was slow to fall asleep, slow to open her eyes at dawn, slow to adjust to the morning light. She slept too much. She slept too little. She never felt rested.

She tried to imagine life in a foreign culture—speaking Japanese, eating Japanese food, and practicing Japanese customs. The future she had envisioned slipped further and further away. She would not attend an American university, or vote in an American election, or marry an American man, or raise American children. Emptiness and fatigue had set her adrift, like an unmoored boat on a stagnant lagoon.

Only school motivated her to get out of bed in the morning. She spent most days studying, attending temple service, or canoodling with Albert. Except for no longer permitting him to suck on her neck, she gave her body willingly and allowed him a single or a double on her bases. Within, she felt numb and empty.

Now, on her bed reading, her mind wandered to where Albert's hands had wandered the night before. Strange how she hadn't noticed his hands brushing close to her vestibule until she returned to herself and felt his fingers slip inside of her panties. Poor Albert. She hoped she hadn't hurt him too badly.

Her father was at the table writing another sermon that might never be delivered. Outside, she heard people talking excitedly in loud voices.

Something was amiss.

She jumped off of her bunk and went outside with her father.

Hundreds of people had swarmed from their barracks, like termites surging from dark crevices and into fresh air for the first time. Some covered their faces with both hands. Some with clouded gazes searched the crowd—maybe for other people, maybe for clarity. Some fell to their knees. Some screamed, "It can't be." Some talked in hushed fragments, or not at all. "Unthinkable." "How can Japan hold on?" Some wept. Others wailed. "My family is there!"

She followed behind her father who stopped to speak to a friend. Words, sentence fragments, and questions jumbled in her mind as she stared into the crowd.

"What is it?" Father asked the man.

"Hiroshima. Bombed. Destroyed."

Her father's shoulders seemed to shrink into his body. She looked to him for answers. He had none.

• • •

Headlines screamed from newsprint in the days that followed.

NEW BOMB BLASTS JAPAN!

FOUR SQUARE MILES OF HIROSHIMA DESTROYED BY A SINGLE ATOM BOMB.

ATOMIC ENERGY UNLEASED!

An eerie silence engulfed the camp as people digested the unimaginable. Ruby read a printed transcript of President Truman's address.

"A short-time ago an American airplane dropped one bomb on Hiroshima and destroyed its usefulness to the enemy. That bomb had more power than 20,000 tons of TNT. The Japanese began the war at Pearl Harbor. They have been repaid many-fold. And the end is not yet. It is an atomic bomb. It is a harnessing of the basic power of the universe. The force from which the sun draws its power has been loosed against those who brought war. This bomb added a new and revolutionary increase in destruction to supplement the growing

power of our armed forces. These bombs are now in production and even more powerful forms are in development. This is the greatest achievement of organized science in history. It was to spare the Japanese people from utter destruction. If they do not now accept our terms they may expect a rain of ruin from the air the like of which has never been seen on this earth."

Everything had changed so fast and yet seemed to unfold in slow motion. Ruby felt like a dried sea sponge thrown into a wave, crashing and bobbing directionless on the surface. She absorbed the loss of a family she had never known and her father's grief. She absorbed the loss of her faith in America's honor and how wrong she had been to argue faith in America to her classmates—the United States was indeed capable of unthinkable acts. And she absorbed the certain conclusion of war and the uncertainty of her future. Overflowing and incapable of absorbing more, the sponge descended home to the ocean floor.

PASSAGEWAYS

August 1945 – Hiroshima, Japan

Constructed of elm with iron rivets, the weathered sliding doors of Koji's house creaked as they opened and closed on rotting wooden wheels. The constant movement of the doors reminded him of the elegant brass-framed revolving doors at Fukuya Department Store, whooshing thousands of customers through and into its elegant interior. People had hustled in and bustled out all day in search of beauty products, *mochi* confections filled with sweetened red bean paste, infant layettes, and essentials and extravagances.

Koji had lost track of the number of people who had entered and exited their home in the past twenty-four hours. Some left as immortal souls passing over the doorsill beyond death's doors, leaving this life for the next. Others remained, having escaped Hiroshima's hopeless ruin to find hospice. Few left under their own power. And not a single one had whooshed and bustled among beauty.

As he removed another batch of sterile bandages from a pot of boiling water and dumped the water in the kitchen sink, he wondered if Fukuya was still standing amid the rubble. The incessant creaking of the door opening and closing grated his already frazzled nerves. Unlike the shoppers in Fukuya, the guests in his home weren't able to purchase what they needed for any amount of money. Money couldn't regenerate their burned skin. Money couldn't straighten their twisted limbs. Money couldn't return their loved ones from the dead. The vulnerable who crossed the threshold into his home had found a soft and secure landing to die, like sick and injured animals found safety in the brush.

Under the neckerchief tied over his nose and mouth, he held his breath against the smells of death lingering in the trapped humid air. The faucet dripped. He hung the bandages to dry from a clothesline draped across the kitchen.

Drip.

He set a fresh pot on the stove.

Drip... Drip.

Impatient, he stared at the water, as more water dripped behind him, and watched for bubbles. *Why did it take so long for water to boil when watching?*

Drip... Drip. Each ping of water struck the center of the tender nervous system restraining his suppressed torment.

Drip... Drip... Drip.

He tore off the neckerchief, left the now boiling water and dripping faucet behind, bolted out of the kitchen, jumped over an obstacle course of mutilated and incapacitated bodies, pushed the door open to the outside, and ran fast and far until he collapsed face down on the dirt road.

No one came by. No one saw him. No one cared. Everyone was cocooned within their own grief. Sprawled in the dirt like road kill, he inhaled heavy breaths of dust, and wished for an enormous truck to run him over and end his misery. Minutes dragged. The truck never came, and he couldn't imagine where it would come from, anyway.

Finally, he yielded to his impotence, spat out dirt, and trudged back to the house. Incapable of returning to his responsibilities, he sought the solitude and darkness of the root cellar and flung himself on the earthen floor. The sweet memory of Emi's jasmine perfume somehow replaced the root cellar's mustiness as he breathed in memories. He recalled moments playing hide-and-seek through the bamboo grove, picnicking on the hills of Hiji Park, and brushing crumbs off of her delicately pointed chin after lunch. Words from their private talks filled his mind. They had revealed their future hopes—his to graduate from college and work in diplomacy, hers to finish school and raise a family of strong, independent daughters who believed they could accomplish anything in life a man could attain.

They had teased each other, told jokes, and talked about what they ate for dinner. He loved her mind and sense of humor. He loved her confidence and that she drove trams. He loved most that he could be himself with her.

Koji had forgotten their last conversation, yet he would never forget her gruesome death. His kneecaps crushed against his broken heart. She was gone, and yesterday's attack forever changed his future. He filled the root cellar with heart-wrenching wails demanding to understand. To know *why?*

The door opened to a faint stream of light. His mother entered, sat beside him and pulled his head into her bosom. He stammered, "Why her?"

Running her fingers through his hair, saturated with perspiration, his mother offered what few words of comfort she seemed able to muster. "Nothing makes sense in times of war. Her death, this nightmare... senseless. We must trust the universe."

She rocked him in her arms. "Koji... exhale the nightmare."

Finding solace in *Okāsan's* arms, he quieted.

But he knew. Beyond the door and in the broad daylight, the nightmare continued.

• • •

As one finds it impossible to look away from a train wreck, Koji felt obligated to see the full extent of this tragedy for himself. Days after the bombing, he volunteered to walk into the city. After much debate, his parents permitted him to go. They, too, were desperate for supplies and starved for information about the powerful blast, relief efforts, and availability of food. Too nervous to eat, he left his uneaten breakfast in his bowl, shoved a snack in his pocket, and said goodbye to his parents.

He stopped to pet the family donkey braying at a fence. "Hey, boy," he said, rubbing the donkey's soft and pointed ears.

The donkey nudged with his nose.

He scratched the donkey's head. "To you, everything is normal, isn't it?"

Leaving the donkey behind, Koji stepped into Fuchu's green foliage, which soon gave way to the lifeless terrain of Hiroshima's outskirts. Where leafy trees once stood, burnt sticks jutted from the ground. Remnants of collapsed and burned houses replaced the wood-frame homes nestled along the hillside. Ahead of him, a steady stream of refugees swarmed from the city. Wearing shreds and tormented expressions, parents herded small children, teenagers helped grandparents, and lone persons wandered aimlessly forward. He assumed they had lost everything and hoped they found comfort somewhere. Koji was one of few people walking toward the city.

A man approached, pushing his expressionless wife and child in a wagon. The woman's upper body nakedness revealed deep red burns across her chest and arms. The child's face hid under gauze bandages.

Noticing a *zōri* fall from the child's foot and disappear under the wagon, he approached the family. "*Sumimasen*, wait. Pardon my interruption, but your child's sandal." He picked up the *zōri* and placed it back on the child's muddy foot.

"*Arigatō gozaimasu*," the man said, expressing thanks for his kindness. I don't know where you're going, young man, but turn back." He glanced over his shoulder. "There's nothing there but death and despair."

Koji acknowledged the man's warning with a nod and turned to leave. Steps later, he tripped in the rubble trying to avoid smacking into a small boy and his father. Their clothing was torn and filthy, and their faces lacerated and smudged with black soot and dirt. The toddler held an uneaten rice ball in his dirty hands, his fingers digging into it with unconscious regard. Koji continued on and stumbled upon a relief center in Higashi Ward, where he found a volunteer collecting information on survivors and distributing rice balls. Other than limited supplies of gauze, saline, and Mercurochrome, the center offered no medical supplies. He declined a rice ball when offered, leaving it for another who needed it more than he did, and filled his pockets with what little else was offered, registered his household for rations, and provided the names of their houseguests who had been well enough to speak.

He overheard a robust conversation between men hypothesizing about the mystery bomb. Or was it a bomb? A scrawny old man in a tattered kimono argued, "The Americans sprayed magnesium powder all over Hiroshima and then lit the explosion."

A younger man argued, "You're wrong. A bomb burst in the air to inflict mass genocide with murderous force. I'm right, you'll see."

But for their energetic sparring, a miasma of despair hung over the relief center.

Koji left the center. He wandered past crushed houses, leveled storefronts, a sea of blistered roof tiles swept away by the blast, and stopped to pick up a discolored, broken roof tile. Normal red clay tile felt smooth. These tiles felt rough to the touch. Fragments lay scattered everywhere, grayed with burns.

He forced himself to keep moving against the flow of people fleeing the city. Grief-stricken parents, carrying their dead children, came his way. He didn't want to stare, but it wasn't possible to look away. The pit of his gut tightened as he stepped into what seemed to be a realm of torment, incineration, and destruction. Hell.

He rounded an area where a street corner used to be, walking toward the Enko River and Hiroshima Station, and peeked inside a destroyed *sushi* restaurant. Once popular with commuters, it was now ghostly. The blast had blown out the entrance door and windows, and destroyed the entire interior, although the metal stools remained bolted to the floor.

Before rationing, patrons would have occupied the stools, shoving the delicious balls of vinegar-flavored rice, topped with thin slices of fresh fish, into their mouths. Customers would never sit at those stools again. Outside of the restaurant, smoke from open-air crematoriums polluted the humid air. Open-bed trucks rumbled past, loaded with injured survivors, bound for unknown destinations.

Incredulity and shock hit him at Hiroshima Station, where the explosion had concussed the station's masonry walls and blew out the windows. He stared at the ruins his parents had escaped. "How on earth did *Okāsan* and *Otōsan* survive this?"

His words met with an unexpected response. "Hey, kid! Get out of here! It's not safe!"

He didn't need to be told twice.

Block after block, the heat from smoldering ruins penetrated the thick soles of his boots leading him toward Hiroshima Castle. The national treasure where lords and military leaders lived and worked had been obliterated, reduced to ash. Only the stone embankments of the castle's moat remained. Here, he had played *shogunate* warrior as a boy, and just days ago, this had been the pulse of southern Japan's military establishment. He realized the Army Logistics clerk he had duped might well be dead, along with all the high-ranking officers. The file of requisitions now ash.

Did any military leaders remain in charge? Who was in charge?

He passed under the upright pillars of the *torii* gate at the Shrine for the War Dead, sturdy and determined among crushed concrete, unidentifiable fragments, the tines of a gardener's rake, a pushcart. A vacant wilderness of twisted steel frames lay before him. Carbonized wooden utility poles no longer carried overhead power and telephone lines. In the distance, the few remaining masonry structures leaned awry as though pulled by a tremendous gravitational force.

Before him, lying prone among the splintered and harsh edged debris, lay the soft curvature of a naked human form. Unsure if the man was alive, he turned the body to discover his nose, mouth, and ears burned off—his features now suppurating, maggot-infested holes. Remorseful and revolted, he rolled the man over. He vomited, wiped his mouth with his sleeve, and walked farther into silence and isolation, stepping deliberately to avoid touching charred and contorted corpses scattering the debris field. In front of him, a decrepit old man stood staring into nothingness, as though detached from reality. With nothing to offer, Koji continued.

He gulped water from his canteen before attempting to cross the Aioi Bridge. Careful to avoid giant gaps in the lifted roadway, he hurdled a drainage pipe that had punctured the road. The parapets were bent outward on both sides of the bridge, and a sizeable chunk had impaled the riverbed below. He rushed to cross before the bridge collapsed, dumping him into the river's channel of death.

At the Prefectural Industry Promotion Hall, memories and displaced tombstone fragments—flung from an adjacent cemetery—stopped his feet from moving. Standing before the scorched stone-and-concrete facade, he looked through the curved front window openings at the five-story dome's ghostly skeleton and was baffled by the inconsistency of destruction. The building's perimeter walls remained, along with random interior masonry walls, supporting beams, and the frame of the dome. Everything else—windows, walls, floors, furniture, toilets, doors, and the employees who worked here—gone. The building's lifeless and dismal core, hollow. A warped metal spiral staircase led nowhere, except to the afterlife for all of the souls who had perished within these walls. He remembered visiting here with Emi and learning she loved music and musical instruments. Although she never learned to play an instrument, he hoped peaceful melodies serenaded her in rebirth, when she completed her transition to her next life. He moved on.

The Motoyasu River's once sapphire-green waters flowed muddied with death. Injured victims, incapable of moving and sprawled on the river's banks, appeared to watch the tugboats pull barges upriver. For a moment he squinted at the loaded barge decks, trying to see what they carried. He assumed supplies, but soon understood they carried bodies. Hundreds of bodies.

A wounded girl, lying on the ground beside a dead woman, groaned a pathetic beg. "Water, please water." He assumed the lifeless woman was her mother. The girl's injuries told him she wouldn't remain an orphan in this world for long, and he knew the paltry amount remaining in his canteen wouldn't save her, but knowing that did little to ease his shame. He distanced himself from the river and the girl's desperate pleas.

He breathed a sigh of relief when he neared the Red Cross Hospital, functioning despite the collapse of its southeastern wall and blown-out windows. His weary legs carried him past the injured, writhing in pain, many with their bones exposed. A woman crawled toward the hospital entrance. With no energy to continue, she collapsed in front of the building. Isolated in their suffering, others lay naked in urine and feces, dying for their Emperor. He imagined this was what hell looked like. Hiroshima was *naraku* on earth.

He shied away from their nakedness, but there was no escaping the putrid intensity invading his mouth and sickening his stomach. He watched two nurses assess injuries, determine the treatable from the untreatable, take pulses of the breathing, and cover the pulseless. The dead would be collected and burned. A hospital orderly wrote names on the bare skin of those capable of giving their names. He peeked inside where the injured lay next to one another, filling every gurney and meter of floor space. It seemed the medical protocol was the same for all—clean the wounds and apply tincture-soaked gauze.

Without thinking, he blurted, "Why is everyone here? Can't someone take these poor people to other hospitals?"

A weary nurse looked up from her patient. "*This* is the single remaining hospital in the city. *That's* why."

His face flushed with embarrassment.

He stepped outside and walked around the side of the hospital where human automatons cleared debris and carried the deceased to the wide clearing on the side of the hospital for cremation. An unkempt soldier kept a watchful eye on other soldiers and attendants responsible for the burning. They placed ashes in envelopes with the deceased person's name and filed them in a metal box. Koji's throat choked with sadness for the nameless, as their loved ones would never have ashes to honor. He bowed to honor the dead and the heroes handling this unfathomable duty and then borrowed a pen and wrote his name on his forearm.

His feet hurt. It was time to head home over the flattened plain where black, barren trees dotted the land, freakish amid the rubble. Shells of buildings, their outlines sharp and shadowed, stood in the foreground of the peaceful, distant mountains luring him home. He stumbled northeast through the city, wending through debris of twisted tram tracks, rusted drums, broken glass, and wires.

He tripped over a busted sewer pipe and fell into the filthy cavity of an open sewer. As he pulled himself out, something shiny caught his eye. He scavenged among the rubble and found a pocket watch. After scraping off the charred residue, he discovered the owner's family crest engraved on the back. The numbers were faint, but the time was unmistakable—8:15—the time of the blast when it seemed all clocks stopped running.

By the late afternoon, the sky darkened and large clouds moved toward him. He quickened his pace as rain began to drizzle, then pour as he arrived at the Bank of Japan. The new bank building was constructed of reinforced concrete, and although fire damaged, the building remained. Its windows were gone, and mysterious marks darkened the entrance pillars. He ran up the entry stairs, incredulous to find the bank transacting business. Exposed sky replaced the ornate glass roof. Bank employees held umbrellas against the rain as a surge of men and women withdrew money.

He overheard snippets of conversations.

"The basement vault is undamaged."

"Business resumed two days ago. We are fortunate this building survived. Only shells remain of Yasuda Fuji Bank, Sanwa Bank, and Mitsui Bank."

"Someone saw a human shadow imprinted on the stone steps of the Sumitomo Bank. How spooky—a ghost waiting for the bank to open."

A bank manager called for everyone's attention from the second-floor balcony overlooking the atrium. "It happened again! Another mega-bomb! This time on Nagasaki. They obliterated the city!" A gasp escaped the customers who stood in an orderly line, waiting for service with extraordinary patience. "And the Soviets invaded us in Manchuria, declaring war against Japan! Our Emperor says we must be strong and not let these events weaken our will to fight."

The people stared at each other in disbelief. An old lady covered her ears. A man beside Koji whispered, "Impossible."

The customers and employees murmured among themselves, but even in the midst of the unthinkable, not a person dared speak out loud against Japan or the Emperor. Koji wanted to scream. Needing out, he ran from the bank. The sky soon cleared and steam rose from the rubble. Discordant sounds ricocheted from the fallen walls of surrounding structures and assaulted his senses. Images of death. Erratic movements. Desperate to turn off the noise, he squatted with his hands over his head, now between his legs.

Nagasaki destroyed!

He raised his eyes to a man passing with a demarcation about five centimeters wide on the skin of his unclothed back. The line, a strip of pale skin, divided his back from the area burned raw. Koji realized the strip was where the man's shoulder-bag strap had been.

He looked away and toward the clocktower teetering above the tilted shell of Shimomura Watch and Jewelry store. The gigantic clock was gone. Hon Dori was reduced to rubble, the blast consigning its lovely lanterns to oblivion. An open-air cremation center operated where Fukuya Department Store once stood. The store's revolving door no longer revolved. People had entered, but never left. Only ashes with not a soul to claim them remained.

By the time he reached the west building of Fukuro-machi Elementary, his stomach was telling him that he was missing dinner. The school had survived and now operated as an improvised relief center. Survivors with ashen and dazed faces huddled in small groups outside together. Maybe they knew each other, maybe not. Many were barefoot. The lucky wore closed shoes or boots. Like everyone, they were filthy and wore tattered clothes. Women hid under torn pieces of cloth draped over their heads, likely concealing injuries to their once-lovely faces. An old man's suspenders supported his shredded pants and seemed to hold up his exhausted body.

Koji ventured inside, where desperate people scrawled chalk messages on the soot-covered walls of an open stairwell. A man announced his wife's passing and where their children could find him. A stranger posted a message for someone he had met. A teenage girl wrote her intentions to stay with a friend in the country. A boy told his mother, in childlike scrawl, he was with auntie. A woman, soot covering her exquisite features, said she would meet her lover in the grove of evergreen oaks. Koji wondered if the trees survived.

At dusk, he trudged into the Fuchu hills. In the lingering heat, he stopped and watched over the funeral pyres below, where children, mothers, fathers, spouses, or siblings burned at the hands of strangers. If he hadn't known better, he might have mistaken the flames as the joyful firelight of a festival. Instead, the fires dotted an annihilated landscape. He knelt and tried to digest the horror.

The lump in his throat and prickly sensation behind his closed eyes told him humankind had taken an irrevocable step. Out of respect, he stayed with the feeling for as long as he could and lost track of time.

When he opened his eyes, he met the blank stare of a small child, crouched beside him, eating weeds.

"What's your name?" he asked the boy. The child didn't answer, but approached him with a look of hunger. Koji removed the snacks from his pockets. On the hillside, overlooking all that kindled, raged, and smoldered, the boy gobbled down the dried bread and radishes and then drank the remaining sips in Koji's canteen.

He would take the boy home with him tonight and return to the Higashi and Fuchu-machi relief centers tomorrow to post the boy's whereabouts and register him with the authorities. This was the least he could do.

Koji stood and set his gaze on the sanctuary of home where he would tell his parents about today and then never speak of it again. For whatever reason, the universe had spared him and the boy. Facing the city on the darkening horizon, he bowed his deepest and humblest of bows to the destruction below.

He took the child by the hand and began walking home. The boy stumbled, trying to keep up with Koji's stride. Koji stopped and knelt before the boy.

He offered the boy a weak smile, "Piggy-back ride?"

The boy climbed onto his back.

The burden of carrying him was quickly offset by the comfort Koji felt from the boy—his arms wrapped around Koji's neck, his warm breath on Koji's head, and his beating heart on Koji's back.

Under a canopy of stars, light emerged from Fuchu's distant hillside homes and businesses. In the outskirts of devastation, electricity had been restored.

SURRENDER

August 1945 – Hiroshima, Japan

Weeks later, neighbors joined those convalescing at Koji's house. Nervous chitchat about Emperor Hirohito's unprecedented radio broadcast filled the living room. The Japanese had never heard the Emperor's voice, and they were hungry to listen to him address the country at noon. Most everyone expected him to reinforce Japan's commitment to winning the war, but not a single person lacked for an opinion. An old man who lived down the road reported to the neighborhood, "Just days ago, newspaper articles spewed more military propaganda."

A man from a nearby farm stood and cleared his throat. His voice was confident. "Perhaps, but the United States violated international law with the force of their bombs dropped here and on Nagasaki. One account says they used poison gas. Our fierce military will strike back."

His son chimed in. "And fight until we're all dead."

"They can't kill us all," the boy's exhausted father replied.

"Maybe if we bombed New York," a neighbor suggested.

"How long will this go on? So many dead in Hiroshima and Nagasaki. Even with no visible burns or wounds, people die from the sheer exhaustion of war," another man said.

Otōsan spoke. "With the massive bombings and the Soviets' declaration of war on Japan, how can our government expect us to continue sacrificing to support the war? Not that we have anything left to offer. I can't imagine what the Emperor will say."

The radio crackled and a high-pitched buzz signaled the Emperor was about to speak, silencing the room. Those able went down on their knees and bowed at the somber sound of the stilted and jeweled voice.

"To our good and loyal subjects: After pondering deeply the general trends of the world and the actual conditions in our Empire today, we have ordered our Government to communicate to the Governments of the United States, Great Britain, China, and the Soviet Union that our Empire accepts the provisions of their joint declaration. The enemy has begun to employ a new and most cruel bomb, the power of which to do damage is, indeed, incalculable, taking the toll of many innocent lives. Should we continue to fight, it would not only result in an ultimate collapse and obliteration of the Japanese nation, but also it would lead to the total extinction of human civilization. We have resolved to disarm our military and pave the way for a grand peace for all generations to come by enduring the unendurable and suffering what is not sufferable. Cultivate the ways of rectitude, foster nobility of spirit, and work with resolution so that you may enhance the innate glory of the Imperial State and keep pace with the progress of the world."

The war was over.

Koji glanced around the silent room.

Stunned by the extraordinary announcement, heads slumped into hands, eyes stared into other eyes, and no one spoke. Some wept, their hearts broken to have suffered so long for nothing.

A teenager who Koji didn't know was the first to speak. "Defeated?"

The man who earlier suggested that Japan bomb New York seemed agitated. "But our Emperor *never* used the word *surrender.*"

"He didn't have to," *Otōsan* said. "His message was clear."

"Unthinkable."

"Now what?" one of the neighbors asked.

"America will soon take over and decide Japan's future," someone answered.

A meek neighbor lady, whose son was a *kamikaze* pilot buried at sea, whispered, "I hope our conquerors treat us with fairness and compassion.

They've already taken so much."

Koji sincerely hoped so too.

• • •

Days after the Emperor's radio address, Koji learned many Japanese military leaders had committed *seppuku,* in quick succession. But there would be no suicide for Emperor Hirohito. He would remain on the throne.

PETROGLYPHS

1945 – Tule Lake, CA

Sadness, anger, hurt
Petroglyphs on Castle Rock
Did you feel them too?
—Reiko Odate

In the final weeks of August, people at Tule Lake learned shocking yet sketchy details about the severity of the destruction in Hiroshima. Chiko's body sagged when learning that his mother and entire family were presumed dead. The family's ancestral temple was two kilometers from the hypocenter—the temple and its grounds destroyed, including the grave of Ruby's mother. Even the dead had died another death in Hiroshima.

Summer had turned to autumn and America's incarceration camps closed or were closing. Yet the majority of Tule Lake's 18,000 inhabitants remained, including Ruby. On September 2, General Douglas MacArthur had accepted Japan's signed instrument of surrender aboard the teak decks of the USS Missouri in Tokyo Bay. While people danced in the streets across America, Tule Lake's incarcerees planted cool-weather vegetables in their small gardens to sustain them for another possible season of detention. The siren's scream announcing Japan's surrender shook the very foundation of those who believed Japan would never give up, never lose, leaving them—including Taeko Ishimaru—incredulous. Even the tender lettuce leaves drooped after the sirens had gone silent.

In October, Ruby—a life member of the National Honor Society—had walked across the stage and accepted her high school diploma. When a ship with over 6,000 Tule Lake prisoners sailed to Japan in November, the Ishimaru family was not aboard. Chiko's birth city of Hiroshima was destroyed and his family dead. Now, Japan had nothing to offer him. While the ship was at sea, Chiko learned his original parole order required him to remain resident in a War Relocation Project. Something in his file— perhaps a single piece of paper—was missing, lost in the massive War Department bureaucracy. They were stuck in Tule Lake.

On a late December morning, Tule Lake woke to a blanket of fresh snow. Against a gray and heavy sky, the waxing crescent moon pinpointed the ebb and flow of the changing season. Its mysterious far side faced the inhospitable, black expanse of the universe. Mount Shasta stood firm in the distance, shrouded by clouds, like the resolute patience of Tule Lake's remaining inhabitants. Castle Rock's unyielding mass seemed to press harder into the camp. Silhouettes of lone sentries kept watch from wood skeleton towers, their icy stares as unrelenting as Castle Rock. Rigid utility poles and spiked barbed-wire fences punctuated the delicate snowfall, like the bare bones of the jagged trees remaining in Hiroshima.

The absolute stillness and beauty of the snow exacerbated the camp's stark ugliness. Men lit tinder in rusted drums, the fires igniting into bright flames, then licking into ashen hues. Those who would leave that day tossed unwanted memories into the fires. As their memories incinerated, embers and smoke curled into the gray sky and ashes fell to the bottom of the steely drums.

One week earlier, the Ishimarus were suddenly among those preparing to leave. Chiko's parole order that limited his freedom was swept away within the bureaucratic engine. Inside Unit 5401-A, Ruby finished packing. Soon, her family would depart by bus and then board a ship to Hawaii. Ruby tightened the straps on her tattered footlocker where she packed the precious few items she had brought to camp, her yearbook, diploma, and letters from Velvet and Mari. She closed the door on Tule Lake and stepped outside. Snow had drifted against the tattered barracks. Tiny snowflakes fell and melted on her eyelashes, each as unique as every person who had suffered the years of incarceration, died in combat, or in the Hiroshima and

Nagasaki bombings. Desperate to leave incarceration behind, she walked to a drum, threw her diary into the fire, and watched her most personal thoughts burn to haunting ash.

Ruby continued walking, carrying a permanent petroglyph of Tule Lake on her soul. Each footstep trampled a fresh imprint over the footprints of the hundreds of people she followed toward the waiting buses and trains. Their slushy imprints would melt, but the marks of human suffering would remain. Years later, Tule Lake's bony skeleton would be dismantled, leaving behind a flat and treeless terrain, where winds create surface waves across the tules and sagebrush, and echoes of the Japanese American spirit dwell for eternity.

KAMON

December 4, 1945 – Hiroshima, Japan

The mourners gathered around the monuments at a small cemetery high on a Fuchu ridge, bordered by graceful mountains. Unchanged for thousands of years, the foothills seemed to caress the edges of the dead city, as if to comfort its annihilation. Koji placed the ceramic urn containing his father's ashes in the open chamber at the base of the family's stone monument. He replaced and sealed the door to the crypt, carved with the family *kamon*, having delivered *Otōsan's* remains to rest with their ancestors.

As friends and distant relatives made their way back down the hill, he stayed behind. It had been forty-nine days since *Otōsan* died, along with another 25,000 people following Japan's surrender. 145,000 dead in his city. They would never know if his father had died of cancer or the mysterious sickness inflicted on bomb survivors. Many otherwise healthy individuals with no cuts or bruises who were well one day, had become gravely ill with strange symptoms the next. Their hair fell out, fever raged, blood spots covered their bodies, blood disorders and gum lesions appeared, and healthy white cells dwindled. Diarrhea. Nausea. Fatigue. They learned the blast was atomic, and doctors familiar with the power of X-rays determined that people were dying from an illness caused by the bomb's release of radiation. Having learned this frightening news, *Okāsan* began mixing herbs and minerals, much as she had when she administered *kampō* treatments to *Otōsan*. Not a morning passed without *Okāsan* insisting that Koji and Naoki swallow her potions.

Koji stooped and studied his family's *kamon*. Within its hexagonal borders, overlapping bamboo leaves formed three diamonds. *Otōsan* had long ago explained the family crest's unique symbolism. Tortoises wore hexagonal markings on their shells, and the species enjoyed the longest survival of any animal. The diamonds symbolized excellence, and the bamboo, resilience. He was fond of quoting an ancient Japanese proverb: *In time, even the strongest wind tires itself out, but bamboo remains standing tall.* The crest's symbolism—longevity, excellence, and resilience—defined *Otōsan's* story well. Koji picked up a handful of loose dirt and sifted it through his fingers, contemplating his ability to model *Otōsan's* example and his unwillingness to live a life soiled by this war. Like bamboo, he would spring back from these hardships, resolved to flex and not fracture.

Seven

1946 – 1950

ALOHA FROM HAWAII

1946-1947 – Honolulu, Hawaii

January 10, 1946

Dear Mari,

Greetings and Happy Belated New Year from Honolulu, where I am safe and sound, having arrived yesterday! I must catch you up.

I honestly thought we'd never get out of that filthy hovel. Yet somehow, the glitch in Father's parole order was resolved, and we were approved to leave Tule Lake on the next bus to Oakland. Father had been corresponding with his old friend, Reverend Miyamoto, who was released from camp six months earlier and resumed his duties at the Hongwanji temple here in Honolulu. Months ago, the Reverend extended an open invitation to help us find housing while Father sorts things out. We're living with Mr. and Mrs. Ito, members of the Reverend's congregation, in a small house near Kapena Falls. It's a lovely white bungalow with large windows that face swaying palms and lush flower gardens. Last night, I took my first bath in three years! Surrounded by fragrant bubbles, I soaked until long after the water had chilled.

I was relieved to sail into the sunny harbor and smell Hawaii. Remember the first time we saw Aloha Tower together? It's still grand! But this time, instead of heading toward bruising incarceration, I was headed home, a place outside of the fences where I would be free again. Sadly, the fences haunt my dreams. Do they haunt yours too?

I will close now so I can post this letter today. I hope my words find you well and enjoying your dressmaking job. Breathe in the aroma of the enclosed ginger blossom, and please find time to respond with news from Los Angeles between tucks and hems.

Love, Ruby

P.S. Are Mr. and Mrs. Okada still treating you kindly?

• • •

April 1, 1946

Dear Velvet,

No fooling… I'm out of that hell hole and, at long last, am back in Hawaii! I meant to write you weeks ago, but time got away from me. My family was FINALLY released in December and we are living with members of a sister congregation to my father's former temple. They are lovely people and are helping me find work and a pathway to college.

Thank you for sharing your new Sacramento address in your Christmas card, which I received a few days before leaving camp. I simply don't know what I would do if we lost track of one another! Our friendship is one of the few positive memories from my time in Jerome. When you write back, please tell me about your cross-country trip from New Jersey. Have you noticed how much nicer travel is when you're headed some place wonderful and can raise the shades whenever you want? I couldn't get enough of the scenery between

Tule Lake and Oakland—the wilderness is magnificent. For all of its ugliness, America is spectacularly beautiful.

I also want to hear about how things are in Sacramento. My sister told me of storefront signs in Los Angeles that say JAPS NOT WANTED and NO JAPS ALLOWED. Is it like that in Sacramento too? Do you think all of the west coast is a stronghold of prejudice? We have none of that here in Hawaii. Many ethnicities populate the islands and live peacefully here, much like a colorful ethnic rainbow. Interestingly, most of the Japanese here never went to camp because their leaving would have taken away a major part of the state's workforce and devastated its economy. Politics! Anyway, the Japanese here don't understand what we went through. I wish you were here, because you know how it feels to be stripped of your identity and unjustly confined.

Sorry. Enough gloom and doom. The plumerias are blooming. I hope the enclosed blossom keeps some of its fragrance for you. Do take care and write me soon and often!

Love, Ruby

• • •

June 19, 1946

Dear Mari,

Thanks for your letter and parcel, and congratulations on your promotion to lead seamstress. How wonderful for you! The fabric remnants from your shop are gorgeous. The blue floral on the red ground and the red and white polka dot are my favorites! I'm in desperate need of new dresses and will get started right away cutting patterns.

I have big news! Father's been assigned to a temple on the Big Island. Gosh, did you hear about the dreadful tsunami there in April? It destroyed coastal villages and killed many people. Thankfully, the temple survived. Father spent months resolving his banking issues, and the bank in Waimea finally unfroze his account, so he and Okāsan left last week for Hilo. Yay, she's GONE! But not without having pushed and pushed and PUSHED Father for a new assignment! She helped him write letters, organize his sermons, and develop a new Japanese language curriculum. I swear, finding a new assignment seemed more important to her than to him! And it seemed she was always pushing him toward opportunities in locations away from me. Whatever! I'm happy for Father.

Mr. and Mrs. Ito have been lifesavers. They introduced me to their friends, Mr. and Mrs. Howard Becker, who I now live with and work for as a domestic. The Beckers are kind and soft-spoken, and sympathetic to my incarceration. Mr. Becker is a lawyer and leaves for the office at the crack of dawn. He wears a straw hat and a freshly pressed seersucker suit and totes a leather briefcase. When he comes home from work, the bubbly, short, and round Mrs. Becker greets him at the door with a martini, which he gulps down. She is quick to refill his glass, and he sips that one a bit more slowly while smoking his pipe on the porch where they discuss news of the day. Have you ever had a martini, Mari? The glasses are glamorous, and the clear liquid looks delicious. Someday, I'll try one!

And I saved the best news for last! Mr. and Mrs. Ito helped me find a way to attend college. I passed the University of Hawaii entrance exam and begin classes this September. Since the school is a territorial university, the tuition is free! My job with the Beckers covers my room and board, and I will babysit to pay for my books.

Mari, I wish you could go to college with me. I remember college was something you always wanted. I miss you and Mama more than I can say. But I feel surrounded here by your presence. I smell Mama among the plumerias. I hear her whispering "sweet dreams" and your soft snoring amid the crickets' lullaby. Last night, I sat on the beach, watched the stars, and remembered the times we did that together, with our toes buried in the sand. The gravitational pull to Mama and to you, my dear sister, is strong. I see you and her everywhere.

I must close now. A pile of ironing awaits me at dawn. Please write again soon!

Love, Ruby

P.S. I'm planning to major in education and be an elementary school teacher!

P.P.S. Mrs. Becker has a brand-new Singer sewing machine, so she gave me her old electric. It's in perfect condition and I can't wait to run the polka dots under the foot and listen to the gentle hum of the whirling motor. I'll be the best dressed coed at the university!

• • •

September 20, 1946

Dear Velvet,

Congratulations on acceptance to UC Davis! I don't think it matters that you don't quite know what you want to do with your life. That's what college is for. Even if you do nothing other than be someone's wife and mother, you'll be an educated woman.

The campus here is quite large and a bit confusing, but I'm finding my way around. *Do you want to hear about my experience? It doesn't matter, I'm going to tell you, anyway!* Last week, during my health screening at the University Health Center, the nurse asked for my health records. Of course, I don't have any records and told her I had been in an incarceration camp. She asked me what internment was like. She, like most others, are ignorant about it. They don't seem to understand that internment applies only to enemy aliens, not to the imprisonment of our citizens. I guess the word internment makes what happened to us more palatable among the masses? Anyway, after I told her, she had the nerve to comment that I had it better during the war than she did as a navy nurse! Do you believe that? And you won't believe what she said when I asked her if the government had frozen her bank account, confiscated her radio, and locked her up for years within barbed wire. She said, "Well, at least no one shot at you!" The nerve of her! I guess it takes all kinds. Even if there are a few imbeciles, I think college is the most fabulous place in the world! How ironic that one of my first encounters within an institution of higher learning was with a stupid person!

My eyes refuse to stay open a moment longer, so goodbye for now. Write soon!

Love, Ruby

• • •

March 20, 1947

Dear Mari,

Happy Birthday, dear sister and my forever birthday buddy! Your early birthday gift arrived yesterday. The full-skirted dress with the sheer overlay on the bodice is divine, and I thank you with all of my heart. My goodness, it must have taken you hours to press and sew *all of those perfectly perfect pleats! I hope you receive this letter in time for your birthday and you enjoy the shell necklace I made for you. How I miss celebrating our birthdays together!*

Sorry I haven't written since New Year's. The spring semester is in full swing, and I'm busy from dawn until long after the crickets begin their concert, so there is little time for a social life. Meaning, I have no boyfriend, so please stop asking. Mr. and Mrs. Becker continue to treat me kindly, but they are a handful to keep up with, especially when they entertain guests—which is often! You won't believe this, but they have an entire cabinet full of martini glasses! Imagine! I tried one by the way. Yuck!

My favorite thing is to come home and find a letter from you. Please make my day again soon!

Love, Ruby

P.S. My fall semester's grades are straight A's!

PINKY SWEAR

December 9, 1947 – Hiroshima, Japan

Koji glanced at his watch. Mere minutes had passed since he last checked. Beyond the train's window, towns, rice paddies, and waterways blurred by, forming a vague and meaningless landscape. Wearing his father's best suit and hoping to fill his shoes someday, he wondered what *Otōsan* would think of his decision.

The compartment door of the crowded train opened and George Sato returned to his seat beside him. George was a baffling contradiction. With a confident demeanor, chiseled features, thick ebony hair, and an Asian face, he spoke perfect English and wore the uniform of the United States. He was the American nephew of a family friend and traveled to Hiroshima from Sasebo Naval Base on the island of Kyushu to hear Emperor Hirohito's speech in person. Born in Texas to *Issei* parents, George also spoke fluent Japanese. Introduced by *Okāsan's* friend, they had become fast friends in ways Koji never could have imagined from the moment George showed up at their house a few days ago.

Together with the masses, they had witnessed history as the Emperor stood on a raised wooden platform surrounded by Hiroshima's flattened city and waved his hat to a crowd of roaring, captivated spectators. The ghostly dome of the Prefectural Industrial Promotion Hall stood in the background as the sea of people waited to hear his divine voice. Although Japan's postwar Constitution stripped Hirohito of all authority, the Japanese continued revering him as the symbol of Japan and unifier of the Japanese people.

The Emperor's visit to Hiroshima was just one stop on his infamous tour of war-torn Japan and coincided with the anniversary of Pearl Harbor's attack, creating a fascinating paradox. Koji struggled to imagine what the Emperor was thinking. Was the victorious assault on Pearl Harbor worth the devastation America delivered in retaliation?

After the speech, the two men shared their wartime experiences. Sensing Koji's reluctance to talk about the bombing and sensitive to the horrors he had experienced, George kept his questions to the U.S. occupation and Japan's recovery. Koji shared with George how many Japanese floundered in their fear of the unknown, complicated by their difficulty to recognize the good guys from the bad guys when opposing forces rushed in to occupy the power vacuum following the surrender.

George had listened intently when Koji shared stories of how the *Yakuza* had taken advantage of Japan's vulnerabilities, looting surviving armaments from military installations and purchasing the remaining inventories from factory owners at record-low prices. Starvation and chaos fueled the mafia organization's flourishing black markets. And they'd seduced thousands of orphaned children into their service to shine shoes, sell drugs, and prostitute their innocence. His thoughts went to the small boy he had taken home with him the day he walked among Hiroshima's ruins, forever grateful that the boy's parents had claimed him at the Higashi relief center and saved their child from *Yakuza* life.

Koji also told George about his friend, Toma, who had joined the *Yakuza's* local gang. He hadn't seen Toma since the morning of the bombing until the previous week outside of Hiroshima Station, when he had cringed at the sight of Toma's pinky finger. The fingertip was missing above the last joint, cut off at the displeasure of his *Yakuza* boss. No matter. Toma pledged absolute loyalty to the *Yakuza* and persisted in recruiting Koji, offering his other little finger to swear to the prosperous way of life in the organization—a pinky-swear promise that, if broken, resulted in a missing finger. Koji had dismissed Toma's offer. Things were bad, but not bad enough to ingratiate himself with thugs. No doubt Toma had found other recruits.

The people of Hiroshima were afraid of everyone and trusted no one.

Fearful parents sent their young daughters to the countryside to hide from American soldiers. They knew the atrocities Japan's military had inflicted in Korea and China—murdering civilians, raping women, and stealing or destroying property on a massive scale—and expected the worst from the Americans. But most Americans proved kind, some handing candy to youngsters on the street. Koji had witnessed good and profound changes under General Douglas MacArthur. With the government and military dismantled, war-crime trials had convened in Tokyo. The U.S. government was introducing reforms to reduce the influence of wealthy landowners, implementing a new Constitution, and strengthening the parliamentary system with the abolishment of the Emperor's political control. Progress was slow, but Hiroshima was rebuilding bridges and roads, and people were rebuilding their lives.

Over dinner after the Emperor's speech, Koji told George about his U.S. citizenship and hopeless frustration with the bleak opportunities in war-ravaged Japan. Except for Naoki, this was the first time Koji had told anyone his story. George proved to be a trustworthy and sensitive listener. He examined Koji's birth certificate and encouraged Koji to return to America to finish high school. With *Okāsan's* blessing, and by the time she served dessert, they had a plan. Only two days remained in George's leave, and time was of the essence. George promised to make inquiries the following day into the process for Koji's return to the United States. His friend had come through. Koji didn't know how he could ever repay the universe for bringing George into his life or repay him for his generous friendship.

The conductor announced the next stop and the train hissed and screeched as it slowed at the Osaka station. Within the hour, they would meet with representatives at the U.S. Consulate. Koji wiped his sweaty palms on his trouser legs. "George, what if they say no? Everything will work out like you said. Right?"

With sincerity in his eyes, George extended his hand and stuck out his little finger. "Pinky swear."

A RISING JUNIOR

June 1948 – Honolulu, Hawaii

June 10, 1948

Dear Velvet,

I'm sorry I haven't written. That's it. An apology. No excuses!

Do you love college as much as I do? With thousands of students enrolled here, the campus buzzes with lectures, pep rallies, and fraternity parties of dreadful drunkenness (not that I attend). I recently began wondering about something. Do you realize how ignorant we really are? Each day I learn something new or see something different, and I realize I don't know what I don't know! I suppose this means learning is a lifetime proposition, and I wonder when I might catch up to my inflated opinion of myself! I guess I didn't realize that by majoring in education I would become educated in how under-educated I am.

Like in the camps, I'm not a joiner. But I enjoy seeing the sophomores show aloha spirit and compete for such silly things as designing muumuus from flour bags. Some of the transformations were elaborate, loud, and unusual. Oh, what a lark! You'll be happy to know I'm trying to make friends, and I forced myself to attend a Christmas party, a merry post-exam dance in February (straight A's, thank you very much), and a spring picnic.

Mrs. Becker said it would be fine for you to visit this summer. Will you be able to make it? Gosh, I hope so. We can tell stories long into the night, picnic at Waikiki Beach with plate lunches, and watch the waves from under a palm tree (I still try to stay out of the sun). I'll introduce you to the best macaroni salad on the island (mine).

That's all for now. Write soon with word you're coming to visit!

Love, Ruby

P.S. Mrs. Becker redecorated the house (again) and gave me her chenille bedspread and dotted-swiss curtains (like new, but Mrs. Becker says they're old) for my room. I'm planning to paint the walls a luscious shade of pale coral—the perfect backdrop for my shell collection.

BETWEEN THE TRAPEZES

February 1949 – The Pacific Ocean

Koji said goodbye to Japan as he lost sight of Yokohama's shore. Seven days later, the *General Gordon V-15E* bobbed upon the fierce ocean swells against darkening and gloomy skies. The turbulent rise and fall of the ocean, caused by the storm two days ago, had made his body tremble and teeth chatter. And now, another storm brewed in the Pacific—he hoped less tempestuous than the previous one. Seasick the entire voyage, he leaned over the railing and emptied his stomach, once again. The rolling clouds grew so dense, they became one with the water as angry waves dwarfed the massive ocean liner. The seething skies opened again and the ship's horn blasted a signal for passengers to return to their quarters.

He returned below to his third-class cabin and climbed into his bunk to ride out the storm. Relentless swells, howling winds, and thunderclaps stoked the fires of his fear and anxiety. Snuggled under a scratchy wool blanket, he wondered what lay in the depths of the inky sea—shipwrecks with untold stories and discoveries in their holds, diverse and fascinating life forms, and plates converging to cause earthquakes and new realities.

Much later, the calmer sea delivered the precious gift of a settled stomach. He climbed to the deck. Stars freckled and dazzled the infinite velvet sky. The full moon blazed a silver path of light across the tranquil and rippling surface. The shimmers of light, smell of briny vapors, and rhythm of the soft breaking waves beguiled, soothed, and intoxicated him.

It had taken a year for the American Consulate to approve his return to the United States and for him to secure his travel and living arrangements. He placed his palm over his heart, swollen with gratitude for his mother's support. As the eldest son, tradition required him to assume responsibility for her care. Loving him more than herself, she wrote letter after letter to friends, and then friends of friends, to find a respectable family willing to sponsor him in the United States, so he might complete high school. Most Japanese Americans were experiencing severe hardship trying to reestablish their lives after release from camps and were not capable of taking in a stranger. But through *Okāsan's* tenacity and her connections with the temple, the Tanaka family in Sacramento, California invited him to live with them, work as their houseboy, and attend Sacramento High School. George Sato, happily married and living back in his home state of Texas, came through once again, sending Koji money for his one-way fare to San Francisco.

His mind drifted to Emi and the teams of scientists who had swarmed Hiroshima since the bombing. Had she survived her monstrous injuries, people would have labeled her *hibakusha*. She would have been shunned by the Japanese people as a bomb-affected person and subjected to observation and study by the U.S.-led Atomic Bomb Casualty Commission, its reputation growing more horrid each day for gathering information yet doing nothing to help people.

The Commission had forced the twelve-year-old sister of Koji's friend to walk into the light, in an otherwise dark examining room, and drop her gown in front of male scientists, exposing her young and naked body covered in keloids for the benefit of their research. His heart ached when he thought of how mortifying that experience must have been for the young girl. Although he took comfort knowing Emi had already passed on to her next life, free from the markings and pain of thick scars and sympathetic ostracism, he missed her and wondered, *what if.* What if the United States had invaded, rather than dropped the bomb? Would either of them have survived? And for what kind of a life?

Sailing between two trapezes, he was letting go of Japan, but had yet to grab onto his new life in America. In between his past and future, at the mercy of the ship and with no land in sight, his optimism and pessimism vacillated.

•••

After three weeks at sea, on the day the ship was due to arrive in San Francisco, the golden light of the winter sun rose on the calm water, shimmering yellow, coral, and pink rays on the horizon. A pod of playful dolphins greeted the day, jumping and spinning in the air, while greedy seabirds fed on the ocean's bounty. Awake before dawn, Koji stood on deck with his small suitcase.

After living at sea for twenty-one days, he craved land and his new start. Tanaka-*san* would meet his ship and identify himself by holding a sign with Koji's name. Koji knew little English and was nervous about attending an English-speaking high school with students five years his junior. But he was smart and motivated to learn and there was nothing like immersion, forcing one's failure or success. The past was over and he wouldn't let anything impede his education or promising future ever again. He would forge ahead and not look back.

He removed a piece of paper from his left pocket. Within its folds was a *haiku* he had written for Emi, but had never given to her.

I fall into you,
Mesmeric we become one,
The power of love.

Koji crumpled the paper into a ball and tossed it into the ocean swells below. Swallowed by a wave, his declaration of love was pulled by the currents into its final resting place. "Goodbye, my sweet Emi."

He reached in his right pocket for his Japanese-English pocket dictionary and patted it in place, alongside his cherished *Jizō*.

•••

His eyes focused on the horizon, and soon the *General Gordon* held course across the Gulf of the Farallones, busy with shipping traffic and working boats. Her decks buzzed with activity. Suitcases lined up, passengers arrived wearing their best clothing, and the crew prepared to enter port.

In the distance, the soaring red towers and lengthy suspension spans of the Golden Gate Bridge came into focus—an unmistakable and welcoming symbol of American determination and perseverance.

CALIFORNIA OR BUST

1949-1950 – Sacramento, CA

Koji walked down the ship's gangway and away from everything he'd lost—his father, his city, and the Japanese education he'd always imagined. Having celebrated his twentieth birthday aboard the dank ship, he raised his face to the sunshine and stepped onto American soil, a full-grown, wiry man with a shock of wavy black hair and a wide head full of big ideas. To him, America represented a land of limitless opportunity where he had everything to gain and nothing to lose.

His eyes followed the undulating topography gently framing San Francisco and tumbling into the bay. The grace of the hills softened the city and adorned the empty sky like nature's jewelry. He wondered what adventures lay beyond, but he knew his eyes mustn't linger.

Koji searched the crowd, his eyes darting from person to person. On the pier jammed with people searching for their friends and family to disembark, he was a stranger looking for another stranger. He made his way through a mass of people—heads bobbing, arms waving, and bodies falling into the arms of lovers. As he looked for the Japanese man named Tanaka, who he hoped was looking for him, he was startled to realize nearly everyone looked Japanese. That made sense since most of the passengers were of Japanese descent, but his mind had conjured a vision of a white America. He pushed forward, shaking off the unsettling sensations of rolling and swaying, as if he were still at sea.

At the end of the pier, he spotted a man leaning against the terminal building, blowing smoke rings into the air, and holding a sign with black letters: MATSUO. Koji hadn't realized he'd been holding his breath the entire length of the pier, until he exhaled.

"Tanaka-*san*?"

"*Hai!*"

Koji was relieved to hear the man continue in their native tongue, "Welcome to America!"

His instinctive attempt to bow was blocked by the thrust of Mr. Tanaka's extended hand. "Americans shake hands, not bow."

After shaking hands, Mr. Tanaka crushed the cigarette under his shoe and reached for one of Koji's suitcases. "I'm parked over there," he said, pointing across the street.

They crossed the wide promenade and main boulevard and walked past several side streets to his two-door, pheasant-red Mercury Eight. With its wide, round fenders, and smudge-less chrome grill, it looked like a curvy, painted and powdered lady of the evening. Koji had never seen such a beautiful automobile before. They stored Koji's luggage in the trunk and slid onto the caramel leather seats.

"Nice day," Mr. Tanaka said, cranking down his window. "Smoke?"

Koji accepted the cigarette and took a deep and satisfying drag, having run out of cigarettes days ago.

"How about a quick tour of the city, or are you too tired?"

Koji exhaled. "Yes."

"You're too tired?"

"No. I mean yes, a tour, please."

They zoomed up and down the hilly streets beside cable cars with clanging bells. Driving up one precipitous hill, Koji felt his back pressing into the seat and he feared the car might lose its power and fly backward. He turned and looked behind him. At the bottom of the steep hill, it seemed the city flowed into the hills rising in the distance.

"You'll get used to it," Mr. Tanaka said.

With the fresh air blowing in the windows, they drove past narrow, three-story homes with sharply pitched roofs. On Market Street, Mr. Tanaka pulled over and pointed out Koji's window. "City Hall."

The handsome Beaux Arts dome resembled the U.S. Capitol building

Koji had studied and seen in pictures, and he wondered if every American city enjoyed such opulent architecture. Having left a ravaged Japan, Koji thought it strange to see people, many with Asian faces, walking around the vibrant city—safe, healthy, and well-fed. The men wore suits, ties, and hats, and many carried briefcases. Women wore smart hats and suits or full, belted coats, and carried pocketbooks and shopping bags over their wrists. He was surprised at the number of women as tall as his five-foot, eight-inch frame, and his gaze followed their high-heeled shoes to linger on their slender ankles.

San Francisco smelled intoxicating, and he took a deep breath of its irresistible aroma.

On the corner of Grant and Bush Streets, Mr. Tanaka pulled over and pointed to a three-roofed, green dragon gate. "Chinatown." He tapped his fingers on the steering wheel. "Japantown's not what it used to be. Many people didn't come back." His shoulders raised to a half-hearted shrug. "It's lunchtime. Are you hungry?"

Koji was starving. "Yes."

Mr. Tanaka steered the car away from the curb, turned on California Avenue, and parked across the street from the neon sign of the Tadich Grill. "Best seafood in the city. Been here since before California was even a state."

The café curtains dressing the large window offered diners privacy from the street. Inside, surrounded by formality, waiters wearing white coats, served food on white china over white tablecloths. People drank cocktails and a piano player's fingers lifted soft music into the air. The host seated them, and a waiter filled their glasses with the clink of ice water. Another approached the table with menus and a nod.

Mr. Tanaka was a man of elegance in speech, dress, and demeanor who oddly didn't seem capable of talking without hand gestures, somehow making his words more declarative, clear, believable. Koji fiddled with his collar and glanced around the restaurant to see if anyone had noticed his wrinkled and outdated attire. Unsure how to behave, he followed Mr. Tanaka's lead. He put his napkin in his lap. He wiped his hands on the warm towels presented by yet another waiter. He said thank you. He stared at the silverware and wondered how on earth to use it.

No one was eating with chopsticks, and he didn't dare ask for any. In what Koji imagined was perfect English, Mr. Tanaka ordered a feast for them—cracked crab, broiled Alaskan black cod, corn fritters, crusty sourdough, and sage pudding and stewed figs for dessert. Koji fumbled through lunch, using a knife and fork for the first time in his life, and savored every bite of the delicious food. Between their sips of water, yet another waiter hustled to the table from out of nowhere to fill their glasses.

Over lunch, Mr. Tanaka told his story. He had lived in California since his family emigrated from Japan's Yamaguchi Prefecture when he was five years old. He became an optometrist and had run his own office before the attack on Pearl Harbor. After the Exclusion Order was signed, the government forced him and his wife into the Walega Assembly Center, where they lived in a small camp. They were grateful to have slept on cots in newly-constructed barracks, as others before them had slept in mucked-out horse stalls. Months later, they boarded a train for an incarceration camp where they lived until their release. Good-hearted neighbors had watched their house and tended their yard while they were gone. Upon returning, Mr. Tanaka worked odd jobs until he was hired into an optometry practice.

Mr. Tanaka rested his utensils on his plate, placed a hand on his belly, and took a deep breath. "You know what? The United States has never found a single spy or saboteur of Japanese descent. Not one."

Koji struggled to understand how a government founded on justice, freedom, and liberty so easily imprisoned its citizens. He found Mr. Tanaka a man he could look up to and learn from—a man stripped of his rights and dignity, who had persevered with distinguished strength and resilience.

After lunch, they headed northwest on Route 40. Mr. Tanaka reached into the glove box and handed Koji a map. "We're here. Follow along."

Koji studied the one-dimensional representation of the three-dimensional world he would now call home, fascinated by the web of red and yellow highways connecting the Pacific Ocean to landlocked towns and cities, including Sacramento. Having always lived near the water, he couldn't imagine living inland.

Two hours later, they parked in front of a large, white three-story house surrounded by beds of golden daffodils. Mrs. Tanaka stepped out of the door, wiped her hands on her apron, and greeted them on the porch. She was a tiny woman, with a kind face and black hair softly streaked with gray. "Come with me, young man. I have food on the stove."

That night, Koji lay on his bed in a small room off the kitchen. His belly was full. He had never slept above the floor before and hoped he wouldn't roll off and create a disturbance. To the low hum of the refrigerator outside of his door, he rewound the day's events and the flow of the fine house where he now lived, with its roaring fireplace, central heating that delivered warm air through carved wooden vents in the floor, and a western-style bathtub where one emptied the water when finished, unlike in Japan where they washed first and then took turns soaking in the *ofuro*. The window was open a crack, allowing the evening breeze and sounds of darkness to filter in. He wondered how people slept amid the sirens interrupting the constant hum of traffic along 34th Street.

Begging his body to relax and fall into slumber, Koji descended into the serenity of Japan's natural world within. A transparent *shōji* in his mind opened to a dense bamboo grove with sunlight filtering through the stalks and leaves. He meandered along the path to the philosophical beauty of a carefully tended Zen garden, adjacent to a stream where calm water trickled over rocks. Without meditation—something he had practiced since the bombing—he'd lose himself to the horrific images he had chosen to erase.

• • •

For the next year, Koji hardly wandered beyond his immediate neighborhood where the snap-snap-snap of playing cards on bicycle spokes were heard before dawn, signaling the newspaper delivery and start of a new day. He rose early to sweep, garden, and complete any other chores Mrs. Tanaka had listed on the pad in the kitchen.

At Sacramento High School, he was a non-English-speaking man among polite teenage students who observed him with curiosity. They all had the same wide-eyed question—what was *it* like? Knowing he could never adequately describe the bomb that had blistered Hiroshima, and choosing not to relive the experience, Koji delivered his incisive response without flourish. "My family was fortunate. My parents were in an underground tunnel at the train station, and a small mountain protected my brother and me from the blast."

Teachers were too well-mannered to ask, and gave special attention to him, along with the librarian who introduced him to yellow pencils and the Dewey Decimal and card systems. In the library, among the smells of knowledge and the sounds of whispered voices and stamps on book pockets, Koji developed an insatiable hunger for and love of books.

At the community center, with the help of a volunteer language teacher, he learned English beyond the basic ABCs, excuse me, and thank you. He found English challenging to learn and was baffled by the unusual sounds, inconsistent pronunciations like *dough* and *tough*, and contradictory rules like *I before E except after C*, yet words like *conscience* and *forfeit* were correctly spelled. He scratched his head over homophones. How could a *wound* mean injury when thread was *wound* around a spool?

Fatigued, struggling for good grades, and feeling much the outsider, he embraced his chores and studies, having decided the punishing schedule was worth the opportunity afforded by this country. In the summer, he continued his studies with a tutor, and picked pears and peaches for the Del Monte Cannery, where he met Bob Yasuko. Bob was born in Sacramento, spoke perfect English, had spent his high school years in incarceration camp, and was Koji's supervisor.

It was after one of their shifts that Bob invited Koji out for his first hamburger. In Bob's beat-up tan Chevrolet truck, they swung into the parking lot of Doc's Place, a walk-up-to-the-window restaurant in East Sacramento, where a delicious whiff of diner cooking rushed up and delighted Koji's nose. With hamburger juice running down his face, he had fallen in love with yet another delectable slice of America.

Before 1949 rang into 1950, Bob had taken up with a girl named Velvet, and Koji had embraced both of them. Koji never rejected their invitations to eat hamburgers or go to a movie at the Starlite Drive-in Theatre, where, from within the bed of Bob's truck, movies transported the three of them to another time and place with Lawrence Olivier in *Hamlet* and Ingrid Bergman in *Joan of Arc.*

Velvet fancied herself a matchmaker and sometimes brought along a friend to introduce to Koji, none of whom had Velvet's sparkle. He couldn't imagine being interested in one of her boring, intellectual friends. She was one of the most effervescent and beautiful women he'd ever met, and she was no dummy, about to graduate from college with her sights set on Stanford Law. And she was funny. At an electrifying moment of *Sorry, Wrong Number*, Velvet stuck her finger into Koji's rib cage, scaring his un-popped kernels from their hulls. It seemed she, like most Americans, was good at the art of distraction. That, and surprising people.

Eight

1950 - 1955

PEARLS

June 1950 – Honolulu, Hawaii

June 1, 1950

Dear Mari,

Happy June! Not only did I graduate, but I graduated summa cum laude! Under my cap and gown, I wore the prettiest graduation dress of the entire class of 1950! How on earth did you sew all of those tiny pearls along the airy organza neckline? The dress fit like an enchantress had waved her fit-to-a-princess-perfection wand over me. Oh Mari, I'm so grateful for your generosity and sisterhood, and I have no words to describe how important you are to me.

Speaking of pearls, dear sister, I appreciate the pearls of wisdom you offered in your last letter. I understand you want me to forgive the past and move on, but your experience was different than mine. Shikata ga nai is a bunch of hooey. You were older. You had Warren, if only for a little while. You got away from HER. You were released earlier and created a new life. I know I sound petty, and I don't mean to. I truly don't begrudge you the life you've made for yourself. But I can't erase HER abuse, Father's refusal to stop HER, and spending three years locked up. Nor can I erase the pain from my heart. Maybe I'll get there someday, maybe not. Please know I'm trying.

Sorry. I'll move onto more positive news. The University accepted me for a fifth year to earn my certificate as a teacher in the Hawaii public school system. Certification is the equivalent to a master's degree in education. I'll continue to live with and work for Mr. & Mrs. Becker while I attend classes in the fall. Next spring, the school system will assign my internship and I may have to move, so I must save my pennies!

Wasn't Mr. and Mrs. Becker's graduation gift generous? Wow! A cruise-liner ticket to California. Although I wish I could spend that time with you this summer, I understand it's not a good time to visit, so I'm planning to visit Velvet in Sacramento. I do hope Mrs. Okada recovers from her stroke, for you and for her. You must be exhausted working all day and then caregiving for Mrs. Okada well into the night. Hang in there, dear sister. I'll miss seeing you this summer.

All my love,
Ruby

CUT LOOSE

July 1950 – Sacramento, CA

Koji's hammering hangover did little to quash his deep sense of conviction. After completing his morning chores and showering, he followed his nose to the aroma of sizzling bacon in the kitchen and poured himself a cup of coffee. Seated at the table, Mr. Tanaka lowered his newspaper and gave Koji a puzzled look. "Aren't you working today?"

Koji swallowed an enjoyable gulp of the steaming caffeine. "Bob's picking me up in a few minutes. We're registering with the Selective Service today." Last night as he and Bob had a few too many beers and cheered the dazzling Fourth of July fireworks bursting into the sky, they toasted each other and America. A week ago, President Truman ordered U.S. military intervention in the Korean conflict, and men of Selective Service age were registering and preparing to fight yet another war.

"It's the right and honorable thing to do," Mr. Tanaka said.

As Mrs. Tanaka placed a bowl of scrambled eggs on the table, her worried expression suggested otherwise. "But what about school?"

"Bob's ready to put on the uniform if called, but I'm planning to request a one-year deferral so I can graduate."

"Good plan," Mr. Tanaka said.

Through the open windows, Koji heard the unmistakable sound of an exhausted exhaust system, followed by the double honk of the horn. "Gotta go."

Mrs. Tanaka piled bacon strips and eggs on top of buttered toast, making two sandwiches. "One second." She wrapped the sandwiches in wax paper. "You boys have to eat."

Koji grabbed the sandwiches, pushed through the screen door, and called back into the house, "*Arigatō*! Wish us luck!"

Outside, Koji found Bob smoking a cigarette and leaning against the side of the idling truck belching black smoke. "Man, I can smell that bacon all the way out here."

Koji handed him one of the sandwiches.

"Damn, does your head hurt as much as mine?" Bob asked.

Koji winced his reply and they sped down 34th Street.

Fifteen minutes later, at the Sacramento Armory, they joined the end of a line stretching along the thinning lawn and wrapping around the corner. It was lunchtime when they finished completing the forms. Hungry for greasy hamburgers, they headed to Doc's Place.

Koji chased his hamburger and aspirin with cold Coca-Cola. "When does Velvet get back from her aunt's house in San Francisco?"

"Not for a couple more weeks. But I should warn you," Bob said, rubbing his temples, "she's not returning empty-handed."

"Empty-handed?"

"Her friend is coming to visit, and Velvet wants you to meet her. Velvet says she's a real looker."

Koji shook his head and chuckled. "Here we go again."

• • •

For weeks, Koji had dodged meeting Velvet's friend. Busy with summer school and work, he didn't want to invest time in another one of her setups. But Bob had said Velvet would be disappointed if the foursome wasn't able to take in *Sunset Boulevard* together, and he finally bribed Koji into submission with a hamburger. Despite his reluctance and low expectations, Koji had visited the barber earlier in the day and dressed in a freshly pressed suit.

He and Bob were waiting for Velvet and her friend in front of the Colonial Theatre when the girls turned the corner from 10th Street onto Stockton Boulevard. In the fading twilight, Koji caught his first glimpse of Velvet's friend mere moments before he knew she had noticed him too.

Her blouse with a deep neckline was tucked into a full skirt, accentuating her tiny waist. A long strand of pearls fell from her elegant neck, where a vibrant scarf was knotted below side-swept layers of black hair. Her petite frame seemed to carry the proudest of demeanors, and Koji was taken by her chiseled beauty. Her prominent cheekbones flowed like sunset-kissed peaks into the valleys of the loveliest eyes he'd ever seen, and red lipstick drew his attention to her determined mouth.

He followed blindly behind Bob, who kissed Velvet on the cheek, before making the introduction.

As Koji extended his hand to shake Ruby's, Velvet delivered a quick elbow to Ruby's ribs, and he overheard Velvet's whisper, "See, I told you he was a dreamboat."

Flustered to learn embarrassment leaked through one's palms so quickly, he moistened Ruby's hand with his own and stumbled, *"Hajimemashite...* I'm... nice to meet you."

Her dazzling smile spoke a split second before her words. "I know what it means silly. Nice to meet you, too."

Koji struggled to make small talk while waiting in the ticket line. The girl had tied his tongue in a knot. "You're a teacher... right?"

Her voice was clearer than glass. "I will be."

They entered the theatre. While the girls found seats, Koji and Bob followed the aroma of popping corn to the concession counter.

"She seems like a great girl," Bob said. "You like her?"

"I'm not sure." But his thoughts said otherwise.

They joined the girls in the back row of the darkened theatre, and Koji sat beside Ruby. He handed her a bottle of Coke and offered to share a bag of buttered popcorn. While watching previews of coming attractions, Koji and Ruby's hands fumbled around in the popcorn bag, fingers gliding together, until they found their rhythm of sharing. Koji loved the taste of oily, salty movie popcorn, and now his fingers tasted better from having touched hers.

The subtlety of *Sunset Boulevard* was difficult for him to decipher, the menacing music increased his nervousness, and the film's dark humor was lost on him due to his limited command of English. He found himself comparing the characters, Joe and Betty, and their stories to his reality. Betty's wholesomeness reminded him of Emi—innocent and fresh as an apricot blossom with the sweet fragrance of honey. A girl determined to succeed. A girl with a pure heart. A girl fascinated by the dance of a dragonfly.

Yet, when Joe suggested Betty knew nothing about him, but knew exactly what *she* wanted, Koji wondered what Ruby knew about him and what *she* wanted in life. He caught himself glancing at Ruby when he should have been watching the movie, thinking Ruby might be more like the Norma Desmond character—mature, magnetic, and anything but mediocre, her petals held high within the regal structure of a purple chrysanthemum.

When Ruby returned his gaze with a smile, his eyes darted back to the screen. In the scene where Joe asked Betty, "What happened?" and she responded, "You did," Koji was lured into thinking maybe that's how it happens—a person meets another person at random and falls hopelessly in love.

At the end of the evening, after enjoying ice cream floats and making the next day's plans to picnic and swim at Putah Creek, he and Bob walked the girls to the door of Velvet's house. While Bob kissed Velvet goodnight, Koji took Ruby's hand. He didn't know if she expected more than the cordial handshake, but he assumed she was a nice girl and he wasn't taking any chances. Maybe it was the way she bit her lip or the way her voice seemed to drop when she said goodnight, but Koji walked away feeling she might be more than slightly disappointed.

• • •

The next morning, Koji and Bob drove to Velvet's house where the girls waited on the front porch with blankets and picnic baskets. Within minutes, Koji sat among the picnic supplies in the truck bed behind the cab the girls shared with Bob. They headed west, past Davis toward the Vaca Mountains. The dry, hot day was like most other summer days in the valley. Koji found California's arid summers so unlike the uncomfortable humidity of Hiroshima and worth waiting for after the winter rains.

With brilliant sunshine on his face and the warm wind in his hair, they passed landscapes of parched vegetation and brush, and his thoughts turned to Ruby. He wished she was in the sunshine with him. Instead, the back of his head faced the back of her head, with a mere pane of dusty glass separating them. Having already graduated from college, she somehow managed to put him on the edge of his abilities, and he wondered how long it would take for him to catch up to her, if he were to ever catch the tail of her whirlwind. She was incredibly beautiful, with a persona that seemed to be carved of ice and an icicle-sharp intellect. He wanted to ask her questions—what she stood for, what she dreamed of, what she might regret.

Two hours after leaving Sacramento, they parked on a narrow dirt road under towering oak trees. They hiked through thriving cottonwood, tules, and willows to a path feathered with flowering yarrow that opened to a clearing where the ground was sunbaked and cracked. Both girls screamed when a blotchy yellow and brown snake slithered its six-foot body across the path in search of prey.

Koji jumped away. "Is that a rattlesnake?" he asked, his voice embarrassingly shrill.

Unfazed, Bob continued walking. "Nah, I think it's a gopher."

"Gopher? I thought gopher was furry... a rat... no, a rodent?"

Bob laughed. "Yup. Gophers are rodents, but there's also a snake called a gopher."

Doubtful he would ever understand the English language, Koji shook his head.

The path led to the creek below, framed with massive boulders softened by lush vegetation. "How'd you find this place?" Koji asked, as they opened the blankets along the bank.

"It's a famous skinny-dipping hole with the Davis students," Velvet said.

"Skinny-dipping?"

Bob snickered. "Naked swimming."

Koji looked at Ruby, whose wide eyes were trained on Velvet. He couldn't imagine. And yet, he could.

With the picnic set, the girls went behind the boulder to change into their swimsuits, leaving Koji and Bob to undress to their trunks and wade into the crystal-clear creek. Koji's thoughts stayed with Ruby undressing behind the boulder. Entering the cool water had become both urgent and necessary.

• • •

On the other side of the boulder, Ruby grabbed Velvet by the arm. "Hey, you're not serious about skinny-dipping, are you?"

"No, silly! But you're on vacation... cut loose a little, will you?"

Cutting loose was not in Ruby's repertoire. Although she was enjoying her time with Velvet, she hadn't anticipated the painful memories that stirred when she stepped off the ship and onto the solid ground of the mainland. While her eyes searched for Velvet, who met her at the dock, she saw only the sneers of the angry mob who had taunted her thirteen-year-old self. This time, instead of a banana peel thrown at her head, Velvet met her with a bouquet of wildflowers and a radiant smile, still wearing the same heart-shaped necklace from her girlhood. Even though she would probably never again see the man who called her an adorable dirty little Jap, she found herself looking around corners for the tormentor who resided inside her.

Things were different now. She was busy and not looking for romance. She was here on holiday and would soon return to a Hawaii classroom. Yet she couldn't deny Koji made her mouth water like a child waiting for a slice of strawberry shortcake.

"Yoo-hoo, Earth to Ruby," Velvet said, returning Ruby's attention to her friend, standing naked before her, with her bathing suit dangling off of her finger.

"Ditch the pensive mood and spill," she said, placing her folded clothes on a ledge of the boulder. "I've waited long enough."

"Waited for what?"

"What do *you* think about Koji?"

"How come you haven't told me about him before?"

"You were in Hawaii. Why would I have told you about him when he's here in Sacramento?"

"He's cute," she said, knowing there was no harm in being honest with Velvet.

"Cute. That's it?"

"Okay, I can't *believe* I came here to visit *you*, and *you* introduce me to *that, that...* boy... with a minute's warning."

"Minute's warning?"

"Jeez, Velvet. About how dreamy he is." They laughed.

"So, you do like him!"

"Well if you must know, I feel myself blushing every time I look at him. And last night at the movies... what movie did we see anyway? Sitting in the dark theatre next to him... with our fingers in the same popcorn bag. I'm embarrassed to say what thoughts were going through my head."

Velvet playfully shimmied her bare breasts at Ruby. "Yeah, like what?"

"I'm not going to tell you!"

"Well, you're the one who brought it up."

"Velvet, they're on the other side of this rock. They know we're taking off our clothes and I... never mind."

Velvet's voice was bathed in sarcasm. "Is Miss Ruby going to wear a bathing suit?"

"Of course, I'm going to wear a bathing suit! I don't know those boys. I'm not swimming naked in front of two men I just met. I'd swim naked in front of you. I wouldn't care about that. But not them!"

"Well, aren't you prissy!"

Ruby put her hands on her hips. "I'm *not* prissy."

"You most certainly are! And you know what? I changed my mind." Velvet tossed the bathing suit that had been dangling on her finger onto the ground. "I'm not wearing a bathing suit."

"You wouldn't dare."

"Watch me!"

Incredulous, Ruby watched Velvet strut her beautiful, naked body from the shelter of the boulder while yelling, "Ready or not, here I come!"

Sounds of splashing and triumphant, unrestrained laughter followed.

"Oh boy," Ruby muttered, shaking her forehead into the palm of her hand. What was Velvet thinking? Ruby couldn't possibly fathom joining her. A proper girl... does not do *that*. She loved Velvet, but no way was she doing that! And she liked Koji so much that she didn't want him to get the wrong idea about her—to think she was *loose*. But Ruby couldn't help but wonder, what if Koji and Bob were naked too? Unable to bear the thought, she put on her bathing suit.

When the ruckus from Velvet's entrance on the other side had quieted down, Ruby braved her first steps. She wore a new two-piece red swimsuit, with a brassiere top tied behind her neck. Red was her signature color, and she hoped Koji liked the way she looked. She found him floating on his back in the creek, gazing overhead at the canopy of tree tops whispering in the relaxed breeze. He wore bathing trunks and Bob and Velvet were out of sight. Ruby offered a soft thanks to the universe and waded into the water.

"Where'd they go?" she asked.

Koji swam toward her and smiled, pointing upstream. "That way."

"Great," she said, releasing an exasperated sigh. "Maybe we could go the other way?"

"Good idea. *That*... was kind of awkward."

Ruby began relaxing. "It was awkward for me too. I love Velvet, but seriously! Sometimes I don't know what gets into her."

Koji's smile washed away all of her concerns.

They swam with and against the creek's gentle downstream flow and climbed out of the water following large, flat rocks—a staircase placed by nature. Sitting on a creek-side boulder, Ruby shook the water from her hair and tousled its waves among her fingers, while Koji approached a patch of goldenrod blooming along the streambank. He picked one of the bright yellow clusters, returned to where she sat, and tucked the flower gently behind her ear, his touch purposeful and gentle. The muscles in his arms bulged as he lowered himself beside her on the rock. The contrast of muscularity within his small frame gave Ruby a magical feeling, as if she were sitting beside a strong and sensitive *samurai*—a warrior who would fight to protect her.

"Oh look. Grapes," he said, reaching to pluck wild grapes from vines twisting around the base of a nearby tree.

Ruby lowered her back to the coolness of the rock, feeling her heart beat toward the sunlight skipping through the irregularly crowned sycamore trees. Koji was so handsome, and she could tell he was intelligent with some underlying passion she didn't yet understand. She wanted to know him better, to see below his unrevealing concrete facade. Except for her make-out sessions with Albert, she was completely inexperienced in the art of relationships and sexuality, and had not been attracted to anyone for years. Until now.

He returned and lay beside her, and propped up on an elbow. "Grape?"

"Thanks," she said, opening her mouth to the sweet and juicy fruit he placed between her lips. She gazed into his eyes, where they lingered in penetrating, infinite pools of brown. Koji returned her look with one suggesting the universe had choreographed their meeting, but he broke the spell when his fingers tickled her rib cage, giving rise to her spontaneous laughter.

"Hey," he said, looking at her mouth curiously, "you're missing a tooth in the back."

Ruby covered her mouth with her hand. "Oh, don't look back there."

"Why? It's cute."

"I hate my missing tooth," she said, her hand still over her mouth.

"Is there a story?"

The water suddenly tumbled from rock to rock with increased vitality. A breeze had picked up and the gentle whisper of leaves now swished and rustled. A cloud passed overhead and obscured the sun. It was dark, and she was backing away from the glint of pliers in the moonlight. Ruby pushed off the rock with her trembling hands, sat cross-legged so he could no longer peer into her mouth, and stared into the woods.

"Of course, there's a story," she said, with a wave of her hand. "There's a story behind everything, isn't there?"

"But honestly, I don't know anything about you. You know, Velvet fancies herself a matchmaker. Has she done this with you before?"

She leaned in for his answer.

"Once in a while."

"So, tell me a little about yourself."

Koji popped another grape into his mouth, taking his time responding. "She didn't tell you *anything* about me?"

"Not much. Your name and that you're from Japan."

He nodded. "Bob says you've graduated from college."

She wondered why he was deflecting. "Yes. In Hawaii."

"Education is everything. I'm sure your family is proud of you."

Wanting to know Koji's story, Ruby laid back down and propped herself up on her elbow facing him. "I guess. But tell me about your family, what brought you all here and when?"

"Oh, my family isn't here. I'm here by myself. My father died of cancer. I left my mother and brother behind and came here to finish high school. All the schools were destroyed when my city was bombed, you know."

"Gosh, I'm sorry. Which city? Not Hiroshima or Nagasaki?"

"Hiroshima."

Why hadn't Velvet told her he was from Hiroshima, the place where her mother's ashes had rested? She wanted to tell him that, but she was suddenly flustered. "Oh, I'm so sorry."

"It's okay."

"It's *not* okay!"

"Ruby, I've moved on."

Koji popped another grape into his mouth.

She pushed herself off the rock and lurched forward. "You lost... your city was bombed. You lost everything. How can you sit here eating grapes with indifference, saying it's okay?"

"Because war is brutal. It doesn't make sense to me to argue over acceptable ways of killing. Dead is dead."

The goldenrod tucked behind her ear suddenly smelled of crushed black licorice. She grabbed the flower to throw it in the creek, but somehow the blossom found its way into the pocket of her bathing suit. "War is brutal... no kidding. You don't have to tell me. I lived in an incarceration camp, did Velvet tell you?"

Koji sat up and tried to take her hand, but she pulled away.

"I know," he said. "Bob and Velvet did too. And I don't understand how America could do that to you, given the ideals it stands for. But bad things happen in war."

"How can you say that? Dismiss the unthinkable with bad things happen during war! I read the newspapers... people vaporized and turned to ash. And I know what it feels like to be an American who was treated like..." She paused, now shaking. "Koji, I was just a kid starting junior high school when they locked me up."

She stared at the uneaten grapes and contemplated the intimacy they'd shared moments before. Their vibration had changed fast and she wasn't sure what to do about it, if anything, except maybe change the subject. Koji had no way of knowing what she'd been through. He, too, must have gone through hell. Or worse.

She offered a nervous smile. "Anyway, let's get off that stuff. How long have you been here?"

"About a year and a half."

"And did you finish high school?"

He looked down, away from her gaze. "Next year. I have big plans."

She tried to put herself in his shoes and imagine how hard it must have been for him to witness unimaginable destruction, leave his family, and start over in a foreign country. Their brief tiff had not erased her interest in him. Nor, she hoped, his interest in her. "I'd like to know your plans, if you'll tell me."

He leaned into a more relaxed posture. "I knew little English when I came here. Now it's broken but I get by, and I work hard to earn money and to get good grades."

She reached into her pocket and rubbed her fingers along the goldenrod cluster, happy she hadn't tossed it in the water. The things that seemed important to him, she silently acknowledged, were the things important to her.

He continued, "And my deferral was approved so I can finish."

Wait a minute, she thought. "What do you mean, your deferral was approved?"

"Well, I'm an American citizen too. I was born in California, something my parents hid from me until I was twelve years old."

"That's amazing! I can't believe you were born here and didn't know it, living your whole life in Japan. That's really something."

"One foot here, one foot there."

"Me too, I guess."

"You have a foot in Japan?"

"Well no, but we almost moved there. That's what my father and stepmother wanted. Sometimes I feel trapped between the two cultures, but I'm an American girl. I like to go to the movies and listen to Tommy Dorsey and Frank Sinatra. I dreaded the thought of moving to Japan. The bomb changed everything for me too."

"Well, I'm happy to have left Japan for America."

"That makes sense to me, but having never been there, can you tell me your reasons?"

"*This* is the land of opportunity," he said, hands gesturing to the space around them.

His naivete and utopian view of America was borderline laughable, but she tried to be polite. "For some. Do you think it will be fair to you? It hasn't been fair to us. I mean to the Japanese people."

"It can be. Wars end and people move on, one way or another. *Shikata ga nai*, right?"

There was *that* phrase again. Things *could* be helped!

"Seriously, Koji? I lived behind barbed-wire fences for years. Armed guards yelled at me. I was just a little girl. None of that was right. Those years were stolen from us."

"That may be so, but in Japan, the government dictated what we learned, what we ate, and how much we got to eat. They starved the country to build a military intent on controlling all of Asia. It got us nowhere. Japan was decimated. It's a shell of a country now."

Ruby paused, slightly ashamed by her ignorance. "I guess I didn't think of it that way. I'm sorry, I truly am. Let's talk about your deferral. That's good. What would they call you, a conscientious objector? I guess you did that so you can return to your family in Japan?"

Ruby interpreted Koji's gaze going distant as confusion. She was about to explain her question when he rubbed his chin and responded. "No. I don't want to go back to Japan. As eldest son, my mother is my responsibility, so the decision to leave wasn't easy. I don't know if I'll ever go back. I want to be here. The deferral is so I can finish high school. Then I'll honor my duty and serve this country."

Ruby stared at the waters navigating the rough edges in the rocks, trying to make sense of what he said. Within moments, her emotions had taken a sharp turn. "Wait a minute. Why should you fight America's war? Why should you go? I don't think any Japanese should fight for another war! My sister's husband enlisted in the U.S. Army and was killed in Italy while his family and my sister remained imprisoned. He was foolish to do that, and you're foolish too. How could you possibly fight for the country that dropped an atomic bomb on your city *and* killed my father's family who lived there *and* destroyed my mother's grave? That's the craziest thing I've ever heard. What's the point? What will you fight for? Do you know what this country REALLY stands for? How could you? You're... you're just a high school boy who doesn't know anything!"

Koji slid off the boulder, picked up a rock, and skipped it across the creek. "It's my duty."

Was he for real? Was it possible to be so cavalier about war that you can talk about it and skip rocks at the same time?

She boiled inside. "That's absolutely ridiculous! It's not your duty. You came here a year ago. How is it possibly your duty?"

"I was born here, I chose to come back and build my life here, and that means I need to pay my dues. America is the world I want to live in and if enlisting is what I have to do as an American, then that's the price I will pay."

"You are so placid. How can you be so willing to follow what a government does? This government did horrible things to my family and unthinkable things to your people. How *can* you?"

Koji's eyes bore into her. "You don't have to understand me. But understand this," he said in a measured voice and with an unflinching demeanor.

"I've moved on from suffering and this is how my future will unfold and how I think it's *best* to unfold. You choose to suffer. Maybe, just maybe, you might want to consider letting go of everything that makes you so angry. It's not very attractive."

She jumped to her feet without ever taking her eyes off of his.

"Don't you preach to me. Don't you *dare* preach to me! Yes, you've had your pain but you don't know what it was like to be betrayed by the country you love so much. *You* don't know what betrayal is like."

"I do know what it's like. Japan was an aggressor and betrayed its citizens for decades and decades. You may think this is a horrible country to live in, but I think it might be the greatest country in the world. You just try and see if you can live in Japan. You would die there! Maybe you experienced some hardship during the war, but that's life. Put it behind you and move on, or bitterness will settle into your root system and shrivel your soul. There's lots of life yet to live, and if you're looking in the past, you can't move forward. I don't know about you, but I intend to put the war as far behind me as I can."

Ruby tasted blood on her lips. Who in the hell did this boy think he was talking to her this way?

"How dare you tell me how I should feel!" she yelled.

The creek's burble now seemed to thunder.

Storm clouds bulging with frustration rolled through Ruby and overcame the rational part of her brain. These were no ordinary clouds, but the unstable kind, from which tornados spun. Her core twisted with an intensity and immediacy from which she had no control, as the swirling vortex unleashed its fury.

"*Shikata ga nai* this... you... you... foolish, foolish Japanese," she cried, as she stripped off her bathing suit top and threw it into Koji's face. "Nobody, not anybody, tells me what to think, especially not some under-educated high school boy!"

Not intending to give him any opportunity to respond, she jumped in the creek, straightened her spine, and began swimming upstream.

WINDWARD

1950-1955 – Hawaii

Ruby returned to Honolulu and found refuge on her island haven, distant from the mainland and its remembrances of feeling small and angry. With the fall semester underway and studies consuming her mind, she intended to forget the moments that had eroded her confidence and the infuriating high school boy who had ruined a perfectly lovely afternoon. Even so, she tucked the withered goldenrod into the crevice of a conch shell where it would be safely out of her sight.

For the next five years, hands sped around the clock face as she checked the boxes of her accomplishments. She finished her studies and spent the spring of 1951 in Kauai completing her internship at Koloa Elementary School. While on the island, she visited Waimea and discovered that Pig Lady had died. She concluded her childhood memories were too painful to revisit.

From occasional postcards, she learned her father and stepmother had left Hilo for Berkeley, California, where Father was appointed Reverend to a temple. Settling into contented widowhood, Mari continued working as a dressmaker and caring for her aging in-laws. Immersed in her classes at Stanford Law, Velvet's cards and missives had trailed away—much like Bob, who had been drafted by the army and deployed to Korea. Ruby's thoughts drifted to Koji, wondering if he, too, had joined or been called into service.

In the fall of 1951, Ruby was assigned to a school in Waimānalo on Oahu, where she taught second grade in a classroom that opened to gorgeous mountain views and lived rent-free in a cottage with other unmarried teachers. As the days and seasons passed, the steady calm of Hawaii's blissful energy spirited her away and nourished her island soul. She turned her attention inward and reconnected to herself. In the evenings, sitting under a large banyan tree behind the cottage, she graded word problems and cursive practices and reflected on her students. She was firm, but kind, in building the fragile self-esteem of her family of seven-year-olds, as they developed vocabularies and abilities to understand right from wrong.

She spent Saturday afternoons facing clear, open waters. With sand granules nestled between her toes, she watched young families build castles and play in the surf and wondered if someday she might be a mother teaching her children about the ocean's joys and dangers. The acts of mothering were constant—rescuing dropped sandwiches from the sand, chasing snorkels and flippers into the sea, posing with children while fathers snapped photographs.

But it was seeing the way the mothers cared for their injured children that made her ribcage spasm. The woman who cradled her son when he twisted his ankle running along the undulating sand. The woman who quieted her daughter's screams with tender soothing when the older brother smashed her sandcastle. The woman who dried her child's tears and rubbed away the burn of a jellyfish sting. The love and tenderness of a real mother—a mother like Mama.

Resting on the white sand of the windward shores where the ocean waves were the bluest in Hawaii, Ruby had been oblivious to the shifting current within her. Now, she allowed the current to linger. The current radiated in her chest and then into the back of her throat where a familiar lump formed.

She gazed across the berm where the salt water returned home. The waves crashed and the surface rippled to the blur of the horizon. A shimmer of light. A soft breath. *Let it go.*

With her eyes closed, she surrendered. Warmth flooded her jaw, her cheeks, the orbs of her eyes, and then flowed through her as gentle waves. Salty tears spilled down her face. Not tears of sadness. Not tears of bitterness. Not tears of anger. But tears of healing. Tears of cherished memories that glistened and refreshed. Tears that only love can bring.

WILD BLUE YONDER

1951 – 1955

Koji enlisted in the U.S. Air Force the morning after graduating from high school. Earlier that day, he mailed George Sato a letter of gratitude, along with a money order repaying George for financing his fare from Japan to San Francisco. He left Sacramento for Fort Polk, Louisiana, debt-free and with a patriotic spirit ready to serve America.

A year later, he stood on a massive slab of rock that shifting tectonic plates had advanced above the Earth's calm, reflective sea. In the dream, he faced another formation of equal size, miles away on the opposite side of a large body of water. He fixed his gaze on the flat surface at the formation's highest ground—a helicopter pad. But for whom he wondered? And why? He reached into his pocket for his sunglasses. The lenses filtered the glare and enabled him to distinguish a circular pattern of rocks paving the pad's surface, perhaps placed by an ancient culture.

He was tasked with engineering a system to cross the water and he delved into the toolkit of his intellect. Building a bridge wasn't possible, so he drifted deeper into his dream and visualized people crossing in chairs suspended from ropes that moved them along a pulley system. Smaller rock formations, close enough together to walk among them, peeked from under the surface, revealing a fraction of their true size. Was the tide out or in? Was he seeing everything possible to see, or a mere glimpse of what might be seen?

Compelled forward, he stepped onto the first of many rocks. As he continued, the surroundings changed and began to appear as though painted by the universe with a brush dipped in magic. Though the skies were clear where he paused, a mountain range rose in distant fog. Intermittent hunger pangs turned to a steady ache. He checked his watch, confirming he'd lost track of time. Now, he needed to decide. Should he turn back or continue to the other side, risking the unknown? The rock beneath him swayed.

Before falling into the abyss, he pulled himself from the vivid dream and awoke in his bunk to the steady pitch of his ship somewhere in the Pacific headed to Japan, where he was assigned to U.S. Far East Headquarters in Tokyo. In the early dawn, enveloped in the snores of his bunkmates, he reflected on the all-too-real dream while it was still fresh in his mind. Pick a side. Risk the unknown. The feeling was indeed unsteady. He closed his eyes moistened with tears to recall more clearly small details from his past—Naoki's snores, his mother's *udon* soup, his childhood home where the family had cared for the dying and the dead. Painful memories of young lives wasted muddied his throat.

He stretched fuzz from his restless mind and body and rolled to reach under his cot where his *Jizō* was tucked inside of a duffel bag. Stroking its verdigris finish seemed to polish Koji's pride in all he had accomplished since leaving Japan and nourish the intensity of his spirit. The small statue triggered the nostalgic memory of Naoki's wisecrack that day long ago on Miyajima—*lucky yours is metal.* Koji missed his brother, now nineteen years old, managing the farm and attending Hiroshima's upper secondary school.

As the ship groaned and his bunkmates stirred, he caught a glimpse of his mate's pinup calendar, featuring a sultry redhead whose massive breasts spilled from her lacy lingerie. Never had he enjoyed the nipples of a woman with breasts that large. *Someday, maybe?* He returned to the place where the souvenirs of his mind and his dreams coalesced.

•••

He was greeted in Tokyo by Japan's polite, punctual culture and a dissolved Empire rebuilding its systems and economy. The heady smell of fish markets transported him back in time.

Months passed before he had accumulated enough leave to visit his mother and brother. The Hiroshima-bound train from Tokyo departed precisely on the half-hour and whizzed him past Mount Fuji hours later. The volcano's perfect symmetry and snow-capped peak, sharp against the clear sky, stood unchanging, harboring immortal secrets and symbolizing the perfection of Japan's culture.

The next day, when the train pulled into Hiroshima Station, his legs were stiff and his stomach empty. Outside of the station, the delicious aroma of *yaki imo* drifted in the humid air and unlocked blurred memories of the sweet potato he had shared with Emi. His eyes feasted on a city rising from the ashes of its char. The glistening late afternoon sunlight of reconstruction had replaced the dismal shadows that once covered the lifeless city with weary hopelessness. From the rubble and aftereffects of energy that had traveled and destroyed at the speed of light, seedlings sprouted into oleanders and camphor trees sprouted new branches—budding sources of resilience and hope. Hovering under the station's newly constructed canopy and checking his hair in the reflection of a window, stood his brother. Naoki had sprouted into the full-grown frame of a man with a strong resemblance to their father.

Koji waved and Naoki looked his way. The affection etched on Naoki's face made clear that he had seen Koji, and Koji's beaming smile responded in kind.

"*Okaerinasai*," Naoki said, welcoming his older brother home with a respectful bow.

Koji smacked his brother on the back with the light touch of his palm, his casual manner of saying it was good to be home.

On the drive to Fuchu, Naoki explained the locals' novel description of distance—now, every location was measured in the meters or kilometers from the hypocenter. Hiroshima's modern streets now crisscrossed in a dependable grid, replacing its once-winding streets and alleys. New housing, where families slept peacefully, replaced scrappy huts that had been constructed with boards and tin. New schools, where children learned the values of democracy and played without fear, replaced battered open-air buildings. New specialty shops, where people purchased goods and services without rationing, replaced stores destroyed to rubble. Children and families splashed and swam in the rivers brimming with life.

Soon, they were winding through the landscape of Koji's childhood, and it was time for him to release the words weighing him down.

"Naoki, would you mind pulling over for a few minutes? There's something I want to talk to you about before we see *Okāsan*."

Naoki parked the car.

Koji reached for the cigarettes in his shirt pocket. "Want one?"

Naoki's smile was relaxed. "Nah."

"I want to thank you for taking care of things while I was gone. When I left Japan, it was for the opportunity to finish high school, something that wasn't possible for me here. I'm relieved the occupation reformed the schools and you are now close to graduating. I'm proud of you, Naoki, and of the way you stepped up to work the farm, take care of *Okāsan*, and get good grades in school. My leaving required sacrifice from you and there are few ways for me express my gratitude."

Koji took a deep, calming drag and watched the smoke curl from the tip of his cigarette.

"When I lived here, I always wondered what it was like in America. Over the past few years, I've fallen in love with the country—her government, her strength, her opportunity. And as an American, I am proud to serve her in the Air Force. It's ironic she returned me to Japan for service, isn't it?"

Their eyes met, and Naoki nodded.

He extinguished the cigarette in the ash tray.

Koji continued. "I know my responsibility as *chōnan* is here in Japan. But I don't want my life here. I want a life in America. Naoki, I intend to discharge my oldest-son obligation and the ultimate authority of the family to you, including my interest in all of our land, if you'll allow me to do so. Our property will be yours to do with as you please, as long as you promise to care for our mother."

Naoki's graceful nod accepting Koji's decision showed it was something he had been expecting.

• • •

The house hadn't changed. Their mother was waiting on the *engawa* when they arrived. Save for a few gray hairs, she looked younger and more relaxed than when Koji had said goodbye to her. She touched the side of his face with her warm, gentle hand.

After stuffing himself with *Okāsan's miso* soup, grilled mackerel, and *sunomono*, and while Naoki busied himself with washing dishes, Koji retreated to the privacy of his old room. He pushed the *tansu* aside, pried open the loose floorboard, and unburied the American leaflets that had warned of impending doom and promised a new and peaceful Japan would follow the war. Japan hadn't heeded the warning, but America had fulfilled her promise and his childhood wish that the war would lead to a better life.

He tucked the leaflets into his bag, moved the *tansu* back into place, and then entered the bathroom first and one last time as *chōnan*. There, he scrubbed his exhausted body with the long-handled soapy brush, immersed himself in the *ofuro's* warm water, and drowned any residual memory that need not be remembered into the recesses of his mind.

The next day, Koji climbed the hill to the cemetery and sat before his family's monument. Studying the family *kamon*, he reconnected with memories of his father and permitted his grief to flow in a way that wasn't possible six years ago when *Otōsan's* ashes were interred. He trusted *Otōsan* would respect his decision to return to and stay in the United States, but how would he find the words to rebel against the convention of his familial obligation and tell *Okāsan*?

The breeze whispered through the trees and approaching footsteps rustled.

"I thought I'd find you here," his mother said, now standing behind him. She cupped his shoulder with her warm hand.

He turned to face her. "*Okāsan*, there's something I must ask you." His voice cracked. "I can't seem to find the words."

"It's okay, Koji. I know you chose America. You go. You be happy."

• • •

A few days later, Koji kissed his mother goodbye and returned to Tokyo.

Time passed. In June 1955, he unpacked his bags and settled into his sparsely furnished apartment in Berkeley, California. With great pride, he displayed his Staff Sergeant's stripes and the Korean Service, UN Service, and National Defense Service medals on a small shelf by the bed, grateful to the nation that would provide him with the education assistance under the G.I Bill to attend the University of California.

Nine

1957 – 1958

OH, MY STARS

1957 – Berkeley, CA

Koji rested his pen on the table, its surface gilded smooth by the touch of hands, books, and papers. He straightened his back, relieving the pain and tightness.

He turned his head to the left until he felt the welcome stretch of tissue and bones moving over each other, repeated to the right where his eyes rested on leather-bound volumes organized on polished bookshelves, and then leaned his neck backward with his face to the soaring barrel-vaulted ceiling of the north reading room. Silence filled his ears and he breathed in the familiar aroma of beeswax, knowledge, and success.

With his head square over his shoulders, he watched the morning drizzle trickle down the Roman-arched window capping the far end of the room, and his thoughts drifted to Gene Kelly dancing in the rain. Seeing the lighthearted movie had been a welcome break from his demanding studies at UC Berkeley, but his date with Suzie the floozy had come to a screeching halt when she caught the eye of a fraternity man in an expensively tailored sport coat. No matter. Suzie was a mere distraction and raised no feelings, at least not within his heart.

Koji's eyes wandered the room that had come to life since his pre-dawn arrival. Head-down students under bronze task lights were spread among tables stretching the enormous length and width of the room, while others searched within the drawers of the card catalog for research materials and literary treasures. He returned to his comparative politics paper and ignored the grumbling in his stomach and the sound of clicking heels, as someone walked past and then returned.

Now, the person who stood over him silently nagged for his attention. He raised his eyes to the face he'd never forgotten, the one that stirred turbulence in his stomach.

The face of Ruby Ishimaru.

"Hello, Koji."

Seven years had passed since he last saw her. Koji liked to believe he was in control of his life, his words, his emotions. Yet here he sat, at a loss for words, on the wood library chair that seemed to splinter his control, staring at Ruby for an overlong moment.

"Ruby. What are you doing here?"

"May I sit down? Just for a few minutes."

He rose and offered her the chair opposite him. Her exquisite face was even more chiseled than he remembered, and her waist tinier above the fuller curve of her hips.

"I was reluctant to interrupt you when I saw you sitting here," she said, her cheeks in a hot blush. "But I had to... to apologize for my indecent behavior that day. You know, at the swimming hole."

Embarrassment seemed to soften her otherwise stony demeanor. Feeling sorry for her, he lied. "Ancient history, Ruby. Forgotten long ago."

"I appreciate your graciousness, Koji. But truly, I've felt the shame of that day for years."

"Apology accepted. Are you a student here too?"

"No. I love to visit this library when I have the time. I moved to Berkeley two years ago after I finished graduate school and my first years of teaching in Hawaii. I teach elementary school now, here in Berkeley. Tell me about you. You're a student?"

"Yes, for almost two years since I was discharged from the Air Force."

She shook her head with a look that radiated haughtiness. "So, you joined."

"Yes, right after graduation. I spent most of my four years in Tokyo at a desk job and began my studies here right after returning. I have a lot of time to make up for, so I maintain a heavy course load and go year-round."

"Well, good for you. Sounds like your plan is on track. What are you studying?"

"Political Science. I'm hoping to go into diplomacy with the State Department, perhaps at the U.S. Embassy in Japan."

"Oh, so you want to return to Japan after all?"

"Not permanently, but I would as a springboard to something bigger and better. I want to get to Washington, D.C. first. I'll see where that takes me. How about you? You like it here?"

"It's okay. My father and stepmother live in Berkeley, and my father convinced me to move here. He said I'd have more opportunities for career advancement and community connection than I would on the islands. But I don't appreciate the California mindset. Do you believe that during my interview with the school superintendent, he proclaimed me the first *Nisei* to work in the elementary school? It was as if he said that to make me feel grateful for the job or something. But I'm here, at least for now."

What was it about this woman? Koji didn't understand why she found it so hard to let things go, why her instinct was to lean into combat, fighting the war within.

"Well, thanks for stopping and for your apology," he said, rifling his papers.

"Sure. I'll let you get back to your studies. Good seeing you, Koji."

"You too. Don't catch cold. It's wet out there today."

"That's January," she said, pushing back her chair.

Ruby walked away, but quickly returned to his table.

"I'm a member of the Young Buddhist Society that meets at my father's temple. Maybe you'd like to come to our meeting sometime." She picked up his pen and notebook and scribbled *1524 Oregon Street* in the top margin. "We're meeting tomorrow night."

"Thanks, but I can't make it."

She offered a weak smile. "Well, some other time then. We meet the fourth Thursday of each month."

"I'll think about it."

As Ruby walked away, his eyes lingered on her shapely legs and elegant carriage.

• • •

Later, Koji crossed the lawn from the library satisfied with the draft of his paper. The drizzle had stopped. After three days of rain, everyone seemed to crave the outdoors and the campus grounds were alive with activity. Students studied or played catch. Lovers kissed on a nearby bench. Mothers from the neighborhood pushed baby carriages, while holding the tiny hands of their toddlers. He laid his jacket on the damp ground at the base of the Campanile and leaned against the clock tower as its bell struck five o'clock.

Surrounded by life, Koji was unable to grasp the withering feeling of aloneness stirring in his gut. Thinking it must be hunger, and with little time to eat before his evening class, he reached into his pocket for the squashed peanut butter and jelly sandwich. Night was falling. If the cloud cover cleared, he might walk home later under a star-filled sky. His mind wandered to Ruby, a woman as sharp as the points of a star, whose beauty dazzled in the fringes of clandestine shadows.

Distracted by a banging noise, Koji's eyes followed the sound to a toddler trying to force an object into the hole of a shape-sorter toy. The boy's mother chatted with the woman beside her, ignoring her son's frustration. Koji finished his sandwich and started walking toward the boy on his way to Bacon Hall. As he approached, he was able to see the boy's mind in motion and his determination to push a star into a round opening. Impossible, thought Koji. As he was about to offer to help, the boy pried the lid off of the bucket and tossed the star inside with a satisfied smile.

That's right, thought Koji. Some things aren't meant to be forced. He didn't understand why, but he lost a bit of his sanity—feeling more frustrated than happy—when he was with Ruby. He was wise to recognize their incompatibility now, before investing too much time and energy into something not meant to be. He walked with long purposeful steps past the boy and across the damp lawn. Loose grass cuttings stuck to his shoes.

RUST

1957 – Berkeley, CA

A cool evening breeze filtered through the open window of the temple where Ruby greeted over twenty members of the Young Buddhist Association. They were mostly single adults and a few teenagers, people who gave their time and talents to their spiritual family, finding fellowship, unity, and wholeness among others with shared experiences, including the shame of incarceration. Ruby smoothed the lines of her tweed pencil skirt and straightened the wide belt. The snug-fitting turquoise pullover required no smoothing. This outfit—a recent birthday present from Mari—made her feel polished and capable of accomplishing anything.

She called the meeting to order and reviewed the agenda, making eye contact with members in the audience while scanning faces for Koji Matsuo. As with January and February, he hadn't come to this meeting either. Moving on to the new business of transforming a vacant lot to a community garden on Oregon Street near Grant, she began capturing the group's decisions on a portable blackboard in teacher-perfect cursive.

She was confirming the member's name in charge of zoning approval when Koji entered the temple and sat in the back. They established eye contact, and he seemed to hold her gaze for an awkward moment.

After the meeting adjourned, Koji lingered, drinking tea and conversing with strangers who welcomed him warmly. Ruby wanted to thank him for coming before he left, but she was held captive by a woman's incessant gossip. She kept her eye on him and was pleased to see his steady manner and handshakes, not the slightest clumsy or ill at ease. The busybody took a breath, and Ruby used the opportunity to excuse herself and scoot away.

"Koji! Hi! I'm delighted you joined us."

"Thanks for inviting me. The garden sounds like a marvelous community service project. I'd enjoy learning more about it sometime."

"Sure! Would you like to walk there now?" she asked, glancing at her watch. "It's early."

His brow furrowed.

"Not tonight. I have an early class tomorrow. Are you free Saturday afternoon? I can stop by for you at two o'clock."

Ruby had planned to shop for baby clothes with a friend who had left her teaching job when the school discovered she was in the family way. Her friend would understand if they rescheduled for another day.

"Yes."

• • •

Ruby spent two restless nights thinking about Koji, wondering what she would wear on Saturday and where the afternoon might lead. She felt on the brink of something. It wasn't that being attracted to a man made her nervous. It was her intense hope that he like her. Her behavior at the swimming hole had been uncouth, and she feared she might once again say or do something to provoke an argument.

But it was more than that. As much as she liked Koji and wanted him to like her, she didn't want to like him *too* much. After all, liking him might become something more. The kind of something that frightened her. Yet he showed up in her town and at her father's temple, with his wavy hair, firm jaw and confident handshakes, and in two brief interactions, undermined her resolve to go slow and not jump into something she'd regret.

She hoped Koji would arrive before her father and stepmother returned from running errands to spare him their scrutiny. Her last boyfriend had been chronically late, and it had been nothing for her to stew for an hour waiting for him. How dare he have put a higher premium on his time than her own. When the boyfriend stood her up, she was no longer willing to put up with his rude and inconsiderate behavior, and she ended the relationship by refusing to accept his calls. The doorbell rang at two o'clock sharp. Ruby opened the door with a pleased smile.

"The florist said they should blossom soon in a sunny window," Koji said, presenting her with a small potted daffodil.

Her heart fluttered. "How sweet," she said, admiring his smart casual attire, validating her choice to wear slacks. She placed the daffodils on the entry table, joined him on the porch, and pulled the door closed.

At the vacant lot on Oregon Street, the only hint of a community garden was a colorful sign, SOUTH BERKELEY COMMUNITY GARDEN COMING SOON. Ruby described the committee's many plans for the parcel and appreciated Koji's interest in the project that meant so much to her. His years of farming made him a terrific resource, and she hoped for his involvement. "Thanks for coming here with me," she said. "What are your plans for the rest of the day?"

"It's such a nice day, I thought we'd go for ice cream."

"Sure, you lead."

Walking alongside Koji, Ruby didn't care where they went for ice cream. They strolled along Shattuck Avenue, window shopping its bustling stores and inhaling the savory aroma of roasted garlic wafting from Giovanni's Restaurant. Koji steered the conversation to Ruby's time at the University of Hawaii and her teaching assignments since graduation.

Approaching the viridescent arch of the university's Sather Gate, Koji pointed to a jovial older gentleman in a white cap and smock, tending his ice cream cart. "There's the Crunchy-Munchy Man. Best ice cream around."

Crunchy-Munchy Man acknowledged passersby with a tip of his hat to the ladies and a salute to the gentlemen. He listened with his eyes, talked with his hands, and lit the faces of children by delivering their cones with a flourish.

"What's your favorite?" Koji asked.

She dipped into her pocket for coins. "Strawberry. Shall we go Dutch?"

"Thanks, but I've got it. I saved most of my pay when I was in the service."

The man accepted Koji's quarters and delivered change from the coin dispenser worn on his belt.

They found a nearby bench, and he asked about the community garden—how will you get permission from the lot owner, where will the water come from, who may use the garden, who will fund it, and what will they plant? By the time she finished answering his many questions, her ice cream was melting.

"Here, let me." Koji dabbed the cream from around her lips with his handkerchief, his tender touch lulling her body into a warm and creamy pool.

She held his gaze, which conveyed a certain seriousness.

An elderly couple sat on the bench opposite them and held hands while sharing a single cone. When the man smiled at the woman, his smile radiated an adoration that reached deep into the crinkles of his eyes. "Gosh, they're cute," Ruby said. "Isn't it lovely how some people enjoy their entire lives together?"

Koji told her about his parents' tender relationship and how his father had died a few short months after the bombing. She told him about losing her mother when she was ten years old and how Mama had already missed most of her life and would miss all of her future.

"Does it hurt when you remember your father?" she asked.

"Sometimes, but not like it used to."

"Somedays it hurts so much, it feels like Mama just died. I tell myself that as long as sorrow is in my heart, her love remains."

"But it's been so long. How many years since she died?"

"Eighteen years this month," she said, with a painful longing for her mother's touch.

"Doesn't holding onto sorrow for that long make you... well, kind of rusty?"

Suddenly, her heart pounded. "What do you mean?" Her voice suggested an answer was unnecessary.

"It seems to me holding onto that kind of grief dissolves joy, like rust dissolves metal."

"Well, at least I know it's there. Hidden rust is more harmful."

Koji shrugged, walked away a few steps, stooped down, and reached

322

for something on the sidewalk. "Look, a penny." He held the coin to the sunlight. "1939."

The year Mama died.

"What's that Frank Sinatra song about pennies?" he asked.

She felt a tingling in her chest recalling Sinatra's voice.

"So, when you hear it thunder
Don't run under a tree
There'll be pennies from heaven
For you and me."

Nearby, the bells of the Campanile struck four o'clock and Ruby felt a slight chill.

"I'd better get home and help with supper," she said.

As she turned to leave, the words tumbled from her mouth. "Do you want to help with the garden?"

"It's a terrific project, but I'm pretty busy with school. I don't think so."

"Will I see you again?" she asked, staring at the shiny pennies in his loafers.

"I don't know, Ruby. It seems we have little in common except hardship and death."

She struggled to find the right words. "If only that weren't true."

She walked away with her head held high, forcing herself to focus on anything except why this man brought out the worst in her.

TRICK? OR TREAT?

1957 – Berkeley, CA

Koji followed a crowd of students out of the lecture hall and walked down the South Hall's magnificent central stairway. His palm glided over the wood banister, mellowed over time by thousands of students who had come before him. He appreciated the air of intelligence the university's architect had incorporated into the classical design.

Stepping outside, he smelled the early autumn air and made his way to an empty bench where he opened his notebook to a document torn along the fold lines. He unfolded the paper, and once again, reviewed the requirements of his degree program. Organized by general requirements, requirements for his major, and electives, this tattered sheet was Koji's map, where he plotted and tracked completed classes and classes yet to complete, with earned credits and credits yet to earn. Three composition credits, plus three history credits, plus three political science credits, tallied semester after semester, to attain that necessary cumulative total of one hundred twenty. A mere thirty-six credits to record and on track to graduate in the spring, he realized his academic accomplishments had snuck up on him, much like a deep tan accumulates over the summer.

September had become his favorite month. The verdant leaves of Japanese maple trees changed to vibrant scarlet. Fresh produce transitioned from watermelon, peppers, and tomatoes to collard greens, beets, and onions. His mind drifted to the community garden. He had wandered past the garden over the summer months and observed much progress. Community volunteers had cleared the lot, tilled bed plots, and nurtured seedlings to yield a seasonal bounty. Childhood memories of farming flooded his heart as he studied his clean hands—now missing the gritty sift of dirt. Before he knew it, his feet were taking him to the intersection of Oregon and Grant.

The community garden's colorful sign came into focus. On the opposite side of the street, a teacher herded a line of young schoolchildren swinging plastic buckets and carrying small gardening tools. The woman's stern voice was borderline bossy, yet she carried herself with the classic grace of a Japanese woman. While the children waited to cross the street, two boys began sword fighting with hand trowels. Before the teacher broke up the commotion, a trowel had connected with its target. Koji quickened his pace and then ducked behind the panels of a large parked truck.

Hidden by the truck, he peeked to get a better look.

At Ruby.

"Children… quiet." Ruby took the arm of the offending child. "Tommy, sit on the grass."

She knelt in front of the crying boy. "Johnnie, where does it hurt?"

The boy pulled up his shirt and showed her his belly.

She patted the spot with a certain tenderness, and the boy's cries quieted to gasps.

"Better?"

Johnnie nodded. She rubbed her fingers through the child's hair and then held her palms over his cheeks, looking into his eyes and speaking words Koji couldn't hear. She took Johnnie's hand, and they approached Tommy. He, too, was crying.

Koji envisioned her negotiating the apology that preceded the shaking of hands between the boys.

Ruby instructed the children to look both ways for traffic. She stepped off the curb, walked into the center of the road, and stretched her arms wide. "Children, I won't tolerate any more nonsense today. Now stay in line as you cross the road. I'll meet you in the garden."

With the last child safely across the street, she glanced in Koji's direction before following the children, seeming to take no notice of him.

Koji sat on the truck's bumper and lit a cigarette. As smoke curled skyward from the embers, he imagined Ruby at the garden, teaching her young students how to grow lettuce from seed, how to pick wax beans, how to harvest pumpkins in time to light up Halloween and fill pies at Thanksgiving, and how to care for something that's alive. And he imagined she would someday make a wonderful mother. Why did she keep finding her way into his life? Or had he found his way into hers? The woman annoyed and yet tantalized him, leaving him restless and craving paper-thin slices of *fugu*, a lethal delicacy.

He crushed the cigarette butt under the heel of his shoe and walked away.

• • •

Ruby closed her book, *Peyton Place*, a sexy novel about the scandals and tense social anatomy of a small New England town. She squirmed in her seat and looked out the window to the lemon tree in the front yard bursting with plump fruit. A certain ache flooded her body as she imagined what it would feel like to give her fragile heart to a man and share her inner world and body with him. In her fantasy, she wore a blush peignoir set. His gaze penetrated her eyes as his fingers caressed her arms and unbuttoned the tiniest of covered buttons. As the silk fell from her shoulders, his fingers trailed toward her breasts, now revealed through the sheer bodice of her nightgown. How exquisite to feel so beautiful at the precise moment he promised gentleness when they became one.

Alone in the quiet house, Ruby jumped at the piercing ring of the telephone resting on the marred walnut table across the living room. An unrelenting timbre followed and then reverberated, faded, and started again. And again. She wondered who the caller might be. Perhaps it was that arrogant lawyer her father had pushed on her. How long must she continue tolerating her Father's introductions to his highly educated and professional acquaintances, mostly *Kibei* educated in Japan? The proper husband material. She wanted to end her dates with these men as soon as the date started, wishing time would speed up, so she might go home, only to wish time would slow as she contemplated turning twenty-nine on her next birthday. She had disliked each of the men, and she looked for any excuse to avoid them.

She didn't answer at first, hoping the caller would give up. But the ringing continued, demanding to be answered, demanding her to cross the room and pick up the receiver, heavy and cold to her touch. "Hello."

"Hi, Ruby?" the familiar voice said.

Why was Koji calling her when he had made it abundantly clear they were not right for one another?

"Yes, this is she."

"This is Koji Matsuo. How are you?"

Her grip on the receiver strengthened. This man was a recipe for uncomfortable feelings.

"I'm fine, thank you. And you?" she asked, oozing politeness.

"Good. I'm calling to see if you might enjoy going to a dance with me on October twelfth?"

Her hand sweated against the now warm receiver and her mind raced. She liked Koji, but was frustrated by his ambivalence—he seemed to like her one moment, then reject her the next.

Pinning the receiver between her shoulder and her ear, she twisted her moist hands together, considering and delaying her response.

"It's at the American Legion," he said. "I'm a member now. I'll pick you up at seven thirty if you'd like to go."

"That sounds lovely." She thought the Veterans Memorial building was a bit too far for high heels. "Are we walking?"

"No. We'll go with my friend, Tony, from the Legion, and his date, Patty. Tony has a car."

The paper pad kept by the telephone was covered with the swirls, flowers, and hearts she had doodled while they concluded the call with pleasantries. She tore the sheet from the pad and used it to replace her bookmark in *Peyton Place*.

• • •

Two weeks later, Koji arrived on time for the dance. Regrettably, Ruby's father and stepmother were home. She had told her parents a bit about him earlier in the day, tolerating their negativity. They hadn't met Koji, yet they had already judged him unworthy of her, a farm boy with no college degree. After quick introductions, bows, and head nods, Ruby and Koji escaped the uncomfortable once-over for the car and more friendly introductions between Ruby, Tony, and Patty.

"Thank you," Ruby said, as Koji opened the car door and offered his hand to her. She slid onto the back seat and smoothed the chiffon folds of her dress. The florist's white box with the pink ribbon on the seat didn't escape her attention.

Minutes later, Tony parked the car and they walked down Center Street. The facade of the officious Veterans Memorial building commemorated three wars—the Civil, Spanish-American, and World War I, its imposing concrete supporting the weight of past and future conflicts.

They joined two other couples at one of many eight-top tables in the crowded, smoke-filled dance hall. Pumpkin centerpieces overflowed with yellow and orange chrysanthemums and lilies, tucked among colorful leaves. Whiskey sours flowed from a tiered glass fountain. Balloon bouquets flanked the stage and dangled among curly ribbons and streamers above the tuxedo-clad band members warming their instruments.

The band leader stepped to the microphone.

"Good evening, ladies and gentlemen! I'm Leo Everett and we are the Everett Brothers. We have a special evening planned for you, and we'll get things started with a gentle Sinatra medley."

Leo Everett cued the band with his baton, and they began playing "I've Got You Under My Skin."

Koji pushed his chair back. "Would you like to dance?"

She took his hand, and he led her to the dance floor. He positioned his body, clasped his left hand over her right, placed his other hand at the curve of her back, and stepped forward with a self-assured movement that said he was no stranger to taking partners in his arms. His hair smelled of fresh pomade, his suit of grassy wool, and his breath of cigarettes. She sensed a stiffness in his body that soon relaxed into hers, as they moved together and their breaths mingled.

"Do you like Frank Sinatra?" he asked.

"I do. Just not 'Don't Fence Me In.'"

"But that's a terrific song."

"Not when you've spent years behind fences."

They continued swaying to the music, but an awkward silence filled the space between them.

"I understand," he said. "No longer fenced in, yet still fenced off."

She fought the sadness tightening in her chest. "Yes, I suppose. But I don't mean to be."

He pressed his palm at her waist to draw her closer, and her knees went weak.

The band finished the set and everyone applauded.

"May I get you something to drink?" he asked.

"Thank you. I'd love a whiskey sour. Extra cherries, please."

She excused herself to the ladies' room, powdered her nose, and touched up her lipstick. Koji was waiting for her at the table with her drink and a Coke when she returned. "No whiskey sour for you?"

"I drink little. It makes me sleepy."

Was it really the alcohol? Or maybe he didn't like feeling too relaxed or the least bit out of control. Either way, she was pleased he wasn't a big drinker. She also admired that he was on time, gracious, and honest, all signaling a certain sense of honor.

They sipped their drinks and watched Tony and Patty spin around the dance floor to the Cha-Cha and the Tango. "They're fantastic dancers!" Ruby said, admiring the perfect form and backward extension of Patty's leg as her upper body stretched seductively forward, her lips a heartbeat from Tony's, and her spine as flexible as an accordion. The dance ended when Tony dipped Patty's fully extended body inches from the floor. By then, other dancers who had stopped to marvel at and applaud their sultry finesse surrounded the couple.

The music mellowed.

"How are your classes, Koji?"

"Good. I have a full load and I'll graduate in the spring."

"And then... are you off to D.C.?"

"That's the plan."

Having never been farther east than Arkansas, Ruby wondered how different the east coast was from the west. To her, Washington, D.C. was a city of decisive power, where important men wielded authority and influence. What was it about Washington that attracted him?

"By the way, where do you live?" she asked.

"In a tiny studio above a shoe-repair shop on Center Street. It's not much, but it serves my needs—a bed, bathroom, and small cooktop."

She imagined Koji in his apartment, scuffing around in his slippers. "You cook?"

"Simple things... *soba, udon*. But when I have time, I make a mean *tamagoyaki*."

"Wow, that's pretty impressive," she said, acknowledging the patience required to roll and grill those egg omelets.

They rejoined the dance in a jitterbug that left them breathless and ended the night dancing cheek-to-cheek to "Earth Angel."

Later, the car pulled in front of Ruby's house.

Koji offered Tony a friendly smack on the shoulder. "Thanks for the ride, man. You and Patty go on. I'll walk home from here."

Once again, he opened the car door and extended his hand to her. "Here, let me help you with your wrap, it's chilly." He draped the wrap over her bare shoulders, being careful not to smash her corsage.

"Thank you again for the beautiful flower. Orchids are one of my favorites."

"My pleasure. The florist recommended white since it goes with everything." He looked up at the sky full of stars. "How wondrous is our universe?"

Minutes passed as they paused on the sidewalk gazing into the twinkling cosmos. "The night sky reminds me of a great celestial prairie and the infinite possibilities in our world," she said.

A strand of her hair had come loose from her updo.

"Here, allow me." His hand brushed her cheek as he tucked the strand behind her ear.

Although she hadn't moved, she felt herself falling into him.

They walked up the porch steps and he held the screen door open while she unlocked the interior door.

"I'd better be going," he said.

"Thank you for a lovely evening, Koji. I don't know when I've enjoyed myself this much."

"Me too." He turned to leave.

Halfway down the steps, he stopped and came back to the door.

They stood on opposite sides of the screen door, inches apart.

She raised her palms to the screen. "Earth Angel" hummed in her head, *I'm just a fool. A fool in love with you.*

He raised his hands to hers and their fingertips met, a touch that thrilled and signaled to her life was about to change.

She held the gaze of his serious eyes, their connection one of pure desire.

Their foreheads touched.

She smiled bravely. "Odd we're both here. Do you think destiny brought us together?"

"I don't know if any path is pre-determined, especially since our past tell us life is unpredictable. We only have the moment we're in. But maybe, just maybe, the universe has something in store for us we don't yet understand."

His body straightened and he backed away from the door preparing to leave. She raised her forehead from the screen, but her fingertips remained where his had been, tingling from his touch. With a whispered "good night," he stepped off the porch.

Ruby closed the door and listened to his steps until they could no longer be heard.

• • •

With fall came the goblins and mischief of Halloween. This was Koji's third Halloween in Berkeley and his first giving out candy to trick-or-treaters. Porch lights illuminated the quiet residential neighborhood, alive with costumed children parading the street, ringing doorbells, and threatening to trick people who didn't give them the treats they hunted, albeit ever so politely. He didn't understand the silly holiday. In Japan, one would think it ridiculous to bother another, especially a total stranger.

He liked watching Ruby greet the children—many of whom were or had been her students in prior years—and hand them lollipops. She complimented the homemade costumes of cowboys, princesses, vampires, and bunnies. She straightened Davy Crockett's crooked raccoon cap. She was friendly and respectful to chaperoning parents. When a child forgot his manners—almost always a boy—she reminded him to say please and thank you.

After a few hours, the flow of trick-or-treaters dwindled, and Ruby joined Koji on the glider. "Whatcha think?" she asked, offering him the almost-empty bowl of lollipops.

Koji had to admit, the kids were cute. And Ruby was cute with them. He envisioned her an excellent teacher—firm, patient, and kind. "It was fun. Thanks for inviting me and showing me the ropes of this strange holiday."

He popped a root beer-flavored lollipop into his mouth, and she unwrapped a strawberry one for herself. Her bare lips curled around the pink sucker before pulling it from her mouth and giving it a long and playful lick with the tip of her tongue. *There she goes again.* She'd done it the night of the dance, too, the innocent, yet arousing way she relished her whiskey sour—poking the cherry with the cocktail stick, running the cherry over her lips, licking the cherry juice from her lips, and savoring the cherry whole. Yes, he enjoyed watching her. He enjoyed watching her do simple things with an innocence he found irresistible.

The screen door creaked open, and her father stepped out on the porch. "All over?"

"Probably," Ruby said. "We might have another stray or two before the night ends."

Her father sat down. "Koji... Ruby tells me you're from Hiroshima and you went to Hiroshima Itchu. I, too, was a student there."

Well that's something, Koji thought. Maybe this was an indicator he and the Reverend would hit it off.

"Yes, Sir. For a while, until I was mobilized to factory work."

"Well now," Reverend Ishimaru exhaled, stretching his legs as if to lengthen time before he continued. "So many young lives interrupted and sacrificed." He rubbed his chin. "My family's temple was destroyed... the Mangyoji temple. You know it?"

"Yes, Sir. I'm sorry for your loss."

"You've been past there since the bombing?"

"Yes, Sir. There's nothing left."

Ruby's father nodded his head.

"But your family... all survived, right?" he asked.

"Yes, Sir."

"How? Where were you?"

Koji gritted his teeth, cracking the last remaining sliver of root-beer lollipop between his molars. "My parents were in the underground passageway at Hiroshima station."

The Reverend leaned in. "Amazing... so close to where the bomb fell. Your parents? Unharmed?"

"Yes, Sir. They were able to escape the building before it was consumed by fire." He paused. "But my father died a few months later."

Ruby gently placed her hand on his bicep, her touch comforting. "My younger brother and I had been at work at the rifle factory, protected by Hiji Park."

"Younger brother? You're *chōnan*?"

"Yes, Sir."

"But you're here. Who cares for your mother?"

"My brother, Sir."

"I see," he said, with a grimace that Koji interpreted as sudden displeasure. The Reverend got up from the chair. "Ruby, let's not keep the light on too long and encourage the older misfits in the neighborhood. Good night now."

Koji felt naked, believing Ruby's father thought him a shirker. Perhaps there was something to Halloween after all—wearing masks and costumes as protection from ghosts.

SUNSET

1957 – Berkeley, CA

The following Saturday, Ruby carried a picnic basket to the Botanical Garden where she was meeting Koji at the Japanese Pool exhibit. Under the brilliant sun, she followed a path meandering through fragrant gardens of winter iris, delicate Chinese plumbago, and fuchsia to the serene waterfalls, stepping stones, lanterns, and pool.

She spotted Koji on a flat boulder just off the water's edge. He wore sunglasses and lay on his back with his feet flat on the rock, knees and face to the heavens, just as he'd done back at the swimming hole long ago. *What went through his mind? Did he think about some obscure philosophy? Was he building the foundation of a research paper in his mind? Or might he be thinking about her?*

She'd tiptoed down the path, as she had tiptoed out of the house to avoid her father's questions about where she was going and with whom. Father thought it shameful how Koji had walked away from his eldest-son responsibilities, and he had given her an earful after Koji left on Halloween. Until she understood where this relationship was going, best to keep her dates with Koji quiet. The small waterfall muffled her footsteps, yet Koji turned to her. *Was she wearing too much perfume?*

He stood and faced her. "Here, allow me," he said, offering to take the basket from her with one hand and help her to the rock with the other.

"I'm curious," she said. "What were you thinking about before I arrived?"

"What you prepared for lunch. I'm starved!" He laughed.

She'd been certain his brain had been hard at work, and yet she was dead wrong. The only thing hard at work was the grumbling of the man's stomach.

"Well mister, you better eat something before you fade away."

He helped her spread a small blanket over the boulder. "What's this?" he asked, removing her Scrabble game from the basket.

"I thought we might play after lunch. Have you played before?"

He shook his head.

"I'll teach you. It's fun."

She wrapped her arms around the front of her knees and admired the surroundings, a haven of mindful, spiritual, and tranquil elements. "How is it I've never visited this part of the gardens before? It's gorgeous."

"A perfect place for centering and quiet." He rubbed his palms together. "What's for lunch?"

She unpacked deviled eggs and *sushi* prepared with eggs, Spam, and rice, and wrapped in *nori*.

Koji dug in. "It's delicious! I really like the way you prepared the Spam."

"How do you prepare it?"

"Fried, in a pan. This Spam tastes different."

"It's marinated in soy sauce with brown sugar."

He licked his lips.

She unfolded the Scrabble board, explained the rules, distributed tiles, and methodically arranged hers on a tile rack. Koji followed her lead, caught on fast, and they spent the next few hours engaged with words.

Ruby won the first game, having earned sixty-six points with a lucky first play, using all seven of her tiles, spelling VICIOUS. Koji followed with SAVAGE, and she with INSANE.

"Powerful words," he said.

She giggled. "Random letters. Luck of the draw."

In the second game, Ruby placed TULIP over a double-letter square, crossed her fingers, and ignored the little voice inside of her cautioning of the nearby triple and double word squares. It was a close game, and soon the bag was empty of tiles. An X remained un-played. She hoped Koji wouldn't play the valuable tile before she went out. But he had proved himself quite clever, and there was no mistaking the sudden gleam in his eyes. From the I, Koji placed his tiles, slow and deliberate, and completed the word AXIOM—over a triple-word square.

"I won!" he whooped.

"Congratulations! Lucky play *and* beginner's luck! Wanna play again?"

"Nah... wanna head over to the bay and watch the sunset?"

How often had she fantasized about watching the sunset with an attractive man? But was she ready?

"I can't think of anything nicer."

They strolled through the garden's changing fall foliage to the exit and cut across campus.

"Do you want to leave the basket at my apartment?" he asked, approaching Center Street. "It's off of Shattuck."

"Good idea."

A few minutes later, Koji waved hello to Ernest, the shoe cobbler at Ernest's Shoe Repair. "Would you like to come up?" Koji asked.

Yes, she wanted to go up! She'd been dying to see where and how he lived.

"Sure," she said, cool as glass.

They entered a door to the side of Ernest's and climbed the stairs to the second floor. Koji unlocked and held the door for her. "Home, sweet home," he said.

She stepped into the small room. The late afternoon sunlight flooded through an open window above an apron sink, where a few clean dishes rested on the drainboard and a folded towel draped over the apron. He'd taped an Ernest's Shoe Repair calendar to dingy yellow walls that wept for a fresh coat of paint. A single lightbulb hung from the center of the ceiling. Quaker oatmeal, jars of noodles and rice, and cans of Campbell's soup were organized behind glass in the few cabinets. His textbooks were stacked with the largest on the bottom and smallest on the top, next to a beat-up Remington typewriter on the small table. On the opposite side of the room, a single bed ran the length of the wall. He'd made his bed with crisp military corners and folded a wool blanket at the bottom. A lamp, alarm clock, and a small statue rested on his nightstand below a small shelf where an old clay jar and his military medals were displayed.

The ancient markings on the clay jar caught her eye. "What's this jar?"

"Oh, I found that buried in my backyard when my brother and I dug our bomb shelter. It was full of old silver coins which I sold years ago to help pay for some of my expenses."

She couldn't imagine her safety depending on a homemade bomb shelter. "That's incredible, Koji. There so much about you I still don't know. But I'd like to."

He smiled. "All in good time, Ruby."

She picked up the statue. "Who's your little friend?"

"That's *Jizō*. My father bought him for me when I was ten as a reward for good grades. He goes where I go."

"I'm that way about my sea glass and shells, especially the shell I discovered with my mother. It has the luminosity of sunrise."

• • •

An hour later, after a quick bus ride across University Avenue, they faced San Francisco with their legs dangling off a pier. It was the golden hour when saffron light bathed the city skyline and glistened on the surface of the steely water.

He took her hand. "I'll never tire of looking at this."

"Tell me about Japan sunsets."

"Ah… Hiroshima's bay and mountains are similar to San Francisco. But the spectacular sunsets are at Miyajima, where the sun ends its day behind the forested mountains and its afterglow illuminates the red *torii* gate. Maybe you'll see it someday."

Having tried so hard over the years to avoid Japan, she'd never considered she might visit there.

"What's it like in Japan? My father told you how his family perished in the bombing, but he didn't say my mother was from Ehime Prefecture. My grandparents used to write and send my sister and me gifts, but we stopped hearing from them as soon as my father returned from finding a new wife."

She sighed. "He was gone for six months, if you can imagine that. Anyway, I don't think there's much reason for me to go there." She rubbed her hands together and stared at her crossed ankles.

Koji put his arm around her and pulled her into his warm body. "I'm sorry about your family and mother dying, your father leaving you at such a young age, your losses. So many years to be hurting."

She nodded.

"My father used to say life is fleeting, like cherry blossoms, and so we must embrace life while we have it," he said.

"With a Buddhist minister father, I should probably know better than to ignore how every day is precious."

They swayed to the rhythm of the surface waves.

"Yes, about your father. You must know he didn't want to leave you or hurt you. He did what he thought he had to do. Don't you see, he wasn't capable of raising you alone. Life is complicated, Ruby. We're all flawed. Everything isn't about you."

"I know."

"So, what do you need? What are you waiting for?"

For years, she had wrapped her brittle heart with distractions—educating herself and now educating her students. Was she ready to take a chance and risk more heartbreak? "I don't know exactly."

Koji's fingertip found its way under her chin and gently raised her head. His face was so close to hers, she felt the warmth of his breath. She wondered if the smell of her after-lunch peppermint lingered. Her eyes met the intention in his. Could he see the vulnerability there? Her heart beat faster. He kissed her softly, and then with the parting of lips, his tongue cracked her heart wide open, as if he had opened an oyster shell and explored with great tenderness to find the most exquisite of pearls.

They caught their breath and Koji lay on the pier with his head in her lap.

She held his gaze until his eyes closed.

Across the bay, tall buildings and spires reached into the tangerine blaze of billowing clouds.

"Is forgiveness on the horizon?" he asked.

She stroked his forehead and temples, and his face relaxed under her fingertips.

"Maybe," she whispered.

"You never answered my question," she said, changing the subject.

"What question?"

"I asked what Japan is like."

"Oh, that. Much as you might imagine. Battered, bruised, with a rich history defining its hardworking, formal, and respectful culture."

"That's a textbook response." She felt so close to him and yet so far away. "I've only heard your stock answers, and I want to know. What was the bombing like for you?"

He crossed his arms over his chest. "Unimaginable."

"It must have been. Maybe it would be helpful for you to open up a little."

His eyes remained closed, and he took a deep breath, as if the words that followed might suffocate him.

"I was working in the rifle factory and saw the flash. It was blinding. The roof collapsed around me and knocked me out. When I came to, I saw the mushroom cloud. Fires. Naked and burned bodies floating down rivers. Our family was unharmed, and we cared for desperate friends, family, and strangers. I carried my dead childhood friend and dozens of others to a funeral pyre. Death was everywhere. The atomic bomb crushed hopes, dreams, and futures. But not people's strength and resilience. I guess that's why I enjoy beautiful sunsets and appreciate what I have, even if it's not much. I've seen firsthand it can all disappear in a flash."

Ruby's soul swelled with compassion for this determined man who somehow retained the positive, having witnessed a devastation she couldn't comprehend, protecting himself by shutting out the bad like one might chain a rabid dog.

The fiery sun disappeared below the horizon before either of them spoke again.

He sat beside her and held her hand. "Ruby, all countries, good and bad, make mistakes. Same with people. I've made mistakes. Your father's made mistakes. You've made mistakes. Mistakes are important lessons of life, as long as we learn from them, forgive them, and commit to doing better."

This once undereducated high school boy now possessed an intelligence and wisdom that seemingly dwarfed hers. Perhaps her grumbling and inability to forgive was ill-mannered, but she couldn't deny her grudges. Some pushed darkness down. Others pushed darkness out. Either way, darkness cut one in half.

The sky morphed into twilight hues of lilac, and the ebbing tide entranced her as gravity pulled at the bay and took its waters farther out to sea. Nighttime would soon yield to another day.

HOME FOR THE HOLIDAYS

1957 – Berkeley, CA

On Thanksgiving Day, alone in his darkening apartment, Koji's stomach grumbled. The aroma of roasted turkey mingled with the sweet scent of baking and wafted through the plaster crevices from adjacent apartments. Families across America gathered in thanks that day, and his body twinged with a sudden pang of melancholic longing for his mother and Naoki.

He closed his eyes and sent loving energy across the Pacific, along with profound gratefulness to *Okāsan* for permitting him to explore his American birthright and to his brother for his selfless caring for their mother. Had he been selfish to blaze his path in America by abandoning his *chōnan* responsibilities? Had he disturbed a centuries-old cultural order by not preserving its strict hierarchical system? Had he dishonored his ancestors and the unborn son of his dreams, by turning his back on the future he might have built in Japan?

The atomic bomb had destroyed, fragmented, and changed everything. With Japan's economy, landscape, and educational systems decimated, and the years he'd already lost to the war, he wasn't able to see beyond the ravaged terrain. He believed he could provide for his family from afar.

Soon, he would achieve his lifelong ambition of graduating from college, a joy he never would have realized in Hiroshima. Wasn't seeking one's best self and happiness something to feel proud of rather than guilty about? Wasn't loving his family better than resenting them for shackling him with duty, even if it meant being away from them? But arguing these points in his head would never change one thing. He would be negatively judged for shirking his responsibilities by people who mattered to him—men like Reverend Ishimaru. And he needed to live with that.

Over the last few weeks, he and Ruby had spent most weekend afternoons together—walking, playing card games, and listening to the 49ers on the radio. On weeknights, they fell into a rhythm at the library, Ruby grading papers and Koji studying. He had secretly hoped for a Thanksgiving dinner invitation to the Ishimaru home and was disappointed when Ruby didn't ask him. Maybe her family wanted an intimate family dinner, maybe her father didn't like or respect him, or maybe Ruby didn't like him enough to include him in family functions. He imagined turkey roasted crisp and golden brown, sides of stuffing *and* rice, and pumpkin pie garnished with whipped cream. His memory floated to the rifle factory when he'd traded pumpkin for rice, never imagining Americans created fragrant custard filling with its flesh.

A knock at the door interrupted his reach for a can of chicken noodle soup. He answered to find Ruby, her face glowing, basket in hand.

"Happy Thanksgiving, handsome."

"Happy Thanksgiving to you, too, beautiful. This is a surprise." He licked a trickle of drool from the corner of his mouth and they kissed. "What's in the basket?"

"I bring sustenance to the hardworking student. Hungry?"

"Starved!"

She entered, placed the basket on the table, and walked straight to his cupboard for a plate. "I'll plate this while it's hot. Whatcha working on?"

He cleared books from the table. "Completing exam study cards."

She set a plate overflowing with a drumstick, slices of tender white meat, stuffing, rice, brussels sprouts, and cranberry sauce in front of him. "Bon appétit, mister."

He was right. They had made stuffing *and* rice. "Thank you. This looks so good. Did you do all the cooking?"

"I made the turkey and pie. *Okāsan* and I prepared everything else together."

The stepmother caused Ruby great angst, so he was pleased to hear they had cooked together. "I take it your relationship with your stepmother is... softening?"

"Maybe. I think I've figured her out."

"How so?"

"She's far more educated than most Japanese women of her time and steeped in Buddhism as a priestess. Her ego is huge and she needs to be in charge. All of that was pulled out from under her when she moved to America. I suppose I've found the tiniest bit of empathy for how hard things must have been for her, and I forgive her for the harm she caused me. I really do. She simply isn't capable of being different. We will never like each other, and she honestly doesn't matter to me anymore. For now, we live in the same house and breathe the polite air of cordiality for Father's sake."

Koji knew better than to step further into this situation. "To the chefs!" he said, devouring the delicious food, even if they were leftovers.

"While you're eating, I'll tell you all about our Thanksgiving activities at school. The children traced their hands onto construction paper creating the cutest turkeys to hang on the wall of our classroom. We practiced all week for their skit, reenacting the first Thanksgiving. Except for a few lost lines, their performance was perfect, and they looked darling in their handmade headdresses and pilgrim hats. Some mothers baked pumpkin cupcakes and donated candy corn and other treats for our class party. It was a fun week."

He pictured Ruby encouraging and bossing the children around from the stage wings and teaching them this bit of history in a lighthearted way—a lack of seriousness unheard of in Japan's schools.

"Best to let that settle before pumpkin pie," she said. "What can I do to help you study?"

"You any good at typing?"

"Fifty-five words per minute," she said, with a satisfied grin.

He read aloud his handwritten American Culture research paper, and the clickety-clack of the keys, the dings, and the confident sound of carriage returns filled the room. She was quick with the eraser to correct her few mistakes and finished typing the fifteen-page paper in no time.

"I almost forgot," she said, holding one end of a forked bone from the turkey. "Time to make a wish."

"A wish?"

"Thanksgiving tradition. We each grab a side and snap the bone apart while making a wish. Whoever gets the bigger piece of the bone will have their wish come true."

"What if it cracks in equal pieces?"

"Well, it never does, but if so then I guess we both win! Close your eyes and pull on the count of three."

He peeked with one eye and chuckled as she squinched her eyes shut. She seemed determined to win.

"One. Two. Three."

Snap!

"I win!" she said, raising the bigger bone in triumph.

"What'd you wish for?"

"I wished for a Christmas tree."

"Doesn't everyone in America have a tree at Christmas?"

"We used to when I was little. Mama... she loved Christmas." Her look turned scornful. "But *Okāsan* has *never* permitted a dead tree in the house."

Clearly, she still nursed a grudge toward her stepmother.

Ruby curled her leg under her bottom into a relaxed pose. "How about you? What did you wish for?"

"Good grades," he lied.

The unmistakable symptoms were there—he thought of her all the time, missed her when they weren't together, and imagined her in his future. He was falling for her, and he wished his feelings for her were mutual. Only her deep-seated resentments held him back.

"You work so hard, Koji. You'll do well."

"That's the rule I follow—always do my best."

• • •

A few days before Christmas, Koji had taken his last exam and cleaned his apartment top to bottom. He went to places in Berkeley he had never ventured before and dropped a nickel in the red kettle of every Salvation Army bell ringer he met.

On Christmas Eve, he set the draped table with his two plates, the lacquered chopsticks his mother had given him, and two jelly jars he substituted as glasses. After spending the entire day preparing a special dinner of *maki* and *sushi, wasabi,* pickled ginger, and *ohitashi,* he placed the *sushi* platter—a cutting board covered with aluminum foil—on the center of the table. On the cooktop, the *sake* warmed to mask its price tag.

He answered the knock on his door at the exact time he had invited Ruby for dinner. He raced to answer, as he imagined a small child might race down the stairs on Christmas morning, and opened the door to find her removing a silk scarf covering her head, giving him an idea.

"Hi," she said, with a broad smile, her painted crimson lips never failing to arouse him.

"Hi yourself. May I borrow that?" he asked.

"My scarf?"

"Yes. Just for a minute... close your eyes."

She did as he instructed, and he covered her eyes with the scarf and tied it from behind.

"Now turn around, and watch your step," he said, taking her hand.

He led her into the apartment and turned her around three times.

She giggled. "What are we doing? Playing pin the tail on the donkey?"

"Something like that."

When he removed the blindfold, her eyes reflected the five-foot fir tree he'd bought at the corner lot and decorated with multi-colored balls and lights purchased at the five-and-dime store.

She stood as still as a statue, staring at the tree as if in a daze, her cheeks and neck flushing to match her lips. Her eyes were wet when they met his.

"Merry Christmas, Ruby."

She stepped closer to the tree, ran her fingers over the garland, and touched every ornament as if each held a story.

"No one has ever done anything this special for me. It's perfect. Thank you."

He pulled her into his arms and she buried her face in his shoulder, where he felt her tears dampening his shirt. He lost himself in her scent—the allure of gardenia, woodlands, and jasmine vines.

"I have a confession," he said.

"What?"

"We aren't finished with the tree yet."

He kissed her forehead.

"Sit down," he said. "I'll pour the *sake* and we'll finish."

Moments later, they clinked glasses, and he handed her a small wrapped present from under the tree. "This is for you. Merry Christmas."

She opened his gift with the reckless giddiness of a child, tearing off the bow and ripping the paper. Inside, she discovered a red ball ornament with her name etched in silver glitter.

Her teary eyes met his, and she blew him the softest of kisses. "Did you make this yourself?"

He nodded. "My first craft project. Your students inspired me."

"I love it."

She crossed the room to where her coat hung and fished in the pocket.

"I have something for you too," she said, presenting him with a small square box wrapped in whimsical paper printed with Santas on bicycles.

He accepted her gift and shook the box, wondering what might be inside. It made no sound.

His eyebrows furrowed. "I bet it's peanuts."

"You're so silly. Open it."

He slid his finger under the tape. "It's a baseball, isn't it?"

She tapped her foot.

He folded back the paper with surgical precision before turning the box over to see the front. "I know... it's a paperweight!"

Ruby scowled. "Open it, will you?"

Even with a scowled expression, she was beautiful.

Nestled in tissue paper was a Golden Bears snow globe. He shook it and the flakes flurried through the water and fell over the grizzly.

"I guessed you might enjoy a little of Japan's snowfall here in Berkeley."

Had he told her about missing Hiroshima's snow? He couldn't remember. A warm contentment washed over his body. "It's great. Thank you."

He leaned into her pursed lips but left them with a mere peck. He had another gift for her. He fumbled under the old scarf he used as a tree skirt and found the box of tinsel.

"I saved the best for last! Let's get our tinsel on!" He opened the box, grabbed a handful, and tossed it on the tree. It landed in a messy wad over an ornament.

"No! You can't do it that way," she cried. "Be neat. Hang one strand at a time, evenly spaced on the branches, and not too close to anything already hanging."

"You mean like this?" he asked, hanging a single strand of tinsel from each of her ears. But the playful exchange took a sudden, serious leap. His eyes lingered on the tinsel, framing her rosy face and reflecting the colorful glow of the tree. His fingertips stroked her earlobes and then his palms stroked her cheeks. Looking deep into her eyes, he knew she was the woman for him.

Her palms rested on his chest. "It's been so long since the Christmas spirit touched me. I'd forgotten what Christmas was like and thought I'd never enjoy the spirit again... the same way I thought I'd never want to feel again. But you changed that. You. You're changing me, Koji."

His lips found hers and he rode her current, allowing an undertow over which he had no control to carry him away.

WHO'S SORRY NOW?

1958 – Berkeley, CA

For Ruby, the holidays had been like drinking a delicious cocktail of effervescent glee, rendering her intoxicated with bubbling butterflies of love. But the crisp excitement of New Year's Eve softened and seemed to fizzle out. In January, their respective commitments were as steady as the rains—she, focused on her students and he, immersed in an intense winter seminar. With February's torrential downpours, Koji plunged into his last semester with challenging, capstone courses. She baked him a lemon birthday cake, but otherwise, they celebrated his special day with little fanfare.

During their limited time together, Koji had carried her away, let her in, and gobbled her up. She had felt safe sharing with him the losses and disappointments in her life, but she hadn't told him about her father's pressure to find and marry an established man with solid roots in Japanese values. And it would hurt Koji to know her father's unfavorable opinion of him. She would continue to keep their relationship quiet until she knew Koji's plans and felt more certain about their relationship. He hadn't mentioned moving to Washington, D.C. since the night of the dance, and she hadn't asked. A lot could happen between now and his graduation in three months, and she didn't see the point now in agitating either man.

Under March's wafting clouds, Ruby dodged puddles and walked past poppies and fawn lilies awakening in neighborhood gardens. Her brain told her to concentrate on the moment and believe her future with Koji would unfold the way the universe intended. She hoped their relationship would continue blooming, but under the darkening sky, she worried it would fade away like the bubbles when champagne has gone flat.

By the end of March, the skies had cleared and spring invigorated the air. Ruby's birthday fell on a Tuesday, a day when Koji's classes finished early. He had invited her to a special birthday dinner at a fancy restaurant and insisted on picking her up at home. She spent hours bathing, massaging lotion in measured upward strokes along her neck, smoothing her hair, and convincing herself Father would be cordial to Koji. His criticism would come later, in private.

She tried on almost every dress in her closet, selected a blue taffeta with a scalloped neckline, and sashayed to the kitchen where her stepmother was preparing supper and her father worked at the table whittling a rabbit, one of a dozen Japanese zodiac animals he'd been working on.

He looked up and smiled. "Aren't you pretty, birthday girl. Is Sasaki-*san* taking you out for your birthday?"

Standing in the doorway, she considered her answer. Kazuo Sasaki was the haughty and opinionated lawyer he had introduced to her in the fall. A real bore. "No. I haven't seen Kazuo for months." She paused before continuing. "Koji's taking me to dinner."

Her father lowered his head, placed the rabbit and his knife on the table, and stared at her. "I thought I made my feelings clear to you about him."

Taeko stopped chopping vegetables, approached the table, and stood behind Father with a reddening face and harrumphed. "A peasant. Even *you* can do better."

Ruby's downcast eyes studied the innocent rabbit beside the knife. The knife was surgical, double-edged. She wanted to pick it up. Instead, she ignored the woman who always made a miserable situation worse.

Her father shushed Taeko with the raise of his index finger to his grimaced lips, and returned his attention to Ruby. "Ruby, I don't mean to be harsh, but you need a good Japanese husband—someone who will provide for you and honor our ways, not a *fumeiyo no hito* with no family values," he said, conveniently switching to Japanese to call Koji a disgraced person.

Koji would be there any second. Ruby dreaded having this conversation now, but the argument spilled from her mouth, anyway. "How can you be so critical of him? You left your family too."

Her blatant insult settled into his furrowed brows. "You know full well my brother is *chōnan* in my family. Enormous responsibility falls on the first son. No honorable man walks away from his responsibility!"

"But this isn't Japan, and I'm twenty-nine years old! I get to choose who to love. Not you. You've already lost one daughter to your uncompromising standards. Must you lose another?"

He sent her a pained stare and shrunk in his chair. "Daughter, as the Buddha said, *'the tongue like a sharp knife, kills without drawing blood.'* You will not be punished for your anger, you will be punished by your anger." He pushed away from the table, walked to his bedroom, and closed the door.

Now, her stepmother's glare was full of judgment. "How dare you disrespect your *Otōsan* that way, under his roof! And for what? A peasant! Get out of my sight!"

Gladly. But a nagging feeling accompanied her into the living room. She sat on the sofa and allowed the fresh air from the open windows to assuage her reddened face and quiet her agitation. The doorbell rang and startled her. How many seconds had passed? A wave of panic washed over her at the thought Koji may have overheard the argument.

She opened the door to find Koji holding a bouquet of daffodils, tied with a yellow ribbon, the brilliance of the yellow flowers in stark contrast to his wounded eyes.

She joined him on the porch.

"You heard?"

"Enough."

A weak "I'm sorry" escaped with the sob trapped in her throat.

"I should go," he said, turning to leave.

"Don't leave. Please let me explain."

His arms fell limp to his sides, and he rested the daffodils on a porch chair, but his body was stiff when he spoke. "I suspected your father wouldn't respect or understand my decision to leave my responsibilities in Japan, but it sounds like I underestimated his disdain."

"I thought with time my father would come around... and you insisted on picking me up today. I didn't know what to do, and I thought it would be okay... that I'd deal with my father later."

His dull eyes turned fiery. "Wait. We've been seeing each other for months. Are you saying you've been seeing me all of this time behind your parents' backs? Is that why you always came to my place or suggested we meet somewhere? Because you are ashamed of me?"

"No, I'm not ashamed of you, but I thought... I guess I was wrong."

She covered her face with her hands. Warm tears moistened her palms.

"Did they know you were bringing Thanksgiving leftovers to me, or am I so beneath you that you hid that from them too?"

"But you don't understand."

"Oh, but I do. At first it was your anger and unforgiving spirit. Now it's your deceit. And even if you hadn't been so deceitful, now it's clear I'll never meet your father's expectations."

"What does that matter? He's an old man with old-world views."

"It matters, because more is going on here than what your father thinks of me."

"But we can figure..." A sob caught her voice. "Figure this out."

"That's where you're wrong. *We* don't need to figure anything out."

He released a deep exhale. "I'm sorry, Ruby, but you're just too hard to be with sometimes, and I'm afraid to be with you."

The curveball spun its way over home plate. "You're breaking up with me?" She grabbed his arm.

The look in his eyes was as desolate as an oyster shell no longer inhabited, washed up on a vacant beach. He pushed her hand away. "This isn't easy for me either. I plan to leave after graduation, anyway. I'd hoped... well, it doesn't matter anymore. Goodbye, Ruby."

When Koji walked away, his back was straight and his stride long. The sun, low on the horizon, wove its beams into strands of his black hair and illuminated the superiority of his posture.

She darted down the steps and front pavement and watched until his body faded into the distance, leaving the sidewalk vacant. "You quitter! I don't need you anyway! I don't need anybody!"

Her chest caved in, and she choked back a strangled sob as he turned the corner and disappeared from sight. She staggered on the front walk, ashamed her screams had echoed throughout the neighborhood. Back on the porch, the daffodils lay on the chair, abandoned like the ginger flowers she and Mari had picked for Mama and tossed aside on the day she died.

She collapsed into a chair and stared at the daffodils, their spathes already withering. Soon, they would turn brown, shrivel, and die. Everything died or left. Koji was no different.

MOVING ON

1958 – Berkeley, CA

Weeks had passed since Koji disappeared around the corner onto McGee Avenue. Days lengthened and fell away in gray light as one drowsy day dawned to the next. Tepid, flat, and bitter wine was all that remained of Ruby's blissful champagne holiday with him, when the new year was bright with promise. The force of April's restless winds equaled her disposition, but the walls in the Ishimaru home sighed with relief as Ruby and her parents entered an unspoken truce, each feeling righteous, yet striking the cordial notes of a tragic opera score. Father had accepted her apology for her sneaky behavior and disrespectful words, and said the breakup was for the best.

Ruby spent her free time at the community garden harvesting snow peas and radishes and tilling the soil for broccoli and mustard greens. Digging, clipping, and weeding did more than dirty her fingernails and produce vegetables. It saved her sanity. Easter had come and gone with the same concocted tradition of decorating and hiding of eggs as the year before, and her students had returned high on the sugar of marshmallow Peeps.

A few weeks later at school, Ruby responded to a ruckus in the cloak room just as Sally Ward delivered a swift kick to Betsy Blair. Betsy cowered to avoid Sally's Buster Browns, and the misdirected kick connected with Betsy's arm.

Betsy howled in pain.

Ruby stepped between the students. "That's enough! Break it up, girls!"

Sally continued to challenge Betsy with a squinched face and an indignant puff of her chest.

This wasn't the first time she'd separated these two third-graders, one a Jehovah's Witness who the other children often teased. But their aggression blurred the role of victim and bully.

"Who started it?" she asked.

Betsy pointed at Sally. "She did!"

"Well, you pulled my hair!"

"That's because you called me a Bogus Hovis!"

Ruby took Sally by the arm. "Were you making fun of Betsy's religion?"

"Yes, Miss Ishimaru."

"Go to the principal's office." She pointed at the door. "Now!"

She turned her attention to Betsy. "Let me see your arm."

"I'm okay, Miss Ishimaru."

"I need to see," Ruby said, pushing up Betsy's sleeve and uncovering a fresh red mark surrounded by clusters of bruises and grab marks covering the girl's arm.

Her tone softened. "Betsy, where did those bruises come from?"

When their eyes met, the girl returned a blank stare, surrounded by the stares of other students who had congregated to witness the action.

"Children, return to your seats." Ruby closed the cloak room door.

She bent down to Betsy's level. "Betsy, are there more? Maybe some I can't see?"

Betsy hung her head and nodded.

"Oh goodness... come here, child."

Ruby wrapped her arms around the girl.

"Who struck you?"

Betsy didn't answer.

"You can trust me, Betsy."

Betsy turned to face the wall. Her entire small body was trembling. "She didn't mean to hurt me."

Ruby understood the girl was terrified. She turned her around gently and put her hands on Betsy's shoulders.

Her voice was soft. "Who didn't mean to hurt you?"

Betsy rubbed her nose. Sniffling, she looked at her shoes. "My... mom," she whispered.

Ruby rubbed her own chest to soothe the sudden, sharp pain.

"Has she hit you before?"

"Yes, but it's my fault." Now, Betsy was crying openly. "It's always my fault."

Ruby considered her choices. Her heart collapsed under the weight of this critical decision, knowing full well the consequences would be painful no matter what she decided.

"Betsy, I'm going to take you to see Nurse Swain. While you're with her, I'll speak with Principal Hudson. I don't know what will happen next, but... "

"No! You can't tell! Promise me you won't."

"Betsy, I can't. As your teacher, I must protect you from harm. Even in your home."

She ran her fingers through Betsy's sweaty hair.

"Listen, I need you to know something."

She raised Betsy's chin and looked into her teary eyes. "You did nothing to deserve being harmed this way. Now, we're going to see the nurse. And while we're sorting this out, I want these bruises to remind you of your bravery. You can and will be okay."

Ruby stayed after school to meet with the principal and social worker, who took Betsy into her care. She had to believe the system would protect the girl.

Once home, she went to her room, kicked off her shoes, and curled into a ball on her bed, filled with resentment for Taeko in the next room and Betsy's mother wherever she was. Betsy would experience a long and troubled road ahead.

She woke the next morning in a tense ball, clothed from the day before. Her swollen eyes adjusted to the early dawn seeping through her windows and focused on the shelf where she kept her white feather, sea glass, and shells. Having stretched the stiffness from her joints, she padded across the room and ran her fingertips over every piece, recalling each memory. She opened a threadbare pouch and emptied the jacks and ball into her palm. The ball had long since lost its bounce, but the jacks remained strong and sharp. Tucked inside the largest of her shells—a conch she had found with Mari—was the withered goldenrod hidden from that long-ago day at the creek.

She breathed in dust from the no longer fragrant flower, and it flooded her heart with remorse. With the shell to her ear, she heard the echo of faint memories. Koji jumping in fear of a snake. Koji practicing his oral presentation on the humanity of international relations. Koji humming "Auld Lang Syne" on New Year's Eve.

Sound waves intensified from within the spine of the shell's pink opalescent lining, and something within Ruby stirred. The universe was trying to tell her something.

Listen, Ruby. Listen.

Tears streamed down her face at the sudden realization. Everything meaningful to her had been reduced to a single shelf of mementos. The cost of so fiercely protecting herself had deprived her of so much that might have been. Defending Betsy had helped her see that.

Her last words to Betsy—*you can and will be okay.*

From beyond her window, she heard the distant tinkle of windchimes. And a whisper. *Gaman, Ruby. You know what to do.*

She recognized how her anger eroded inner peace and caused more pain—buried wounds—a silent wall between her and others. Aired in the open, wounds festered, for all to see and be harmed by the ugliness. She continued listening, and heard Koji's words. *You're just too hard to be with.*

The urge surfaced without warning, and she ran out of the house and down the street.

Twenty minutes later, out of breath and covered in sweat, she knocked on Koji's door. He answered wearing his slippers, a tea towel over his shoulder, and an odd expression.

"Ruby. What you doing here?"

Her teeth, not yet brushed that morning, bit down on her bottom lip.

"Koji, all of this is my fault. I ruined everything. I can't take back what my parents said. But they aren't me. How can I apologize? How can I make this right? How can we fix us?"

She slumped against the doorway.

"You and a nine-year-old helped me see how wrong I've been to push everything and everyone away. Please, forgive me."

Her eyes pooled with tears, and her voice cracked. "I don't want to ruin your life, Koji. How could I? I love you. And loving you makes me... well, more vulnerable than I've ever felt in my life. And I'm afraid of that."

She did nothing to hide or control the steady stream of tears flooding her face.

"I need you, Koji. I want you to love me too."

Silence.

"Please give me another chance."

Several agonizing moments passed.

And still he said nothing, and nothing in his eyes suggested he wanted her to stay.

With the drop of her head, her hair hung in her face and stuck to her skin. "I'm sorry."

Did he not know what to say? Was he afraid to say something he might regret? Was she not worth the energy of his response?

She walked away without knowing, and heard the door close behind her.

● ● ●

The following Sunday, she attended temple service, weak from not eating and exhausted from not sleeping. The ringing of the *bonshō* and the peaceful chants of the congregation did little to pierce her deadened senses or stir her soul, and her father's Dharma message was rendered meaningless as she silently berated herself. The twisted rollercoaster of her life had climbed, fallen, and screeched to a halt, leaving her whipped and numb.

A congregant approached her after the service and asked if she would water the garden for him that day. She forced herself to say yes. At least while gardening, her hands were useful.

That afternoon, she put away her uneaten lunch and left for the garden. Her walk was sluggish. She arrived to find a man, with his back to her, watering the plants. His rubber boots came to his knees, emphasizing his short femurs and long torso. The water sprayed from the hose nozzle he held with one hand. There was a certain distinctive precision and pace to his watering. He seemed to hold the nozzle in one spot for a bit of time before methodically moving the spray to the next spot. She counted. Fifteen seconds each.

From the back, he looked like Koji, but she knew her mind was playing tricks on her again. She saw him everywhere, but it was never him. Why would he be here anyway? He'd never been to the garden without her. This man with the hose could be anyone. She ignored the urge to duck out of sight and continued walking toward him through small puddles. Perhaps the squishing of her footfalls disturbed him. He turned.

Her eyes blinked slowly and registered his backward movement, as if he stepped away to distance himself from the discomfort of pitying her.

"You're watering our kale," she said.

"Someone had to. The leaves were wilting. It appears someone has neglected their responsibilities."

He continued watering.

"Why are you here, Koji?"

"Mindless work. It clears my head."

"Where on earth did you get those ridiculous boots?" she asked.

"These? Don't make fun of my boots. These are my *Jiji* boots. They belonged to my grandfather. He wore them into the rice paddies every day. Fit me perfect. Made in Japan. Good quality. Will never wear out."

Her rope was fraying and her body twisted and tied into knots. "What are you really doing here?"

He released his hand from the lever and rested the nozzle on the ground and walked toward her. Pressure increased in her chest with each of his measured steps forward, and she felt she might explode. It seemed an eternity before he stood in front of her.

"I have news. I received a job offer from the Library of Congress in

Washington, D.C. I start work there in July."

She pressed her palm into her abdomen and swallowed the hard lump that had formed. Except for the breeze lifting his hair at the temples, he was perfectly still.

"The thing is," he said, "you're the one I wanted to share my news with."

"I thought you were afraid to be with me."

"I'm more afraid of being without you."

"Then why did you let me leave, without saying a word?"

"I needed to be sure. You know I take hours to pick out a pair of socks." She wanted to wring his neck with the hose.

"And are you?... Sure, I mean."

His eye contact was strong, unblinking. He nodded, "You made me... "

Rather than finish his sentence, he lifted her into the air by her waist and held her above him—close enough to feel his breath, yet far enough away to preserve the delicate balance of non-commitment. She hovered motionless, wondering if he heard the violent beat of her heart, afraid for the moment to end. Once he lowered her, a choice would be made and there would be no turning back.

"You didn't finish. What were you going to say?" she asked.

As he lowered her ever so gently to her feet, his steady eyes suggested he was estimating his response. His lips brushed against hers, breaking away long enough to answer. "You made me face the reality of loving you. I think I've loved you since the moment you turned the corner from Tenth onto Stockton."

A tidal wave crashed over her, tumbled her about, and untied all of her knots. She melted into his body and became small in his arms.

"I love you too. I never believed I could feel this way."

Then, he claimed her mouth, flooding her with pleasure. He tasted of garden mint and smelled of rosemary. Somehow, his touch richly aromatic.

When his lips released hers, he held her face in his palms and looked deep into her eyes.

"Do you remember being together on the rock at the river?" he asked.

She smiled. "You fed me grapes."

"The sun filtered through the tree tops and warmed our faces. I remember thinking you were the most beautiful girl in the world."

Ruby often longed to return to that rock and start over with Koji, without her defensiveness, without making a fool of herself, without running away.

"It's from those moments we find ourselves here. Ruby, we are an intersection of opposites. Apart, we undermine the natural order."

He dropped to one knee and took her hand.

"You're the love of my life. I promise to be at your side always and never abandon you, if you'll have me. Will you marry me?"

The certainty in her heart came with the knowledge that her love for Koji was a once-in-a-lifetime love.

Tears trickled over her wide smile. "Yes. I'll marry you."

Later, as they rolled up the hose and put it away, she asked him the question she'd been afraid to ask. "My father will be hurt if you don't ask for his permission. If he says no, it won't change my decision to marry you. Will you ask him anyway?"

Koji cocked his head to one side, and smiled with a glint of mischief. "I already asked."

REBIRTH

1958 – Berkeley, CA

The snow of yesterday
That fell like cherry blossoms
Is water once again.
—Gozan Bungaku

On a glorious day in mid-May, a warm breeze carried proud whispers across the University of California at Berkeley Memorial Stadium. Above a few wispy clouds, the sun reflected on the beaming faces of thousands of graduates. The traditional notes of "Pomp and Circumstance" filled the air smelling of achievement and promise. Dignitaries and distinguished scholars in full-hooded academic regalia observed from their dais seats with decorum and detachment.

A bright bird, originally from the hillside community of Fuchu in southern Japan, sat among a row of other feathered spectators perched on the stadium's scoreboard in the red-winged body the man now inhabited. The bird fluffed his regal feathers when Koji crossed the stage and accepted his diploma and soared overhead when Koji shifted his tassel from the left to the right of his cap. And then Akio was gone, flying toward the horizon, leaving his son to bask in the pride of having graduated with high distinction. Education had always been Koji's oxygen, nourishing each cell in his body. Now, his veins were fueled with the knowledge and soaring spirit to achieve the full promise of his future.

A month later, on a day equal in its glory to Koji's graduation ceremony, he and Ruby prepared for their wedding. In the small house next to the temple, Mari provided for Ruby, as Ruby had provided for her sister on her wedding day. Mari zipped the back of Ruby's modest tea-length wedding dress and lowered the mesh from her silk headband, covering the bride's soft brown eyes in a veil of pure innocence. She placed a lei of white carnations she'd strung together over Ruby's head, kissed her cheek, and wished her a happy life. Before entering the temple where Koji waited with a single white carnation pinned to the lapel of his navy suit, Mari took the bride's hand and said, "Mama was our bedrock of goodness. She always looked after us. Somehow, she will be present today smiling with pride."

Ruby knew her sister's words to be true.

Forgiveness and peace permeated the temple with the ringing of the *bonshō*. Reverend Ishimaru officiated the ceremony, and the people who mattered most to the bride and groom witnessed the nuptials, including Mari, who weeks earlier had reconciled with her father. Bob, his wife, and baby girl had traveled from Sacramento, as did Velvet and her new husband, a judge from Los Angeles. Except for Taeko, who witnessed with stoic indifference, everyone smiled as Koji and Ruby exchanged vows and they applauded when he placed the simple gold band on her steady finger. Even her father was pleased, having heard what Koji had to say when he visited to ask for Ruby's hand. He had been wrong about Koji. He was a fine man who worked hard to achieve his education and place in the world. He may have walked away from his *chōnan* responsibilities, but not without deep reflection and honor.

Showered in rice, the newlyweds raced to the faded Chevy sedan Koji had purchased used. Earlier, Koji had placed Ruby's tattered footlocker, safeguarding her precious mementos, in the trunk beside their remaining possessions. And he had tucked *Jizō* inside the glove box, alongside a United States roadmap to guide their cross-country journey. Maps distort reality. No roadmap encompasses the circumference of the earth. But this roadmap, with their route highlighted in yellow crayon, would guide them to Washington, D.C., and was the only roadmap they needed. For now.

The bridegroom started the engine and beamed at his bride.

"Do you have any plans for later?" she asked.

"Well, I was thinking of this," he said, kissing her softly. "Ready, Mrs. Matsuo?"

"Ready, Mr. Matsuo."

Friends and family waved goodbye as the couple drove away with the clatter of tin cans attached to the bumper trailing behind.

Standing among the others on the sidewalk, Reverend Ishimaru scratched his head. "How odd. Why's a red bathing brassiere tied to their antenna?" he asked his oldest daughter.

"Father, I can't imagine."

EPILOGUE

1995 – Tokyo, Japan

I can lead you
to the truth,
but you must
find it for yourself.
Then you'll get the seal.
—*Kobun Otogawa*

The lavish cherry blossoms in Tokyo's Chidorigafuchi Park outside of Ruby's open hotel window mesmerized her with their delicate transience, releasing a jumble of thoughts and emotions. Exhilarated with anticipation, Ruby breathed in the blossoms' faint fragrance to ground her sensibilities and reflected on how she had ended up here. How *they* had ended up here.

The injustices of the war years seemed like a distant memory. Yet for Ruby, and for many Japanese Americans, they remained a shameful part of life only acknowledged by the United States as a wrong five years earlier. The formal apology from President Bush and the $20,000 Ruby received in reparation from the U.S. government as one of the living Japanese Americans incarcerated during the war was insignificant and inadequate. It was wrong to have rounded up those of Japanese descent, separated families, and incarcerated innocent people in the middle of nowhere, in the middle of anywhere—indefinitely.

Shikata ga nai. Ruby had scoffed at the Japanese belief her entire life. It *could* have been helped. Something *could* have been done about it. Something *should* have been done about it. But something *wasn't* done about it, until forty-five years later. She refused any personal financial benefit by contributing her share to help rebuild her childhood temple, leveled when Hurricane Iniki had swept over and destroyed large swaths of Kauai.

She released her breath.

Ruby now enjoyed the extravagances of simple joys—pride in her children's accomplishments, teaching, gardening, and cooking. Over time, she made peace with the injustice and no longer allowed it to dominate her emotions, her thoughts, her behaviors. In a world filled with challenges, unfairness, beauty, and possibility, everything in life mattered and nothing in life mattered. She reminded herself that life is constantly moving and shifting. Righteousness, shame, reconciliation, and forgiveness all mattered. Each had its place. She also appreciated life's ironies—her conviction never to set foot in Japan and her father's opinion that Koji was beneath her. Beneath him.

She inspected this sixty-six year old version of herself in the full-length mirror. Her suit elegant, her hair now silvered, and her pearl necklace— since repaired by a Tokyo jeweler—back close to her heart. The familiar pearls looked different to her now. Iridescent. Like life when viewed from a different angle, their meaning had changed. At this moment, luster outshined the pain of long ago.

The door opened and Koji entered their suite. He bowed and offered Ruby a corsage of orchids, as he had done for every special occasion in their thirty-seven years of marriage. One of their dates at the Lincoln Memorial. Purchasing their first home. The birth of each of their three children. She brought the corsage closer, its aroma taking her further back in time—her mother's funeral, everyone wearing white, the temple bathed in candlelight, a lei of orchids over the frame of her mother's photograph. We are born. We live. We die. We come and we go, as she and Koji had come together in Berkeley and gone to Washington, D.C. in 1958.

Since then, Ruby's life with Koji had been a blur. She taught in the local school system and supported Koji's career at the Library of Congress, celebrating his promotions from mailroom, to librarian, to head of a new position in Tokyo curating Library material, to Head of the Library's Japanese Section in Washington, D.C., and later to acting Head of the Library's entire Asian Division. While Head of the Japanese Section, Japanese royalty visited the Library. The moments were heavy with irony as Koji came face to face with the eldest son of the Emperor, who many of his generation revered. After a deep bow, Koji had shown Emperor Akihito and Empress Michiko certain Library treasures, including the second-oldest extant example of printing in the world, dated from 700 A.D., and the Sketchbooks of Ando Hiroshige, the *Hiroshige gacho*.

Oddly, to Ruby, Koji seemed content every step of the way, even though the war years were incredibly painful for him too. He had never shared his thoughts, let alone his feelings. He endured the hardship of those war years, lived as an American among the enemy, and witnessed the horror of the bombing with dignity and the resolve to live the American dream. He seemed to know—to *believe*—everything in life mattered and nothing in life mattered. She took another deep breath.

In one hour, Koji—proud, intelligent, dignified—would receive one of Japan's highest civilian honors, The Order of the Sacred Treasure: Gold Rays with Neck Ribbon, for his exemplary service and contributions to U.S.-Japan understanding and relations, a rare accolade for a non-Japanese citizen. The irony. A single American citizen of Japanese descent. Raised in Japan by a nation that believed the Emperor was divine and Americans were the enemy. He was but a small speck with a foot in each country on opposite sides of the globe, one of billions of inhabitants spinning on the infinitely flawed planet. Yet, he had contributed to uniting these former enemies and making the world a better place, for himself, for her, for their children and grandchildren.

True to their ancestors' culture, neither of them had ever spoken with their children about the bombing, the incarceration, their hardships, what the war was like for them, or their feelings. Now, entering the twilight of their lives in this distant country, they recognized a stifling silence might echo through generations, leaving their children and grandchildren with a trivialized and hazy perception of what they had experienced and who they were. Surrounded by ancient Japanese history and culture, they summoned the courage to share their hearts and stories with their children when they returned home. Ruby would open her tattered footlocker to the sunlight. Koji would tell his story of the blinding flash. Someday, the children would inherit his *Jizō* and his rubber *Jiji* boots, along with the meaning of the small statue and the truth of whose boots they would walk in. Ruby and Koji had traversed the cruelties of America's war with Japan, loved America with their whole hearts, and raised their children to do the same. Of white ashes, they *gaman*.

They departed the hotel for the Imperial Palace and stepped into the sunshine under a shower of fragrant cherry blossoms, their fragile petals shimmering with each twirl and welcoming spring after the long cold winter. Exquisite. Graceful. Fleeting.

Glossary of
Japanese Words

Amida: A Buddha who rules over paradise, enjoying endless and infinite bliss

Arigatō: Thank you (informal)

Arigatō gozaimasu: Thank you (formal)

Baishakunin: Matchmaker

Bakayarō: Phrase for "stupid fool" (slang)

Beigoma: A traditional, small Japanese toy—a top often decorated with Chinese characters

Bentō: A single portion, home-packed meal, often for lunch

Bonsai: An ornamental tree or shrub grown in a pot and artificially prevented from reaching its normal size

Bonshō: A large bell found in Buddhist temples throughout Japan, used to summon the monks to prayer and to demarcate periods of time

Butsudan: Buddhist altar

chan: Suffix for a child

Chōnan: Eldest son

Daikon: Radish

Daimyō: Feudal lord

Engawa: Porch or edging strip of flooring usually of wood or bamboo

Fugu: A fish delicacy with lethal organs

Fumeiyo no hito: A disgraced person

Furoshiki: Traditional Japanese wrapping cloth used to transport clothes, gifts, or other goods

Gaman: Japanese phrase for "enduring the seemingly unbearable with patience and dignity"

Genkan: A traditional Japanese entry area for a house, apartment, or building

Giri: Self-sacrificing devotion, duty, or obligation

Gō: An abstract strategy board game using white and black stones

Gomennasai: Phrase for "I'm sorry"

Gyokusai: Honorable and gallant of deaths

Hachimaki: Japanese headband

Hai: Phrase for "yes"

Haiku: Japanese form of poetry

Hajimemashite: Phrase for "Nice to meet you (for the first time)"

Hi no maru bento: A bowl of rice with red plum in the center resembling the Japanese flag

Hi no maru: The Japanese flag

Hibakusha: Atomic bomb-affected survivor

Hiragana: Japanese phonetic lettering system

Ichi, ni, san, shi, go: Phrase for counting "One, two, three, four, five"

Ikebana: The art of flower arranging

Irasshaimase: Phrase for "Welcome"

Issei: A Japanese immigrant to North America

Itadakimasu: An expression of gratitude before meals

Jizō: A guardian deity who looks over children and travelers

Jōdan deshō: Phrase for "Are you kidding me?"

Juzu: A string of prayer beads

Kabocha: Squash

Kamon: Family crest

Kampō: Japanese variant of traditional Chinese herbal medicines

Kanji: Chinese characters that are used in the Japanese writing system

Katakana: Japanese syllabic writing or alphabet used for foreign words and sounds

Katana: Saber

Kendō: A form of fencing with two-handed bamboo swords, originally developed as a safe form of sword training for samurai

Kenzoku: Deepest friendship

Kibei: A son or daughter of Issei parents who is born in America and especially in the U.S. and educated largely in Japan

Kokutai no Hongi: Qualities that make Japanese uniquely Japanese

Konnichiwa: Phrase for "Hello, good afternoon"

kun: Suffix for Japanese boys

Kuso: Phrase for "Damn!"

Kyōiku ni Kansuru Chokugo: The guiding principles of education in effect through the war years (1890-1948), especially the virtues of cultivating loyalty to Japan, the Emperor, parents, elders, and ancestors

Manji: The Buddhist symbol of prosperity and eternity

Minka: A traditional home-building style

Miso: Fermented soybean paste

Mochi: A sweet, dough-like mass made from cooked and pounded rice

Musubi: A Japanese rice ball that is mixed, filled, or topped with a variety of ingredients and sometimes wrapped in dried seaweed

Namu Amida Butsu: Phrase for "I take refuge in Amida Buddha"

Naraku: Hell

Nisei: A person born in the U.S. to immigrant parents from Japan

Nori: Dried seaweed

Ofuro: A bath

Ohayō goziamasu: Phrase for "Good morning"

Ohitashi: Wrung-out spinach

Okāsan: Mother

Okaerinasai: Phrase for "Welcome home" (formal)

Okonomiyaki: Savory pancakes with various ingredients

Om Amideva Hrīh: Tibetan term for Buddhist mantra to overcome all obstacles

Oni: Folklore ogre

Origami: Art of folding paper into decorative shapes and figures

Otōsan: Father

Ozōni: A special broth soup enjoyed in the morning on New Year's Day in Japan

Sake: Alcoholic beverage made by fermenting rice

Samurai: Member of a powerful military caste in feudal Japan

san: Common honorific title, similar to Mrs. and Mr.

Sate: Phrase meaning "so, now, or well then"

Sayonara: Goodbye

Seiza: Traditional way of sitting in an upright, kneeling position

Senbei: Rice crackers

Sencha: Green tea

Senninbari: A belt or cloth stitched by one thousand persons, sometimes by women to protect departing warriors, or a cloth with one thousand stitches

Sensei: Teacher and also a suffix (-sensei) used for doctors, teachers, and religious leaders

Seppuku: A form of Japanese ritual suicide by disembowelment

Shikata ga nai: Phrase for "It cannot be helped"

Shinai: A fencing stick, usually made of bamboo

Shizukani: Expression for "Be quiet"

Soba: Buckwheat noodles

Shogunate: The administration of a shogun who is the supreme military leader of feudal Japan

Shōji: A door, window, or room divider used in traditional Japanese architecture, consisting of translucent (or transparent) sheets on a lattice frame

Shōyu: Soy sauce

Sōdesune: Phrase for "I agree with you"

Sōdesuka: Phrase for "That is right," or "That is so"

Sofubo: Grandparents

Sunomono: Vinegar-based dish, usually a cucumber salad

Sumi-e: Japanese ink art or painting

Sumimasen: Excuse me

Sushi: Anything made with vinegared rice (may also contain vegetables, spices, fish, or other delicacies)

Tadaima: Expression for "I am home"

Taisō: Calisthenics

Tamagoyaki: Fried egg omelette

Tansu: Chest of drawers

Tatami: Straw mat

Torii: A traditional Japanese gate most commonly found at the entrance of or within a Shinto shrine, where it symbolically marks the transition from the mundane to the sacred

Udon: Wheat flour noodles

Umeboshi: Salted, pickled plum

Wasen: Traditional Japanese boat

Washi: Japanese paper

Wasshoi: Expression or chant "Heave ho!" symbolizing unity

Yaki imo: Roasted or baked sweet potato

Yakuza: Organized crime syndicates originating in Japan

Yoi nihonjin: Phrase for a good Japanese citizen

Zaibatsu: A large business conglomerate

Zōri: Thonged sandals usually made of rice straw, cloth and leather

Authors' Note

This book is a work of fiction, inspired by true events experienced by Hisao Matsumoto and Reiko Odate Matsumoto, two ordinary people whose lives were shaped by extraordinary circumstances. Individually and together, they personify the spirit of *Gaman*—enduring the seemingly unbearable with dignity and patience. May their stories endure in our hearts and minds. May they forever rest in peace.

Giving

A percentage of author royalties will be donated to the Japanese American Memorial Pilgrimages (JAMP) organization, a centralized resource for promoting pilgrimages and educating people about the World War II Japanese American incarceration camps. JAMP is in partnership with Northwest Film Forum, a registered 501(c)(3) non-profit organization. www.jampilgrimages.com

Acknowledgments

We endeavored to write this book with integrity for historical accuracy and are indebted to the National Archives and Records Administration, the Pearl Harbor National Memorial, the Japanese American National Museum, the Smithsonian Institution, the Hiroshima Peace Memorial Museum, the Japanese American Memorial Pilgrimages, the West Kaua'i Heritage Center, Densho, and the many authors, photographers, and filmmakers who have documented these historical moments.

Our thanks go to everyone at Apprentice House Press for bringing this book to publication, and we offer special thanks to Mary Velazquez for her editing and director Kevin Atticks for his extraordinary leadership of the AHP team.

While writing the manuscript, we enjoyed the good fortune of participating in a small Baltimore County Public Library critique group whose members championed this work from the beginning, critiqued with rigor and love, and saw us through our writers' highs and lows.

To our readers—Ellen Prentiss Campbell, Joan Davidson, Marsha Engstrom, Eugenia Kim, Katie Aiken Ritter, Claudia Katayanagi, and Deborah Lambert—we are grateful for your investment in the manuscript and in us.

We extend deep appreciation to our editors Kathryn Johnson for her early guidance and Karen Osborn whose kindness, belief in this book, and comprehensive pearls of wisdom brought *Of White Ashes* to life.

With loving gratitude, we thank Wakako Odate Baker for trusting us with her seldom-told recollections and stories.

For the graceful leaf that flitters through time in the Shenandoah Valley and the pragmatic speck in the universe seeking Walter Cronkite, we hope we have made you proud.

About the Authors

Constance Hays Matsumoto

A native Marylander, Connie empty-nests in Greenville, Delaware with her husband, Kent, and their adorable Westie. She is a former corporate and interior design devotee who later embraced the art and rigor of creative writing. Inspired by Shakespeare's "What's past is prologue," Connie writes stories and poetry intended to influence positive change in our world. Connie earned her B.A. from Notre Dame of Maryland University and M.S. in Business from Johns Hopkins University. She is a member of the Authors Guild, Eastern Shore Writers' Association, Historical Novel Society, and Women's National Book Association, and served on the Board of Directors of the Maryland Writers' Association as Communications Chair and as President of the Baltimore Chapter.

Kent Matsumoto

Kent, a third-generation Japanese American, was born in Virginia and spent his formative years living in Japan where he attended the American School. He earned his degrees from the University of Virginia and University of Michigan Law School, and has worked in law firms and private and public companies. He currently serves on the boards of a publicly traded community bank and the non-profit Head Start Washington County (Maryland). He has authored articles for professional publications and spoken before numerous professional organizations.

Apprentice House Press

Loyola University Maryland

Apprentice House is the country's only campus-based, student-staffed book publishing company. Directed by professors and industry professionals, it is a nonprofit activity of the Communication Department at Loyola University Maryland.

Using state-of-the-art technology and an experiential learning model of education, Apprentice House publishes books in untraditional ways. This dual responsibility as publishers and educators creates an unprecedented collaborative environment among faculty and students, while teaching tomorrow's editors, designers, and marketers.

Eclectic and provocative, Apprentice House titles intend to entertain as well as spark dialogue on a variety of topics. Financial contributions to sustain the press's work are welcomed. Contributions are tax deductible to the fullest extent allowed by the IRS.

To learn more about Apprentice House books or to obtain submission guidelines, please visit www.apprenticehouse.com.

Apprentice House
Communication Department
Loyola University Maryland
4501 N. Charles Street
Baltimore, MD 21210
410-617-5265
info@apprenticehouse.com
www.apprenticehouse.com

Printed in the USA
CPSIA information can be obtained
at www.ICGtesting.com
LVHW091228121223
766157LV00002B/26